Love Eternal by H. Rider Haggard

Sir Henry Rider Haggard, KBE was born on June 22nd, 1856 at Bradenham in Norfolk, England.

After his education he was pushed towards an Army career but failed the entrance exam. Next Haggard was positioned to work for the British Foreign Office but he seems not to have sat that exam. Using family connections, he was sent to Southern Africa by his father in search of a further opportunity of a career.

Haggard spent six years there before a return to England and marriage. He had begun to write and publish some non-fiction in Africa but it was only after studying Law in the hope it might prove to be the proper career his father wanted for him that Haggard began to write fiction, using his African experiences as the basis.

His first fiction was published in 1885 and the following year King Solomon's Mines was published. It was a phenomenal success. His career was set.

Haggard wrote well and wrote often. He managed to sympathise with the local populations even though they were exploited and manipulated by Europeans intent on amassing fortunes in money, people and resources. His writing career covered the great sprint to Empire of several European powers and both reflects and criticizes these events through his well-loved characters including Allan Quatermain and Ayesha.

In his later years Haggard pursued much in the way social reform as well as standing for Parliament and writing a great many letters to The Times.

Henry Rider Haggard died on May 14th, 1925 at the age of 68. His ashes were buried at Ditchingham Church.

Index of Contents

CHAPTER I

HONEST JOHN

More than thirty years ago two atoms of the eternal Energy sped forth from the heart of it which we call God, and incarnated themselves in the human shapes that were destined to hold them for a while, as vases hold perfumes, or goblets wine, or as sparks of everlasting radium inhabit the bowels of the rock. Perhaps these two atoms, or essences, or monads indestructible, did but repeat an adventure, or many, many adventures. Perhaps again and again they had proceeded from that Home august and imperishable on certain mornings of the days of Time, to return thither at noon or nightfall, laden with the fruits of gained experience. So at least one of them seemed to tell the other before all was done and that other came to believe. If so, over what fields did they roam throughout the æons, they who having no end, could have no beginning? Not those of this world only, we may be sure. It is so small and there are so many others, millions upon millions of them, and such an infinite variety of knowledge is needed to shape the soul of man, even though it remain as yet imperfect and but a shadow of what it shall be.

Godfrey Knight was born the first, six months later she followed (her name was Isobel Blake), as though to search for him, or because whither he went, thither she must come, that being her doom and his.

Their circumstances, or rather those of their parents, were very different but, as it chanced, the houses in which they dwelt stood scarcely three hundred yards apart.

Between the rivers Blackwater and Crouch in Essex, is a great stretch of land, flat for the most part and rather dreary, which, however, to judge from what they have left us, our ancestors thought of much importance because of its situation, its trade and the corn it grew. So it came about that they built great houses there and reared beautiful abbeys and churches for the welfare of their souls. Amongst these, not very far from the coast, is that of Monk's Acre, still a beautiful fane though they be but few that worship there to-day. The old Abbey house adjacent is now the rectory. It has been greatly altered, and the outbuildings are shut up or used as granaries and so forth by arrangement with a neighbouring farmer. Still its grey walls contain some fine but rather unfurnished chambers, reputed by the vulgar to be haunted. It was for this reason, so says tradition, that the son of the original grantee of Monk's Acre Abbey, who bought it for a small sum from Henry VIII at the Dissolution of the Monasteries, turned the Abbey house into a rectory and went himself to dwell in another known as Hawk's Hall, situate on the bank of the little stream of that name, Hawk's Creek it is called, which finds its way to the Blackwater.

Parsons, he said, were better fitted to deal with ghosts than laymen, especially if the said laymen had dispossessed the originals of the ghosts of their earthly heritage.

The ancient Hawk's Hall, a timber building of the sort common in Essex as some of its premises still show, has long since disappeared. About the beginning of the Victorian era a fish-merchant of the name of Brown, erected on its site a commodious, comfortable, but particularly hideous mansion of white brick, where he dwelt in affluence in the midst of the large estate that had once belonged to the monks. An attempt to corner herrings, or something of the sort, brought this worthy, or unworthy tradesman to disaster, and the Hall was leased to a Harwich smack-owner of the name of Blake, a shrewd person, whose origin was humble. He had one son named John, of whom he was determined to "make a gentleman." With this view John was sent to a good public school, and to college. But of him nothing could make a gentleman, because true gentility and his nature were far apart. He remained, notwithstanding all his advantages, a cunning, and in his way an able man of business, like his father before him. For the rest, he was big, florid and presentable, with the bluff and hearty manner which sometimes distinguishes a faux bonhomme. "Honest John" they called him in the neighbourhood, a soubriquet which was of service to him in many ways.

Suddenly Honest John's father died, leaving him well off, though not so rich as he would have liked to be. At first he thought of leaving Hawk's Hall and going to live at Harwich, where most of his business interests were. But, remembering that the occupation of it gave him a certain standing in the county, whereas in Harwich he would have been only a superior tradesman, he gave up the idea. It was replaced by another—to marry well.

Now John Blake was not an idealist, nor in any sense romantic; therefore, from marriage he expected little. He did not even ask that his wife should be good-looking, knowing that any aspirations which he had towards beauty could be satisfied otherwise. Nor did he seek money, being well aware that he could make this for himself. What he desired were birth and associations. After a little waiting he found exactly what he wanted.

A certain Lord Lynfield from the South of England, who lived in London, and was a director of many Boards, took a pheasant-shooting in the neighbourhood of Hawk's Hall, and with it a house. Here he lived more or less during the winter months, going up to town when necessary, to attend his Boards. Lord Lynfield was cursed with several extravagant sons, with whom John Blake, who was a good shot, soon became friendly. Also he made himself useful by lending one of them a considerable sum of money. When this came to Lord Lynfield's ears, as Honest John was careful that it should, he was disturbed and offered repayment, though as a matter of fact he did not know where to turn for the cash. In his bluffest and heartiest way Blake refused to hear of such a thing.

"No, no, my Lord, let it stand. Your son will repay me one day, and if he doesn't, what will a trifle like that matter?"

"He certainly shall repay you. But all the same, Mr. Blake, you have behaved very well and I thank you much," replied his Lordship courteously.

Thus did John Blake become an intimate of that aristocratic family.

Now Lord Lynfield, who was a widower, had one unmarried daughter. She was an odd and timid little person, with strong religious views, who adored secretly a high-church curate in London. This, indeed, was the reason why she had been brought to Essex when her infatuation was discovered by one of her married sisters, who, like the rest of the family, was extremely "low." Lady Jane was small in body and shrinking and delicate in character, somewhat mouselike indeed. Even her eyes were large and timid as are those of a mouse. In her John Blake perceived the exact parti whom he desired for a wife.

It is not necessary to follow the pitiful story to its inevitable end, one, happily, more common at that time than it is to-day. Mr. Blake played the earnest, ardent lover, and on all occasions proclaimed his own unworthiness at the top of his loud voice. Also he hinted at large settlements to the married sisters, who put the matter before Jane very plainly indeed. In the end, after a few words with her father, who pointed out that the provision which could be made for her was but small, and that he would die more happily if he knew her to be comfortably settled in life with a really trustworthy and generous man such as Mr. Blake had proved himself to be, she gave way, and in due course they were married.

In fact, the tragedy was complete, since Jane loathed her husband, whose real nature she had read from the beginning, as much as she adored the high-church curate from whom in some terrible hour she parted with broken words. Even when he died a few years later, she continued to adore him, so much that her one hope was that she might meet him again in the land where there is no marrying or giving in marriage. But all of this she kept locked in her poor little heart, and meanwhile did her duty by her husband with an untroubled brow, though those mouse-like eyes of hers grew ever more piteous.

He, for his part, did not do his duty by her. Of one side of his conduct she was careless, being totally indifferent as to whom he admired. Others she found it hard to bear. The man was by nature a bully, one who found pleasure in oppressing the helpless, and who loved, in the privacy of his home, to wreak the ill-temper which he was forced to conceal abroad. In company, and especially before any of her people, he treated her with the greatest deference, and would even make loud laudatory remarks concerning her; when they were alone there was a different tale to tell, particularly if she had in any way failed in promoting that social advancement for which he had married her.

"What do you suppose I give you all those jewels and fine clothes for, to say nothing of the money you waste in keeping up the house?" he would ask brutally.

Jane made no answer; silence was her only shield, but her heart burned within her. It is probable, notwithstanding her somewhat exaggerated ideas of duty and wifely obedience, that she would have plucked up her courage and left him, even if she must earn her own living as a sempstress, had it not been for one circumstance. That circumstance was the arrival in the world of her daughter, Isobel. In some ways this event did not add to her happiness, if that can be added to which does not exist, for the reason that her husband never forgave her because this child, her only one, was not a boy. Nor did he lose any opportunity of telling her this to her face, as though the matter were one over which she had control. In others, however, for the first time in her battered little life, she drank deep of the cup of joy. She loved that infant, and from the first it loved her and her only, while to the father it was indifferent, and at times antagonistic.

From the cradle Isobel showed herself to be an individual of character. Even as a little girl she knew what she wanted and formed her own opinions quite independently of those of others. Moreover, in a certain way she was a good-looking child, but of a stamp totally different from that of either of her parents. Her eyes were not restless and prominent, like her father's, or dark and plaintive, like her mother's, but large, grey and steady, with long curved lashes. In fact, they were fine, but it was her only beauty, since the brow above them was almost too pronounced for that of a woman, the mouth was a little large, and the nose somewhat irregular. Her hair, too, though long and thick, was straight and rather light-coloured. For the rest she was well-ground and vigorous, with a strong, full voice, and as she approached maturity she developed a fine figure.

When she was not much more than ten Isobel had her first trouble with her father. Something had gone wrong with one of his shipping speculations, and as usual, he vented it upon his wife. So cruelly did he speak to her on a household matter for which she was not the least to blame, that the poor woman at last rose and left the room to hide her tears. Isobel, however, remained behind, and walking up to her father, who stood with his back to the fire, asked him why he treated her mother thus.

"Mind your own business, you impertinent brat," he answered.

"Mummy is my business, and you are—a brute," she exclaimed, clenching her little fists. He lifted his hand as though to strike her, then changed his mind and went away. She had conquered. Thenceforward Mr. Blake was careful not to maltreat his wife in Isobel's presence. He complained to her, however, of the child's conduct, which, he said, was due to her bringing up and encouragement, and Lady Jane in turn, scolded her in her gentle fashion for her "wicked words."

Isobel listened, then asked, without attempting to defend herself,

"Were not father's words to you wicked also, Mummy? It was not your fault if James forgot to bring round the dog-cart and made him miss the train to London. Ought you to be sworn at for that?"

"No, dear, but you see, he is my husband, and husbands can say what they wish to their wives."

"Then I will never have a husband; at least, not one like father," Isobel announced with decision.

There the matter ended. Or rather it did not end, since from that moment Isobel began to reflect much on matrimony and other civilized institutions, as to which at last she formed views that were not common among girls of her generation. In short, she took the first step towards Radicalism, and entered on the road of rebellion against the Existing and Acknowledged.

During the governess era which followed this scene Isobel travelled far and fast along that road. The lady, or rather the ladies, hired by her father, for his wife was allowed no voice in their selection, were of the other known as "determined"; disciplinarians of the first water. For one reason or another they did not stay. Isobel, though a quick and able child, very fond of reading moreover, proved unamenable under discipline as understood by those formidable females, and owing to her possession of a curious tenacity of purpose, ended by wearing them down. Also they did not care for the atmosphere of the house, which was depressing.

One of them once tried to strike Isobel. This was when she was nearly thirteen. Isobel replied with the schoolroom inkpot. She was an adept at stone-throwing, and other athletic arts. It caught her instructress fair upon her gentle bosom, spoiled her dress, filled her mouth and eyes with ink, and nearly knocked her down.

"I shall tell your father to flog you," gasped the lady when she recovered her breath.

"I should advise you not," said Isobel. "And what is more," she added after reflection, "if you do I shall advise him not to listen to you."

Then the governess thought better of it and gave notice instead. To be just to John Blake he never attempted to resort to violence against his daughter. This may have been because he knew by instinct that it would not be safe to do so or tend to his own comfort. Or perhaps, it was for the reason that in his way he was fond of her, looking on her with pride not quite untouched by fear. Like all bullies he was a coward at heart, and respected anyone who dared to stand up to him, even although she were but a girl, and his own daughter.

After the victim of the inkpot incident departed, threatening actions at law and proclaiming that her pupil would come to a bad end, questions arose as to Isobel's future education. Evidently the governess experiment had broken down and was not worth repeating. Although she trembled at the idea of parting with her only joy and consolation in life, Lady Jane suggested that she should be sent to school. It was fortunate for her that she did so, since as the idea came from his wife, Mr. Blake negatived it at once firmly and finally, a decision which she accepted with an outward sigh of resignation, having learned the necessity of guile, and inward delight. Indeed, for it that evening she thanked God upon her knees.

It may be also that her father did not wish that Isobel should go away. Lady Jane bored him to distraction, since kicking a cushion soon becomes poor sport. So much did she bore him indeed that for this and other reasons he passed most of his time in London or at Harwich, in both of which places he had offices where he transacted his shipping business, only spending the week-ends at Hawk's Hall. It was his custom to bring with him parties of friends, business men as a rule, to whom, for sundry purposes, he wished to appear in the character of a family man and local magnate. Isobel, who was quick and vivacious even while she was still a child, helped to make these parties pass off well, whereas without her he felt that they would have been a failure. Also she was useful during the shooting season. So it came about that she was kept at home.

It was at this juncture that an idea came to Mr. Blake. A few years before, at the very depth of the terrible agricultural depression of the period, he had purchased at a forced sale by the mortgagees, the entire Monk's Acre estate, at about £12 the acre, which was less than the cost of the buildings that stood upon the land. This, as he explained to all and sundry, he had done at great personal loss in the interest of the tenants and labourers, but as a matter of fact, even at the existing rents, the investment paid him a fair rate of interest, and was one which, as a business man he knew must increase in value when times changed. With the property went the advowson of Monk's Acre, and it chanced that a year later the living fell vacant through the resignation of the incumbent. Mr. Blake, now as always seeking popularity, consulted the bishop, consulted the church- wardens, consulted the parishioners, and in the end consulted his own interests by nominating the nephew of a wealthy baronet of his acquaintance whom he was anxious to secure as a director upon the Board of a certain company in which he had large holdings.

"I have never seen this clerical gentleman and know nothing of his views, or anything about him. But if you recommend him, my dear Sir Samuel, it is enough for me, since I always judge of a man by his friends. Perhaps you will furnish me, or rather my lawyers, with the necessary particulars, and I will see that the matter is put through. Now, to come to more important business, as to this Board of which I am chairman," &c.

The end of it was that Sir Samuel, flattered by such deference, became a member of the Board and Sir Samuel's nephew became rector of Monk's Acre.

Such appointments, like marriages, are made in Heaven—at least that seems to be the doctrine of the English Church, which is content to act thereon. In this particular instance the results were quite good. The Rev. Mr. Knight, the nephew of the opulent Sir Samuel, proved to be an excellent and hard-working clergyman. He was low-church, and narrow almost to the point of Calvinism, but intensely earnest and conscientious; one who looked upon the world as a place of sin and woe through which we must labour and pass on, a difficult path beset with rocks and thorns, leading to the unmeasured plains of Heaven. Also he was an educated man who had taken high degrees at college, and really learned in his way. While he was a curate, working very hard in a great seaport town, he had married the daughter of another clergyman of the city, who died in a sudden fashion as the result of an accident, leaving the girl an orphan. She was not pure English as her mother had been a Dane, but on both sides her descent was high, as indeed was that of Mr. Knight himself.

This union, contracted on the husband's part largely from motives that might be called charitable, since he had promised his deceased colleague on his death bed to befriend the daughter, was but moderately successful. The wife had the characteristics of her race; largeness and liberality of view, high aspirations for humanity, considerable intelligence, and a certain tendency towards mysticism of the Swedenborgian type, qualities that her husband neither shared nor could appreciate. It was perhaps as well, therefore that she died at the birth of her only son, Godfrey, three years after her marriage.

Mr. Knight never married again. Matrimony was not a state which appealed to his somewhat shrunken nature. Although he admitted its necessity to the human race, of it in his heart he did not approve, nor would he ever have undertaken it at all had it not been for a sense of obligation. This attitude, because it made for virtue as he understood it, he set down to virtue, as we are all apt to do, a sacrifice of the things of earth and of the flesh to the things of heaven, and of the spirit. In fact, it was nothing of the sort, but only the outcome of individual physical and mental conditions. Towards female society, however hallowed and approved its form, he had no leanings. Also the child was a difficulty, so great indeed that at times almost he regretted that a wise Providence had not thought fit to take it straight to the joys of heaven with its mother, though afterwards, as the boy's intelligence unfolded, he developed interest in him. This, however, he was careful to keep in check, lest he should fall into the sin of inordinate affection, denounced by St. Paul in common with other errors.

Finally, he found an elderly widow, named Parsons, who acted as his housekeeper, and took charge of his son. Fortunately for Godfrey her sense of parenthood was more pronounced than that of his father, and she, who had lost two children of her own, played the part of mother to him with a warm and loyal heart. From the first she loved him, and he loved her; it was an affection that continued throughout their lives.

When Godfrey was about nine his father's health broke down. He was still a curate in his seaport town, for good, as goodness is understood, and hard-working as he was, no promotion had come his way. Perhaps this was because the bishop and his other superiors, recognising his lack of sympathy and his narrowness of outlook, did not think him a suitable man to put in charge of a parish. At any rate, so it happened.

Thus arose his appeal to his wealthy and powerful relative, Sir Samuel, and his final nomination to a country benefice, for in the country the doctor said that he must live—unless he wished to die. Convinced though he was of the enormous advantages of Heaven over an earth which he knew to be extremely sinful, the Rev. Mr. Knight, like the rest of the world, shrank from the second alternative, which, as he stated in a letter of thanks to Sir Samuel, however much it might benefit him personally, would cut short his period of terrestrial usefulness to others. So he accepted the rectorship of Monk's Acre with gratitude.

In one way there was not much for which to be grateful, seeing that in those days of depreciated tithes the living was not worth more than £250 a year and his own resources, which came from his wife's small fortune, were very limited. It should have been valuable, but the great tithes were alienated with the landed property of the Abbey by Henry VIII, and now belonged to the lay rector, Mr. Blake, who showed no signs of using them to increase the incumbent's stipend.

Still there was a good house with an excellent garden, too good indeed, with its beautiful and ancient rooms which a former rector of archæological knowledge and means had in part restored to their pristine state, while for the rest his tastes were simple and his needs few, for, of course, he neither drank wine nor smoked. Therefore, as has been said, he took the living with thankfulness and determined to make the best of it on a total income of about £350 a year.

CHAPTER II

ISOBEL KISSES GODFREY

On the whole Monk's Acre suited Mr. Knight fairly well. It is true that he did not like the Abbey, as it was still called, of which the associations and architectural beauty made no appeal to him, and thought often with affection of the lodging-house-like abode in which he had dwelt in his southern seaport town amid the Victorian surroundings that were suited to his Victorian nature. The glorious church, too, irritated him, partly because it was so glorious, and notwithstanding all that the Reformation had done to mar it, so suggestive of papistical practice and errors, and partly because the congregation was so scanty in that great expanse of nave and aisle, to say nothing of the chancel and sundry chapels, that they looked like a few wandering sheep left by themselves in a vast and almost emptied fold. Nor was this strange, seeing that the total population of the parish was but one hundred and forty-seven souls.

Of his squire and patron he saw but little. Occasionally Mr. Blake attended church and as lay-rector was accommodated in an ugly oak box in the chancel, where his big body and florid countenance reminded Godfrey of Farmer Johnson's prize polled ox in its stall. These state visits were not however very frequent and depended largely upon the guests who were staying for the week-end at the Hall. If Mr. Blake discovered that these gentlemen were religiously inclined, he went to church. If otherwise, and this was more common, acting on his principle of being all things to all men, he stopped away.

Personally he did not bother his head about the matter which, in secret, he looked upon as one of the ramifications of the great edifice of British cant. The vast majority of people in his view went to church, not because they believed in anything or wished for instruction or spiritual consolation, but because it looked respectable, which was exactly why he did so himself. Even then nearly always he sat alone in the oak box, his visitors generally preferring to occupy the pew in the nave which was frequented by Lady Jane and Isobel.

Nor did the two often meet socially since their natures were antipathetic. In the bosom of his family Mr. Blake would refer to Mr. Knight as the "little parson rat," while in his bosom Mr. Knight would think of

Mr. Blake as "that bull of Bashan." Further, after some troubles had arisen about a question of tithe, also about the upkeep of the chancel, Blake discovered that beneath his meek exterior the clergyman had a strong will and very clear ideas of the difference between right and wrong, in short, that he was not a man to be trifled with, and less still one of whom he could make a tool. Having ascertained these things he left him alone as much as possible.

Mr. Knight very soon became aware first that his income was insufficient to his needs, and secondly, especially now when his health was much improved, that after a busy and hard-working life, time at Monk's Acre hung heavily upon his hands. The latter trouble to some extent he palliated by beginning the great work that he had planned ever since he became a deacon, for which his undoubted scholarship gave him certain qualifications. Its provisional title was, "Babylon Unveiled" (he would have liked to substitute "The Scarlet Woman" for Babylon) and its apparent object an elaborate attack upon the Roman Church, which in fact was but a cover for the real onslaught. With the Romans, although perhaps he did not know it himself, he had certain sympathies, for instance, in the matter of celibacy. Nor did he entirely disapprove of the monastic orders. Then he found nothing shocking in the tenets and methods of the Jesuits working for what they conceived to be a good end. The real targets of his animosity were his high-church brethren of the Church of England, wretches who, whilst retaining all the privileges of the Anglican Establishment, such as marriage, did not hesitate to adopt almost every error of Rome and to make use of her secret power over the souls of men by the practice of Confession and otherwise.

As this monumental treatise began in the times of the Early Fathers and was planned to fill ten volumes of at least a hundred thousand words apiece, no one will be surprised to learn that it never reached the stage of publication, or indeed, to be accurate, that it came to final stop somewhere about the time of Athanasius.

Realizing that the work was likely to equal that of Gibbon both in length and the years necessary to its completion; also that from it could be expected no immediate pecuniary profits, Mr. Knight looked round to find some other way of occupying his leisure, and adding to his income. Although a reserved person, on a certain Sunday when he went to lunch at the Hall, in the absence of Mr. Blake who was spending the week-end somewhere else, he confided his difficulties to Lady Jane whom he felt to be sympathetic.

"The house is so big," he complained. "Mrs. Parsons" (Godfrey's old nurse and his housekeeper) "and one girl cannot even keep it clean. It was most foolish of my predecessor in the living to restore that old refectory and all the southern dormitories upon which I am told he spent no less than £1,500 of his own money, never reflecting on the expense which his successors must incur merely to keep them in order, since being once there they are liable for charges for dilapidations. It would have been better, after permission obtained, to let them go to ruin."

"No doubt, but they are very beautiful, are they not?" remarked Lady Jane feebly.

"Beauty is a luxury and, I may add, a snare. It is a mistaken love of beauty and pomp, baits that the Evil One well knows how to use, which have led so large a section of our Church astray," he replied sipping at his tumbler of water.

A silence followed, for Lady Jane, who from early and tender associations loved high-church practices, did not know what to answer. It was broken by Isobel who had been listening to the conversation in her acute way, and now said in her clear, strong voice:

"Why don't you keep a school, Mr. Knight? There's lots of room for it in the Abbey."

"A school!" he said. "A school! I never thought of that. No, it is ridiculous. Still, pupils perhaps. Out of the mouth of babes and sucklings, &c. Well, it is time for me to be going. I will think the matter over after church."

Mr. Knight did think the matter over and after consultation with his housekeeper, Mrs. Parsons, an advertisement appeared in The Times and The Spectator inviting parents and guardians to entrust two or three lads to the advertiser's care to receive preliminary education, together with his own son. It proved fruitful, and after an exchange of the "highest references," two little boys appeared at Monk's Acre, both of them rather delicate in health. This was shortly before the crisis arose as to the future teaching of Isobel, when the last governess, wishing her "a better spirit," had bidden her a frigid farewell and shaken the dust of Hawk's Hall off her feet.

One day Isobel was sent with a note to the Abbey House. She rang the bell but no one came, for Mr. Knight was out walking with his pupils and Mrs. Parsons and the parlour-maid were elsewhere. Tired of waiting, she wandered round the grey old building in the hope of finding someone to whom she could deliver the letter, and came to the refectory which had a separate entrance. The door was open and she peeped in. At first, after the brilliant sunlight without, she saw nothing except the great emptiness of the place with its splendid oak roof on the repair of which the late incumbent had spent so much, since as is common in monkish buildings, the windows were high and narrow. Presently, however, she perceived a little figure seated in the shadow at the end of the long oaken refectory table, that at which the monks had eaten, which still remained where it had stood for hundreds of years, one of the fixtures of the house, and knew it for that of Godfrey, Mr. Knight's son. Gliding towards him quietly she saw that he was asleep and stopped to study him.

He was a beautiful boy, pale just now for he had recovered but recently from some childish illness. His hair was dark and curling, dark, too, were his eyes, though these she could not see, and the lashes over them, while his hands were long and fine. He looked most lonely and pathetic, there in the big oak chair that had so often accommodated the portly forms of departed abbots, and her warm heart went out towards him. Of course Isobel knew him, but not very well, for he was a shy lad and her father had never encouraged intimacy between the Abbey House and the Hall.

Somehow she had the idea that he was unhappy, for indeed he looked so even in his sleep, though perhaps this was to be accounted for by a paper of unfinished sums before him. Sympathy welled up in Isobel, who remembered the oppressions of the last governess—her of the inkpot. Sympathy, yes, and more than sympathy, for of a sudden she felt as she had never felt before. She loved the little lad as though he were her brother. A strange affinity for him came home to her, although she did not define it thus; it was as if she knew that her spirit was intimate with his, yes, and always had been and always would be intimate.

This subtle knowledge went through Isobel like fire and shook her. She turned pale, her nostrils expanded, her large eyes opened and she sighed. She did more indeed. Drawn by some over-mastering impulse she drew near to Godfrey and kissed him gently on the forehead, then glided back again frightened and ashamed at her own act.

Now he woke up; she felt his dark eyes looking at her. Then he spoke in a slow, puzzled voice, saying:

"I have had such a funny dream. I dreamed that a spirit came and kissed me. I did not see it, but I think it must have been my mother's."

"Why?" asked Isobel.

"Because no one else ever cared enough for me to kiss me, except Mrs. Parsons, and she has given it up now that the other boys are here."

"Does not your father kiss you?" she asked.

"Yes, once a week, on Sunday evening when I go to bed. Because I don't count that."

"No, I understand," said Isobel, thinking of her own father, then added hastily, "it must be sad not to have a mother."

"It is," he answered, "especially when one is ill as I have been, and must lie so long in bed with pains in the head. You know I had an abscess in the ear and it hurt very much."

"I didn't know. We heard you were ill and mother wanted to come to see you. Father wouldn't let her. He thought it might be measles and he is afraid of catching things."

"Yes," replied Godfrey without surprise. "It wasn't measles, but if it had been you might have caught them, so of course he was right to be careful."

"Oh! he wasn't thinking of me or Mummy, he was thinking of himself," blurted out Isobel with the candour of youth.

"Big, strong men don't catch measles," said Godfrey in mild astonishment.

"He says they do, and that they are very dangerous when you are grown up. Why are you alone here, and what are you working at?"

"My father has kept me in as a punishment because I did my sums wrong. The other boys have gone out bird-nesting, but I have to stop here until I get them right. I don't know when that will be," he added with a sigh, "as I hate rule of three and can't do it."

"Rule of three," said Isobel, "I'm quite good at it. You see I like figures. My father says it is the family business instinct. Here, let me try. Move to the other side of that big chair, there's plenty of room for two, and show it to me."

He obeyed with alacrity and soon the brown head and the fair one were bent together over the scrawled sheet. Isobel, who had really a budding talent for mathematics, worked out the sum, or rather the sums, without difficulty and then, with guile acquired under the governess régime, made him copy them and destroyed all traces of her own handiwork.

"Are you as stupid at everything as you are at sums?" she asked when he had finished, rising from the chair and seating herself on the edge of the table.

"What a rude thing to ask! Of course not," he replied indignantly. "I am very good at Latin and history, which I like. But you see father doesn't care much for them. He was a Wrangler, you know."

"A Wrangler! How dreadful. I suppose that is why he argues so much in his sermons. I hate history. It's full of dates and the names of kings who were all bad. I can't make out why people put up with kings," she added reflectively.

"Because they ought to, 'God bless our gracious Queen,' you know."

"Well, God may bless her but I don't see why I should as she never did anything for me, though Father does hope she will make him something one day. I'd like to be a Republican with a President as they have in America."

"You must be what father calls a wicked Radical," said Godfrey staring at her, "one of those people who want to disestablish the Church."

"I daresay," she replied, nodding her head. "That is if you mean making clergymen work like other people, instead of spying and gossiping and playing games as they do about here."

Godfrey did not pursue the argument, but remarked immorally:

"It's a pity you don't come to our class, for then I could do your history papers and you could do my sums."

She started, but all she said was:

"This would be a good place to learn history. Now I must be going. Don't forget to give the note. I shall have to say that I waited a long while before I found anyone. Goodbye, Godfrey."

"Goodbye, Isobel," he answered, but she was gone.

"I hope he did dream that it was his mother who kissed him," Isobel reflected to herself, for now the full enormity of her performance came home to her. Young as she was, a mere child with no knowledge of the great animating forces of life and of the mysteries behind them, she wondered why she had done this thing; what it was that forced her to do it. For she knew well that something had forced her, something outside of herself, as she understood herself. It was as though another entity that was in her and yet not herself had taken possession of her and made her act as uninfluenced, she never would have acted. Thus she pondered in her calm fashion, then, being able to make nothing of the business, shrugged her shoulders and let it go by. After all it mattered nothing since Godfrey had dreamed that the ghost of his mother had visited him and would not suspect her of being that ghost, and she was certain that never would she do such a thing again. The trouble was that she had done it once and that the deed signified some change in her which her childish mind could not understand.

On reaching the Hall, or rather shortly afterwards, she saw her father who was waiting for the carriage in which to go to the station to meet some particularly important week-end guest. He asked if she had brought any answer to his note to Mr. Knight, and she told him that she had left it in the schoolroom, as she called the refectory, because he was out.

"I hope he will get it," grumbled Mr. Blake. "One of my friends who is coming down to-night thinks he understands architecture and I want the parson to show him over the Abbey House. Indeed that's why he has come, for you see he is an American who thinks a lot of such old things."

"Well, it is beautiful, isn't it, Father?" she said. "Even I felt that it would be easy to learn in that big old room with a roof like that of a church."

An idea struck him.

"Would you like to go to school there, Isobel?"

"I think so, Father, as I must go to school somewhere and I hate those horrible governesses."

"Well," he replied, "you couldn't throw inkpots at the holy Knight, as you did at Miss Hook. Lord! what a rage she was in," he added with a chuckle. "I had to pay her £5 for a new dress. But it was better to do that than to risk a County Court action."

Then the carriage came and he departed.

The upshot of it all was that Isobel became another of Mr. Knight's pupils. When Mr. Blake suggested the arrangement to his wife, she raised certain objections, among them that associating with these little lads might make a tomboy of the girl, adding that she had been taught with children of her own sex. He retorted in his rough marital fashion, that if it made something different of Isobel to what she, the mother, was, he would be glad. Indeed, as usual, Lady Jane's opposition settled the matter.

Now for the next few years of Isobel's life there is little to be told. Mr. Knight was an able man and a good teacher, and being a clever girl she learned a great deal from him, especially in the way of mathematics, for which, as has been said, she had a natural leaning.

Indeed very soon she outstripped Godfrey and the other lads in this and sundry other branches of study, sitting at a table by herself on what once had been the dais of the old hall. In the intervals of lessons, however, it was their custom to take walks together and then it was that she always found herself at the side of Godfrey. Indeed they became inseparable, at any rate in mind. A strange and most uncommon intimacy existed between these young creatures, almost might it have been called a friendship of the spirit. Yet, and this was the curious part of it, they were dissimilar in almost everything that goes to make up a human being. Even in childhood there was scarcely a subject on which they thought alike, scarcely a point upon which they would not argue.

Godfrey was fond of poetry; it bored Isobel. His tendencies were towards religion though of a very different type from that preached and practised by his father; hers were anti-religious. In fact she would have been inclined to endorse the saying of that other schoolgirl who defined faith as "the art of believing those things which we know to be untrue," while to him on the other hand they were profoundly true, though often enough not in the way that they are generally accepted. Had he possessed any powers of definition at that age, probably he would have described our accepted beliefs as shadows of the Truth, distorted and fantastically shaped, like those thrown by changeful, ragged clouds behind which the eternal sun is shining, shadows that vary in length and character according to the hour and weather of the mortal day.

Isobel for her part took little heed of shadows. Her clear, scientific stamp of mind searched for ascertainable facts, and on these she built up her philosophy of life and of the death that ends it. Of course all such contradictions may often be found in a single mind which believes at one time and rejects at another and sees two, or twenty sides of everything with a painful and bewildering clearness.

Such a character is apt to end in profound dissatisfaction with the self from which it cannot be free. Much more then would one have imagined that these two must have been dissatisfied with each other and sought the opportunities of escape which were open to them. But it was not so in the least. They argued and contradicted until they had nothing more to say, and then lapsed into long periods of weary but good-natured silence. In a sense each completed each by the addition of its opposite, as the darkness completes the light, thus making the round of the perfect day.

As yet this deep affection and remarkable oneness showed no signs of the end to which obviously it was drifting. That kiss which the girl had given to the boy was pure sisterly, or one might almost say, motherly, and indeed this quality inspired their relationship for much longer than might have been expected. So much was this so that no one connected with them on either side ever had the slightest suspicion that they cared for each other in any way except as friends and fellow pupils.

So the years went by till the pair were seventeen, young man and young woman, though still called boy and girl. They were good-looking in their respective ways though yet unformed; tall and straight, too, both of them, but singularly dissimilar in appearance as well as in mind. Godfrey was dark, pale and thoughtful-faced. Isobel was fair, vivacious, open-natured, amusing, and given to saying the first thing that came to her tongue. She had few reservations; her thoughts might be read in her large grey eyes before they were heard from her lips, which generally was not long afterwards. Also she was very able. She read and understood the papers and followed all the movements of the day with a lively interest, especially if these had to do with national affairs or with women and their status.

Business, too, came naturally to her, so much so that her father would consult her about his undertakings, that is, about those of them which were absolutely above board and beyond suspicion of sharp dealing. The others he was far too wise to bring within her ken, knowing exactly what he would have heard from her upon the subject. And yet notwithstanding all his care she suspected him, by instinct, not by knowledge. For his part he was proud of her and would listen with pleasure when, still a mere child, she engaged his guests boldly in argument, for instance a bishop or a dean on theology, or a statesman on current politics. Already he had formed great plans for her future; she was to marry a peer who took an active part in things, or at any rate a leading politician, and to become a power in the land. But of this, too, wisely he said nothing to Isobel, for the time had not yet come.

During these years things had prospered exceedingly with John Blake who was now a very rich man with ships owned, or partly owned by him on every sea. On several occasions he had been asked to stand for Parliament and declined the honour. He knew himself to be no speaker, and was sure also that he could not attend both to the affairs of the country and to those of his ever-spreading business. So he took another course and began to support the Conservative Party, which he selected as the safest, by means of large subscriptions.

He did more, he bought a baronetcy, for only thus can the transaction be described. When a General Election was drawing near, one evening after dinner at Hawk's Hall he had a purely business conversation with a political Whip who, perhaps not without motive, had been complaining to him of the depleted state of the Party Chest.

"Well," said Mr. Blake, "you know that my principles are yours and that I should like to help your, or rather our cause. Money is tight with me just now and the outlook is very bad in my trade, but I'm a man who always backs his fancy; in short, would £15,000 be of use?"

The Whip intimated that it would be of the greatest use.

"Of course," continued Mr. Blake, "I presume that the usual acknowledgment would follow?"

"What acknowledgment?" asked the Whip sipping his port wearily, for such negotiations were no new thing to him. "I mean, how do you spell it?"

"With a P," said Mr. Blake boldly, acting on his usual principle of asking for more than he hoped to get.

The Whip contemplated him through his eyeglass with a mild and interested stare.

"Out of the question, my dear fellow," he said. "That box is full and locked, and there's a long outside list waiting as well. Perhaps you mean with a K. You know money isn't everything, as some of you gentlemen seem to think, and if it were, you would have said fifty instead of fifteen."

"K be damned!" replied Mr. Blake. "I'm not a mayor or an actor- manager. Let's say B, that stands for Beginning as well as Baronet; also it comes before P, doesn't it?"

"Well, let's see. You haven't a son, have you? Then perhaps it might be managed," replied the Whip with gentle but pointed insolence, for Mr. Blake annoyed him. "I'll make inquiries, and now, shall we join the ladies? I want to continue my conversation with your daughter about the corruption which some enemy, taking advantage of her innocence, has persuaded her exists in the Conservative Party. She is a clever young lady and makes out a good case against us, though I am sure I do not know whence she got her information. Not from you, I suppose, Sir John—I beg your pardon, Mr. Blake."

So the matter was settled, as both of them knew it would be when they left the room. The cash found its way into some nebulous account that nobody could have identified with any party, and in the Dissolution Honours, John Blake, Esq., J.P., was transformed into Sir John Blake, Bart.; information that left tens of thousands of the students of the list mildly marvelling why. As the same wonder struck them regarding the vast majority of the names which appeared therein, this, however, did not matter. They presumed, good, easy souls, that John Blake, Esq., J.P., and the rest were patriots who for long years had been working for the good of their country, and that what they had done in secret had been discovered in high places and was now proclaimed from the housetops.

Lady Jane was inclined to share this view. She knew that a great deal of her husband's money went into mysterious channels of which she was unable to trace the ends, and concluded in her Victorian-wife kind of fashion, or at any rate hoped, that it was spent in alleviating the distress of the "Submerged Tenth" which at that time was much in evidence. Hence no doubt the gracious recognition that had come to him. John Blake himself, who paid over the cash, naturally had no such delusions, and unfortunately in that moment of exultation, when he contemplated his own name adorning the lists in every newspaper, let out the truth at breakfast at which Isobel was his sole companion. For by this time Lady Jane had grown too delicate to come down early.

"Well, you've got a baronet for a father now, my girl"—to be accurate he called it a "bart."—he said puffing himself out like a great toad before the fire, as he threw down the Daily News in which his name was icily ignored in a spiteful leaderette about the Honours List, upon the top of The Times, The Standard, and The Morning Post.

"Oh!" said Isobel in an interested voice and paused.

"It's wonderful what money can do," went on her father, who was inclined for a discussion, and saw no other way of opening up the subject. "Certain qualifications of which it does not become me to speak, and a good subscription to the Party funds, and there you are with Bart. instead of Esq. after your name and Sir before it. I wonder when I shall get the Patent? You know baronets do not receive the accolade."

"Don't they?" commented Isobel. "Well, that saves the Queen some trouble of which she must be glad as she does not get the subscription. I know all about the accolade," she added; "for Godfrey has told me. Only the other day he was showing me in the Abbey Church where the warriors who were to receive it, knelt all night before the altar. But they didn't give subscriptions, they prayed and afterwards took a cold bath."

"Times are changed," he answered.

"Yes, of course. I can't see you kneeling all night with a white robe on, Father, in prayer before an altar. But tell me, would they have made you a baronet if you hadn't given the subscription?"

Sir John chuckled till his great form shook—he had grown very stout of late years.

"I think you are sharp enough to answer that question for yourself. I have observed, Isobel, that you know as much of the world as most young girls of your age."

"So you bought the thing," she exclaimed with a flash of her grey eyes. "I thought that honours were given because they were earned."

"Did you?" said Sir John, chuckling again. "Well, now you know better. Look here, Isobel, don't be a fool. Honours, or most of them, like other things, are for those who can pay for them in this way or that. Nobody bothers how they come so long as they do come. Now, listen. Unfortunately, as a girl, you can't inherit this title. But it doesn't matter much, since it will be easy for you to get one for yourself."

Isobel turned red and uttered an exclamation, but enjoining silence on her with a wave of his fat hand, her father went on:

"I haven't done so badly, my dear, considering my chances. I don't mind telling you that I am a rich man now, indeed a very rich man as things go, and I shall be much richer, for nothing pays like ships, especially if you man them with foreign crews. Also I am a Bart," and he pointed to the pile of newspapers on the floor, "and if my Party gets in again, before long I shall be a Lord, which would make you an Honourable. Anyway, my girl, although you ain't exactly a beauty," here he considered her with a critical eye, "you'll make a fine figure of a woman and with your money, you should be able to get any husband you like. What's more," and he banged his fist upon the table, "I expect you to do it; that's your part of the family business. Do you understand?"

"I understand, Father, that you expect me to get any husband I like. Well, I'll promise that."

"I think you ought to come into the office, you are so smart," replied Sir John with sarcasm. "But don't you try it on me, for I'm smarter. You know very well that I mean any husband I like, when I say 'any husband you like.' Now do you understand?"

"Yes," replied Isobel icily. "I understand that you want to buy me a husband as you have bought a title. Well, titles and husbands are alike in one thing; once taken you can never be rid of them day or night. So I'll say at once, to save trouble afterwards, that I would rather earn my living as a farm girl, and as for your money, Father, you can do what you wish with it."

Then looking him straight in the eyes, she turned and left the room.

"An odd child!" thought Sir John to himself as he stared after her. "Anyway, she has got spirit and no doubt will come all right in time when she learns what's what."

CHAPTER III

THE PLANTAGENET LADY

In the course of these years of adolescence, Godfrey Knight had developed into a rather unusual stamp of youth. In some ways he was clever, for instance at the classics and history which he had always liked; in others and especially where figures were concerned, he was stupid, or as his father called him, idle. In company he was apt to be shy and dull, unless some subject interested him, when to the astonishment of those present, he would hold forth and show knowledge and powers of reflection beyond his years. By nature he was intensely proud; the one thing he never forgot was a rebuff, or forgave, was an insult. Sir John Blake soon found this out, and not liking the lad, whose character was antagonistic to his own in every way, never lost an opportunity of what he called "putting him in his place," perhaps because something warned him that this awkward, handsome boy would become a stumbling-block to his successful feet.

Godfrey and Isobel were both great readers. Nor did they lack for books, for as it chanced there was a good library at Hawk's Hall, which had been formed by the previous owner and taken over like the pictures, when Mr. Blake bought the house. Also it was added to constantly, as an order was given to a large London bookseller to supply all the important new works that came out. Although he never opened a book himself, Sir John liked to appear intellectual by displaying them about the rooms for the benefit of his visitors. These publications Isobel read and lent to Godfrey; indeed they perused a great deal which young people generally are supposed to leave alone, and this in various schools of thought, including those that are known as "free."

It was seldom that such studies led to unanimity between them, but to argument, which sharpened their intellects, they did lead, followed invariably by a charitable agreement to differ.

About the time of the addition of the name of John Blake to the roll of British Chivalry, a book on Mars came their way—it was one by a speculative astronomer which suggests that the red planet is the home of reasoning beings akin to humanity. Isobel read it and was not impressed. Indeed, in the vigorous language of youth, she opined that it was all "made-up rot."

Godfrey read it also and came to quite a different conclusion. The idea fired him and opened a wide door in his imagination, a quality with which he was well provided. He stared at Mars through the large Hall telescope, and saw, or imagined that he saw the canals, also the snow-caps and the red herbage. Isobel stared too and saw, or swore that she saw—nothing at all—after which they argued until their throats were dry.

"It's all nonsense," said Isobel. "If only you'll study the rocks and biology, and Darwin's 'Origin of Species,' and lots of other things, you will see how man came to develop on this planet. He is just an accident of Nature, that's all."

"And why shouldn't there be an accident of Nature on Mars and elsewhere?" queried Godfrey.

"Perhaps, but if so, it is quite another accident and has nothing to do with us."

"I don't know," he answered. "Sometimes," here his voice became dreamy as it had a way of doing, "I think that we pass on, all of us, from star to star. At least I know I often feel as if I had done so."

"You mean from planet to planet, Godfrey; stars are hot places, you know. You should not swallow all that theosophical bosh which is based on nothing."

"There's the Bible," went on Godfrey, "which tells us the same thing, that we live eternally—"

"Then we must always have lived, since eternity is a circle."

"Why not, Isobel? That is what I was trying to say. Well, if we live eternally, we must live somewhere, perhaps in those planets, or others, which it would be a waste to keep empty."

"I daresay—though Nature does not mind waste, or what seems to be waste. But why should you think of living eternally at all? Many people live a great deal too long as it is, and it is horrible to believe that they go on for ever."

"You see they might grow to something splendid in the end, Isobel. You must not judge them by what they are now."

"Oh! I know, the caterpillar and the butterfly, and all the rest of it."

"The Bible"—continued Godfrey imperturbably—when she cut him short.

"Well, what of the Bible? How do you know that it is true?"

"Because I do know it, though the truth in it may be different for everyone. What is more, I know that one day you will agree with me."

She looked at him curiously in the flashing way that was peculiar to her, for something in his tone and manner impressed her.

"Perhaps. I hope so, Godfrey, but at present I often feel as though I believed in nothing, except that I am I and you are you, and my father is—there he's calling me. Goodbye," and she was gone.

This particular conversation, one of many, had, as it happened, important results on the lives of these two young creatures. Isobel, in whom the love of Truth, however ugly it might be and however destructive of hope, faith, charity and all the virtues, was a burning, inbred passion, took to the secret study of theology in order to find out why Godfrey was so convinced as to the teachings of the Bible. She was not old or mellowed enough to understand that the real reason must be discovered, not in the letter but in the spirit, that is in the esoteric meaning of the sayings as to receiving the Kingdom of Heaven like a child and the necessity of being born again. Therefore with a fierce intensity, thrusting aside the spirit and its promptings which perhaps are shadows of the only real truths, she wrestled with the letter. She read the Divines, also much of the Higher Criticism, the lives of Saints, the Sacred Books themselves and many other things, only to arise bewildered, and to a great extent unbelieving.

"Why should I believe what I cannot prove?" she cried in her heart, and once with her lips to Godfrey.

He made her a very wise answer, although at the moment it did not strike either of them in that light.

"When you tell me of anything that you can really prove, I will show you why," he said. To this he added a suggestion that was most unwise, namely, that she should consult his father.

Now Mr. Knight was, it is true, a skilled theologian of a certain, narrow school and learned in his way. It is probable, however, that in all the wide world it would have been difficult to find any man less sympathetic to a mind like Isobel's or more likely to antagonize her eager and budding intelligence. Every doubt he met with intolerant denial; every argument with offensive contradiction; every query with references to texts.

Finally, he lost his temper, for be it acknowledged, that this girl was persistent, far from humble, and in a way as dogmatic as himself. He told her that she was not a Christian, and in her wrath she agreed with him. He said that she had no right to be in church. She replied that if this were so she would not come and, her father being indifferent upon the point (Lady Jane did not count in such matters), ceased her attendance. It was the old story of a strait-minded bigot forcing a large-minded doubter out of the fold that ought to have been wide enough for both of them. Moreover, this difference of opinion on matters of public and spiritual interest ended in a private and mundane animosity. Mr. Knight could never forgive a pupil of his own, whose ability he recognized, who dared to question his pontifical announcements. To him the matter was personal rather than one of religious truth, for there are certain minds in whose crucibles everything is resolved individually, and his was one of them. He was the largest matters through his own special and highly-magnifying spectacles. So, to be brief, they quarrelled once and for all, and thenceforward never attempted to conceal their cordial dislike of each other.

Such was one result of this unlucky discussion as to the exact conditions of the planet Mars, god of war. Another was that Godfrey developed a strong interest in the study of the heavenly bodies and when some domestic debate arose as to his future career, announced with mild firmness that he intended to be an astronomer. His father, to whom the heavenly bodies were less than the dust beneath his human feet and who believed in his heart that they had been created, every one of them, to give a certain amount of light to the inhabitants of this world when there was no moon, was furious in his arctic fashion, especially as he was aware that with a few distinguished exceptions, these hosts of heaven did not reward their votaries with either wealth or honour.

"I intend you for my own profession, the Church," he said bluntly. "If you choose to star-gaze in the intervals of your religious duties, it is no affair of mine. But please understand, Godfrey, that either you enter the Church or I wash my hands of you. In that event you may seek your living in any way you like."

Godfrey remonstrated meekly to the effect that he had not made up his mind as to his fitness for Holy Orders or his wish to undertake them.

"You mean," replied his father, "that you have been infected by that pernicious girl, Isobel. Well, at any rate, I will remove you from her evil influence. I am glad to say that owing to the fact that my little school here has prospered, I am in a position to do this. I will send you for a year to a worthy Swiss pastor whom I met as a delegate to the recent Evangelical Congress, to learn French. He told me he desired an English pupil to be instructed in that tongue and general knowledge. I will write to him at once. I hope that in new surroundings you will forget all these wild ideas and, after your course at college, settle down to be a good and useful man in the walk of life to which you are so clearly called."

Godfrey, who on such occasions knew how to be silent, made no answer, although the attack upon Isobel provoked him sorely. In his heart indeed he reflected that a year's separation from his parent would not be difficult to bear, especially beneath the shadow of the Swiss mountains which secretly he longed to climb. Also he really wished to acquire French, being a lad with some desire for knowledge and appreciation of its advantages. So he looked humble merely and took the first opportunity to slip from the presence of the fierce little man with small eyes, straight, sandy hair and a slit where his lips should be, through whose agency, although it was hard to believe it, he had appeared in this disagreeable and yet most interesting world.

In point of fact he had an assignation, of an innocent sort. Of course it was with the "pernicious" Isobel and the place appointed was the beautiful old Abbey Church. Here they knew that they would be undisturbed, as Mr. Knight was to sleep at a county town twenty miles away, where on the following morning he had business as the examiner of a local Grammar School, and must leave at once to catch his train. So, when watching from an upper window, he had seen the gig well on the road, Godfrey departed to his tryst.

Arriving in the dim and beauteous old fane, the first thing he saw was Isobel standing alone in the chancel, right in the heart of a shaft of light that fell on her through the rich-coloured glass of the great west window, for now it was late in the afternoon. She wore a very unusual white garment that became her well, but had no hat on her head. Perhaps this was because she had taken the fancy to do her plentiful fair hair in the old Plantagenet fashion, that is in two horns, which, with much ingenuity she had copied more or less correctly from the brass of an ancient, noble lady, whereof the two intended to take an impression. Also she had imitated some of the other peculiarities of that picturesque costume, including the long, hanging sleeves. In short, she wore a fancy dress which she proposed to use afterwards at a dance, and one of the objects of the rubbing they were about to make, was that she might study the details more carefully. At least, that was her object. Godfrey's was to obtain an impression of the crabbed inscription at the foot of the effigy.

There she stood, tall and imposing, her arms folded on her young breast, the painted lights striking full on her broad, intellectual forehead and large grey eyes, shining too in a patch of crimson above her heart. Lost in thought and perfectly still, she looked strange thus, almost unearthly, so much so that the impressionable and imaginative Godfrey, seeing her suddenly from the shadow, halted, startled and almost frightened.

What did she resemble? What might she not be? he queried to himself. His quick mind suggested an answer. The ghost of some lady dead ages since, killed, for there was the patch of blood upon her bosom, standing above the tomb wherein her bones crumbled, and dreaming of someone from whom she had been divorced by doom and violence.

He sickened a little at the thought; some dread fell upon him like a shadow of Fate's uplifted and pointed finger, stopping his breath and causing his knees to loosen. In a moment it was gone, to be replaced by another that was nearer and more natural. He was to be sent away for a year, and this meant that he would not see Isobel for a year. It would be a very long year in which he did not see Isobel. He had forgotten that when his father told him that he was to go to Switzerland. Now the fact was painfully present.

He came on up the long nave and Isobel, awakening, saw him.

"You are late," she said in a softer voice than was usual to her. "Well, I don't mind, for I have been dreaming. I think I went to sleep upon my feet. I dreamed," she added, pointing to the brass, "that I was that lady and—oh! all sorts of things. Well, she had her day no doubt, and I mean to have mine before I am as dead and forgotten as she is. Only I would like to be buried here. I'll be cremated and have my ashes put under that stone; they won't hurt her."

"Don't talk like that," he said with a little shiver, for her words jarred upon him.

"Why not? It is as well to face things. Look at all these monuments about us, and inscriptions, a lot of them to young people, though now it doesn't matter if they were old or young. Gone, every one of them and quite forgotten, though some were great folk in their time. Gone utterly and for always, nothing left, except perhaps descendants in a labourer's cottage here and there who never even heard of them."

"I don't believe it," he said almost passionately, I believe that they are living for ever and ever, perhaps as you and I, perhaps elsewhere."

"I wish I could," she answered, smiling, "for then my dream might have been true, and you might have been that knight whose brass is lost," and she pointed to an empty matrix alongside that of the great Plantagenet lady.

Godfrey glanced at the inscription which was left when the Cromwellians tore up the brass.

"He was her husband," he said, translating, "who died on the field of Crecy in 1346."

"Oh!" exclaimed Isobel, and was silent.

Meanwhile Godfrey, quite undisturbed, was spelling out the inscription beneath the figure of the knight's wife, and remarked presently:

"She seems to have died a year before him. Yes, just after marriage, the monkish Latin says, and—what is it? Oh! I see, 'in sanguine,' that is, in blood, whatever that may mean. Perhaps she was murdered. I say, Isobel, I wish you would copy someone else's dress for your party."

"Nonsense," she answered. "I think its awfully interesting. I wonder what happened to her."

"I don't know. I can't remember anything in the old history, and it would be almost impossible to find out. There are no coats of arms, and what is more, no surname is given in either inscription. The one says, 'Pray for the soul of Edmundus, Knight, husband of Phillippa, and the other, 'Pray for the soul of Phillippa, Dame, wife of Edmundus.' It looks as though the surnames had been left out on purpose, perhaps because of some queer story about the pair which their relations wished to be forgotten."

"Then why do they say that one died in blood and the other on the field of Crecy?"

Godfrey shook his head because he did not know. Nor indeed was he ever able to find out. That secret was lost hundreds of years ago. Then the conversation died away and they got to their work.

At length the rubbing, as it is termed technically, was finished and the two prepared to depart out of the gloom of the great church which had gathered about them as the evening closed in. Solitary and small they looked in it surrounded by all those mementoes of the dead, enveloped as it were in the very atmosphere of death. Who has not felt that atmosphere standing alone at nightfall in one of our ancient English churches that embody in baptism, marriage and burial the hopes, the desires, and the fears of unnumbered generations?

For remember, that in a majority of instances, long before the Cross rose above these sites, they had been the sacred places of faith after faith. Sun-worshippers, Nature-worshippers, Druids, votaries of Jove and Venus, servants of Odin, Thor and Friga, early Christians who were half one thing and half another, all have here bowed their brows to earth in adoration of God as they understood Him, and in these hallowed spots lies mingled the dust of every one of them.

So Godfrey felt in that hour and the same influences impinged upon and affected even the girl's bold, denying soul. She acknowledged them to herself, and after a woman's way, turned and almost fiercely laid the blame upon her companion.

"You have infected me with your silly superstitions," she said, stamping her foot as they shut and locked the door of the church. "I feel afraid of something, I don't know what, and I was never afraid of anything before."

"What superstitions?" he asked, apologetically. "I don't remember mentioning any."

"There is no need for you to mention them, they ooze out of you. As though I could not read your mind! There's no need for you to talk to tell me what you are thinking of, death—and separations which are as bad, and unknown things to come, and all sorts of horrors."

"That's odd," he remarked, still without emotion, for he was used to these attacks from Isobel which, as he knew, when she was upset, always meant anything but what she said, "for as a matter of fact I was thinking of a separation. I am going away, Isobel, or rather, my father is sending me away."

He turned, and pointing to the stormy western sky where the day died in splendour, added simply in the poetic imagery that so often springs to the lips of youth:

"There sets our sun; at least it is the last we shall look upon together for a whole year. You go to London to-morrow, don't you? Before you come back I shall be gone."

"Gone! Why? Where? Oh! what's the use of asking? I knew something of the sort was coming. I felt it in that horrible old church. And after all, why should I mind? What does it matter if you go away for a year or ten years—except that you are the only friend I have—especially as no doubt you are glad to get out of this dreadful hole? Don't stand there looking at me like a moon-calf, whatever that may be, but tell me what you mean, or I'll, I'll—" and she stopped.

Then he told her—well, not quite everything, for he omitted his father's disparaging remarks about herself.

She listened in her intent fashion, and filled in the gaps without difficulty.

"I see," she said. "Your father thinks that I am corrupting you about religion, as though anybody could corrupt you when you have got an idea into your stupid head; at least, on those subjects. Oh! I hate him, worse even than I do my own, worse than you do yourself."

Godfrey, thinking aloud, began to quote the Fourth Commandment. She cut him short:

"Honour my father!" she said. "Why should we honour our fathers unless they are worthy of honour? What have we to thank them for?"

"Life," suggested Godfrey.

"Why? You believe that life comes from God, and so do I in a way. If so, what has a father to do with it who is just a father and no more? With mothers perhaps it is different, but you see I love my mother and he treats her like—like a dog, or worse," and her grey eyes filled with tears. "However, it is your father we are talking of, and there is no commandment telling me to honour him. I say I hate him and he hates me, and that's why he is sending you away. Well, I hope you won't find anyone to contaminate you in Switzerland."

"Oh! Isobel, Isobel," he broke out, "don't be so bitter, especially as it is of no use. Besides after all you have got everything that a girl can have—money and position and looks—"

"Looks!" she exclaimed, seizing on the last word, "when you know I am as ugly as a toad."

He stared at her.

"I don't know it; I think you beautiful."

"Wait till you see someone else and you will change your mind," she snapped, flushing.

"And you are going to come out," he went on hastily.

"Yes, at a fancy ball in this Plantagenet lady's dress, but I almost wish I was—to go out instead—like her."

"And I daresay you will soon be married," he blurted, losing his head for she bewildered him.

"Married! Oh! you idiot. Do you know what marriage means—to a woman? Married! I can bear no more of this. Goodbye," and turning she walked, or rather ran into the darkness, leaving him amazed and alone.

This was the last time that Godfrey spoke with Isobel for a long while. Next morning he received a note addressed in her clear and peculiar writing, which from the angular formation of the letters and their regularity, at a distance looked not unlike a sheet of figures.

It was short and ran:—

Dear Old Godfrey,—Don't be vexed with me because I was so cross this evening. Something in that old church upset me, and you know I have a dreadful temper. I didn't mean anything I said. I daresay it is a good thing you should go away and see the world instead of sticking in this horrid place. Leave your address with Mother Parsons, and I will write to you; but mind you answer my letters or I shan't write any more. Good-bye, old boy. Your affectionate Isobel. Who is always thinking of you.

P.S.—I'll get this to the Abbey with your milk. Can't leave it myself, as we are starting for town at half-past seven to-morrow morning to catch the early train.

CHAPTER IV

THE GARDEN IN THE SQUARE

As it chanced Godfrey did see Isobel once more before he left England. It was arranged that he was to leave Charing Cross for Switzerland early on a certain Wednesday morning. Late on the Tuesday afternoon, Mr. Knight brought the lad to the Charing Cross Hotel. There, having taken his ticket and made all other necessary arrangements, he left him, returning himself to Essex by the evening train. Their farewell was somewhat disconcerting, at any rate to the mind of the youth.

His father retired with him to his room at the top of the hotel, and there administered a carefully prepared lecture which touched upon every point of the earnest Christian's duty, ending up with admonitions on the dangers of the world, the flesh, and the devil, and a strong caution against frivolous, unbelieving and evil-disposed persons, especially such as were young, good-looking and wore petticoats.

"Woman," said Mr. Knight, "is the great danger of man. She is the Devil's favourite bait, at least to some natures of which I fear yours is one, though that is strange, as I may say that on the whole I have always disliked the sex, and I married for other reasons than those which are supposed to be common. Woman," he went on, warming to his topic, "although allowed upon the world as a necessary evil, is a painted snare, full of [he meant baited with] guile. You will remember that the first woman, in her wicked desire to make him as bad as herself, tempted Adam until he ate the apple, no doubt under threats of estranging herself from him if he did not, and all the results that came from her iniquity, one of which is that men have had to work hard ever since."

Here Godfrey reflected that there was someone behind who tempted the woman, also that it is better to work than to sit in a garden in eternal idleness, and lastly, that a desire for knowledge is natural and praiseworthy. Had Isobel been in his place she would have advanced these arguments, probably in vigorous and pointed language, but, having learnt something of Adam's lesson, he was wiser and held his tongue.

"There is this peculiarity about women," continued his parent, "which I beg you always to remember. It is that when you think she is doing what you want and that she loves you, you are doing what she wants and really she only loves herself. Therefore you must never pay attention to her soft words, and especially beware of her tears which are her strongest weapon given to her by the father of deceit to enable her to make fools of men. Do you understand?"

"Yes," said Godfrey, with hesitation, "but—" this burst from him involuntarily, "but, Father, if you have always avoided women, as you say, how do you know all this about them?"

For a moment Mr. Knight was staggered. Then he rose to the occasion.

"I know it, Godfrey, by observing the effect of their arts on others, as I have done frequently."

A picture rose in Godfrey's mind of his father with his eye to keyholes, or peering through fences with wide-open ears, but wisely he did not pursue the subject.

"My son," continued and ended Mr. Knight, "I have watched you closely and I am sure that your weakness lies this way. Woman is and always will be the sin that doth so easily beset you. Even as a child you loved Mrs. Parsons much more than you did me, because, although old and unsightly, she is still female. When you left your home this morning for the first time, who was it that you grieved to part from? Not your companions, the other boys, but Mrs. Parsons again, whom I found you embracing in that foolish fashion, yes, and mingling your tears with hers, of which at your age you should be ashamed. Indeed I believe that you feel being separated from that garrulous person, who is but a servant, more than you do from me, your father."

Here he waited for Godfrey's contradiction, but as none came, went on with added acerbity:

"Of that anguis in herba, that viper, Isobel, who turns the pure milk of the Word to poison and bites the hand that fed her, I will say nothing, nothing," (here Godfrey reflected that Isobel would have been better described as a lion in the path rather than as a snake in the grass) "except that I rejoice that you are to be separated from her, and I strictly forbid any communication between you and her, bold, godless and revolutionary as she is. I had rather see any man for whose welfare I cared, married to a virtuous and pious-minded housemaid, than to this young lady, as she is called, with all her wealth and position, who would eat out his soul with her acid unbelief and turn the world upside down to satisfy her fancy. Now I must go or I shall miss my train. Here is a present for you, of which I direct you to read a chapter every day," and he produced out of a brown paper parcel a large French Bible. "It will both do you good and improve your knowledge of the French tongue. I especially commend your attention to certain verses in Proverbs dealing with the dangers on which I have touched, that I have marked with a blue pencil. Do you hear?"

"Yes, Father. Solomon wrote Proverbs, didn't he?"

"It is believed so and his wide—experience—gives a special value to his counsel. You will write to me once a week, and when you have had your dinner get to bed at once. On no account are you to go out into the streets. Goodbye."

Then he planted a frosty kiss upon Godfrey's brow and departed, leaving that youth full of reflections, but to tell the truth, somewhat relieved.

Shortly afterwards Godfrey descended to the coffee-room and ate his dinner. Here it was that the universal temptress against whom he had been warned so urgently, put in a first appearance in the person of a pleasant and elderly lady who was seated alongside of him. Noting this good-looking and lonely lad, she began to talk to him, and being a woman of the world, soon knew all about him, his name, who he was, whither he was going, etc. When she found out that it was to Lucerne, or rather its immediate neighbourhood, she grew quite interested, since, as it happened, she—her name was Miss Ogilvy—had a house there where she was accustomed to spend most of the year. Indeed, she was returning by the same train that Godfrey was to take on the following morning.

"We shall be travelling companions," she said when she had explained all this.

"I am afraid not," he answered, glancing at the many evidences of wealth upon her person. "You see," he added colouring, "I am going second and have to spend as little as possible. Indeed I have brought some food with me in a basket so that I shall not need to buy any meals at the stations."

Miss Ogilvy was touched, but laughed the matter off in her charming way, saying that he would have to be careful that the Custom-house officers did not think he was smuggling something in his basket, and as she knew them all must look to her to help him if he got into difficulties on the journey. Then she went on chatting and drawing him out, and what is more, made him take several glasses of some delicious white wine she was drinking. It was not very strong wine, but except for a little small beer, practically Godfrey had been brought up as a teetotaller for economy's sake, and it went to his head. He became rather effusive; he told her of Sir John Blake about whom she seemed to know everything already, and something of his friendship with Isobel, who, he added, was coming out that very night at a fancy dress ball in London.

"I know," said Miss Ogilvy, "at the de Lisles' in Grosvenor Square. I was asked to it, but could not go as I am starting to-morrow."

Then she rose and said "Good-night," bidding him be sure not to be late for the train, as she would want him to help her with her luggage.

So off she went looking very charming and gracious, although she was over forty, and leaving Godfrey quite flattered by her attention.

Not knowing what to do he put on his hat and, walking across the station yard, took his stand by a gateway pillar and watched the tide of London life roll by. There he remained for nearly an hour, since the strange sight fascinated him who had never been in town before, the object of some attention from a policeman, although of this he was unaware. Also some rather odd ladies spoke to him from time to time which he thought kind of them, although they smelt so peculiar and seemed to have paint upon their faces. In answer to the inquiries of two of them as to his health he told them that he was very well. Also he agreed cordially with a third as to the extreme fineness of the night, and assured a fourth that he had no wish to take a walk as he was shortly going to bed, a statement which caused her to break into uncalled-for laughter.

It was at this point that the doubting policeman suggested that he should move on.

"Where to?" asked Godfrey of that officer of the law.

"To 'ell if you like," he replied. Then struck with curiosity, he inquired, "Where do you want to go to? This pillar ain't a leaning post."

Godfrey considered the matter and said with the verve of slight intoxication:

"Only two places appeal to me at present, heaven (not hell as you suggested), and Grosvenor Square. Perhaps, however, they are the same; at any rate, there is an angel in both of them."

The policeman stared at him but could find no fault with the perfect sobriety of his appearance.

"Young luny, I suspect," he muttered to himself, then said aloud: "Well, the Strand doesn't lead to 'eaven so far as I have noticed, rather t'other way indeed. But if you want Grosvenor Square, it's over there," and he waved his hand vaguely towards the west.

"Thank you," said Godfrey, taking off his hat with much politeness. "If that is so, I will leave heaven to itself for the present and content myself with Grosvenor Square."

Off he started in the direction indicated, and, as it seemed to him, walked for many miles through a long and bewildering series of brilliant streets, continually seeking new information as to his goal. The end of it was that at about a quarter to eleven he found himself somewhere in the neighbourhood of the Edgware Road, utterly stranded as it were, since his mind seemed incapable of appreciating further indications of locality.

"Look here, young man," said a breezy costermonger to whom he had appealed, "I think you had better take a 'ansom for the 'orse will know more about London than you seem to do. There's one 'andy."

"That is an idea," said Godfrey, and entered the cab, giving the address of Grosvenor Square.

"What number?" asked the driver.

"I don't know," replied Godfrey, "the Ball, Grosvenor Square."

Off they went, and in due course, reaching the square, drove round it until they came to a great house where there were signs of festivity in the shape of an awning above the entrance and a carpet on the pavement.

The cab stopped with a jerk and a voice from above—never having been in a hansom before, at first Godfrey could not locate it—exclaimed:

"Here's your Ball, young gent. Now you'd better hop out and dance."

His fare began to explain the situation through the little trap in the roof, demonstrating to the Jehu that his object was to observe the ball from without, not to dance at it within, and that it was necessary for him to drive on a little further. That worthy grew indignant.

"Blowed if I don't believe you're a bilk," he shouted through the hole. "Here, you pay me my fare and hook it, young codger."

Godfrey descended and commenced a search for money, only to remember that he had left his purse in his bag at the hotel. This also he explained with many apologies to the infuriated cabby, two gorgeous flunkeys who by now had arrived to escort him into the house, and a group of idlers who had collected round the door.

"I told yer he was a bilk. You look after your spoons, Thomas; I expect that's wot he's come for. Now you find that bob, Sonny, or I fetches the perlice."

Then an inspiration flashed on Godfrey's bewildered mind. Suddenly he recollected that, by the direction of heaven, Mrs. Parsons had sewn a ten shilling piece into the lining of his waistcoat, "in case he should ever want any money sudden-like." He undid that garment and heedless of the mockery of the audience, began to feel wildly at its interior calico. Joy! there it was in the lefthand corner.

"I have money here if only I can get it out," he gasped.

A woman in the gathering crowd, perhaps from pity, or curiosity, in the most unexpected way produced a pair of scissors from her pocket with which he began to hack at the waistcoat, gashing it sadly. At length the job was done and the half-sovereign appeared wrapped in a piece of cotton wool.

"Take it," said Godfrey, "and go away. Let it teach you to have more trust in your fellow creatures, Mr. Cabman."

The man seized the coin, examined it by the light of his lamp, tasted it, bit it, threw it on the top of the cab to see that it rang true, then with a "Well, I'm blowed!" whipped up his horse and went off.

Godfrey followed his example, as the flunkeys and the audience supposed to recover his change, though the last thing he was thinking of at that moment was change—except of locality. He ran a hundred yards or more to a part of the square where there was no lamp, then paused to consider.

"I have made a fool of myself," he reflected, "as Isobel always says I do when I get the chance. I have come all this way and been abused and laughed at for nothing."

Then his native determination began to assert itself. Why should it be for nothing? There was the house, and in it was Isobel, and oh! he wanted to see her. He crossed to the square-garden side and walked down in the shadow of the trees which grew there.

Under one of these he took his stand, squeezing himself against the railings, and watched the glowing house that was opposite, from which came the sounds of music, of dancing feet, of laughter and the tinkling of glasses. It had balconies, and on these appeared people dressed in all sorts of costumes. Among them he tried to recognise Isobel, but could not. Either she did not come or he was too far off to see her.

A dance was ending, the music grew faster and faster, then ceased with a flourish. More people appeared on the balconies. Others crowded into the hall, which he could see, for the door was open. Presently a pair came onto the steps. One of them was dressed as a knight in shining armour. He was a fine, tall young man, and his face was handsome, as the watcher could perceive, for he had taken off his plumed helm and carried it in his hand. The other was Isobel in her Plantagenet costume, to which were added one rose and a necklet of pink pearls. They stood on the steps a little while laughing and talking. Then he heard her say:

"Let us go into the square. It will be cooler. The key is hanging on the nail."

She vanished for a moment, doubtless to fetch the key. Then they walked down the steps, over the spread carpet, and across the roadway. Within three paces of where Godfrey stood there was a gate. She gave the key to the knight, and after one or two attempts the gate swung open. Whilst he was fumbling at the lock she stood looking about her, and presently caught sight of Godfrey's slim figure crouched against the railings in the deepest of the shadows.

"There is someone there, Lord Charles," she said.

"Is there?" he answered, indifferently. "A cab-tout or a beggar, I expect. They always hang about parties. Come on, it is open at last."

They passed into the garden and vanished. A wild jealousy seized Godfrey, and he slipped after them with the intention of revealing himself to Isobel. Inside the railings was a broad belt of shrubs bordered by a gravel path. The pair walked along the path, Godfrey following at a distance, till they came to a recessed seat on which they sat down. He halted behind a lilac bush ten paces or so away, not that he wanted to listen, but because he was ashamed to show himself. Indeed, he stopped his ears with his fingers that he might not overhear their talk. But he did not shut his eyes, and as the path curved here and the moon shone on them, he could see them well. They seemed very merry and to be playing some game.

At any rate, first with her finger she counted the air-holes in the knight's helmet which he held up to her. Then with his finger he counted the pearls upon her neck. When he had finished she clapped her hands as though she had won a bet. After this they began to whisper to each other, at least he whispered and she smiled and shook her head. Finally, she seemed to give way, for she unfastened the flower which she wore in the breast of her dress, and presented to him. Godfrey started at the sight which caused him to take his fingers from his ears and clutch the bush. A dry twig broke with a loud crack.

"What's that?" said Isobel.

"Don't know," answered Lord Charles. "What a funny girl you are, always seeing and hearing things. A stray cat, I expect; London squares are full of them. Now I have won my lady's favour and she must fasten it to my helm after the ancient fashion."

"Can't," said Isobel. "There are no pins in Plantagenet dresses."

"Then I must do it for myself. Kiss it first, that was the rule, you know."

"Very well," said Isobel. "We must keep up the game, and there are worse things to kiss than roses."

He held the flower to her and she bent forward to touch it with her lips. Suddenly he did the same, and their lips came very close together on either side of the rose.

This was too much for Godfrey. He glided forward, as the stray cat might have done, of which the fine knight had spoken, meaning to interrupt them.

Then he remembered suddenly that he had no right to interfere; that it was no affair of his with whom Isobel chose to kiss roses in a garden, and that he was doing a mean thing in spying upon her. So he halted behind another bush, but not without noise. His handsome young face was thrust forward, and on it were written grief, surprise and shame. The moonlight caught it, but nothing else of him. Isobel looked up and saw.

He knew that she had seen and turning, slipped away into the darkness back to the gate. As he went he heard the knight called Lord Charles, exclaim:

"What's the matter with you?" and Isobel answer, "Nothing. I have seen a ghost, that's all. It's this horrible dress!"

He glanced back and saw her rise, snatch the rose from the knight's hand, throw it down and stamp upon it. Then he saw and heard no more for he was through the gate and running down the square. At its end, as he turned into some street, he was surprised to hear a gruff voice calling to him to stop. On looking up he saw that it came from his enemy, the hansom-cab man, who was apparently keeping a lookout on the square from his lofty perch.

"Hi! young sir," he said, "I've been watching for you and thinking of wot you said to me. You gave me half a quid, you did. Jump in and I'll drive you wherever you want to go, for my fare was only a bob."

"I have no more money," replied Godfrey, "for you kept the change."

"I wasn't asking for none," said the cabby. "Hop in and name where it is to be."

Godfrey told him and presently was being rattled back to the Charing Cross Hotel, which they reached a little later. He got out of the cab to go into the hotel when once again the man addressed him.

"I owe you something," he said, and tendered the half-sovereign.

"I have no change," said Godfrey.

"Nor 'ain't I," said the cabman, "and if I had I wouldn't give it you. I played a dirty trick on you and a dirtier one still when I took your half sov, I did, seeing that I ought to have known that you ere just an obfusticated youngster and no bilk as I called you to them flunkeys. What you said made me ashamed, though I wouldn't own it before the flunkeys. So I determined to pay you back if I could, since otherwise I shouldn't have slept well to-night. Now we're quits, and goodbye, and do you always think kindly of Thomas Sims, though I don't suppose I shall drive you no more in this world."

"Goodbye, Mr. Sims," said Godfrey, who was touched. Moreover Mr. Sims seemed to be familiar to him, at the moment he could not remember how, or why.

The man wheeled his cab round, whipping the horse which was a spirited animal, and started at a fast pace.

Godfrey, looking after him, heard a crash as he emerged from the gates, and ran to see what was the matter. He found the cab overturned and the horse with a 'bus pole driven deep into its side, kicking on the pavement. Thomas Sims lay beneath the cab. When the police and others dragged him clear, he was quite dead!

Godfrey went to bed that night a very weary and chastened youth, for never before had he experienced so many emotions in a few short hours. Moreover, he could not sleep well. Nightmares haunted him in which he was being hunted and mocked by a jeering crowd, until Sims arrived and rescued him in the cab. Only it was the dead Sims that drove with staring eyes and fallen jaw, and the side of the horse was torn open.

Next he saw Isobel and the Knight in Armour, who kept pace on either side of the ghostly cab and mocked at him, tossing roses to each other as they sped along, until finally his father appeared, called Isobel a young serpent, at which she laughed loudly, and bore off Sims to be buried in the vault with the Plantagenet lady at Monk's Acre.

Godfrey woke up shaking with fear, wet with perspiration, and reflected earnestly on his latter end, which seemed to be at hand. If that great, burly, raucous-voiced Sims had died so suddenly, why should not he, Godfrey?

He wondered where Sims had gone to, and what he was doing now. Explaining the matter of the half-sovereign to St. Peter, perhaps, and hoping humbly that it and others would be overlooked, "since after all he had done the right thing by the young gent."

Poor Sims, he was sorry for him, but it might have been worse. He might have been in the cab himself and now be offering explanations of his own as to a wild desire to kill that knight in armour, and Isobel as well. Oh! what a fool he had been. What business was it of his if Isobel chose to give roses to some friend of hers at a dance? She was not his property, but only a girl with whom he chanced to have been brought up, and who found him a pleasant companion when there was no one else at hand.

By nature, as has been recorded, Godfrey was intensely proud, and then and there he made a resolution that he would have nothing more to do with Isobel. Never again would he hang about the skirts of that fine and rich young lady, who on the night that he was going away could give roses to another man, just because he was a lord and good-looking—yes, and kiss them too. His father was quite right about women, and he would take his advice to the letter, and begin to study Proverbs forthwith, especially the marked passages.

Having come to this conclusion, and thus eased his troubled mind, he went to sleep in good earnest, for he was very tired. The next thing of which he became aware was that someone was hammering at the door, and calling out that a lady downstairs said he must get up at once if he meant to be in time. He looked at his watch, a seven-and-sixpenny article that he had been given off a Christmas tree at Hawk's Hall, and observed, with horror, that he had just ten minutes in which to dress, pack, and catch the train. Somehow he did it, for fortunately his bill had been paid. Always in after days a tumultuous vision remained in his mind of himself, a long, lank youth with unbrushed hair and unbuttoned waistcoat, carrying a bag and a coat, followed by an hotel porter with his luggage, rushing wildly down an interminable platform with his ticket in his teeth towards an already moving train. At an open carriage door stood a lady in whom he recognized Miss Ogilvy, who was imploring the guard to hold the train.

"Can't do it, ma'am, any longer," said the guard, between blasts of his whistle and wavings of his green flag. "It's all my place is worth to delay the Continental Express for more than a minute. Thank you kindly, ma'am. Here he comes," and the flag paused for a few seconds. "In you go, young gentleman."

A heave, a struggle, an avalanche of baggage, and Godfrey found himself in the arms of Miss Ogilvy in a reserved first-class carriage. From those kind supporting arms he slid gently and slowly to the floor.

"Well," said that lady, contemplating him with his back resting against a portmanteau, "you cut things rather fine."

Still seated on the floor, Godfrey pulled out his watch and looked at it, then remarked that eleven minutes before he was fast asleep in bed.

"I thought as much," she said severely, "and that's why I told the maid to see if you had been called, which I daresay you forgot to arrange for yourself."

"I did," admitted Godfrey, rising and buttoning his waistcoat. "I have had a very troubled night; all sorts of things happened to me."

"What have you been doing?" asked Miss Ogilvy, whose interest was excited.

Then Godfrey, whose bosom was bursting, told her all, and the story lasted most of the way to Dover.

"You poor boy," she said, when he had finished, "you poor boy!"

"I left the basket with the food behind, and I am so hungry," remarked Godfrey presently.

"There's a restaurant car on the train, come and have some breakfast," said Miss Ogilvy, "for on the boat you may not wish to eat. I shall at any rate."

This was untrue for she had breakfasted already, but that did not matter.

"My father said I was not to take meals on the trains," explained Godfrey, awkwardly, "because of the expense."

"Oh! I'm your father, or rather your mother, now. Besides, I have a table," she added in a nebulous manner.

So Godfrey followed her to the dining car, where he made an excellent meal.

"You don't seem to eat much," he said at length. "You have only had a cup of tea and half a bit of toast."

"I never can when I am going on the sea," she explained. "I expect I shall be very ill, and you will have to look after me, and you know the less you eat, well—the less you can be ill."

"Why did you not tell me that before?" he remarked, contemplating his empty plate with a gloomy eye. "Besides I expect we shall be in different parts of the ship."

"Oh! I daresay it can be arranged," she answered.

And as a matter of fact, it was "arranged," all the way to Lucerne. At Dover station Miss Ogilvy had a hurried interview at the ticket office. Godfrey did not in the least understand what she was doing, but as a result he was her companion throughout the long journey. The crossing was very rough, and it was Godfrey who was ill, excessively ill, not Miss Ogilvy who, with the assistance of her maid and the steward, attended assiduously to him in his agonies.

"And to think," he moaned faintly as they moored alongside of the French pier, "that once I wished to be a sailor."

"Nelson was always sick," said Miss Ogilvy, wiping his damp brow with a scented pocket-handkerchief, while the maid held the smelling-salts to his nose.

"Then he must have been a fool to go to sea," muttered Godfrey, and relapsed into a torpor, from which he awoke only to find himself stretched at length on the cushions of a first-class carriage.

Later on, the journey became very agreeable. Godfrey was interested in everything, being of a quick and receptive mind, and Miss Ogilvy proved a fund of information. When they had exhausted the scenery they conversed on other topics. Soon she knew everything there was to know about him and Isobel, whom it was evident she could not understand.

"Tell me," she said, looking at his dark and rather unusual eyes, "do you ever have dreams, Godfrey?" for now she called him by his Christian name.

"Not at night, when I sleep very soundly, except after that poor cabman was killed. I have seen lots of dead people, because my father always takes me to look at them in the parish, to remind me of my own latter end, as he says, but they never made me dream before."

"Then do you have them at all?"

He hesitated a little.

"Sometimes, at least visions of a sort, when I am walking alone, especially in the evening, or wondering about things. But always when I am alone."

"What are they?" she asked eagerly.

"I can't quite explain," he replied in a slow voice. "They come and they go, and I forget them, because they fade out, just like a dream does, you know."

"You must remember something; try to tell me about them."

"Well, I seem to be among a great many people whom I have never met. Yet I know them and they know me, and talk to me about all sorts of things. For instance, if I am puzzling over anything they will explain it quite clearly, but afterwards I always forget the explanation and am no wiser than I was before. A hand holding a cloth seems to wipe it out of my mind, just as one cleans a slate."

"Is that all?"

"Not quite. Occasionally I meet the people afterwards. For instance, Thomas Sims, the cabman, was one of them, and," he added colouring, "forgive me for saying so, but you are another. I knew it at once, the moment I saw you, and that is what made me feel so friendly."

"How very odd!" she exclaimed, "and how delightful. Because, you see—well never mind—"

He looked at her expectantly, but as she said no more, went on.

"Then now and again I see places before I really do see them. For example, I think that presently we shall pass along a hillside with great mountain slopes above and below us covered with dark trees. Opposite to us also, running up to three peaks with a patch of snow on the centre peak, but not quite at the top." He closed his eyes, and added, "Yes, and there is a village at the bottom of the valley by a swift-running stream, and in it a small white church with a spire and a gilt weathercock with a bird on it. Then," he continued rapidly, "I can see the house where I am going to live, with the Pasteur Boiset, an old white house with woods above and all about it, and the beautiful lake beneath, and beyond, a great mountain. There is a tree in the garden opposite the front door, like a big cherry tree, only the fruit looks larger than cherries," he added with confidence.

"I suppose that no one showed you a photograph of the place?" she asked doubtfully, "for as it happens I know it. It is only about two miles from Lucerne by the short way through the woods. What is more, there is a tree with a delicious fruit, either a big cherry or a small plum, for I have eaten some of it several years ago."

"No," he answered, "no one. My father only told me that the name of the little village is Kleindorf. He wrote it on the label for my bag."

Just then the line went round a bend. "Look," he said, "there is the place I told you we were coming to, with the dark trees, the three peaks, and the stream, and the white church with the cock on top of the spire."

She let down the carriage window, and stared at the scene.

"Yes," she exclaimed, "it is just as you described. Oh! at last I have found what I have been seeking for years. Godfrey, I believe that you have the true gift."

"What gift, Miss Ogilvy?"

"Clairvoyance, of course, and perhaps clairaudience as well."

The lad burst out laughing, and said that he wished it were something more useful.

From all of which it will be guessed that Ethel Ogilvy was a mystic of the first water.

CHAPTER V

MADAME RIENNES

About 11 o'clock on the day following this conversation, Godfrey found himself standing on the platform in the big station of Lucerne.

"How are you going to get to Kleindorf?" Miss Ogilvy asked of him. "It's five miles away by the road. I think you had better come to my house and have some déjeuner. Afterwards I will send you there in the carriage."

As she spoke a tall gaunt man in ultra-clerical attire, with a very large hooked nose and wearing a pair of blue spectacles, came shuffling towards them.

"Madame is Engleesh?" he said, peering at her through the blue glasses. "Oh! it is easy to know it, though I am so blind. Has Madame by chance seen a leetle, leetle Engleesh boy, who should arrive out of this train? I look everywhere and I cannot find him, and the conducteur, he says he not there. No leetle boy in the second class. His name it is Godfrey, the son of an English pasteur, a man who fear God in the right way."

There was something so absurd in the old gentleman's appearance and method of address, that Miss Ogilvy, who had a sense of humour, was obliged to turn away to hide her mirth. Recovering, she answered:

"I think this is your little boy, Monsieur le Pasteur," and she indicated the tall and handsome Godfrey, who stood gazing at his future instructor open-mouthed. Whoever he had met in his visions, the Pasteur Boiset was not one of them. Never, asleep or waking, had he seen anyone in the least like him.

The clergyman peered at Godfrey, studying him from head to foot.

"Mon Dieu!" he exclaimed, "I understood he was quite, quite leetle, not a big young man who will eat much and want many things. Well, he will be bon compagnon for Juliette, and Madame too, she like the big better than the leetle. Il est beau et il a l'air intelligent, n'est ce pas, Madame?" he added confidentially.

"Bien beau et très intelligent," she replied, observing that Godfrey was engaged in retrieving his overcoat which he had left in the carriage. Then she explained that she had become friendly with this young gentleman, and hoped that he would be allowed to visit her whenever he wished. Also she gave her name and address.

"Oh! yes, Mademoiselle Ogilvee, the rich English lady who live in the fine house. I have heard of her. Mais voyons! Mademoiselle is not Catholic, is she, for I promise to protect this lad from that red wolf?"

"No, Monsieur, fear nothing. Whatever I am, I am not Catholic," (though, perhaps, if you knew all, you would think me something much more dangerous, she added to herself.)

Then they said goodbye.

"I say, Miss Ogilvy," exclaimed Godfrey, blushing, "you've been awfully kind to me. If it hadn't been for you I should have missed that train and never heard the last of it. Also, I should have had to go hungry from London here, since I promised my father not to buy anything on the journey, and you know I forgot the basket." (By the way, being addressed, it arrived three days afterwards, a mass of corruption, with six francs to pay on it, and many papers to be signed.)

"Not at all, Godfrey, it was delightful to have you as a companion—and a friend," she added meaningly. "You will come and see me, won't you?"

"Yes, of course, if I can. But meanwhile, please wait a minute," and he pulled out his purse.

"What on earth are you going to do, Godfrey? I don't want your card."

"Card! I haven't got a card. I am going to make you a present."

"Make me a present?" gasped Miss Ogilvy, a vague vision of half-crowns flashing before her mind.

"Yes, it is rather a curious thing. It was found round the neck-bone of an old knight, whose remains they threw out of the Abbey Church when they put in the heating apparatus. I saw it there, and the sexton gave it to me when he discovered that it was only stone. You will see it has a hole in it, so he must have worn it as an ornament. The grave he lay in was that of a Crusader, for the legs are crossed upon his brass, although his name has gone. Oh! here it is," and he produced an oblong piece of black graphite or some such stone, covered with mystical engravings.

She seized the object, and examined it eagerly.

"Why, it is a talisman," she said, "Gnostic, I should think, for there is the cock upon it, and a lot that I can't read, probably a magic formula. No doubt the old Crusader got it in the East, perhaps as a gift from some Saracen in whose family it had descended. Oh! my dear boy, I do thank you. You could not have made me a present that I should value more."

"I am so glad," said Godfrey.

"Yes, but I am ashamed to take it from you. Well, I'll leave it back to you one day."

"Leave it back! Then you must die before me, and why should you do that? You are quite young."

"Because I shall," she answered with a sad little smile. "I look stronger than I am. Meanwhile you will come and tell me all about this talisman."

"I have told you all I know, Miss Ogilvy."

"Do you think so? I don't. But look, your old pasteur is calling that the diligence is coming. Good-bye. I'll send the carriage for you next Sunday in time for déjeuner."

A few minutes later Godfrey found himself packed in a rumbling old diligence amidst a number of peasant women with baskets. Also there was a Roman Catholic priest who sat opposite to the Pasteur. For a while these two eyed each other with evident animosity, just like a pair of rival dogs, Godfrey thought to himself.

At the outskirts of the town they passed a shrine, in which was the image of some saint. The priest crossed himself and bowed so low that he struck the knee of the Pasteur, who remonstrated in an elaborate and sarcastic fashion. Then the fight began, and those two holy men belaboured each other, with words, not fists, for the rest of the journey. Godfrey's French was sadly to seek, still before it was done, he did wonder whether all their language was strictly Christian, for such words as Sapristi, and Nom de Dieu, accompanied by snapping of the fingers, and angry stares, struck him as showing a contentious and even a hostile spirit. Moreover, that was not the end of it, since of the occupants of the diligence, about one half seemed to belong to the party of the priest, and the other half to the party of the Pasteur.

By degrees all of these were drawn into the conflict. They shouted and screamed at each other, they waved their arms, and incidentally their baskets, one of which struck Godfrey on the nose, and indeed nearly came to actual fisticuffs.

Apparently the driver was accustomed to such scenes, for after a glance through his little window he took no further notice. So it went on until at last he pulled up and shouted:

"Voyageurs pour Kleindorf, descendez. Vite, s'il vous plait."

"Here we do get down, young Monsieur," said the Pasteur, suddenly relapsing into a kind of unnatural calm. Indeed, at the door he turned and bowed politely to his adversary, wishing him bon voyage, to which the priest replied with a solemn benediction in the most Catholic form.

"He is not bad of heart, that priest," said the Pasteur, as he led the way to the gate of a little shrubbery, "but he do try to steal my sheep, and I protect them from him, the blood-toothed wolf. Jean, Jean!"

A brawny Swiss appeared and seized the baggage. Then they advanced across the belt of shrubbery to a lawn, through which ran a path. Lo! in the centre of that lawn grew such a fruit-tree, covered with large cherries or small plums, as Godfrey had described to Miss Ogilvy, and beyond it stood the long white house, old, and big, and peaceful looking. What he had not described, because of them his subliminal sense had given him no inkling, were the two ladies, who sat expectant on the verandah, that commanded a beautiful view of the lake and the mountains beyond.

By a kind of instinct distilled from his experience of clergymen's belongings, Godfrey had expected to see a dowdy female, with a red, fat face, and watery eyes, perhaps wearing an apron and a black dress hooked awry, accompanied by a snub-nosed little girl with straight hair, and a cold in the head. In place of these he saw a fashionably- dressed, Parisian-looking lady, who still seemed quite young, very pleasant to behold, with her dark eyes and graceful movements, and a girl, apparently about his own age, who was equally attractive.

She was brown-eyed, with a quick, mobile face, and a lithe and shapely, if as yet somewhat unformed figure. The long thick plait in which her chestnut hair was arranged could not hide its plenitude and beauty, while the smallness of her hands and feet showed breeding, as did her manners and presence. The observant Godfrey, at his first sight of Juliette, for such was her name, marvelled how it was possible that she should be the daughter of that plain and ungainly old pasteur. On this point it is enough to say that others had experienced the same wonder, and remained with their curiosity unsatisfied. But then he might as well have inquired how he, Godfrey, came to be his father's son, since in the whole universe no two creatures could have been more diverse.

Monsieur Boiset waddled forward, with a gait like to that of a superannuated duck, followed at some distance by Godfrey and the stalwart Jean with the luggage.

"My dears," he called out in his high voice, "I have found our new little friend; the train brought him safely. Here he is."

Madame and Juliette looked about them.

"I see him not," said Madame.

"Where is he?" asked Juliette, in a pleasant girlish voice. "Still at the gate? And say then, my father," this in low tones meant not to be overheard, "who is this monsieur?"

"He is the little boy," exclaimed the Pasteur, chuckling at his joke, "but you see he has grown in the train."

"Mon Dieu!" exclaimed Madame, "I wonder if his bed will be long enough?"

"It is very amusing," remarked Juliette.

Then they both descended from the verandah, to greet him with foreign cordiality which, as they spoke rapidly in French, was somewhat lost on Godfrey. Recognizing their kind intentions, however, he took off his hat and bowed to each in turn, remarking as he did so:

"Bonjour, oui. Oui, bonjour," the only words in the Gallic tongue that occurred to him at the moment.

"I speek Engleesh," said Juliette, with solemn grandeur.

"I'm jolly glad to hear it," replied Godfrey, "and I parle Français, or soon shall, I hope."

Such was Godfrey's introduction to his new home at Kleindorf, where very soon he was happy enough. Notwithstanding his strange appearance and his awkwardness, Monsieur Boiset proved himself to be what is called "a dear old gentleman"; moreover, really learned, and this in sundry different directions. Thus, he was an excellent astronomer, and the possessor of a first-rate telescope, mounted in a little observatory, on a rocky peak of ground which rose up a hundred feet or more in the immediate neighbourhood of the house, that itself stood high. This instrument, which its owner had acquired secondhand at some sale, of course was not of the largest size. Still, it was powerful enough for all ordinary observations, and to show many hundreds of the heavenly bodies that are invisible to the naked eye, even in the clear air of Switzerland.

To Godfrey, who had, it will be remembered, a strong liking for astronomy, it was a source of constant delight. What is more, it provided a link of common interest that soon ripened into friendship between himself and his odd old tutor, who had been obliged hitherto to pursue his astral researches in solitude, since to Madame and to Juliette these did not appeal. Night by night, especially after the winter snows began to fall, they would sit by the stove in the little observatory, gazing at the stars, making calculations, in which, notwithstanding his dislike of mathematics, Godfrey soon became expert, and setting down the results of what they learned.

In was in course of these studies that the whole wonder of the universe came home to him for the first time. He looked upon the marvel of the heavens, the mighty procession of the planets, the rising and setting of the vast suns that burn beyond them in the depths of space, weighing their bulk and measuring their differences, and trembled with mingled joy and awe. Were these the heritage of man? Would he ever visit them in some unknown state and age? Or must they remain eternally far and alien? This is what he longed to learn, and to him astronomy was a gateway to knowledge, if only he could discover how to pass the gate.

Godfrey had not the true scientific spirit, or a yearning for information, even about the stars, for its own sake. He wanted to ascertain how these affected him and the human race of which he was a member. In short, he sought an answer to the old question: Are we merely the spawn of our little earth, destined to perish, as the earth itself must do one day, or, through whatever changes we must pass, are we as immortal as the universe and the Might that made it, whatever that may be? That was his problem, the same which perplexes every high and thinking soul, and at this impressionable period of his life it scarcely ever left him. There he would sit with brooding eyes and bent brow seeking the answer, but as yet finding none.

Once Juliette discovered him thus, having come to the observatory to tell him that his dinner had been waiting for half an hour, and for a while watched him unnoted with the little shaded lamp shining on his face. Instantly, in her quick fashion, she christened him, Hibou, and Hibou or Owl, became his nickname in that establishment. Indeed, with his dark eyes and strongly marked features, wrapped in a contemplative calm such as the study of the stars engenders, in that gloom he did look something like an owl, however different may have been his appearance on other occasions.

"What are you thinking of, Monsieur Godfrey?" she asked.

He came back to earth with a start.

"The stars and Man," he answered, colouring.

"Mon Dieu!" she exclaimed, "I think man is enough to study without the stars, which we shall never visit."

"How do you know that, Mademoiselle?"

"I know it because we are here and they are there, far, far away. Also we die and they go on for ever."

"What is space, and what are death and time?" queried Godfrey, with solemnity.

"Mon Dieu!" said Juliette again. "Come to dinner, the chicken it grows cold," but to herself she added, "He is an odd bird, this English hibou, but attractive—when he is not so grave."

Meanwhile Godfrey continued to ponder his mighty problem. When he had mastered enough French in which Madame and Juliette proved efficient instructors, he propounded it to the old Pasteur, who clapped his hand upon a Bible, and said:

"There is the answer, young friend."

"I know," replied Godfrey, "but it does not quite satisfy; I feel that I must find that answer for myself."

Monsieur Boiset removed his blue spectacles and looked at him.

"Such searches are dangerous," he said. "Believe me, Godfrey, it is better to accept."

"Then why do you find fault with the Roman Catholics, Monsieur?"

The question was like a match applied to a haystack. At once the Pasteur took fire:

"Because they accept error, not truth," he began. "What foundation have they for much of their belief? It is not here," and again he slapped the Bible.

Then followed a long tirade, for the one thing this good and tolerant old man could not endure was the Roman Catholic branch of the Christian Faith.

Godfrey listened with patience, till at last the Pasteur, having burnt himself out, asked him if he were not convinced.

"I do not know," he replied. "These quarrels of the Churches and of the different faiths puzzle and tire me. I, too, Monsieur, believe in God and a future life, but I do not think it matters much by what road one travels to them, I mean so long as it is a road."

The Pasteur looked at him alarmed, and exclaimed:

"Surely you will not be a fish caught in the net which already I have observed that cunning and plausible curé trying to throw about you! Oh! what then should I answer to your father?"

"Do not be frightened, Monsieur. I shall never become a Roman Catholic. But all the same I think the Roman Catholics very good people, and that their faith is as well as another, at any rate for those who believe it."

Then he made an excuse to slip away, leaving the Pasteur puzzled.

"He is wrong," he said to himself, "most wrong, but all the same, let it be admitted that the boy has a big mind, and intelligent—yes, intelligent."

It is certain that those who search with sufficient earnestness end in finding something, though the discovered path may run in the wrong direction, or prove impassable, or wind through caverns, or along the edge of precipices, down which sooner or later the traveller falls, or lead at length to some cul-de-sac. The axiom was not varied in Godfrey's case, and the path he found was named—Miss Ogilvy.

On the first Sunday after his arrival at Kleindorf a fine carriage and pair drew up at the shrubbery gate, just as the family were returning from the morning service in the little church where the Pasteur ministered. Madame sighed when she saw it, for she would have loved dearly to possess such an equipage, as indeed, she had done at one period in her career, before an obscure series of circumstances led to her strange union with Monsieur Boiset.

"What beautiful horses," exclaimed Juliette, her hazel eyes sparkling. "Oh! that tenth Commandment, who can keep it? And why should some people have fine horses and others not even a pony? Ma mère, why were you not able to keep that carriage of which you have spoken to me so often?"

Madame bit her lip, and with a whispered "hold your tongue," plunged into conversation about Miss Ogilvy. Then Godfrey entered the carriage and was whirled away in style, looking like the prince in a fairy book, as Juliette remarked, while the Pasteur tried to explain to her how much happier she was without the temptation of such earthly vanities.

Miss Ogilvy's house was a beautiful dwelling of its sort, standing in gardens of its own that ran down to the lake, and commanding fine views of all the glorious scenery which surrounds Lucerne. The rooms were large and lofty, with parquet floors, and in some of them were really good pictures that their owner had inherited, also collections of beautiful old French furniture. In short, it was a stately and refined abode, such as is sometimes to be found abroad in the possession of Americans or English people of wealth, who for their health's sake or other reasons, make their homes upon the Continent.

On hearing the carriage arrive, Miss Ogilvy, who was dressed in a simple, but charming grey gown and, as Godfrey noticed at once, wore round her neck the old Gnostic talisman which he had given her, came from a saloon to meet him in the large, square hall.

"I am glad to see you, Godfrey," she said in her soft, cultivated voice.

"So am I, Miss Ogilvy," he answered, with heartiness, "I mean to see you. But," he added, studying her, "you do not look very well."

She smiled rather pathetically, and said in a quick voice:

"No, I took a cold on that journey. You see I am rather an invalid, which is why I live here—while I do live—what they call poitrinaire."

Godfrey shook his head, the word was beyond him.

"Anglicé consumptive," she explained. "There are lots of us in Switzerland, you know, and on the whole, we are a merry set. It is characteristic of our complaint. But never mind about me. There are two or three people here. I daresay you will think them odd, but they are clever in their way, and you ought to have something in common. Come in."

He followed her into the beautiful cool saloon, with its large, double French windows designed to keep out the bitter winds of winter, but opened now upon the brilliant garden. Never before had he been in so lovely a room, that is of a modern house, and it impressed him with sensations that at the moment he did not try to analyse. All he knew was that they were mingled with some spiritual quality, such as once or twice he had felt in ancient churches, something which suggested both the Past and the Future, and a brooding influence that he could not define. Yet the place was all light and charm, gay with flowers and landscape pictures, in short, lacking any sombre note.

Gathered at its far end where the bow window overlooked the sparkling lake, were three or four people, all elderly. Instantly one of these riveted his attention. She was stout, having her grey hair drawn back from a massive forehead, beneath which shone piercing black eyes. Her rather ungainly figure was clothed in what he thought an ugly green dress, and she wore a necklet of emeralds in an old-fashioned setting, which he also thought ugly but striking. From the moment that he entered the doorway at the far end of that long saloon, he felt those black eyes fixed upon him, and was painfully aware of their owner's presence, so much so, that in a whisper, he asked her name of Miss Ogilvy.

"Oh!" she answered, "that is Madame Riennes, the noted mesmerist and medium."

"Indeed," said Godfrey in a vague voice, for he did not quite understand what was meant by this description.

Also there was a thin, elderly American gentleman to whom Godfrey was introduced, named Colonel Josiah Smith, and a big, blond Dane, who talked English with a German accent, called Professor Petersen. All of these studied Godfrey with the most unusual interest as, overwhelmed with shyness, he was led by Miss Ogilvy to make their acquaintance. He felt that their demeanour portended he knew not what, more at any rate than hope of deriving pleasure from his society; in fact, that they expected to get something out of him. Suddenly he recollected a picture that once he had seen in a pious work which he was given to read on Sundays. It represented a missionary being led by the hand by a smiling woman into the presence of some savages in a South Sea island, who were about to cook and eat him.

In the picture a large pot was already boiling over a fire in the background. Instinctively Godfrey looked for the pot, but saw none, except one of the flowers which stood on a little table in a recess, and round it half a dozen chairs, one of them large, with arms. Had he but known it, that chair was the pot.

No sooner had he made his somewhat awkward bow than luncheon was announced, and they all went into another large and beautiful room, where they were served with a perfect meal. The conversation at table was general, and in English, but presently it drifted into a debate which Godfrey did not understand, on the increase of spirituality among the "initiated" of the earth.

Colonel Josiah Smith, who appeared to associate with remarkable persons whom he called "Masters," who dwelt in the remote places of the world, alleged that such increase was great, which Professor Petersen, who dwelt much among German intellectuals, denied. It appeared that these "intellectuals" were busy in turning their backs on every form of spirituality.

"Ah!" said Miss Ogilvy, with a sigh, "they seek the company of their kindred 'Elementals,' although they do not know it, and soon those Elementals will have the mastery of them and break them to pieces, as the lions did the maligners of Daniel."

In after years Godfrey always remembered this as a very remarkable prophecy, but at the time, not knowing what an Elemental might be, he only marvelled.

At length Madame Riennes, who, it seemed, was half French and half Russian, intervened in a slow, heavy voice:

"What does it matter, friends of my soul?" she asked. Then having paused to drink off a full glass of sparkling Moselle, she went on: "Soon we shall be where the spirituality, or otherwise, of this little world matters nothing to us. Who will be the first to learn the truths, I wonder?" and she stared in turn at the faces of every one of them, a process which seemed to cause general alarm, bearing, as it did, a strong resemblance to the smelling-out of savage witch-doctors.

Indeed, they all began to talk of this or that at hazard, but she was not to be put off by such interruptions. Having investigated Godfrey till he felt cold down the back, Madame turned her searchlight eyes upon Miss Ogilvy, who shrank beneath them. Then of a sudden she exclaimed with a kind of convulsive shudder:

"The Power possesses and guides me. It tells me that you will be the first, Sister Helen. I see you among the immortal Lilies with the Wine of Life flowing through your veins."

On receipt of this information the Wine of Life seemed to cease to flow in poor Miss Ogilvy's face. At any rate, she went deadly pale and rested her hand upon Godfrey's shoulder as if she were about to faint. Recovering a little, she murmured to herself:

"I thought it! Well, what does it matter though the gulf is great and terrible?"

Then with an effort she rose and suggested that they should return to the drawing-room.

They did so, and were served with Turkish coffee and cigarettes, which Madame Riennes smoked one after the other very rapidly. Presently Miss Ogilvy rang the bell, and when the butler appeared to remove the cups, whispered something in French, at which he bowed and departed.

Godfrey thought he heard him lock the door behind him, but was not sure.

CHAPTER VI

"Let us sit round the table and talk," said Madame Riennes.

Thereon the whole party moved into the recess where was the flower-pot that has been mentioned, which Miss Ogilvy took away.

They seated themselves round the little table upon which it had stood. Godfrey, lingering behind, found, whether by design or accident, that the only place left for him was the arm-chair which he hesitated to occupy.

"Be seated, young Monsieur," said the formidable Madame in bell-like tones, whereon he collapsed into the chair. "Sister Helen," she went on, "draw the curtain, it is more private so; yes, and the blind that there may be no unholy glare."

Miss Ogilvy, who seemed to be entirely under Madame's thumb, obeyed. Now to all intents and purposes they were in a tiny, shadowed room cut off from the main apartment.

"Take that talisman from your neck and give it to young Monsieur Knight," commanded Madame.

"But I gave it to her, and do not want it back," ventured Godfrey, who was growing alarmed.

"Do what I say," she said sternly, and he found himself holding the relic.

"Now, young Monsieur, look me in the eyes a little and listen. I request of you that holding that black, engraved stone in your hand, you will be so good as to throw your soul, do you understand, your soul, back, back, back and tell us where it come from, who have it, what part it play in their life, and everything about it."

"How am I to know?" asked Godfrey, with indignation.

Then suddenly everything before him faded, and he saw himself standing in a desert by a lump of black rock, at which a brown man clad only in a waist cloth and a kind of peaked straw hat, was striking with an instrument that seemed to be half chisel and half hammer, fashioned apparently from bronze, or perhaps of greenish-coloured flint. Presently the brown man, who had a squint in one eye and a hurt toe that was bound round with something, picked up a piece of the black rock that he had knocked off, and surveyed it with evident satisfaction. Then the scene vanished.

Godfrey told it with interest to the audience who were apparently also interested.

"The finding of the stone," said Madame. "Continue, young Monsieur."

Another vision rose before Godfrey's mind. He beheld a low room having a kind of verandah, roofed with reeds, and beyond it a little courtyard enclosed by a wall of grey-coloured mud bricks, out of some of which stuck pieces of straw. This courtyard opened onto a narrow street where many oddly-clothed people walked up and down, some of whom wore peaked caps. A little man, old and grey, sat with the fragment of black rock on a low table before him, which Godfrey knew to be the same stone that he had already seen. By him lay graving tools, and he was engaged in polishing the stone, now covered with figures and writing, by help of a stick, a piece of rough cloth and oil. A young man with a curly beard walked into the little courtyard, and to him the old fellow delivered the engraved stone with obeisances, receiving payment in some curious currency.

Then followed picture upon picture in all of which the talisman appeared in the hands of sundry of its owners. Some of these pictures had to do with love, some with religious ceremonies, and some with war. One, too, with its sale, perhaps in a time of siege or scarcity, for a small loaf of black-looking bread, by an aged woman who wept at parting with it.

After this he saw an Arab-looking man finding the stone amongst the crumbling remains of a brick wall that showed signs of having been burnt, which wall he was knocking down with a pick-axe to allow water to flow down an irrigation channel on his garden. Presently a person who wore a turban and was girt about with a large scimitar, rode by, and to him the man showed, and finally presented the stone, which the Saracen placed in the folds of his turban.

The next scene was of this man engaged in battle with a knight clad in mail. The battle was a very fine one, which Godfrey described with much gusto. It ended in the knight killing the Eastern man and hacking off his head with a sword. This violent proceeding disarranged the turban out of which fell the black stone. The knight picked it up and hid it about him. Next Godfrey saw this same knight, grown into an old man and being borne on a bier to burial, clad in the same armour that he had worn in the battle. Upon his breast hung the black stone which had now a hole bored through the top of it.

Lastly there came a picture of the old sexton finding the talisman among the bones of the knight, and giving it to himself, Godfrey, then a small boy, after which everything passed away.

"I guess that either our young friend here has got the vision, or that he will make a first-class novelist," said Colonel Josiah Smith. "Any way, if you care to part with that talisman, Miss Ogilvy, I will be glad to give you five hundred dollars for it on the chance of his integrity."

She smiled and shook her head, stretching out her hand to recover the Gnostic charm.

"Be silent, Brother Josiah Smith," exclaimed Madame Riennes, angrily. "If this were imposture, should I not have discovered it? It is good vision—psychometry is the right term—though of a humbler order such as might be expected from a beginner. Still, there is hope, there is hope. Let us see, now. Young gentleman, be so good as to look me in the eye."

Much against his will Godfrey found himself bound to obey, and looked her "in the eye." A few moments later he felt dizzy, and after that he remembered no more.

When Godfrey awoke again the curtain was drawn, the blinds were pulled up and the butler was bringing in tea. Miss Ogilvy sat by his side, looking at him rather anxiously, while the others were conversing together in a somewhat excited fashion.

"It is splendid, splendid!" Madame was saying. "We have discovered a pearl beyond price, a great treasure. Hush! he awakes."

Godfrey, who experienced a curious feeling of exhaustion and of emptiness of brain, yawned and apologized for having fallen asleep, whereon the professor and the colonel both assured him that it was quite natural on so warm a day. Only Madame Riennes smiled like a sphinx, and asked him if his dreams were pleasant. To this he replied that he remembered none.

Miss Ogilvy, however, who looked rather anxious and guilty, did not speak at all, but busied herself with the tea which Godfrey thought very strong when he drank it. However, it refreshed him wonderfully, which, as it contained some invigorating essence, was not strange. So did the walk in the beautiful garden which he took afterwards, just before the carriage came to drive him back to Kleindorf.

Re-entering the drawing-room to say goodbye, he found the party engaged listening to the contents of a number of sheets of paper closely written in pencil, which were being read to them by Colonel Josiah Smith, who made corrections from time to time.

"Au revoir, my young brother," said Madame Riennes, making some mysterious sign before she took his hand in her fat, cold fingers, "you will come again next Sunday, will you not?"

"I don't know," he answered awkwardly, for he felt afraid of this lady, and did not wish to see her next Sunday.

"Oh! but I do, young brother. You will come, because it gives me so much pleasure to see you," she replied, staring at him with her strange eyes.

Then Godfrey knew that he would come because he must.

"Why does that lady call me 'young brother'?" he asked Miss Ogilvy, who accompanied him to the hall.

"Oh! because it is a way she has. You may have noticed that she called me 'sister'."

"I don't think that I shall call her sister," he remarked with decision. "She is too alarming."

"Not really when you come to know her, for she has the kindest heart and is wonderfully gifted."

"Gifts which make people tell others that they are going to die are not pleasant, Miss Ogilvy."

She shivered a little.

"If her spirit—I mean the truth—comes to her, she must speak it, I suppose. By the way, Godfrey, don't say anything about this talisman and the story you told of it, at Kleindorf, or in writing home."

"Why not?"

"Oh! because people like your dear old Pasteur, and clergymen generally, are so apt to misunderstand. They think that there is only one way of learning things beyond, and that every other must be wrong. Also I am sure that your friend, Isobel Blake, would laugh at you."

"I don't write to Isobel," he exclaimed setting his lips.

"But you may later," she said smiling. "At any rate you will promise, won't you?"

"Yes, if you wish it, Miss Ogilvy, though I can't see what it matters. That kind of nonsense often comes into my head when I touch old things. Isobel says that it is because I have too much imagination."

"Imagination! Ah! what is imagination? Well, goodbye, Godfrey, the carriage will come for you at the same time next Sunday. Perhaps, too, I shall see you before then, as I am going to call upon Madame Boiset."

Then he went, feeling rather uncomfortable, and yet interested, though what it was that interested him he did not quite know. That night he dreamed that Madame Riennes stood by his bed watching him with her burning eyes. It was an unpleasant dream.

He kept his word. When the Boiset family, especially Madame, cross-examined him as to the details of his visit to Miss Ogilvy, he merely described the splendours of that opulent establishment and the intellectual character of its guests. Of their mystic attributes he said nothing at all, only adding that Miss Ogilvy proposed to do herself the honour of calling at the Maison Blanche, as the Boisets' house was called.

About the middle of the week Miss Ogilvy arrived and, as Madame had taken care to be at home in expectation of her visit, was entertained to tea. Afterwards she visited the observatory, which interested her much, and had a long talk with the curious old Pasteur, who also interested her in his way, for as she afterwards remarked to Godfrey, one does not often meet an embodiment of human goodness and charity. When he replied that the latter quality was lacking to the Pasteur where Roman Catholics were concerned, she only smiled and said that every jewel had its flaw; nothing was quite perfect in the world.

In the end she asked Madame and Juliette to come to lunch with her, leaving out Godfrey, because, as she said, she knew that he would be engaged at his studies with the Pasteur. She explained also that she did not ask them to come with him on Sunday because they would be taken up with their religious duties, a remark at which Juliette made what the French call a "mouth," and Madame smiled faintly.

In due course she and her daughter went to lunch and returned delighted, having found themselves fellow-guests of some of the most notable people in Lucerne, though not those whom Miss Ogilvy entertained on Sundays. Needless to say from that time forward Godfrey's intimacy with this charming and wealthy hostess was in every way encouraged by the Boiset family.

The course of this intimacy does not need any very long description. Every Sunday after church the well-appointed carriage and pair appeared and bore Godfrey away to luncheon at the Villa Ogilvy. Here he always met Madame Riennes, Colonel Josiah Smith, and Professor Petersen; also occasionally one or two others with whom these seemed to be sufficiently intimate to admit of their addressing them as "Brother" or "Sister."

Soon Godfrey came to understand that they were all members of some kind of semi-secret society, though what this might be he could not quite ascertain. All he made sure of was that it had to do with matters which were not of this world. Nothing concerning mundane affairs, however important or interesting, seemed to appeal to them; all their conversation was directed towards what might be called spiritual problems, reincarnations, Karmas (it took him a long time to understand what a Karma is), astral shapes, mediumship, telepathic influences, celestial guides, and the rest.

At first this talk with its jargon of words which he did not comprehend, bored him considerably, but by degrees he felt that he was being drawn into a vortex, and began to understand its drift. Even while it was enigmatic it acquired a kind of unholy attraction for him, and he began to seek out its secret meaning in which he found that company ready instructors.

"Young brother," said Madame Riennes, "we deal with the things not of the body, but of the soul. The body, what is it? In a few years it will be dust and ashes, but the soul—it is eternal—and all those stars you study are its inheritance, and you and I, if we cultivate our spiritual parts, shall rule in them."

Then she would roll her big eyes and become in a way magnificent, so that Godfrey forgot her ugliness and the repulsion with which she inspired him.

In the end his outlook on life and the world became different, and this not so much because of what he learned from his esoteric teachers, as through some change in his internal self. He grew to appreciate the vastness of things and the infinite possibilities of existence. Indeed, his spiritual education was a fitting pendant to his physical study of the heavens, peopled with unnumbered worlds, each of them the home, doubtless, of an infinite variety of life, and each of them keeping its awful secrets locked in its floating orb. He trembled in presence of the stupendous Whole, of which thus by degrees he became aware, and though it frightened him, thought with pity of the busy millions of mankind to whom such mysteries are nothing at all; who are lost in their business or idleness, in their eating, drinking, sleeping, love-making, and general satisfaction of the instincts which they possess in common with every other animal. The yearning for wisdom, the desire to know, entered his young heart and possessed it, as once these did that of Solomon, to such a degree indeed, that standing on the threshold of his days, he would have paid them all away, and with them his share in this warm and breathing world, could he have been assured that in exchange he would receive the key of the treasure-house of the Infinite.

Such an attitude was neither healthy nor natural to a normal, vigorous lad just entering upon manhood, and, as will be seen, it did not endure. Like everything else, it had its causes. His astronomical studies were one of these, but a deeper reason was to be found in those Sunday séances at the Villa Ogilvy. For a long while Godfrey did not know what happened to him on these occasions. The party sat round the little table, talking of wonderful things; Madame Riennes looked at him and sometimes took his hand, which he did not like, and then he remembered no more until he woke up, feeling tired, and yet in a way exhilarated, for with the mysteries of hypnotic sleep he was not yet acquainted. Nor did it occur to him that he was being used a medium by certain of the most advanced spiritualists in the world.

By degrees, however, inklings of the truth began to come. Thus, one day his consciousness awoke while his body seemed still to be wrapt in trance, and he saw that there was a person present who had not been of the party when he went to sleep. A young woman, clad in a white robe, with lovely hair flowing down her back, stood by his side and held his supine fingers in her hand.

She was beautiful, and yet unearthly, she wore ornaments also, but as he watched, to his amazement these seemed to change. What had been a fillet of white stones, like diamonds, which bound her hair, turned to one of red stones, like rubies, and as it did so the colour of her eyes, which were large and very tranquil, altered.

She was speaking in a low, rich voice to Miss Ogilvy, who answered, addressing her as Sister Eleanor, but what she said Godfrey could not understand. Something of his inner shock and fear must have reflected itself upon his trance-bound features, for suddenly he heard Madame Riennes exclaim:

"Have done! the medium awakes, and I tell you it is dangerous while our Guide is here. Back to his breast, Eleanor! Thence to your place!"

The tall figure changed; it became misty, shapeless. It seemed to fall on him like a cloud of icy vapour, chilling him to the heart, and through that vapour he could see the ormolu clock which stood on a bracket in the recess, and even note the time, which was thirteen minutes past four. After this he became unconscious, and in due course woke up as usual. The first thing his eyes fell on was the clock, of which the hands now pointed to a quarter to five, and the sight of it brought everything back to him. Then he observed that all the circle seemed much agitated, and distinctly heard Madame Riennes say to Professor Petersen in English:—

"The thing was very near. Had it not been for that medicine of yours—! It was because that speerit do take his hand. She grow fond of him; it happen sometimes if the medium be of the other sex and attractive. She want to carry him away with her, that Control, and I expect she never quite leave him all his life, because, you see, she materialize out of him, and therefore belong to him. Next time she come, I give her my mind. Hush! Our wonderful little brother wake up—quite right this time."

Then Godfrey really opened his eyes; hitherto he had been feigning to be still in trance, but thought it wisest to say nothing. At this moment Miss Ogilvy turned very pale and went into a kind of light faint.

The Professor produced some kind of smelling-bottle from his pocket, which he held to her nostrils. She came to at once, and began to laugh at her own silliness, but begged them all to go away and leave her quiet, which they did. Godfrey was going too, but she stopped him, saying that the carriage would not be ready till after tea, and that it was too wet for him to walk in the garden, for now autumn had come in earnest. The tea arrived, a substantial tea, with poached eggs, of which she made him eat two, as she did always after these sittings. Then suddenly she asked him if he had seen anything. He told her all, adding:

"I am frightened. I do not like this business, Miss Ogilvy. Who and what was that lady in white, who stood by me and held my hand? My fingers are still tingling, and a cold wind seems to blow upon me."

"It was a spirit, Godfrey, but there is no need to be afraid, she will not do you any harm."

"I don't know, and I don't think that you have any right to bring spirits to me, or out of me, as I heard that dreadful Madame say had happened. It is a great liberty."

"Oh! don't be angry with me," she said piteously. "If only you understood. You are a wonderful medium, the most wonderful that any of us has ever known, and through you we have learned things; holy, marvellous things, which till now have not been heard of in the world. Your fame is already great among leading spiritualists of the earth, though of course they do not know who you are."

"That does not better matters," said Godfrey, "you know it is not right."

"Perhaps not, but my dear boy, if only you guessed all it means to me! Listen; I will tell you; you will not betray me, will you? Once I was very fond of someone; he was all my life, and he died, and my heart broke. I only hope and pray that such a thing may never happen to you. Well, from that hour to this I have been trying to find him and failed, always failed, though once or twice I thought—. And now through you I have found him. Yes, he has spoken to me telling me much which proves to me that he still lives elsewhere and awaits me. And oh! I am happy, and do not care how soon I go to join him. And it is all through you. So you will forgive me, will you not?"

"Yes, I suppose so," said Godfrey, "but all the same I don't want to have anything more to do with that white lady who is called Eleanor and changes her jewels so often; especially as Madame said she was growing fond of me and would never leave me. So please don't ask me here again on Sundays."

Miss Ogilvy tried to soothe him.

"You shouldn't be frightened of her," she said. "She is really a delightful spirit, and declares that she knew you very intimately indeed, when you were an early Egyptian, also much before that on the lost continent, which is called Atlantis, to say nothing of deep friendships which have existed between you in other planets."

"I say!" exclaimed Godfrey, "do you believe all this?"

"Well, if you ask me, I must say that I do. I am sure that we have all of us lived many lives, here and elsewhere, and if this is so, it is obvious that in the course of them we must have met an enormous number of people, with certain of whom we have been closely associated in the various relationships of life. Some of these, no doubt, come round with us again, but others do not, though we can get into touch with them under exceptional circumstances. That is your case and Eleanor's. At present you are upon different spheres, but in the future, no doubt, you will find yourselves side by side again, as you have often been, in due course to be driven apart once more by the winds of Destiny, and perhaps, after ages, finally to be united. Meanwhile she plays the part of one of your guardian angels."

"Then I wish she wouldn't," said Godfrey, with vigour. "I don't care for a guardian angel of whom I have no memory, and who seems to fall on you like snow upon a hot day. If anybody does that kind of thing I should prefer a living woman."

"Which doubtless she has been, and will be again. For you see, where she is, she has memory and foreknowledge, which are lacking to the incarnated. Meanwhile, through you, and because of you, she can tell us much. You are the wire which connects us to her in the Unseen."

"Then I hope you will find another wire; I really do, for it upsets me and makes me feel ill. I know that I shall be afraid to go to bed to-night, and even for you, Miss Ogilvy, I won't come next Sunday."

Then, as the carriage was now at the door, he jumped into it and departed without waiting for an answer.

Moreover, on the next Sunday, when, as usual, it arrived to fetch him at Kleindorf, Godfrey kept his word, so that it went back empty. By the coachman he sent an awkwardly worded note to Miss Ogilvy, saying that he was suffering from toothache which had prevented him from sleeping for several nights, and was not well enough to come out.

This note she answered by post, telling him that she had been disappointed not to see him as she was also ill. She added that she would send the carriage on the following Sunday on the chance of his toothache being better, but that if it was not, she would understand and trouble him no more.

During all that week Godfrey fought with himself. He did not wish to have anything more to do with the white and ghostly Eleanor, who changed her gems so constantly, and said that she had known him millenniums ago. Indeed, he felt already as though she were much too near him, especially at night, when he seemed to become aware of her bending over his bed, and generally making her presence known in other uncomfortable ways that caused his hair to stand up and frightened him.

At the same time he was really fond of Miss Ogilvy, and what she said about being ill touched him. Also there was something that drew him; it might be Eleanor, or it might be Madame Riennes. At any rate he felt a great longing to go. Putting everything else aside, these investigations had their delights. What other young fellow of his age could boast an Eleanor, who said she had been fond of him tens of thousands of years before?

Moreover, here was one of the gates to that knowledge which he desired so earnestly, and how could he find the strength to shut it in his own face?

Of course the end of the matter was that by the following Sunday, his toothache had departed, and the carriage did not return empty to the Villa Ogilvy.

He found his hostess looking white and ethereal, an appearance that she had acquired increasingly ever since their first meeting. Her delight at seeing him was obvious, as was that of the others. For this he soon discovered the reason. It appeared that the sitting on the previous Sunday, when he was overcome by toothache, had been an almost total failure. Professor Petersen had tried to fill his place as medium, with the result that when he fell under the influence, the only spirit that broke through his lips was one which discoursed interminably about lager beer and liqueurs of some celestial brew, which, as Madame Riennes, a lady not given to mince her words, told him to his face afterwards, was because he drank too much. Hence the joy of these enthusiasts at the re-appearance of Godfrey.

With considerable reluctance that youth consented to play his usual rôle, and to be put into a charmed sleep by Madame. This time he saw no Eleanor, and knew nothing of what happened until he awoke to be greeted by the horrific spectacle of Miss Ogilvy lying back in her chair bathed in blood. General confusion reigned in the midst of which Madame Riennes alone was calm.

"It is hæmorrhage from the lungs," she said, "which is common among poitrinaires. Brother Petersen, do what you can, and you, Brother Smith, fly for Mademoiselle's doctor, and if he is not at home, bring another."

Later Godfrey heard what had chanced. It seemed that the wraith, or emanation, or the sprite, good or evil, or whatever it may have been, which called itself Eleanor, materialized in a very ugly temper. It complained that it had not been allowed to appear upon the previous Sunday and had been kept away from its brother, i.e. Godfrey. Then it proceeded to threaten all the circle, except Godfrey, who was the real culprit, with divers misfortunes, especially directing its wrath against Miss Ogilvy.

"You will die soon," it said, "and in the spirit world I will pay you back." Thrice it repeated this: "You will die," to which Miss Ogilvy answered with calm dignity:

"I am not afraid to die, nor am I at all afraid of you, Eleanor, who, as I now see, are not good but evil."

While she spoke a torrent of blood burst from her lips, Eleanor disappeared, and almost immediately Godfrey awoke.

In due course the doctor came and announced that the hæmorrhage had ceased, and that the patient was in no imminent danger. As to the future, he could say nothing, except that having been Miss Ogilvy's medical attendant for some years, he had expected something of this sort to happen, and known that her life could not be very long.

Then Godfrey went home very terrified and chastened, blaming himself also for this dreadful event, although in truth no one could have been more innocent. He had grown very fond of Miss Ogilvy, and shuddered to think that she must soon leave the world to seek a dim Unknown, where there were bad spirits as well as good.

He shuddered, too, at the thought of this Eleanor, who made use of him to appear in human form, and on his knees prayed God to protect him from her. This indeed happened, if she had any real existence and was not some mere creation of the brain of Madame Riennes, made visible by the working of laws whereof we have no knowledge. Never again, during all his life, did he actually see any more of Eleanor, and the probability is that he never will, either here or elsewhere.

Three days later Godfrey received a letter from the doctor, saying that Miss Ogilvy wished to see him, and that he recommended him not to delay his visit. Having obtained the permission of the Pasteur, he went in at once by the diligence, and on arrival at the villa, where evidently he was expected, was shown up to a bedroom which commanded a beautiful view of the lake and Mount Pilatus. Here a nurse met him and told him that he must not stay long; a quarter of an hour at the outside. He asked how Mademoiselle was, whereon she answered with an expressive shrug:

"Soon she will be further from the earth than the top of that mountain."

Then she took him to another smaller room, and there upon the bed, looking whiter than the sheets, lay his friend. She smiled very sweetly when she caught sight of him.

"Dear Godfrey," she said, "it is kind of you to come. I wanted to see you very much, for three reasons. First, I wish to beg your pardon for having drawn you into this spiritualism without your knowing that I was doing so. I have told you what my motive was, and therefore I will not repeat it, as my strength is small. Secondly, I wish you to promise me that you will never go to another séance, since now I am quite sure that it is dangerous for the young. To me spiritualism has brought much good and joy, but with others it may be different, especially as among spirits, as on the earth, there are evil beings. Do you promise?"

"Yes, yes," answered Godfrey, "only I am afraid of Madame Riennes."

"You must stand up against her if she troubles you, and seek the help of religion; if necessary consult your old Pasteur, for he is a good man. There is no danger in the world that cannot be escaped if only one is bold enough, or so I think, though, alas! myself I have lacked courage," she added with a gentle sigh.

"Now, dear boy," she went on after pausing to recover strength, "I have a third thing to say to you. I have left you some money, as I know that you will have little. It is not every much, but enough, allowing for accidents and the lessening of capital values, to give you £260 a year clear. I might have given you more, but did not, for two reasons. The first is, that I have observed that young men who have what is called a competence, say £500 or £600 a year, very often are content to try and live on it, and to do nothing for themselves, so that in the end it becomes, not a blessing, but a curse. The second is, that to do so I should be obliged to take away from certain charities and institutions which I wish to benefit. That is all I have to say about money. Oh! no, there is one more thing. I have also left you the talisman you gave me, and with it this house and grounds. Perhaps one day you might like to live here. I have a sort of feeling that it will be useful to you at some great crisis of your fate, and at least it will remind you of me, who have loved and tried to beautify the place. In any case it will always let, and if it becomes a white elephant, you can sell it and the furniture, which is worth something."

Godfrey began to stammer his thanks, but she cut him short with a wave of her hand, murmuring:

"Don't let us waste more time on such things, for soon you must go away. Already I see that nurse looking at me from the doorway of the other room, and I have something more to say to you. You will come to think that all this spiritualism, as it is called, is nothing but a dangerous folly. Well, it is dangerous, like climbing the Alps, but one gets a great view from the top. And, oh! from there how small men look and how near are the heavens. I mean, my dear boy, that although I have asked you to abjure séances and so forth, I do pray of you to cultivate the spiritual. The physical, of course, is always with us, for that is Nature's law, without which it could not continue. But around and beyond it broods the spirit, as once it did upon the face of the waters, encircling all things; the beginning of all things, and the end. Only, as wine cannot be poured into a covered cup, so the spirit cannot flow into a world-sealed heart, and what is the cup without the wine? Open your heart, Godfrey, and receive the spirit, so that when the mortal perishes the immortal may remain and everlastingly increase. For you know, if we choose death we shall die, and if we choose life we shall live; we, and all that is dear to us."

Miss Ogilvy paused a little to get her breath, then went on: "Now, my boy, kiss me and go. But first—one word more. I have taken a strange affection for you, perhaps because we were associated in other existences, I do not know. Well, I want to say that from the land whither I am about to be borne, it shall be my great endeavour, if it is so allowed, to watch over you, to help you if there be need, and in the end to be among the first to greet you there, you, or any whom you may love in this journey of yours through life. Look, the sun is sinking. Now, goodbye till the dawn."

He bent down and kissed her and she kissed him back, throwing her thin and feeble arm about his neck, after which the nurse came and hurried him away weeping. At the door he turned back and saw her smile at him, and, oh! on her wasted face were peace and beauty.

Next day she died.

Forty-eight hours later Godfrey attended her funeral, to which the Pasteur Boiset was also bidden, and after it was over they were both summoned to the office of a notary where her will was read. She was a rich woman, who left behind her property to the value of quite £100,000, most of it in England. Indeed, this Swiss notary was only concerned with her possessions in Lucerne, namely the Villa Ogilvy, its grounds and furniture, and certain moneys that she had in local securities or at the bank. The house, its appurtenances and contents, were left absolutely to Godfrey, the Pasteur Boiset being appointed trustee of the property until the heir came of age, with a legacy of £200, and an annual allowance of £100 for his trouble.

Moreover, with tender care, except for certain bequests to servants, the testatrix devoted all her Swiss moneys to be applied to the upkeep of the place, with the proviso that if it were sold these capital sums should revert to her other heirs in certain proportions. The total of such moneys as would pass with the property, was estimated by the notary to amount to about £4,000 sterling, after the payment of all State charges and legal expenses. The value of the property itself, with the fine old French furniture and pictures which it contained, was also considerable, but unascertained. For the rest it would appear that Godfrey inherited about £12,000 in England, together with a possible further sum of which the amount was not known, as residuary legatee. This bequest was vested in the English trustees of the testatrix who were instructed to apply the interest for his benefit until he reached the age of twenty-five, after which the capital was to be handed over to him absolutely.

Godfrey, whose knowledge of the French tongue was still limited, and who was overcome with grief moreover after the sad scene through which he had just passed, listened to all these details with bewilderment. He was not even elated when the grave notary shook his hand and congratulated him with the respect that is accorded to an heir, at the same time expressing a hope that he would be allowed to remain his legal representative in Switzerland. Indeed, the lad only muttered something and slipped away behind the servants whose sorrow was distracted by the exercise of mental arithmetic as to the amount of their legacies.

After his first stupefaction, however, the Pasteur could not conceal his innocent joy. A legacy of £200, a trusteeship "of the most important," as he called it, and an allowance of £100 for years to come, were to him wonderful wealth and honour.

"Truly, dear young friend," he said to Godfrey, as they left the office, "it was a fortunate hour for me, and for you also, when you entered my humble house. Now I am not only your instructor, but the guardian of your magnificent Lucerne property. I assure you that I will care for it well. To-morrow I will interview those domestics and dismiss at least half of them, for there are far too many."

CHAPTER VII

MR. KNIGHT AND DUTY

The pair returned to Kleindorf by the evening diligence, and among the passengers was that same priest who had been their companion on the day of Godfrey's arrival. As usual he was prepared to be bellicose, and figuratively, trailed the tails of his coat before his ancient enemy. But the Pasteur would not tread on them. Indeed, so mild and conciliatory were his answers that at last the priest, who was a good soul at bottom, grew anxious and inquired if he were ill.

"No, no," said a voice from the recesses of the dark coach, "Monsieur le Pasteur has come into money. Oh, I have heard!"

"Is it so? Now I understand," remarked the priest with a sniff, "I feared that he had lost his health."

Then they arrived at Kleindorf, and the conversation ended with mutual bows.

Great was the excitement of Madame and Juliette at the news which they brought with them. To their ears Godfrey's inheritance sounded a tale of untold wealth, nearly 300,000 francs! Why, they did not know anyone in the neighbourhood of Kleindorf who owned so much. And then that fine house, with its gardens and lovely furniture, which was the talk of Lucerne. And the Pasteur with his 5,000 francs clear to be paid immediately, plus an income of 2,500 for the next eight years. Here were riches indeed. It was wonderful, and all after an acquaintance of only a few months. They looked at Godfrey with admiration. Truly he must be a remarkable youth who was thus able to attract the love of the wealthy.

An idea occurred to Madame. Why should he not marry Juliette? She was vivacious and pretty, fit in every way to become a great lady, even perhaps to adorn the lovely Villa Ogilvy in future years. She would have a word with Juliette, and show her where fortune lay. If the girl had any wit it should be as good as assured, for with her opportunities—

And so, doubtless, it might have chanced had it not been for a certain determined and unconventional young woman far away in England, of whom the persistent memory, however much he might flirt, quite prevented Godfrey from falling in love, as otherwise he ought to, and indeed, probably must have done at his age and in his circumstances.

Perhaps Miss Juliette, who although young was no fool, also had ideas upon the subject, at any rate at this time, especially as she had found l'Hibou always attractive, notwithstanding his star-gazing ways, and the shower of wealth that had descended on him as though direct from the Bon Dieu, did not lessen his charms. If so, who could blame her? When one has been obliged always to look at both sides of a sou and really pretty frocks, such as ladies wear, are almost as unobtainable as Godfrey's stars, money becomes important, especially to a girl with an instinct for dress and a love of life.

Thenceforward, at least, as may be imagined, Monsieur Godfrey became a very prominent person indeed in the Boiset establishment. All his little tastes were consulted; Madame moved him into the best spare bedroom, on the ground that the one he occupied would be cold in winter, which, when he was out, Juliette made a point of adorning with flowers if these were forthcoming, or failing them with graceful sprays of winter berries. Also she worked him some slippers covered with little devils in black silk, which she said he must learn to tread under foot, though whether this might be a covert allusion to his spiritualistic experiences or merely a flight of fancy on her part, Godfrey did not know.

On the evening of the reading of the will, prompted thereto by the Pasteur, that young gentleman wrote a letter to his father, a task which he always thought difficult, to tell him what had happened. As he found explanations impossible, it was brief, though the time occupied in composing drafts, was long. Finally it took the following form:—

"My dear Father,—I think I told you that I travelled out here with a lady named Miss Ogilvy, whom I have often seen since. She has just died and left me, as I understand, about £12,000, which I am to get when I am twenty-five. Meanwhile I am to have the income, so I am glad to say I shall not cost you any more. Also she has left me a large house in Lucerne with a beautiful garden and a lot of fine furniture, and some money to keep it up. As I can't live there, I suppose it will have to be let.

"I hope you are very well. Please give my love to Mrs. Parsons and tell her about this. It is growing very cold here, and the mountains are covered with snow, but there has been little frost. I am getting on well with my French, which I talk with Mademoiselle Juliette, who knows no English, although she thinks she does. She is a pretty girl and sings nicely. Madame, too, is very charming. I work at the other things with the Pasteur, who is kind to me. He will write to you also and I will enclose his letter.

"Your affectionate son, "Godfrey."

The receipt of this epistle caused astonishment in Mr. Knight, not unmixed with irritation. Why could not the boy be more explicit? Who was Miss Ogilvy, whose name, so far as he could recollect, he now heard for the first time, and how did she come to leave Godfrey so much money? The story was so strange that he began to wonder whether it were a joke, or perhaps, an hallucination. If not, there must be a great deal unrevealed. The letter which Godfrey said the Pasteur would write was not enclosed, and if it had been, probably would not have helped him much as he did not understand French, and could scarcely decipher his cramped calligraphy. Lastly, he had heard nothing from any lawyers or trustees.

In his bewilderment he went straight to Hawk's Hall, taking the letter with him, with a view to borrowing books of reference which might enable him to identify Miss Ogilvy. The butler said that he thought Sir John was in and showed him to the morning room, where he found Isobel, who informed him that her father had just gone out. Their meeting was not affectionate, for as has been told, Isobel detested Mr. Knight, and he detested Isobel. Moreover, there was a reason, which shall be explained, which just then made him feel uncomfortable in her presence. Being there, however, he thought it necessary to explain the object of his visit.

"I have had a very strange letter from that odd boy, Godfrey," he said, "which makes me want to borrow a book. Here it is, perhaps you will read it, as it will save time and explanation."

"I don't want to read Godfrey's letters," said Isobel, stiffly.

"It will save time," repeated Mr. Knight, thrusting it towards her.

Then, being overcome by curiosity, she read it. The money part did not greatly interest her; money was such a common thing of which she heard so much. What interested her were, first, Miss Ogilvy and the unexplained reasons of her bequest, and secondly, in a more acute fashion, Mademoiselle Boiset, who was pretty and sang so nicely. Miss Ogilvy, whoever she might have been, at any rate, was dead, but Juliette clearly was much alive, with her prettiness and good voice. No wonder, then, that she had not heard from Godfrey. He was too occupied with the late Miss Ogilvy and the very present Mademoiselle Juliette, in whose father's house he was living as one of the family.

Isobel's face, however, showed none of her wonderings. She read the letter quite composedly, but with such care that afterwards she could have repeated it by heart. Then she handed it back, saying:

"Well, Godfrey seems to have been fortunate."

"Yes, but why? I find no explanation of this bequest—if there is a bequest."

"No doubt there is, Mr. Knight. Godfrey was always most truthful and above-board," she answered, looking at him.

Mr. Knight flinched and coloured at her words, and the steady gaze of those grey eyes. She wondered why though she was not to learn for a long while.

"I thought perhaps you could lend me some book, or books, which would enable me to find out about Miss Ogilvy. I have never heard of her before, though I think that in one of his brief communications Godfrey did mention a lady who was kind to him in the train."

"Certainly, there are lots of them. 'Who's Who'—only she would not be there unless she was very rich, but you might look. Peerages; they're no good as she was Miss Ogilvy, though, of course, she might be the daughter of a baron. 'County Families,' Red Books, etc. Let's try some of them."

So they did try. Various Ogilvys there were, but none who gave them any clue. This was not strange, as both Miss Ogilvy's parents had died in Australia, when she was young, leaving her to be brought up by an aunt of another name in England, who was also long dead.

So Mr. Knight retreated baffled. Next morning, however, a letter arrived addressed "Godfrey Knight, Esq.," which after his pleasing fashion he opened promptly. It proved to be a communication from a well-known firm of lawyers, which enclosed a copy of Miss Ogilvy's will, called special attention to the codicil affecting himself, duly executed before the British Consul and his clerk in Lucerne, gave the names of the English trustees, solicited information as to where the interest on the sum bequeathed was to be paid, and so forth.

To this inquiry Mr. Knight at once replied that the moneys might be paid to him as the father of the legatee, and was furious when all sorts of objections were raised to that course, unless every kind of guarantee were given that they would be used solely and strictly for the benefit of his son. Finally, an account had to be opened on which cheques could be drawn signed by one of the trustees and Mr. Knight. This proviso made the latter even more indignant than before, especially as it was accompanied by an intimation that the trustees would require his son's consent, either by letter or in a personal interview, to any arrangements as to his career, etc., which involved expenditure of the trust moneys. When a somewhat rude and lengthy letter to them to that effect was met with a curt acknowledgment of its receipt and a reference to their previous decision, Mr. Knight's annoyance hardened into a permanent grievance against his son, whom he seemed to hold responsible for what he called an "affront" to himself.

He was a man with large ideas of paternal rights, of which an example may be given that was not without its effect upon the vital interests of others.

When Isobel returned from London, after the fancy-dress ball, at which she thought she had seen a ghost whilst sitting in the square with her young admirer who was dressed as a knight, she waited for a long while expecting to receive a letter from Godfrey. As none came, although she knew from Mrs. Parsons that he had written home several times, she began to wonder as to the cause of his silence. Then an idea occurred to her.

Supposing that what she had seen was no fancy of her mind, but Godfrey himself, who in some mysterious fashion had found his way into that square, perhaps in the hope of seeing her at the ball in order to say goodbye? This was possible, since she had ascertained from some casual remark by his father that he did not leave London until the following morning.

If this had happened, if he had seen her "playing the fool," as she expressed it to herself with that good-looking man in the square, what would he have thought of her? She never paused to remember that he had no right to think anything. Somehow from childhood she acknowledged in her heart that he had every right, though when she said this to herself, she did not in the least understand all that the admission conveyed. Although she bullied and maltreated him at times, yet to herself she always confessed him to be her lord and master. He was the one male creature for whom she cared in the whole world, indeed, putting her mother out of the question, she cared for no other man or woman, and would never learn to do so.

For hers was a singular and very rare instance of almost undivided affection centred on a single object. So far as his sex was concerned Godfrey was her all, a position of which any man might well be proud in the case of any woman, and especially of one who had many opportunities of devoting herself to others. In her example, however, she was not to be thanked, for the reason that she only followed her nature, or perhaps the dictates of that fate which inspires and rules very great love, whether it be between man and woman, between parent and child, between brother and brother, or between friend and friend. Such feelings do not arise, or grow. They simply are; the blossoms of a plant that has its secret roots far away in the soil of Circumstance beyond our ken, and that, mayhap, has pushed its branches through existences without number, and in the climates of many worlds.

So at least it was with Isobel, and so it had always been since she kissed the sleeping child in the old refectory of the Abbey. She was his, and in a way, however much she might doubt or mistrust, her inner sense and instinct told her that he was always hers, that so he had always been and so always would remain. With the advent of womanhood these truths came home to her with an increased force because she knew—again by instinct—that this fact of womanhood multiplied the chances of attainment to the unity which she desired, however partial that might still prove to be.

Yet she knew also that this great mutual attraction did not depend on sex, though by the influence of sex it might be quickened and accentuated. It was something much more deep and wide, something which she did not and perhaps never would understand. The sex element was accidental, so much so that the passage of a few earthly years would rob it of its power to attract and make it as though it had never been, but the perfect friendship between their souls was permanent and without shadow of change. She knew, oh!, she knew, although no word of it had ever been spoken between them, that theirs was the Love Eternal. The quick perception of her woman's mind told her these things, of which Godfrey's in its slower growth was not yet aware.

Animated by this new idea that she had really seen Godfrey, and what was much worse, that Godfrey had really seen her upon an occasion when she would have much preferred to remain invisible to him, she was filled with remorse, and determined to write him a letter. Like that of the young man himself to his father, its composition took her a good deal of time.

Here it is as copied from her third and final draft:—

"My dear old Godfrey,—I have an idea that you were in the Square on the night of the fancy ball when I came out, and wore that horrid Plantagenet dress which, after all, did not fit. (I sent it to a jumble-sale where no one would buy it, so I gave it to Mrs. Smilie, who has nine children, to cut into frocks for her little girls.) If you were there, instead of resting before your long journey as you ought to have done, and saw me with a man in armour and a rose—and the rest, of course you will have understood that this was all part of the game. You see, we had to pretend that we were knights and ladies who, when they were not cutting throats or being carried off with their hair down, seem to have wasted their time in giving each other favours, and all that sort of bosh. (We did not know what a favour was, so we used a rose.)

The truth is that the young man and his armour, especially his spurs which tore my dress, and everything about him bored me, the more so because all the while I was thinking of—well, other things—how you would get through your journey, and like those French people and the rest. So now, if you were there, you won't be cross, and if you were not, and don't understand what I am saying, it isn't worth bothering about. In any case, you had no right to—I mean, be cross. It is I who should be cross with you for poking about in a London square so late and not coming forward to say how do you do and be introduced to the knight. That is all I have to say about the business, so don't write and ask me any questions.

"There is no news here—there never is—except that I haven't been into that church since you left, and don't mean to, which makes your father look at me as sourly as though he had eaten a whole hatful of crab-apples. He hates me, you know, and I rather like him for showing it, as it saves me the trouble of trying to keep up appearances. Do tell me, when you write, how to explain his ever having been your father. If he still wants you to go into the Church I advise you to study the Thirty-nine Articles. I read them all through yesterday, and how anybody can swear to them in this year of grace I'm sure I don't know. They must shut their eyes and open their mouths, like we used to do when we took powders. By the way, did you ever read anything about Buddhism? I've got a book on it which I think rather fine. At any rate, it is a great idea, though I think I should find it difficult to follow 'the Way.'

"I am sorry to say that Mother is not well at all. She coughs a great deal now that Essex is getting so damp, and grows thinner and thinner. The doctor says she ought to go to Egypt, only Father won't hear of it. But I won't write about that or we should have another argument on the fourth Commandment. Good-bye, dear old boy.—Your affectionate Isobel.

"P.S.—When you write don't tell me all about Switzerland and snow- covered mountains and blue, bottomless lakes, etc., which I can read in books. Tell me about yourself and what you are doing and thinking—especially what you are thinking.

"P.P.S.—That man in armour isn't really good-looking; he has a squint. Also he puts scent upon his hair and can't spell. I know because he tried to write a bit of poetry on my programme and got it all wrong."

When she had finished this somewhat laboured epistle Isobel remembered that she had forgotten to ask Godfrey to write down his address. Bethinking her that it would be known to Mrs. Parsons, she took it round to the Abbey House, proposing to add it there. As it happened Mrs. Parsons was out, so she left it with the housemaid, who promised faithfully to give it to her when she returned, with Isobel's message as to writing the address on the sealed envelope. In order that she might not forget, the maid placed it on a table by the back door. By ill luck, however, presently through that door, came, not Mrs. Parsons, but the Rev. Mr. Knight. He saw the letter addressed to Godfrey Knight, Esq., and, though he half pretended to himself that he did not, at once recognized Isobel's large, upright hand. Taking it from the table he carried it with him into his study and there contemplated it for a while.

"That pernicious girl is communicating with Godfrey," he said to himself, "which I particularly wish to prevent."

A desire came upon him to know what was in the letter, and he began to argue with himself as to his "duty"—that was the word he used. Finally he concluded that as Godfrey was still so young and so open to bad influences from that quarter, this duty clearly indicated that he should read the letter before it was forwarded. In obedience to this high impulse he opened and read it, with the result that by the time it was finished there was perhaps no more angry clergyman in the British Empire. The description of himself looking as though he had eaten a hatful of crab-apples; the impious remarks about the Thirty-nine Articles; the suggestion that Godfrey, instead of going to bed as he had ordered him to do that evening, was wandering about London at midnight; the boldly announced intention of the writer of not going to church—indeed, every word of it irritated him beyond bearing.

"Well," he said aloud, "I do not think that I am called upon to spend twopence-halfpenny" (for Isobel had forgotten the stamp) "in forwarding such poisonous trash to a son whom I should guard from evil. Hateful girl! At any rate she shall have no answer to this effusion."

Then he put the letter into a drawer which he locked.

As a consequence, naturally, Isobel did receive "no answer," a fact from which she drew her own conclusions. Indeed, it would not be too much to say that these seared her soul. She had written to Godfrey, she had humbled herself before Godfrey, and he sent her—no answer. It never occurred to her to make inquiries as to the fate of that letter, except once when she asked the housemaid whom she chanced to meet, whether she had given it to Mrs. Parsons. The girl, whose brain, or whatever represented that organ, was entirely fixed upon a young man in the village of whom she was jealous, answered, yes. Perhaps she had entirely forgotten the incident, or perhaps she considered the throwing of the letter upon a table as equivalent to delivery.

At any rate, Isobel, who thought, like most other young people, that when they once have written something, it is conveyed by a magical agency to the addressee, even if left between the leaves of a blotter, accepted the assurance as conclusive. Without doubt the letter had gone and duly arrived, only Godfrey did not choose to answer it, that was all. Perhaps this might be because he was still angry on account of the knight in armour—oh! how she hoped that this was the reason, but, as her cold, common sense, of which she had an unusual share, convinced her, much more probably the explanation was that he was engaged otherwise, and did not think it worth while to take the trouble to write.

Later on, it is true, she did mean to ask Mrs. Parsons whether she had forwarded the letter. But as it chanced, before she did so, that good woman burst into a flood of conversation about Godfrey, saying how happy he seemed to be in his new home with such nice ladies around, who it was plain, thought so much of him, and so forth. This garrulity Isobel took as an intended hint and ceased from her contemplated queries. When some months later Mr. Knight brought her Godfrey's epistle which announced his inheritance, needless to say, everything became plain as a pikestaff to her experienced intelligence.

So it came about that two young people, who adored each other, were estranged for a considerable length of time. For Isobel wrote no more letters, and the proud and outraged Godfrey would rather have died than attempt to open a correspondence—after what he had seen in that London square. It is true that in his brief epistles home, which were all addressed to his father, since Mrs. Parsons was what is called "a poor scholar," he did try in a roundabout way to learn something about Isobel, but these inquiries, for reasons of his own, his parent completely ignored. In short, she might have been dead for all that Godfrey heard of her, as he believed that she was dead—to him.

Meanwhile, Isobel had other things to occupy her. Her mother, as she had said in the letter which Mr. Knight's sense of duty compelled him to steal, became very ill with lung trouble. The doctors announced that she ought to be taken to Egypt or some other warm climate, such as Algeria, for the winter months. Sir John would hear nothing of the sort. For years past he had chosen to consider that his wife was hypochondriacal, and all the medical opinions in London would not have induced him to change that view. The fact was, as may be guessed, that it did not suit him to leave England, and that for sundry reasons which need not be detailed, he did not wish that Isobel should accompany her mother to what he called "foreign parts." In his secret heart he reflected that if Lady Jane died, well, she died, and while heaven gained a saint, earth, or at any rate, Sir John Blake, would be no loser. She had played her part in his life, there was nothing more to be made of her either as a woman as a social asset. What would it matter if one more pale, uninteresting lady of title joined the majority?

Isobel had one of her stormy interviews with Sir John upon this matter of her mother's health.

"She ought to go abroad," she said.

"Who told you that?" asked her father.

"The doctors. I waited for them and asked them."

"Then you had no business to do so. You are an impertinent and interfering chit."

"Is it impertinent and interfering to be anxious about one's mother's health, even if one is a chit?" inquired Isobel, looking him straight in the eyes.

Then he broke out in his coarse way, saying things to his daughter of which he should have been ashamed.

She waited until he ceased, red-faced, and gasping, and replied:

"Were it not for my mother, whom you abuse, although she is such an angel and has always been so kind to you, I would leave you, Father, and earn my own living, or go with my uncle Edgar to Mexico, where he is to be appointed Minister, as he and Aunt Margaret asked me to. As it is I shall stop here, though if anything happens to Mother, because you will not send her abroad, I shall go if I have to run away. Why won't you let her go?" she added with a change of voice. "You need not come; I could look after her. If you think that Egypt or the other place is too far, you know the doctors say that perhaps Switzerland would do her good, and that is quite near."

He caught hold of this suggestion, and exclaimed, with a sneer:

"I know why you want to go to Switzerland, Miss. To run after that whipper-snapper of a parson's son, eh? Well, you shan't. And as for why I won't let her go, it's because I don't believe those doctors, who say one minute that she should go to Egypt, which is hot, and the next to Switzerland, which is cold. Moreover, I mean you to stop in England, and not go fooling about with a lot of strange men in these foreign places. You are grown up now and out, and I have my own plans for your future, which can't come off if you are away. We stop here till Christmas, and then go to London. There, that's all, so have done."

At these insults, especially that which had to do with Godfrey, Isobel turned perfectly scarlet and bit her lip till the blood ran. Then without another word she went away, leaving him, if the truth were known, a little frightened. Still, he would not alter his decision, partly because to do so must interfere with his plans, and he was a very obstinate man, and partly because he refused to be beaten by Isobel. This was, he felt, a trial of strength between them, and if he gave way now, she would be master. His wife's welfare did not enter into his calculations.

So they stopped in Essex, where matters went as the doctors had foretold, only more quickly than they expected. Lady Jane's complaint grew rapidly worse, so rapidly that soon there was no question of her going abroad. At the last moment Sir John grew frightened, as bullies are apt to do, and on receipt of an indignant letter from Lord Lynfield, now an old man, who had been informed of the facts by his grand-daughter, offered to send his wife to Egypt, or anywhere else. Again the doctors were called in to report, and told him with brutal frankness that if their advice had been taken when it was first given, probably she would have lived for some years. As it was, it was impossible for her to travel, since the exertion might cause her death upon the journey, especially if she became seasick.

This verdict came to Isobel's knowledge as the first had done. Indeed, in his confusion, emphasized by several glasses of port, her father blurted it out himself.

"I wonder whether you will ever be sorry," was her sole comment.

Then she sat down to watch her mother die, and to think. Could there be any good God, she wondered, if He allowed such things to happen. Poor girl! it was her first experience of the sort, and as yet she did not know what things are allowed to happen in this world in obedience to the workings of unalterable laws by whoever and for whatever purpose these may be decreed.

Being ignorant, however, and still very young and untaught of life, she could not be expected to take these large views, or to guess at the Hand of Mercy which holds the cup of human woes. She saw her mother fading away because of her father's obstinacy and self-seeking, and it was inconceivable to her that such an unnecessary thing could be allowed by a gentle and loving Providence. Therefore, she turned her back on Providence, as many a strong soul has done before her, rejecting it for the reason that she could not understand.

Had she but guessed, this attitude of hers, which could not be concealed entirely in the case of a nature so frank, was the bitterest drop in her mother's draught of death. She, poor gentle creature, made no complaints, but only excuses for her husband's conduct. Nor, save for Isobel's sake did she desire to live. Her simple faith upbore her through the fears of departure, and assured her of forgiveness for all errors, and of happiness beyond in a land where there was one at least whom she wished to meet.

"I won't try to argue with you, because I am not wise enough to understand such things," she said to Isobel, "but I wish, dearest, that you would not be so certain as to matters which are too high for us."

"I can't help it, Mother," she answered.

Lady Jane looked at her and smiled, and then said:

"No, darling, you can't help it now, but I am sure that a time must come when you will think differently. I say this because something tells me that it is so, and the knowledge makes me very happy. You see we must all of us go through darkness and storms in life; that is if we are worth anything, for, of course, there are people who do not feel. Yet at the end there is light, and love, and peace, for you as well as for me, Isobel; yes, and for all of us who have tried to trust and to repent of what we have done wrong."

"As you believe it I hope that it is true; indeed, I think that it must be true, Mother dear," said Isobel with a little sob.

The subject was never discussed between them again, but although Isobel showed no outward change of attitude, from that time forward till the end, her mother seemed much easier in her mind about her and her views.

"It will all come right. We shall meet again. I know it. I know it," were her last words.

She died quite suddenly on the 27th of December, the day upon which Sir John had announced that they were to move to London.

As a matter of fact, one of the survivors of this trio was to move much further than to London, namely, Isobel herself. It happened thus. The funeral was over; the relatives and the few friends who attended it had departed to their rooms if they were stopping in the house, or elsewhere; Isobel and her father were left alone. She confronted him, a tall, slim figure, whose thick blonde hair and pale face contrasted strikingly with her black dress. Enormous in shape, for so Sir John had grown, carmine-coloured shading to purle about the shaved chin and lips (which were also of rather a curious hue), bald-headed, bold yet shifty-eyed, also clad in black, with a band of crape like to that of a Victorian mute, about his shining tall hat, he leaned against the florid, marble mantelpiece, a huge obese blot upon its whiteness. They were a queer contrast, as dissimilar perhaps as two human beings well could be.

For a while there was silence between them, which he, whose nerves were not so young or strong as his daughter's, was the first to break.

"Well, she's dead, poor dear," he said.

"Yes," answered Isobel, her pent-up indignation bursting forth, "and you killed her."

Then he too burst forth.

"Damn you, what do you mean, you little minx?" he asked. "Why do you say I killed her, because I did what I thought the best for all of us? No woman had a better husband, as I am sure she acknowledges in heaven to-day."

"I don't know what Mother thinks in heaven, if there is one for her, as there ought to be. But I do know what I think on earth," remarked the burning Isobel.

"And I know what I think also," shouted her enraged parent, dashing the new, crape-covered hat on to the table in front of him, "and it is that the further you and I are apart from each other, the better we are likely to get on."

"I agree with you, Father."

"Look here, Isobel, you said that your uncle Edgar, who has been appointed Minister to Mexico, offered to take you with him to be a companion to his daughter, your cousin Emily. Well, you can go if you like. I'll pay the shot and shut up this house for a while. I'm sick of the cursed place, and can get to Harwich just as well from London. Write and make the arrangements, for one year, no more. By that time your temper may have improved," he added with an ugly sneer.

"Thank you, Father, I will."

He stared at her for a little while. She met his gaze unflinchingly, and in the end it was not her eyes that dropped. Then with a smothered exclamation he stamped out of the room, kicking Isobel's little terrier out of the path with his elephantine foot. The poor beast, of which she was very fond, limped to her whining, for it was much hurt. She took it in her arms and kissed it, weeping tears of wrath and pity.

"I wonder what Godfrey would say about the fifth Commandment if he had been here this afternoon, you poor thing," she whispered to the whimpering dog, which was licking its hanging leg. "There is no God. If there had been He would not have given me such a father, or my mother such a husband."

Then still carrying the injured terrier, she went out and glided through the darkness to her mother's grave in the neighbouring churchyard. The sextons had done their work, and the raw, brown earth of the grave, mixed with bits of decayed coffins and fragments of perished human bones, was covered with hot-house flowers. Among these lay a gorgeous wreath of white and purple orchids, to which was tied a card whereon was written: "To my darling wife, from her bereaved husband, John Blake."

Isobel lifted the wreath from its place of honour and threw it over the the churchyard wall. Then she wept and wept as though her heart would break.

CHAPTER VIII

THE PASTEUR TAKES THE FIELD

In due course Godfrey received an epistle of frigid congratulation from his father upon his accession to wealth which, he remarked, would be of assistance to him in his future clerical career. The rest of the letter was full of complaints against the indignities that had been heaped upon him by Miss Ogilvy's executors and trustees, and also against Godfrey himself for not having furnished him with more information concerning the circumstances surrounding his inheritance. Lastly, Mr. Knight enclosed a paper which he requested Godfrey to sign and return, authorizing him to deal with the income of the legacy.

This Godfrey did obediently, only a week or two later to receive a formal notification from the lawyers, sent to him direct this time as his address had been filled in on the Authority, informing him that he had no power to sign such documents, he being in fact under age, and suggesting that he should refrain from doing so in the future. Enclosed were copies of their first letter to him, and of the other documents which Mr. Knight had not thought it worth while to forward because, as he said, they were heavy and foreign postage was so expensive.

Further the trustees announced that they proposed to allow him £50 a year out of the income for his personal needs, which would be paid half-yearly, and enclosed a draft for £25, which was more money than ever Godfrey had possessed before. This draft he was desired to acknowledge, and generally to keep himself in touch with the trustees, and to consult them before taking any step of importance, also as to his future career.

All this, with the sense of independence which it gave him, was agreeable enough to Godfrey, as it would have been to any youth. He acknowledged the draft under the guidance of the Pasteur, saying that he would write again when he had anything to communicate, but that as yet he had not made up his mind as to his future, and proposed to stay where he was, continuing his studies, if his father would allow him to do so. Next he took an opportunity to go to Lucerne with the Pasteur, who wished to inspect the Villa Ogilvy and consult the notary as to an inventory of its contents and arrangements for its upkeep.

Godfrey, who was received by the servants with many bows, and requests that they might be allowed to continue in their employment, wandered through the big rooms which looked so desolate now, and stared until he was tired at examples of beautiful French furniture, of which he understood nothing. Then, oppressed by memories of his kind friend into whose death chamber he had blundered, and, as it seemed to him, by a sense of her presence which he imagined was warning him of something, he left the house, telling the Pasteur, who was peering about him through his blue spectacles in an innocent and interested way, that he would meet him at the five o'clock diligence. Indeed, he had business of his own to do, which seemed to him more important than all this stock-taking and legal discussion. Having plenty of money in his pocket Godfrey wished to spend some of it in presents.

First, he bought a large meerschaum pipe with a flexible stem as a gift to the Pasteur, whom he had heard admire this very pipe in the shop window and express regrets that it was too expensive for his means. Having paid down thirty francs like a man for this treasure, he proceeded to a jeweller's near by. There he acquired a necklace of amethysts set with great taste in local silver work, for Madame to wear, and a charming silver watch of the best Swiss make for Juliette. When he found that these objects involved an expenditure of fourteen sovereigns, he was a little staggered, but again smiled and paid up. There was also a lovely little ring of gold with two turquoise hearts that he bought for £2 to send to Isobel when she wrote to him. But, as Isobel had posted her letter in Mr. Knight's drawer, that ring never reached her finger for many a day.

These gifts safely in his pocket, he began to stroll towards the railway station, whence the diligence started, slowly, as he had plenty of time. As he went he saw, in a shop window, a beautiful stick of olive wood, with an ebony crook. It was marked ten francs, and he coveted it greatly, but reflected with a sigh that having spent so much on others he could afford nothing for himself, for Godfrey was an unselfish soul. Instead he bought a collar of Swiss lace for Mrs. Parsons. Immediately after he left the lace shop he became aware that he was being shadowed. He heard no footfall, and he saw no one, but he knew that this was so; he could feel it down his back, and in a cold wind which blew across his hands, as it had done always at the Villa Ogilvy séances.

The road that he was following led across some public gardens beneath an avenue of trees, which, of course, at this time of the year, were leafless. This avenue was lighted here and there, and beneath one of the gas lamps Godfrey wheeled round to see Madame Riennes advancing on him out of the gloom. Her stout form padded forward noiselessly, except for the occasional crackle of a dead and frosted leaf beneath her foot. She wore a thick cloak of some sort with a black hood that framed her large, white face, making her look like a monk of the Inquisition as depicted in various old prints. Beneath the blackness of this hood and above the rigid line of the set mouth, stared two prominent and glowing eyes, in which the gaslight was reflected. They reminded Godfrey of those of a stalking cat in a dark room. Indeed, from the moment that he caught sight of them he felt like the mouse cowering in a corner, or like a bird in a tree fascinated by the snake that writhes towards it along the bough.

"Ah, mon petit," said Madame, in her thick, creamy voice, that seemed to emerge from her lower regions, "so I have found you. I was walking through the town and a notion came to me that you were here, a—what you call it?—instinct like that which make the dog find its master. Only I master and you dog, eh?"

Godfrey tried to pull himself together, feeling that it would not be wise to show fear of this woman, and greeted her as politely as he could, taking off his hat with a flourish in the foreign fashion.

"Put that hat back on your head, mon petit, or you will catch cold and be ill, you who are much too precious to be ill. Listen, now: I have something to say to you. You have great luck, have you not? Ah! sweet Sister Helen, she go to join the spirits, quite quick, as I tell her a little while ago she will do, and she leaves you much money, though to me, her old friend, her sister in the speerit, she give not one sou, although she know I want it. Well, I think there some mistake, and I wish to talk to Sister Helen about this money business. I think she leave me something, somehow, if I can find out where. And you, dear petit, can help me. Next Sunday you will come to my rooms of which I give you address," and she thrust a card into his hand, "and we will talk with Sister Helen, or at least with Eleanor, your little friend."

Godfrey shook his head vigorously, but she took no notice.

"What have you been buying," she went on, "with Sister Helen's money? Presents, I think. Yes, yes, I see them in your pocket," and she fixed her eyes upon the unhappy Godfrey's pocket, at least that is where he felt them.

"Oh! very pretty presents. Necklace for the fine Madame, of whom I can tell you some stories. Watch for pretty Mees, with the red, pouting lips, so nice to kiss. Pipe for good old Pasteur, to smoke while he think of heaven, where one time he sit all day and do nothing for ever; lace for someone else, I know not who, and I think a charming ring for one who will not wear it just yet; a big girl with a pale face and eyes that flash, but can grow soft. One who would know how to love, eh! Yes, not a doll, but one who would know how to love like a woman should. Am I right?"

The confused Godfrey babbled something about a shop, and was silent.

"Well, never mind the shop, my leetle friend. You come to my shop next Sunday, eh?"

"No," said Godfrey, "I have had enough of spirits."

"Yes, perhaps, though the speerits have been your good friends, taking Sister Helen, who has left something behind her. But those dear speerits, they have not had enough of you; they very faithful souls, especially that pretty Eleanor. I tell you, Mr. Godfrey, you will come to see me next Sunday, and if you not come, I'll fetch you."

"Fetch me! How?"

"Look at my eyes, that's how. I put you to sleep many times now, and I have power to make you come where I want and do what I wish. You do not believe me, eh? Well, now I show you. Come, mon petit, and give your dear godmamma a kiss," and she smiled at him like an ogress.

Now the last thing in the whole world that Godfrey wished to do was to embrace Madame Riennes, whom he loathed so that every fibre of his body shrank from her. Yet, oh horror! a wild impulse to kiss her took possession of him. In vain he struggled; he tried to step backwards, and instead went forwards, he tried to turn his head away, but those glowing eyes held and drew him as a magnet draws a needle. And as the needle rolls across the table ever more quickly towards the magnet, so did the unwilling Godfrey gravitate towards Madame Riennes. And now, oh! now her stout arm was about his neck, and now—he was impressing a fervent embrace upon her dome-like brow.

"There! What did I tell you, you nice, kind, little Godfrey," she gurgled with a hollow laugh. "Your dear godmamma thanks you, and you must run to catch that diligence. Au revoir till Sunday afternoon. Do not trouble about the hour, you will know exactly when to start. Now go."

She made a movement of her big, white hand, with the result that Godfrey felt like a spring which had been suddenly released. Next instant, still pursued by that gurgling laughter, he was running hard towards the diligence.

Fortunately the Pasteur was so full of talk about the house and his business with the notary, that there was no need for Godfrey to speak in the coach, or indeed at dinner. Then after the meal was finished he produced his presents, and with blushes and stammers offered them to the various members of the family. What rapture there was! Madame was delighted with her necklace, which she said and truly, was in the best of taste. Juliette kissed the watch, and looked as though she would like to kiss the donor, as indeed was her case. The Pasteur examined the fine pipe through his blue spectacles, saying that never had he expected to own one so beautiful, then at once filled it and began to smoke. After this they all scolded him for his extravagance.

"You did not buy anything for yourself," said Juliette, reproachfully. "Oh! yes, I see you did," and she pretended to perceive for the first time the little red case containing the ring, which inadvertently he had pulled out of his pocket with the other articles, although in truth she had observed it from the beginning. "Let us learn what it is," she went on, possessing herself of and opening the case. "Oh! a ring, what a pretty ring, with two hearts. For whom is the ring, Monsieur Godfrey? Someone in England?"

Then Godfrey, overcome, told a lie.

"No, for myself," he said.

Juliette looked at him and exclaimed:

"Then you should have told the jeweller to make it big enough. Try and you will see."

He turned red as a boiled lobster. Mademoiselle stood opposite to him, shaking her pretty head, and murmuring: "Quel mensonge! Quel bête mensonge!" while Madame broke into a low and melodious laughter, and as she laughed, looked first at the ring and then at Juliette's shapely hand.

"Make not a mock of our young friend," said the Pasteur, suddenly lifting his glance, or rather his spectacles from a long contemplation of that noble pipe and becoming aware of what was passing. "We all have our presents, which are magnificent. What then is our affair with the ring? Pardon them, and put it in your pocket, Godfrey, and come, let us go to the observatory, for the night is fine, and by now the stove will be warm."

So they went, and soon were engaged in contemplation of the stars, an occupation which absorbed Godfrey so much that for a while he forgot all his troubles.

When the door had shut behind them Madame looked at Juliette, who with her new watch held to her ear, observed her out of the corners of her eyes.

"I find him charming," said Madame presently.

"Yes, Mamma," replied Juliette, "so bright and even the tick is musical."

"Stupid!" exclaimed Madame. "When I was your age—well."

"Pardon!" said Juliette, opening her eyes innocently.

"Child, I meant our young English friend. I repeat that I find him charming."

"Of course, Mamma—after that necklace."

"And you—after that watch?"

"Oh! well enough, though too grave perhaps, and fond of what is far off—I mean stars," she added hurriedly.

"Stars! Pish! It is but because there is nothing nearer. At his age—stars!—well of a sort, perhaps."

She paused while Juliette still looked provokingly innocent. So her mother took a long step forward, for in truth she grew impatient with all this obtuseness in which, for reasons of her own, she did not believe.

"If I were a girl of your age," mused Madame as though to herself, "I do not think that ring would go to England."

"How, Mamma, would you steal it?"

"No, but I would make sure that it was given to me."

Now Juliette could no longer feign not to understand. She said nothing, but turned as red as Godfrey had done a little while before and stood waiting.

"I find him charming," repeated Madame, "though he is so young, which is a fault that will mend," and she fixed her eyes upon her daughter's face with a look of interrogation.

Then Juliette gave a little sigh and answered:

"Good. If you will make me say it, so do I also, at least, sometimes I think so, when he is not dull," and turning she fled from the room.

Madame smiled as the door closed behind her.

"That goes well, and should go better," she said to herself. "Only, for whom is the ring? There must be some girl in England, although of her he says nothing. Peste! There are so many girls. Still, she is far away, and this one is near. But it could be wished that she were more experienced, for then, since she likes him well enough, all would be sure. What does a man count in such a case—especially when he is so young? Pish! nothing at all," and Madame snapped her fingers at the empty air. "It is the woman who holds the cards, if only she knows how to play them."

Now all these things happened on a Wednesday. When Godfrey went to bed that night uncomfortable memories of Madame Riennes, and of the chaste embrace which she had forced him to impress upon her expansive forehead, haunted him for a while, also fears for the future. However, Sunday was still a long way off, so he went to sleep and dreamed that he was buying presents at every shop in Lucerne and giving them all to Madame Riennes.

On Thursday he was quite happy. On Friday he began to suffer from uneasiness, which on Saturday became very pronounced. It seemed to him that already waves of influence were creeping towards him like the fringes of some miasmic mist. Doubtless it was imagination, but he could feel their first frail tentacles wrapping themselves around his will, and drawing him towards Lucerne. As the day went on the tentacles grew stronger, till by evening there might have been a very octopus behind them. If this were so that night, he wondered what would happen on the following day, when the octopus began to pull. On one point he was determined. He would not go; never would he allow Madame Riennes to put him to sleep again, and what was much worse to make him kiss her. At any rate that spirit, Eleanor, was beautiful and attractive—but Madame Riennes! Rather than forgather with her again in this affectionate manner, much as he dreaded it—or her—he would have compounded with the ghost called Eleanor.

Now, although like most young people, Godfrey was indolent and evasive of difficulties, fearful of facing troubles also, he had a bedrock of character. There were points beyond which he would not go, even for the sake of peace. But here a trouble came in; he was well aware that although he would not go—to Madame Riennes to wit—there was something stronger than himself which would make him go. It was the old story over again set out by St. Paul once and for ever, that of the two laws which make a shuttlecock of man so that he must do what he wills not. Having once given way to Madame Riennes, who was to him a kind of sin incarnate, he had become her servant, and if she wished to put him to sleep, or to do anything else with him, well, however much he hated it, he must obey.

The thought terrified him. What could he do? He had tried prayers, never before had he prayed so hard in all his life; but they did not seem to be of the slightest use. No guardian angel, not even Eleanor, appeared to protect him from Madame Riennes, and meanwhile, the fog was creeping on, and the octopus tentacles were gripping tighter. In his emergency there rose the countenance of Miss Ogilvy's dying counsel, welcome and unexpected as light of the moon to a lost traveller on a cloud-clothed night. What had she told him to do? To resist Madame Riennes. He had tried that with lamentable results. To invoke the help of religion. He had tried that with strictly negative results; the Powers above did not seem inclined to intervene in this private affair. To appeal to the Pasteur. That he had not tried but, unpromising as the venture seemed to be, by Jove! he would. In his imminent peril there was nothing to which he would have appealed, even Mumbo-Jumbo itself if it gave him the slightest hope of protection from Madame Riennes.

Accordingly, when they went to the observatory that night, instead of applying his eye to the telescope in the accustomed fashion, Godfrey rushed at the business like a bull at a gate. At first the Pasteur was entirely confused, especially as Godfrey spoke in English, which the preceptor must translate into French in his own mind. By degrees, however, he became extraordinarily interested, so much so that he let the new pipe go out, and what was very rare with him, except in the most moving passages of his own sermons, pushed the blue spectacles from his high nose upwards, till they caught upon the patch of grizzled hair which remained upon his bald head.

"Ah!" he said, answering in French, which by now Godfrey understood fairly well, "this is truly exciting; at last I come in touch with the thing. Know, Godfrey, that you furnish me with a great occasion. Long have I studied this, what you call it—demonology. Of it I know much, though not from actual touch therewith."

Then he began to talk of gnosticism, and witchcraft, and Incubi, and Succubi, and the developments of modern spiritualism, till Godfrey was quite bewildered. At length he paused, relit the new pipe, and said:

"These matters we will study afterwards; they are, I assure you, most entertaining. Meanwhile, we have to deal with your Madame Riennes. All right, oh! quite all right. I will be her match. She will not make me kiss her, no, not at all, not at all! Be tranquil, young friend, if to-morrow you feel the impulse to go, go you shall, but I will go with you. Then we will see. Now to bed and sleep well. For me, I must study; I have many books on this subject, and there are points whereon I would refresh myself. Be not afraid. I know much of Madame Riennes and I will leave her flat as that," and with surprising alacrity he jumped on a large black beetle which, unhappily for itself, just then ran across the observatory floor to enjoy the warmth of the stove. "Wait," he added, as Godfrey was leaving. "First kneel down, I have memory of the ancient prayer, or if I forget bits, I can fill in the holes."

Godfrey obeyed in a rather abject fashion, whereon the old Pasteur, waving the pipe above his head, from which emerged lines of blue smoke such as might have been accessory to an incantation, repeated over him something in Latin, that, owing to the foreign accent, he could not in the least understand. It ended, however, with the sign of the cross made with the bowl of the pipe, which the Pasteur forgot still remained in his hand.

Fortified by the accession of this new ally, Godfrey slept fairly well, till within a little while of dawn, when he was awakened by a sound of rapping. At first he thought that these raps, which seemed very loud and distinct, were made by someone knocking on the door, perhaps to tell him there was a fire, and faintly murmured "Entrez." Then to his horror he became aware that they proceeded, not from the door, but from the back of his wooden bedstead, immediately above him, and at the same time recollected that he had heard similar noises while sitting at the little table in the Villa Ogilvy, which the mystics gathered there declared were produced by spirits.

His hair rose upon his head, a cold perspiration trickled down him; he shook in every limb. He thought of lighting a candle, but reflected that it was on the chest of drawers at the other side of the room, also that he did not know where he had put the matches. He thought of flying to the Pasteur, but remembered that to do so, first he must get out of bed, and perhaps expose his bare legs to the assault of ghostly hands, and next that, to reach the chamber of Monsieur and Madame Boiset, he must pass through the sanctuary of the room occupied by Juliette. So he compromised by retiring under the clothes, much as a tortoise draws its head into its shell.

This expedient proved quite useless, for there beneath the blankets the raps sounded louder than ever. Moreover, of a sudden the bed seemed to be filled with a cold and unnatural air, which blew all about him, especially upon his hands, though he tried to protect these by placing them under his back. Now Godfrey knew something of the inadequate and clumsy methods affected by alleged communicating spirits, and half automatically began to repeat the alphabet. When he got to the letter I, there was a loud rap. He began again, and at A came another rap. Once more he tried, for something seemed to make him do so, and was stopped at M.

"I am," he murmured, and recommenced until the word "here" was spelt out, after which came three rapid raps to signify a full stop.

"Who is here?" he asked in his own mind, at the same time determining that he would leave it at that. It was of no use at all, for the other party evidently intended to go on.

There was a perfect rain of raps, on the bed, off the bed, on the floor, even on the jug by the washstand; indeed, he thought that this and other articles were being moved about the room. To stop this multiform assault once more he took refuge in the alphabet, with the result that the raps unmistakably spelt the word "Eleanor."

"Great Heavens!" he thought to himself, "that dreadful spirit girl here, in my bedroom! How can she? It is most improper, but I don't suppose she cares a sou for that."

In his despair and alarm he tucked the clothes tightly round him, and thrusting out his head, said in trembling accents:

"Please go away. You know I never asked you to come, and really it isn't right," remarks which he thought, though, like all the rest, this may have been fancy, were followed by a sound of ghostly laughter. What was more, the bedclothes suddenly slipped off him, or—oh horror! perhaps they were pulled off. At any rate, they went, and when next he saw them they were lying in a heap by the side of the bed.

Then it would seem that he fainted, overcome by these terrors, real or imaginary. At any rate, when he opened his eyes again it was to see the daylight creeping into the room (never before had he appreciated so thoroughly the beauties of the dawn) and to find himself lying half frozen on the bed with the pillow, which he was clasping affectionately, for his sole covering.

At breakfast that morning he looked so peculiar and dilapidated, that Madame and Juliette made tender inquiries as to his health, to which he replied that his bedclothes had come off in the night and the cold had given him a chill "in the middle." They were very sympathetic, and dosed him with hot café-au-lait, but the Pasteur, studying him through the blue spectacles, said, "Ah, is it so?" in a kind of triumphant tone which Madame designated as "bête." Indeed, to those unacquainted with what was passing in M. Boiset's mind, it must have seemed particularly stupid.

When breakfast was over he possessed himself of Godfrey, and led him to the observatory, where the stove was already lit, though this was not usual in the daytime, especially on Sundays.

"Now, my boy, tell me all about it," he said, and Godfrey told him, feebly suggesting that it might have been a nightmare.

"Nightmare! Nonsense. The witch Riennes has sent her demon to torment you, that is all. I thought she would. It is quite according to rule, a most clear and excellent case. Indeed, I am a lucky student."

"I don't believe in witches," said Godfrey, "I always heard they were rubbish."

"Ah! I don't know. Here in the mountains these Swiss people believe in them, and tell strange stories, some of which I have heard as their Pasteur, especially when I held office among the High Alps. Also the Bible speaks of them often, does it not, and what was, is, and shall be, as Solomon says. Oh! why hesitate? Without doubt this woman is a witch who poses as an innocent modern spiritualist. But she shall not send her pretty female devil after you again, for I will make that room impossible to her."

"Please do," said Godfrey. "And as for Madame Riennes, it is certainly strange that she should have known about the things I had in my pocket the other day, although of course, she may have followed me into the shops."

"Yes, yes, she followed you into the shops, she or her demon, though perhaps you would not see her there. What did you tell me? That in the villa you thought that the dead Mademoiselle was warning you against something? Well, perhaps she was, for she was a good woman, though weak and foolish to trust to spiritualism, and now, without doubt, she sees all, and would protect you of whom she is fond."

"Then I wish she had done it a little better," said Godfrey. "Oh! listen, there's a rap!"

A rap there was certainly, on the hot iron of the stove, a resonant, ringing rap. The Pasteur advanced and made an examination, and while he was doing so there came another. What is more, in a most inexplicable fashion his blue spectacles flew from his nose. Very solemnly he found and replaced them and then, with the utmost dignity, addressing himself to the stove, he cursed and exorcised that article of domestic furniture in his best mediæval Latin. Apparently the effort was successful, for there were no more manifestations.

"Listen, my boy. You do not part from me this day. Presently we go to church, and you sit under me where I can keep my eye on you. If you make one movement towards the door, I descend from the desk or the pulpit, and take you back there with me."

"I don't want to move," said Godfrey.

"No, but there are others who may want to move you. Then after church we dine, and after dinner we take a nice walk through the woods arm in arm. Yes, perhaps we go as far as Lucerne and pay a little visit there, since this afternoon I have arranged that there is no service."

So Godfrey went to church and sat under the cold, blue glare of the Pasteur's spectacles, listening to a really eloquent sermon, for his preaching was excellent. He took his text from the story of Saul and the witch of Endor, and after dwelling on it and its moral, opened up the whole problem of the hidden influences which may, and probably do, affect the human soul. He gave a short but learned account of the history of demonology throughout the ages, which evidently he had at his fingers' ends. He distinguished between good and evil spirits, and while not denying the lawfulness of such research, pointed out the peril that the seeker ran, since in his quest for the good he might find the evil. Finally, he demonstrated that there was a sure refuge from all such demoniacal attacks, which those who suffered from them had but to seek.

Madame dozed during this sermon. Juliette wondered what had sent her father down that road, and the little congregation, those of them who understood, thought it a pleasant change from his usual discourse upon their sins, since they at least had never practised demonology. But to Godfrey, to whom, indeed, it was addressed, it brought much comfort, for in the Pasteur and his pure and beautiful doctrine, he saw a rock on which he might stand secure, defying Madame Riennes and Eleanor, and all the hosts of hell behind them.

Then came dinner. It was towards the middle of this meal that Godfrey began to feel very ill at ease. He fidgeted, he looked towards the door, he half rose and sat down again.

"Do you perchance wish to go out?" asked the Pasteur, who was keeping him under constant observation.

"What of it if he does?" interrupted Madame. "Did not Monsieur Godfrey inform us that he was unwell? Go then, Monsieur Godfrey."

"No, not so," said the Pasteur. "Remain seated. In one minute I will be ready to accompany you."

"Mon Dieu! what for?" exclaimed Madame. "Never did I hear of such a thing," while even Juliette looked amazed.

Meanwhile Godfrey had risen and was making for the door, with a fixed and sickly smile upon his face. The Pasteur swallowed down his vin ordinaire and rushed after him.

"He is ill," said Juliette, with sympathy, "all day he has looked strange."

"Perhaps," said Madame. "That sermon of your father's was enough to turn anybody's stomach, with his talk about devils and witches. But why cannot he leave him alone? A doctor in such a case perhaps, but a clergyman—! Mon Dieu! there they go, the two of them walking towards the woods. What a strange idea! And your father has Monsieur Godfrey by the arm, although assuredly he is not faint for he pulls ahead as though in a great hurry. They must be mad, both of them. I have half a mind—"

"No, no, Mother," said Juliette. "Leave them alone. Doubtless in time they will return. Perhaps it has something to do with the stars."

"Silly girl! Stars at midday!"

"Well, Mamma, you know they are always there even if one cannot see them."

"Nonsense, child. They only come at night. The question is—where are those two going?"

Juliette shook her head and gave it up, and so perforce did her mother.

CHAPTER IX

THE PASTEUR CONQUERS

Meanwhile, following a short cut through the snowy woods that ran over the shoulder of the intervening hill, the pair were wending their way towards Lucerne. Godfrey, a fixed and vacant look upon his face, went first; the Pasteur clinging to his arm like a limpet to a rock, puffed along beside him.

"Heaven!" he gasped, "but this attraction of yours must be strong that it makes you walk so fast immediately after dinner."

"It is, it is!" said Godfrey, in a kind of agony. "I feel as though my inside were being drawn out, and I must follow it. Please hold my arm tight or I shall run."

"Ah! the witch. The great witch!" puffed the Pasteur, "and up this hill too, over snow. Well, it will be better on the down grade. Give me your hand, my boy, for your coat is slipping, and if once you got away how should I catch you?"

They accomplished the walk into Lucerne in absolutely record time. Fortunately, at this after-dinner hour few people were about, but some of those whom they met stared at them, and one called:

"Do you take him to the police-station? Shall I summon the gens- d'arme?"

"No, no," replied the Pasteur, "he goes to keep an assignation, and is in a hurry."

"Then why does he take you with him? Surely a clergyman will make a bad third at such an affair?" ejaculated an outspoken lady who was standing at her house door.

"Where is the street? I do not know it," asked the Pasteur.

"Nor do I," answered Godfrey, "but we shall come there all right. To the left now."

"Oh! the influence! The strong influence!" muttered Monsieur Boiset. "Behold! it leads him."

Truly it did lead him. Round corners and across squares they went into an old part of the town with which neither of them was acquainted, till at length Godfrey, diving beneath an archway, pulled up in front of an antique doorway, saying:

"I think this is the place."

"Look at the writing and make sure," said the Pasteur, "for it seems ridiculous—"

At that moment the door opened mysteriously, and Godfrey disappeared into the passage beyond. Scarcely had the Pasteur time to follow him when it shut again, although he could see no concierge.

"Doubtless it is one of those that works with a wire," he thought to himself, but he had no time to stop to look, for already Godfrey was climbing the stairs. Up he went, three floors, and up after him scrambled the Pasteur. Suddenly Godfrey stopped at a door and not waiting to ring the bell, knocked with his hand. Immediately it opened and Godfrey, with his companion, passed into a very dark hall round which were several other doors. Here in the gloom the Pasteur lost him. Godfrey had gone through one of the doors, but which he could not see. He stood still, listening, and presently heard a deep peculiar voice speaking English with a very foreign accent, say:

"So you have come to see your godmamma, my dear little clever boy. Well, I thought you would, and last night I sent you a pretty messenger to give you remembrance."

Then the Pasteur found the handle of the door and entered the room. It was a curious place draped, not without taste of a bizarre kind, in vivid colours, wherein purple dominated, and it gave an idea of mingled magnificence and squalor. Some of the furniture was very good, as were one or two of the pictures, though all of it was of an odd and unusual make. Thus, the sideboard was shaped like a sarcophagus, and supported on solid sphinxes with gilded faces. In a corner of the room also stood an unwrapped mummy in a glass case.

In the midst of all this stood a common deal table, whereon were a black bottle, and the remains of Madame's meal, which seemed to have consisted of large supplies of underdone meat. In front of the fire was a large, well-worn couch, and by it a small stout table such as spiritualists use, on which gleamed a ball of glass or crystal. On this couch was seated Madame clad in a kind of black dressing-gown and a wide gold scarf tied about her ample waist. Her fat, massive face was painted and powdered; on her head she wore a kind of mantilla also gold-coloured, and about her neck a string of old Egyptian amulets. Anything more unwholesome or uncanny than were her general appearance and surroundings as the bright flames of the fire showed them in this stuffy, shadowed room, it would be impossible to imagine.

"Sit down here by my side, my little son in the speerit, where I have made a place ready for you, and let me hold your hand while you tell me all that you have been doing and if you have been thinking much of me and that beautiful Eleanor whom I sent to see you last night," went on Madame Riennes in her ogreish, purring voice, patting the sofa.

Just then she looked up and caught sight of the Pasteur standing in the shadow. Staring at him with her fierce, prominent eyes, she started violently as though at last she had seen something of which she was afraid.

"Say, my Godfrey," she exclaimed in a rather doubtful voice, "what is this that you have brought with you? Is it a scarecrow from the fields? Or is it a speerit of your own? If so, I should have thought that a young man would have liked better the lovely Eleanor than this old devil."

"Yes, Madame Jezebel," said the Pasteur striding forward, speaking in a loud, high voice and waving a large umbrella, which had come partly unfolded in his hurried walk. "It is a scarecrow—one that scares the crows of hell who seek to pick out the souls of the innocent, like you, Madame Jezebel."

Madame uttered a voluminous oath in some strange tongue, and sprang to her feet with an agility surprising in one so stout.

"Say, who are you?" she ejaculated in French, confronting him.

"I am the Pasteur Boiset who accompany my ward to pay this little call, Madame."

"Oh! indeed. That thief of a clergyman, who got his finger into the pie of dead Mademoiselle, eh? Well, there are no more pickings here, Pasteur, but perhaps you come to have your fortune told. Shall I look in the crystal for you and tell you nice things about—what shall we say? About the past of that handsome Madame of yours, for instance? Oh! I will do it for love, yes, for love. Or shall I make that mummy speak for you? I can, for once I lived in that body of hers—it was a gay life," and she stopped, gasping.

"Hearken, woman," said the Pasteur, "and do not think to frighten me. I know all about my wife, and, if once she was foolish, what of it in a world where none are altogether wise? If you do not wish to visit the police cell, you will do well to leave her alone. As for your tricks of chicanery, I want none of them. What I want is that you take off the spell which you have laid upon this poor boy, as Satan your master has given you the power to do. Now, obey me—or—"

"Or? Or what, you old paid advocate of God?"

"That is a good term. If I am an advocate, I know my Employer's mind, I, who have taken His fee, and am therefore in honour bound to serve Him faithfully. Now I will tell you His mind about you. It is that unless you change your ways and repent, soon you will go to hell. Yes, quite soon, I think, for one so fat cannot be very strong in the heart. Do what I bid you, Madame, or I, the advocate of God, having His authority, will curse you in the Name of God, and in the ancient form of which you may have heard."

"Bah! would you frighten me, the great Madame Riennes who have spirits at my command and who, as you admit, can lay on spells and take them off. A flea for you and your God!"

"Spirits at your command! Yes, some of them in there, I think," and he pointed to the black bottle on the table, "and others too, perhaps; I will not deny it. Well, let them advance, and we will see who is on the top of the mountain, I, the old paid advocate of God, or you and your spirits, Madame," and hooking the handle of the big umbrella over his wrist, he folded his arms and stared at her through the blue spectacles.

Madame Riennes gibbered some invocation, but nothing happened.

"I await your spirits. They cannot have gone to bed so early," remarked the Pasteur like a new Elijah.

Then, also like Elijah, to use a vulgarism, he "sailed in" after a way which even the terrified Godfrey, who was crouching against one of the purple curtains, felt to be really magnificent with such artistic sense as remained to him. In his mediæval Latin which, spoken with a foreign accent, Godfrey, although a good scholar, could scarcely follow save for certain holy names, he cursed Madame Riennes in some archaic but most effective fashion. He consigned, this much Godfrey made out, her soul to hell and her body to a number of the most uncomfortable experiences. He trailed her in the dust at the rear of his theological chariot; he descended from the chariot, so to speak, and jumped upon her as he had done upon the beetle; he tossed up her mangled remains as the holy bull, Apis of the Egyptians, might have done with those of a Greek blasphemer. Then, like a triumphant pugilist, metaphorically he stood over her and asked her if she wanted any more.

For a little while Madame Riennes was crushed, also very evidently frightened, for those who deal in the supernatural are afraid of the supernatural. Indeed, none of us welcome the curse even of a malignant and disappointed beggar, or of the venomous gipsy angered by this or that, and much less that of a righteous man inspired by just and holy indignation. Madame Riennes, an expert in the trade, a dealer in maledictions, was not exempt from this common prejudice. As she would have expressed it, she felt that he had the Power on his side.

But Madame was no common charlatan; she had strength of a sort, though where it came from who could say? Moreover, for all kinds of secret reasons of her own, she desired to keep in her grip this boy Godfrey, who had shown himself to be so wonderful a medium or clairvoyant. To her he meant strength and fortune; also for him she had conceived some kind of unholy liking in the recesses of her dark soul. Therefore, she was not prepared to give him up without a struggle.

Presently Madame seemed to cast off the influences with which the Pasteur had overwhelmed her. While his maledictions were in full flow she sank in a huddled heap upon the couch. Of a sudden she revived; she sprang up; notwithstanding her bulk she leapt into the air like a ballet-dancer. She tore the golden mantilla from her head, letting down a flood of raven hair, streaked with grey, and waved it round her. She called upon the names of spirits or demons, long, resounding names with an Eastern ring about them, to come to her aid. Then she pranced into the centre of the room, crying:

"Dog of a clergyman, I defy you and will overcome you. That boy's soul is mine, not yours. I am the greatest mesmerist in the world and he is in my net. I will show you!"

She turned towards the shrivelled, almost naked mummy in the case, and addressed it:

"O Nofri," she said, "Priestess of Set, great seeress and magician of the old world in whom once my spirit dwelt, send forth your Ka, your everlasting Emanation, to help me. Crush this black hound. Come forth, come forth!"

As she spoke the fearful Godfrey in his corner saw the door of the glass case fly open, also as he thought, probably erroneously, that he saw the mummy move, lifting its stiff legs and champing its iron jaws so that the yellow, ancient teeth caught the light as they moved. Then he heard and saw something else. Suddenly the Pasteur in tones that rang like a trumpet, cried out:

"She seems to hesitate, this mummy of yours, Madame. Let me be polite and help her."

With a single bound he was in front of the case. With the hook of his big umbrella he caught the shrivelled thing round the neck; with his long thin arm he gripped it about the middle, just like somebody leading a lady to the dance, thought Godfrey. Then he bent himself and pulled. Out flew the age-withered corpse. The head came off, the body broke above the hips and fell upon the floor, leaving the legs standing in the case, a ghastly spectacle. On to this severed trunk the Pasteur leapt, again as he had done upon the black beetle. It crunched and crumbled, filling the air with a pungent, resinous dust. Then he stood amidst the débris, and placing his right foot upon what had been the mummy's nose, said mildly:

"Now, Madame, what next? This lady is finished?"

Madame Riennes uttered a stifled scream, more she could not do for rage choked her. Her big eyes rolled, she clenched and unclenched her hands, and bent forward as though she were about to fly at the Pasteur like a wild cat. Still poised upon the fragments of the mummy he lifted the point of the umbrella to receive the charge as it came, and taking advantage of Madame's temporary paralysis of speech, went on:

"Hearken! daughter of Beelzebub. You have the curse and it shall work upon your soul, but, yes, it shall work well. Still your body remains, and of that too I would say something. Know that I have heard much of you—oh! the quiet old Pasteur hears many things, especially if he has members of the secret police among his flock. I think that yonder in an office there is a dossier, yes, an official record concerning you and your doings both in this country and in other lands. It has been allowed to sleep, but it can wake again; if it wakes—well, there is the penitentiary for such as you."

Madame gasped and turned green. If Monsieur had drawn a bow at a venture, evidently that chance arrow had found the bull's-eye, for now she truly was frightened.

"What would you have me do?" she asked in a choking voice.

"Free this youth from your influence, as you can if you will."

"My influence! If I had any with him would not that bald skull of yours by now have been shattered like an egg, seeing that he is strong and holds a stick?"

"I have no time to waste, Madame. The Police Office closes early on Sundays."

Then she gave in.

"Come here," she said sullenly to Godfrey, still speaking in French.

He came and stood before her sneezing, for the pungent dust of the smashed mummy, which the Pasteur still ground beneath his large boots, had floated up his nose.

"Cease that noise, little fool, and look at me."

Godfrey obeyed, but did not stop sneezing, because the mixture of spices and organic matter would not allow him to do so. She stared at him very evilly, muttered some more words, and made mystic upward passes with her hands.

"There now," she said, "you are free, so far as I am concerned. But I do not think that you are done with spirits, since they are guests which once entertained to breakfast, stop to luncheon and to dinner; yes, and pass the night when they are merriest. I think you will see many spirits before you die, and afterwards—ah! who knows, little pig? Put your string about his leg and take your little pig home, Pasteur. He will not be drawn to come here again."

"Good, Madame, for remember, if he does I shall be drawn to call at the Police Office. If Madame will take my advice she will try change of air. Lucerne is cold in the winter, especially for those whose hearts are not too strong. Is it finished?"

"Quite, for my part, but for you, interfering humbug, I do not know. Get out of my room, both of you."

The Pasteur bowed with an old-fashioned politeness, and herding Godfrey in front of him, turned to go. As he passed through the door something hard hit him violently in the back, so that he nearly fell. It was the head of the mummy, which Madame had hurled at him. It fell to the floor, and striking against a chair leg, recoiled through the doorway. Godfrey saw it, and an impulse seized him. Lifting that head, he turned. Madame was standing in the middle of the room with her back to the deal table, uttering short little howls of fury.

Godfrey advanced very politely and saying, "I believe this is your property, Madame," placed the battered remnant of humanity upon the table beside the black bottle. As he did so, he glanced at the mesmerist, then turned and fled, for her face was like to that of a devil.

"Monsieur Boiset," he said, when they reached the street, "something has happened to me. I am quite changed. Not for all the world would I go near Madame Riennes again. Indeed, now I feel as though I wished to run away from her."

"That is good!" said the Pasteur. "Oh! I thought it would be so, for I know how to deal with such witches. But not too fast, not too fast, my Godfrey. I wonder what the old Egyptians put into the heads of their mummies to make them so heavy."

"Bitumen," answered Godfrey, and proceeded in a cheerful voice to give an account of the Egyptian process of mummification to his tutor, which Isobel and he had acquired in the course of their miscellaneous reading at Monk's Acre. Indeed, as he had said, whatever the reason, he was changed and prepared to talk cheerfully about anything. A great burden was lifted from his soul.

From that day forward Godfrey became what a youth of his years and race should be, a high-spirited, athletic, and active young man. Madame Riennes and her visions passed from him like a bad dream. Thoughtful he remained always, for that was his nature; sometimes sad also, when he thought of Isobel, who seemed to have disappeared quite out of his life. But as was natural at his age, this mood weakened by degrees. She was always there in the background, but she ceased to obscure the landscape as she had done before, and was to do in his after life. Had she been a girl of the common type, attractive only because she was a young and vivacious woman, doubtless the eclipse would have been complete. Occasionally, indeed, men do love fools in an enduring fashion, which is perhaps the most evil fate that can be laid upon them. For what can be worse than to waste what is deep and real upon a thing of flesh without a soul, an empty, painted bubble, which evades the hand, or bursts if it is grasped? Those are the real unfortunates, who have sold themselves for a mess of potage, that for the most part they are never even allowed to eat, since before the bell rings it has probably been deposited by heaven knows what hand of Circumstance in someone else's plate, or gone stale and been thrown away.

Godfrey was not one of these, because the hand of Circumstance had managed his affairs otherwise. Isobel was no mess of potage, but with all her faults and failings, a fair and great inheritance for him who could take seisin of her. Still, as he believed, she had first treated him badly, then utterly neglected him whose pride she had outraged, by not even taking the trouble to write him a letter, and finally, had vanished away. And he was young, with manhood advancing in his veins, like the pulse of spring, and women are many in the world, some of whom have pretty faces and proper figures. Also, although the fact is overlooked by convention, it has pleased Nature to make man polygamous in his instincts, though where those instincts end and what is called love begins, is a thing almost impossible to define. Probably in truth the limit lies beyond the borders of sex.

So Isobel's grey eyes faded into the background of Godfrey's mental vision, while the violet eyes of Juliette drew ever nearer to his physical perceptions. And here, to save trouble, it may be said at once, that he never cared in the least for Juliette, except as a male creature cares for a pretty female creature, and that Juliette never cared in the least for him, except as a young woman cares in general for a handsome and attractive young man—with prospects. Indeed, she found him too serious for her taste. She did not understand him, as, for his part, in her he found nothing to understand.

After all, ruling out the primary impulses which would make a scullery maid congenial to a genius upon a desert isle, what was there in a Juliette to appeal to a Godfrey? And, with the same qualification, what was there in a Godfrey to appeal to a Juliette? As once, with an accidental touch of poetry, she said to her mother, when at his side she felt as though she were walking over a snow-covered crevasse in the surrounding Alps. All seemed firm beneath her feet, but she never knew when the crust would break, and he would vanish into unfathomed depths, perchance dragging her with him. Or, feeling her danger she might run from him on to safer ground, where she knew herself to be on good, common rock or soil, and no strange, hollow echoes struck her ears, leaving him to pursue his perilous journey alone.

Her mother laughed, and falling into her humour, answered, that beyond the crevasse and at the foot of the further slope lay the warm and merry human town, the best house of which—not unlike the Villa Ogilvy—could be reached in no other way, and that with such a home waiting to receive her, it was worth while to take a little risk. Thereon Juliette shrugged her white shoulders, and in the intervals of one of the French chansonettes which she was very fond of warbling in her gay voice, remarked that she preferred to make journeys, safe or perilous, in the company of a singing-bird in the sunlight, rather than in that of an owl in the dusk, who always reminded her of the advancing darkness.

At least, that was the substance of what she said, although she did not put it quite so neatly. Then, as though by an afterthought, she asked when her cousin Jules, a young notary of Berne, was coming to stay with them.

The winter wore away, the spring came, and after spring, summer, with its greenery and flowers. Godfrey was happy enough during this time. To begin with, the place suited him. He was very well now, and grew enormously in that pure and trenchant air, broadening as well as lengthening, till, notwithstanding his slimness, he gave promise of becoming a large, athletic man.

Madame Riennes too and her unholy terrors had faded into the background. He no longer thought of spirits, although, it is true that a sense of the immanence and reality of the Unseen was always with him; indeed, as time went on, it increased rather than lessened. Partly, this was owing to the character and natural tendencies of his mind, partly also, without doubt, to the fact that his recent experiences had, as it were, opened a door to him between the Seen and the Hidden, or rather burst a breach in the dividing wall that never was built up again. Also his astronomical studies certainly gave an impetus to thoughts and speculations such as were always present with him. Only now these were of a wholesome and reverent nature, tending towards those ends which are advanced by religion in its truest sense.

He worked hard, too, under the gentle guidance of the learned Pasteur, at the classics, literature, and other subjects, while in French he could not fail to become proficient in the company of the talkative Madame and the sprightly Juliette. Nor did he want for relaxation. There were great woods on the hills behind the Maison Blanche, and in these he obtained leave to shoot rabbits, and, horrible to say, foxes. Juliette and he would set out together towards evening, accompanied by a clever cur which belonged to Jean, the factotum of the house.

They would post themselves at some convenient spot, while the instructed hound ranged the woods above. Then would appear perhaps a rabbit, perhaps a hare, though these in that land of poaching were not common, or occasionally a great, red, stealthy fox. At first, with his English traditions, Godfrey shrank from shooting the last, which he had been taught ought to die in one way only, namely, by being torn to pieces in the jaws of the hounds.

Juliette, however, mocked at him, volubly reciting Reynard's many misdeeds—how he stole chickens; how he tore out the throats of lambs, and, according to local report, was not even above killing a baby if he found that innocent alone. So it came about next time the excited yapping of the cur-dog was heard on the slopes above them, followed by stealthy movements among the fallen pine needles, and at length by the appearance of the beautiful red creature slyly slinking away to shelter, not twenty yards from where they stood behind a tree-trunk, that Juliette whispered:

"Tirez! Tirez!" and he lifted the gun, an old-fashioned, single- barrelled piece, aimed and fired.

Then followed a horrid scene. The big shot with which he had loaded, mortally wounded but did not kill the fox, that with its forepaws broken, rolled, and bit, and made dreadful noises in its agony, its beautiful fur all stained with blood. Godfrey did not know what to do; it was too big and strong to kill with Juliette's little stick, so he tried to batter it to death with the stock of the gun, but without success, and at last withdrew, looking at it horrified.

"What shall I do?" he asked faintly of Juliette.

"Load the gun and shoot it again," replied that practical young woman.

So with some mistakes, for the emergency made him nervous, such as the dropping of the cap among the pine needles, he obeyed. At last the poor beast lay dead, a very disagreeable spectacle, with the cur-dog that had arrived, biting joyously at its quivering form.

Godfrey put down the gun and retired behind a tree, whence presently he emerged, looking very pale, for to tell the truth, he had been ill.

"I do not think I like shooting foxes," he said.

"How strange you are," answered Juliette. "Quite unlike other men. Now my Cousin Jules, there is nothing that he loves better. Go now and cut off his tail, to hang upon the wall. It is beautiful."

"I can't," said Godfrey still more faintly.

"Then give me the knife, for I can."

And she did!

Had Madame but known it, that fox did not die unavenged upon her family, for with it departed from the world all hopes of the alliance which she desired so earnestly.

CHAPTER X

GODFREY BECOMES A HERO

The truth is that Godfrey was no true sportsman, really he did not enjoy exterminating other and kindred life to promote his own amusement. Like most young men, he was delighted if he made a good shot; moreover, he had some aptitude for shooting, but unlike most young men, to him afterwards came reflections. Who gave him the right to kill creatures as sentient, and much more beautiful in their way then himself, just because it was "great fun"? Of course, he was familiar with the common answer, that day by day his body was nourished upon the flesh of other animals destroyed for that purpose. But then this was a matter of necessity, so arranged by a law, that personally, he thought dreadful, but over which he had no manner of control. It was part of the hellish system of a world built upon the foundation stone of death.

Nature told him that he must live, and that to live, not being a vegetarian, which for most of us is difficult in a cold climate, he must kill, or allow others to kill for him. But to his fancy, perhaps meticulous, between such needful slaughter and that carried out for his own amusement, and not really for the purposes of obtaining food, there seemed to be a great gulf fixed. To get food he would have killed anything, and indeed, often did in later days, as he would and also often did in after days, have destroyed noxious animals, such as tigers.

But to inflict death merely to show his own skill or to gratify man's innate passion for hunting, which descends to him from a more primitive period, well, that was another matter. It is true, that he was not logical, since always he remained an ardent fisherman, partly because he had convinced himself from various observations, that fish feel very little, and partly for the reason that there is high authority for fishing, although, be it admitted, with a single exception, always in connection with the obtaining of needful food.

In these conclusions Godfrey was strengthened by two circumstances; first, his reading, especially of Buddhistic literature, that enjoins them so strongly, and in which he found a great deal to admire, and secondly, by the entire concurrence of the Pasteur Boiset, whom he admired even more than he did Buddhistic literature.

"I am delighted, my young friend," said the Pasteur, beaming at him through the blue spectacles, "to find someone who agrees with me. Personally, although you might not believe it, I love the chase with ardour; when I was young I have shot as many as twenty-five—no—twenty-seven blackbirds and thrushes in one day, to say nothing of thirty-one larks, and some other small game. Also, once I wounded a chamois, which a bold hunter with me killed. It was a glorious moment. But now, for the reasons that you mention, I have given up all this sport, which formerly to me was so great an excitement and relaxation. Yet I admit that I still fish. Only last year I caught a large hatful of perch and dace, of which I persuaded Madame to cook some that Juliette would not eat and gave to the cat. Once, too, there was a big trout in the Lake Lucerne. He broke my line, but, my boy, we will go to fish for that trout. No doubt he is still there, for though I was then young, these fishy creatures live for many years, and to catch him would be a glory."

After Godfrey had given up his fox-shooting, not because in itself is a terrible crime, like fishing for salmon with herring roe, but for reasons which most of his countrymen would consider effeminate and absurd, he took to making expeditions, still in company with Juliette, for Madame stretched Continental conventions in his case, in search of certain rare flowers which grew upon the lower slopes of these Alps. In connection with one of these flowers an incident occurred, rather absurd in itself, but which was not without effect upon his fortunes.

The search for a certain floral treasure was long and arduous.

"If only I could find that lovely white bloom," exclaimed Juliette in exasperation at the close of a weary hour of climbing, "why, I would kiss it."

"So would I," said Godfrey, mopping himself with a pocket handkerchief, for the sun was hot, "and with pleasure."

"Hidden flower," invoked Juliette with appropriate heroic gestures, "white, secret, maiden flower, hear us! Discover thyself, O shrinking flower, and thou shalt be kissed by the one that first finds thee."

"I don't know that the flower would care for that," remarked Godfrey, as they renewed their quest.

At length behind a jutting mass of rock, in a miniature valley, not more than a few yards wide that was backed by other rocks, this flower was found. Godfrey and Juliette, passing round either side of the black, projecting mass to the opening of the toy vale beyond, discovered it simultaneously. There it stood, one lovely, lily-like bloom growing alone, virginal, perfect. With a cry of delight they sprang at it, and plucked it from its root, both of them grasping the tall stem.

"I saw it first, and I will kiss it!" cried Juliette, "in token of possession."

"No," said Godfrey, "I did, and I will. I want that flower for my collection."

"So do I, for mine," answered Juliette.

Then they both tried to set this seal of possession upon that lily bloom, with the strange result that their young lips met through its fragile substance and with so much energy that it was crushed and ruined.

"Oh!" said Godfrey with a start, "look what you have done to the flower."

"I! I, wicked one! Well, for the matter of that, look what you have done to my lips. They feel quite bruised."

Then first she laughed, and next looked as though she were going to cry.

"Don't be sad," said Godfrey remorsefully. "No doubt we shall find another, now that we know where they are."

"Perhaps," she answered, "but it is always the first that one remembers, and it is finished," and she threw down the stalk and stamped on it.

Just then they heard a sound of laughter, and looking up, to their horror perceived that they were not alone. For there, seated upon stones at the end of the tiny valley, in composed and comfortable attitudes, which suggested that they had not arrived that moment, were two gentlemen, who appeared to be highly amused.

Godfrey knew them at once, although he had not seen them since the previous autumn. They were Brother Josiah Smith, the spiritualist, and Professor Petersen, the investigating Dane, whom he used to meet at the séances in the Villa Ogilvy.

"I guess, young Brother Knight," said the former, his eyes sparkling with sarcastic merriment, "that there is no paint on you. When you find a flower, you know how to turn it to the best possible use."

"The substance of flowers is fragile, especially if of the lily tribe, and impedes nothing," remarked the learned Dane in considered tones, though what he meant Godfrey did not understand at the moment. On consideration he understood well enough.

"Our mutual friend, Madame Riennes, who is absent in Italy, will be greatly amused when she hears of this episode," said Brother Smith. "She is indeed a remarkable woman, for only this morning I received a letter in which she informed me that very soon I should meet you, young man, under peculiar circumstances, how peculiar she did not add. Well, I congratulate you and the young lady. I assure you, you made quite a pretty picture with nothing but that flower between you, though, I admit, it was rough on the flower. If I remember right you are fond of the classics, as I am, and will recall to mind a Greek poet named Theocritus. I think, had he been wandering here in the Alps to-day, he would have liked to write one of his idylls about you two and that flower."

"Because of the interruption give pardon, for it is owed an apology," said the solemn Professor, adding, "I think it must have been the emanation of Madame Riennes herself which led us to this place, where we did not at all mean to come, for she is very anxious to know how you progress and what you are doing."

"Yes, young friend," broke in Brother Smith, not without a touch of malice, for like the rest he was resentful of Godfrey's desertion of their "circle," "and now we shall be able to tell her."

"Say then," said Juliette, "who are these gentlemen, and of what do they talk?"

"They—are—friends of mine," Godfrey began to explain with awkward hesitation, but she cut him short with:

"I like not your friends. They make a mock of me, and I will never forgive you."

"But Juliette, I—" he began, and got no further, for she turned and ran away. Anxious to explain, he ran after her, pursued by the loud hilarity of the intruding pair. In vain, for Juliette was singularly swift of foot, and he might as well have pursued Atalanta.

She reached the Maison Blanche, which fortunately was empty, a clear ten yards ahead of him, and shut herself in her room, whence, declaring that she had a headache, she did not emerge till the following morning.

Godfrey departed to the observatory where he often worked in summer, feeling very sore and full of reflections. He had not really meant to kiss Juliette, at least he thought not, and it was unthinkable that she meant to kiss him, since, so far as he was aware, no young woman ever wanted to do such a thing, being, every one of them, doubtless, as unapproachable and frigid as the topmost, snowy peak of the Alps. (Such was, and always remained his attitude, where the other sex was concerned, one not without inconvenience in a practical world of disillusions.) No, it was that confounded flower which brought about this pure accident—as though Nature, which designs such accidents, had not always a flower, or something equally serviceable, up her sleeve.

Moreover, had it not been for that accursed pair, sent, doubtless, to spy on him by Madame Riennes, the accident would never have mattered; at least not much. He could have apologized suitably to Juliette, that is, if she wanted an apology, which she showed no signs of doing until she saw the two men. Indeed, at the moment, he thought that she seemed rather amused.

He thought of searching out Brother Smith and Professor Petersen, and explaining to them exactly what had happened in full detail, and should they still continue their ribald jests, of punching their heads, which as a manly young fellow, he was quite capable of doing. Reflection showed him, however, that this course might not be wise, since such adventures are apt to end in the police-court, where the flower, and its fruit, would obtain undue publicity. No, he must leave the business alone, and trust that Juliette would be merciful. Supposing that she were to tell Madame that he had tried to kiss her, though probably she would not mention that he had actually succeeded!

The mere idea made him feel cold down the back. He felt sure that Madame would believe the worst of him; to judge from their conversations, ladies, good as they all were, invariably did seem to believe the worst in such affairs. Should he throw himself upon the mercy of the Pasteur? Again, no. It would be so hard to make him comprehend. Also, if he did, he might suggest that the altar was the only possible expiation. And—and, oh! he must confess it, she was very nice and sweet, but he did not wish to marry Juliette and live with her all his life.

No, there was but one thing to be done: keep the burden of his secret locked in his own breast, though, unfortunately, it was locked as well in those of Juliette and of two uninvited observers, and probably would soon also be locked in the capacious bosom of Madame Riennes. For the rest, towards Juliette in the future, he would observe an attitude of strictest propriety; never more should she have occasion to complain of his conduct, which henceforth would be immaculate. Alas! how easy it is for the most innocent to be misjudged, and apparently, not without reason.

This reflection brought something to Godfrey's mind which had escaped it in his first disturbance, also connected with a flower. There came before him the vision of a London square, and of a tall, pale girl, in an antique dress, giving a rose to a man in knight's armour, which rose both of them kissed simultaneously. Of course, when he saw it he had ruled out the rose and only thought of the kisses, although, now that he came to think of it, a rose is of a much thicker texture than a lily. As he had witnessed that little scene, and drawn his own conclusions, so others had witnessed another little scene that afternoon, and made therefrom deductions which, in his innocent soul, he knew to be totally false. Suppose, then, that his deductions were also false. Oh! it was not possible. Besides, a barrier built of rose leaves was not sufficient, which again, with perfect justice, he remembered was exactly what Brother Smith and Professor Petersen had thought of one composed of lily petals.

There for the time the matter ended. Juliette reappeared on the morrow quite cured of her headache, and as gay and charming as ever. Possibly she had confided in her mamma, who had told her that after all things were not so terrible, even if they had been seen.

At any rate, the equilibrium was restored. Godfrey acted on his solemn resolutions of haughtiness and detachment for quite an hour, after which Juliette threw a kitten at him and asked what was the matter, and then sang him one of her pretty chansonettes to the accompaniment of a guitar with three strings, which closed the incident. Still there were no more flower hunts and no new adventures. Tacitly, but completely, everything of the sort was dropped out of their relationship. They remained excellent friends, on affectionate terms indeed, but that was all.

Meanwhile, owing to his doubts arising out of a singular coincidence concerned with flowers and kisses, Godfrey gradually made up his mind to write to Isobel. Indeed, he had half composed the epistle when at the end of one of his brief letters his father informed him that she had gone to Mexico with her uncle. So it came about that it was never posted, since it is a kind of superstition with young people that letters can only be delivered at the place where the addressee last resided. It rarely occurs to them that these may be forwarded, and ultimately arrive. Nor, indeed, did it occur to Godfrey that as Isobel's uncle was the British Minister to a certain country, an envelope addressed to her in his care in that country probably would have reached her.

She was gone and there was an end; it was of no use to think more of the matter. Still, he was sorry, because in that same letter his father had alluded casually to the death of Lady Jane, which had caused Hawk's Hall to be shut up for a while, and he would have liked to condole with Isobel on her loss. He knew that she loved her mother dearly, and of this gentle lady he himself had very affectionate remembrances, since she had always been most kind to him. Yet for the reasons stated, he never did so.

About a fortnight after the flower episode a chance came Godfrey's way of making an Alp-climbing expedition in the company of some mountaineers. They were friends of the Pasteur who joined the party himself, but stayed in a village at the foot of the mountains they were to climb, since for such exercise he had lost the taste. The first two expeditions went off very successfully, Godfrey showing himself most agile at the sport which suited his adventurous spirit and delighted him. By nature, notwithstanding his dreamy characteristics, he was fearless, at any rate where his personal safety was concerned, and having a good head, it gave him pleasure to creep along the edge of precipices, or up slippery ice slopes, cutting niches with an axe for his feet.

Then came the third attempt, up a really difficult peak which had not yet been conquered that year. The details of the expedition do not matter, but the end of it was that at a particularly perilous place one of the party lost his head or his breath and rolled from the path.

There he lay half senseless, on the brink of a gulf, with a drop of a thousand feet or more beneath him. As it happened, they were climbing in lots of three, each of which lots was roped together, but at some distance between the parties, that with the guide being a good way ahead.

Godfrey was leading his party along the track made by the other, but their progress was not very rapid owing to the weakness of the man who had fallen who, as it afterwards transpired, suffered from his heart, and was affected by the altitude. The climber behind Godfrey was strong and bold; also, as it chanced at the moment of the fall, this man's feet were planted upon a lump of projecting rock, so firmly that by throwing himself forward against the snow slope, grasping another lump of rock with his left hand and bearing on to the alpenstock with his right, he was able to sustain the weight of their companion. But the rope which bound them together, though strong, was thin; moreover, at the point where most of the strain came it rested on a knife-like edge of ice, so sharp that there was momentarily danger of its fraying through as the movements of the weight beneath rubbed it against the edge.

When a shout and the stoppage warned Godfrey of what had happened, he turned round and studied the position. Even to his inexperienced eye it was obvious that a catastrophe was imminent. Now there were two things which might be done; one was to stay in his place and help to bear the strain of the swinging body, for almost immediately the fainting man slipped from the ledge, and hung above the gulf. The other was to trust to number two to hold his weight, and go to his assistance in the hope of being able to support him until the guide could return to the first party. As by a flash-like working of the mind Godfrey weighed these alternatives, his quick eye saw what looked like a little bit of fluff appear from the underside of the rope, which told him that one at least of the strands must have severed upon the edge of ice. Then almost instinctively he made his choice.

"Can you hold him?" he said swiftly to number two, who answered, "Yes, I think so," in a muffled voice.

"Then I go to help him."

"If you slip, I cannot bear you both," said the muffled voice.

"No," answered Godfrey, and drawing the sheath knife he wore, deliberately cut the rope which joined him to number two.

Then he scrambled down to the ledge without much difficulty, reaching it, but just in time, for now the razor blade of the ice had cut half through the rope, and very soon the swinging of the senseless weight beneath must complete its work. This ledge, being broad, though sloping, was not a particularly bad place; moreover, on it were little hummocks of ice, resulting from snow that had melted and frozen again, against one of which Godfrey was able to rest his left shoulder, and even to pass his arm round it. But here came the rub. He could not get sufficient grip of the thin rope with his right hand beyond the point where it was cut, to enable him to support even half the weight that hung below. Should it sever, as it must do very shortly, it would be torn from his grasp.

What then could be done? Godfrey peered over the edge. The man was swinging not more than two feet below its brink, that is to say, the updrawn loop of his stout leather belt, to which the rope was fastened, was about that distance from the brink, and on either side of it he hung down like a sack tied round the middle, quite motionless in his swoon, his head to one side and his feet to the other.

Could he reach and grasp that leather belt without falling himself, and if so, could he bear the man's weight and not be dragged over? Godfrey shrank from the attempt; his blood curdled. Then he pictured, again in a mind-flash, his poor companion whirling down through space to be dashed to pulp at the bottom, and the agony of his wife and children whom he knew, and who had wished to prevent him from climbing that day. Oh! he would try. But still a paralysing fear overcame him, making him weak and nervous. Then it was in Godfrey's extremity that his imagination produced a very curious illusion. Quite distinctly he seemed to hear a voice, that of Miss Ogilvy, say to him:

"Do it, Godfrey, at once, or it will be too late. We will help you."

This phantasy, or whatever it was, seemed to give him back his nerve and courage. Coolly he tightened the grip of his left arm about the knob of ice, and drawing himself forward a little, so that his neck and part of his chest were over the edge, reached his right hand downwards. His fingers touched the belt; to grasp it he must have another inch and a half, or two inches. He let himself down that distance. Oh! how easy it seemed to do so—and thrust his fingers beneath the belt. As he closed them round it, the rope parted and all the weight that it had borne came upon Godfrey's arm!

How long did he support it, he often wondered afterwards. For ages it seemed. He felt as though his right arm was being torn from the socket, while the ice cut into the muscles of his left like active torture. He filled himself with air, blowing out his lower part so that its muscles might enable him to get some extra hold of the rough ground; he dug his toes deep into the icy snow. His hat fell from his head, rested for a moment in a ridiculous fashion upon the swinging body beneath, then floated off composedly into space, the tall feather in it sticking upwards and fluttering a little. He heard voices approaching, and above them the shouts of the guide, though what these said conveyed no meaning to him. He must loose his hold and go too. No, he would not. He would not, although now he felt as though his shoulder-joint were dislocated, also that his left arm was slipping. He would die like a brave man—like a brave man. Surely this was death! He was gone—everything passed away.

Godfrey woke again to find himself lying upon a flat piece of snow. Recollection came back to him with a pang, and he thought that he must have fallen.

Then he heard voices, and saw faces looking at him as through a mist, also he felt something in his mouth and throat, which seemed to burn them. One of the voices, it was that of the guide, said:

"Good, good! He finds himself, this young English hero. See, his eyes open; more cognac, it will make him happy, and prevent the shock. Never mind the other one; he is all right, the stupid."

Godfrey sat up and tried to lift his arm to thrust away the flask which he saw approaching him, but he could not.

"Take that burning stuff away, Karl, confound you," he said.

Then Karl, a good honest fellow, who was on his knees beside him, threw his arms about him, and embraced him in a way that Godfrey thought theatrical and unpleasant, while all the others, except the rescued man, who lay semi-comatose, set up a kind of pæan of praise, like a Greek chorus.

"Oh! shut up!" said Godfrey, "if we waste so much time we shall never get to the top," a remark at which they all burst out laughing.

"They talk of Providence on the Alps," shouted Karl in stentorian tones, while he performed a kind of war-dance, "but that's the kind of providence for me," and he pointed to Godfrey. "Many things have I seen in my trade as guide, but never one like this. What? To cut the rope for the sake of Monsieur there," and he pointed to number two, whose share in the great adventure was being overlooked, "before giving himself to almost certain death for the sake of Monsieur with the weak heart, who had no business on a mountain; to stretch over the precipice as the line parted, and hold Monsieur with the weak heart for all that while, till I could get a noose round him—yes, to go on holding him after he himself was almost dead—without a mind! Good God! never has there been such a story in my lifetime on these Alps, or in that of my father before me."

Then came the descent, Godfrey supported on the shoulder of the stalwart Karl, who, full of delight at this great escape from tragedy, and at having a tale to tell which would last him for the rest of his life, "jodelled" spontaneously at intervals in his best "large tip" voice, and occasionally skipped about like a young camel, while "Monsieur with the weak heart" was carried in a chair provided to bear elderly ladies up the lower slopes of the Alps.

Some swift-footed mountaineer had sped down to the village ahead of them and told all the story, with the result that when they reached the outskirts of the place, an excited crowd was waiting to greet them, including two local reporters for Swiss journals.

One of these, who contributed items of interest to the English press also, either by mistake, or in order to make his narrative more interesting, added to a fairly correct description of the incident, a statement that the person rescued by Godfrey was a young lady. At least, so the story appeared in the London papers next morning, under the heading of "Heroic Rescue on the Alps," or in some instances of, "A Young English Hero."

Among the crowd was the Pasteur, who beamed at Godfrey through his blue spectacles, but took no part in these excited demonstrations. When they were back at their hotel, and the doctor who examined Godfrey, had announced that he was suffering from nothing except exhaustion and badly sprained muscles, he said simply:

"I do not compliment you, my dear boy, like those others, because you acted only as I should have expected of you in the conditions. Still, I am glad that in this case another was not added to my long list of disappointments."

"I didn't act at all, Pasteur," blurted out Godfrey. "A voice, I thought it was Miss Ogilvy's, told me what to do, and I obeyed."

The old gentleman smiled and shook his head, as he answered:

"It is ever thus, young Friend. When we wish to do good we hear a voice prompting us, which we think that of an angel, and when we wish to do evil, another voice, which we think that of a devil, but believe me, the lips that utter both of them are in our own hearts. The rest comes only from the excitement of the instant. There in our hearts the angel and the devil dwell, side by side, like the two figures in a village weather-clock, ready to appear, now one and now the other, as the breath of our nature blows them."

"But I heard her," said Godfrey stubbornly.

"The excitement of the instant!" repeated the Pasteur blandly. "Had I been so situated I am quite certain that I should have heard all the deceased whom I have ever known," and he patted Godfrey's dark hair with his long, thin hand, thanking God in his heart for the brave spirit which He had been pleased to give to this young man, who had grown so dear to one who lacked a son. Only this he did in silence, nor did he ever allude to the subject afterwards, except as a commonplace matter-of-course event.

Notwithstanding the "jodellings" which continued outside his window to a late hour, and the bouquet of flowers which was sent to him by the wife of the mayor, who felt that a distinction had been conferred upon their village that would bring them many visitors in future seasons, and ought to be suitably acknowledged, Godfrey soon dropped into a deep sleep. But in the middle of the night it passed from him, and he awoke full of terrors. Now, for the first time, he understood what he had escaped, and how near he had been to lying, not in a comfortable bed, but a heap of splintered bones and mangled flesh at the foot of a precipice, whence, perhaps, it would have been impossible ever to recover his remains. In short, his nerves re-acted, and he felt anything but a hero, rather indeed, a coward among cowards. Nor did he wish ever to climb another Alp; the taste had quite departed from him. To tell the truth, a full month went by before he was himself again, and during that month he was as timid as a kitten, and as careful of his personal safety as a well-to-do old lady unaccustomed to travel.

CHAPTER XI

JULIETTE'S FAREWELL

When Godfrey returned to the Maison Blanche, wearing a handsome gold watch, which had been presented to him with an effusive letter of thanks by the gentleman whom he had rescued and his relatives, he found himself quite a celebrity. Most of the Pasteur's congregation met him when he descended from the diligence, and waved their hats, but as he thanked heaven, did not "jodel."

Leaving the Pasteur to make some acknowledgment, he fled to the house, only to find Madame, Juliette, a number of friends, to say nothing of Jean, the cook and the servant girl, awaiting him there. Madame beamed, and looked as though she were about to kiss him; the fresh and charming Juliette shook his hand, and murmured into his ear that she had no idea he was so brave, also that every night she thanked the Bon Dieu for his escape; while the others said something appropriate—or the reverse.

Once more he fled, this time to his bedroom. There upon his dressing-table lay two letters, one from his father and one addressed in a curious pointed hand-writing, which he did not know. This he opened at once. It was in French, and ran, as translated:

"Ah! Little Brother,—I know all that has happened to you, nor did your godmother need to wait to read about it in the journals. Indeed, I saw it in my crystal before it happened; you with the man hanging to your arm and the rest. But then a cloud came over the crystal, and I could not see the end. I hoped that he would pull you over the edge, so that in one short minute you became nothing but a red plum-pudding at the bottom of the gulf. For you know that the sweetest-tempered fairy godmother can be made cross by wicked ingratitude and evil treatment. Do not think, little Brother, that I have forgiven you for bringing that old pasteur-fool to insult and threaten me. Not so. I pray the speerits night and day to pay you back in your own coin, you who have insulted them also. Indeed, it was they who arranged this little incident, but they tell me that some other speerit interfered at the last moment and saved you. If so, better luck next time, for do not think you shall escape me and them. Had you been true to us you should have had great good fortune and everything you desire in life, including, perhaps, something that you desire most of all. As it is, you shall have much trouble and lose what you desire most of all. Have you been kissing that pretty Mademoiselle again and trying to make her as bad as her mother? Well, I hope you will, because it will hurt that old fool-pasteur. Wherever you go, remember that eyes follow you, mine and those of the speerits. Hate and bad luck to you, my little Brother, from your dear godmamma, whose good heart you have so outraged. So fare ill till you hear from me again, yes and always. Now you will guess my name, so I need not sign it.

"P.S.—Eleanor also sends you her hate from another sphere."

This precious epistle, filled with malignity, reaching him in the midst of so many congratulations, struck upon Godfrey like a blast of icy wind at the zenith of a summer day. To tell the truth also, it frightened him.

He had tried to forget all about Madame Riennes and now here she was stabbing him from afar, for the letter bore a Venice postmark. It may be foolish, but few of us care to be the object of a concentrated, personal hate. Perhaps this is due to the inherited superstitions of our race, not long emerged from the blackness of barbarism, but at least we still feel as our forefathers did; as though the will to work evil had the power to bring about the evil desired. It is nonsense, since were it true, none could escape the direst misfortune, as every one of us is at some time or another the object of the hate or jealousy of other human beings. Moreover, as most of us believe, there is a being, not human, that hates us individually and collectively, and certainly would compass our destruction, had he the power, which happily he has not, unless we ourselves give it to him.

Godfrey comforted himself with this reflection, also, with another; that in this instance the issue of his peril had been far different from what his enemy desired. Yet, with his nerves still shaken both by his spiritualistic experiences, and by those of the danger which he had passed, the letter undoubtedly did affect him in the way that it was meant to do, and the worst of it was that he could not consult his friend and guide, the Pasteur, because of the allusion to the scene with Juliette.

Throwing it down as though it were a venomous snake, which indeed, it was, he opened that from his father, which was brief. It congratulated him coldly on his escape, whereof Mr. Knight said he had heard, not in the way that he would have expected, from himself, but through the papers. This, it may be explained, was not strange, since the account was telegraphed long before Godfrey had time to write. As a matter of fact, however, he had not written, for who cares to indite epistles to an unsympathetic and critical recipient? Most people only compose letters for the benefit of those who like to receive them and, by intuition, read in them a great deal more than the sender records in black and white. For letter-writing, at its best, is an allusive art, something that suggests rather than describes. It was because Godfrey appreciated this truth in a half unconscious fashion, that he did not care to undertake an active correspondence with his father. It is the exception also, for young men to care to correspond with their fathers; the respective outlooks, and often, the respective interests, are too diverse. With mothers it is different, at any rate, sometimes, for in their case the relationship is more intimate. In the instance of the male parent, throughout the realm of nature, it is apt to have an accidental aspect or to acquire one as time goes by.

The letter went on to request that he would climb no more Alps, since he had been sent to Switzerland, to scale not mountains, but the peaks of knowledge. It added, with that naive selfishness from which sometimes even the most pious are not exempt, "had you been killed, in addition to losing your own life, which would not so much have mattered, since I trust that you would have passed to a better, you would have done a wrong to your family. In that event, as you are not yet of age, I believe the money which your friend left to you recently, would have returned to her estate instead of going to benefit your natural heirs."

Godfrey pondered over the words "natural heirs," wondering who these might be. Coming finally to the conclusion that he had but one, namely his father, which accounted for the solicitude expressed so earnestly in the letter, he uttered an expletive, which should not have passed his youthful lips, and threw it down upon the top of that of Madame Riennes.

After this he left the room much depressed, and watching his opportunity, for the merry party in the salon who had gathered to greet him were still there drinking heavy white wine, he slipped through the back door to walk in the woods. These woods were lonely, but then they suited his mood. In truth, never had he felt more alone in his life. His father and he were utterly different, and estranged, and he had no other relatives. In friends he was equally lacking. Miss Ogilvy, whom he had begun to love, was dead, and a friend in heaven is some way off, although he did think he had heard her voice when he was so near to joining her.

There remained no one save the Pasteur, of whom he was growing truly fond, so much so, that he wished that the old gentleman had been appointed to be his father according to the flesh. The rest of the world was a blank to him, except for Isobel, who had deserted him.

Besides, some new sentiment had entered into his relations with Isobel, whereby these were half spoiled. Of course, although he did not altogether understand it, this was the eternal complication of sex which curses more than it blesses in the world; of sex, the eating fire that is so beautiful but burns. For when that fire has passed over the flowers of friendship, they are changed into some new growth, that however gorgeous it may be, yet always smells of flame. Sex being the origin of life is necessarily also the origin of trouble, since life and trouble are inseparable, and devours the gentle joys of friendship, as a kite devours little singing birds. These go to its sustenance, it is true, and both are birds, but the kite is a very different creature from the nightingale or the lark. One of the great advantages of matrimony, if it endures long enough, is that when the sex attraction, which was its cause, has faded, or practically died, once more it makes friendship possible.

Perhaps the best thing of the little we have been told about heaven, is that in it there will be no sex. If there were, it is doubtful whether it could remain heaven, as we define that state, since then must come desires, and jealousies, and selfishness, and disappointment; also births and deaths, since we cannot conceive sex- love without an object, or a beginning without an end. From all of which troubles we learn that the angels are relieved.

Now this wondrous, burning mantle of sex had fallen on Godfrey and Isobel, as he had learned when he saw her with the knight in armour in the garden, and everything was changed beneath its fiery, smothering folds, and for him there was no Isobel. His friend had gone, and he was left wandering alone. His distress was deep, and since he was too young to mask his feelings, as people must learn to do in life, it showed itself upon his face. At supper that night, all of the little party observed it, for he who should have been gay, was sad and spoke little. Afterwards, when the Pasteur and Godfrey went to the observatory to resume their astronomical studies, the former looked at him a while, and said:

"What is the matter, Godfrey? Tell me."

"I cannot," he replied, colouring.

"Is it so bad as that then? I thought that perhaps you had only received a letter, or letters."

"I received two of them. One was from my father, who scolds me because I was nearly killed."

"Indeed. He seems fond of scolding, your father. But that is no new thing, and one to which you should be used. How about the other letter? Was it, perchance, from Madame Riennes?"

"It is not signed, but I think so."

"Really. It is odd, but, I too, have had a letter from Madame Riennes, also unsigned, and I think, after reading it, that you may safely show me yours, and then tell me the truth of all these accusations she makes concerning you and Juliette."

Now Godfrey turned crimson.

"How can I?" he murmured. "For myself I do not care, but it seems like betraying—someone else."

"It is difficult, my boy, to betray that which is already well known, to me, among others. Had this letter, perchance, something to do with an expedition which you two young people made to search for flowers, and nothing else? Ah! I see it is so. Then you may safely show it to me, since I know all about that expedition."

So Godfrey produced the epistle, for at the moment he forgot that it contained allusions to Madame also, and holding it gingerly between his thumb and finger, handed it to him. The Pasteur read it through without showing the slightest emotion.

"Ah!" he said, when he had finished, "in her way she is quite magnificent, that old witch. But, surely, one day, unless she repents, she will be accommodated with some particular hell of her own, since there are few worthy to share it with her. You see, my boy, what she says about Madame. Well, as I think I told her, that dear wife of mine may have had her foolish moments, like most others, if all the truth were known. But note this—there is a great difference between those who have foolish moments, of whatever sort, and those who make it their business to seek such moments; further, between those who repent of their errors and those who glory in, and try to continue them. If you have any doubt of that study the Bible, and read amongst others, of David, who lived to write the Psalms, and of Mary Magdalene, who became a saint. Also, although this did not occur to that tiger of a woman, I may have known of those moments, and even done my best to help my wife out of them, and been well rewarded"—here his kind old face beamed like the sun—"oh! yes, most gloriously rewarded. So a fig for the old witch and her tales of Madame! And now tell me the truth about yourself and Juliette, with a mind at ease, for Juliette has told it to me already, and I wish to compare the stories."

So Godfrey told him everything, and a ridiculous little tale it was. When he had finished the Pasteur burst out laughing.

"You are indeed sinners, you two," he said, "so great, that surely you should stand dressed in white sheets, one on either side of the altar, with the crushed flower in the middle. Ah! that is what I regret, this flower, for it is very rare. Only once have I found it in all my life, and then, as there was no lady present, I left it where it grew. Hearken, all this is a pack of nonsense.

"Hearken again, Godfrey. Everybody things me an old fool. How can it be helped with such a face as mine, and these blue spectacles, which I must wear? But even an old fool sees things sometimes. Thus, I have seen that Madame, who had once plenty of money to play with, and longs, poor dear, for the fine things of life, is very anxious that her Juliette should make a good marriage. I have seen, too, that she has thought of you, whom she thinks much richer than you are, as a good match for Juliette, and has done her best to make Juliette think as she does, all of which is quite natural in her, and indeed, praiseworthy, especially if she likes and respects the young man. But, my boy, it is the greatest nonsense. To begin with, you do not, and never will, care for Juliette, and she does not, and never will, care for you. Your natures, ah! they are quite different. You have something big in the you, and Juliette—well, she has not. Marriage with her would be for you a misery, and for Juliette a misery also, since what have you in common? Besides, even if it were otherwise, do you think I would allow such a thing, with you so young and in my charge? Bah! be good friends with that pretty girl, and go hunt for flowers with her as much as you like, for nothing will come of it. Only, bet no more in kisses, for they are dangerous, and sparks sometimes set fire to haystacks."

"Indeed, I will not," exclaimed Godfrey with fervour.

"There, then, that trouble is finished." (Here, although he did not know it, the Pasteur was mistaken.) "And now, as to the rest of this letter. It is malignant, malignant, and its writer will always seek to do you ill, and perhaps, sometimes succeed. It is the price which you must pay for having mixed with such a person who mixes with the devil, though that was no fault of yours, my boy. Still, always, always in the world we are suffering from the faults of others. It is a law, the law of vicarious sacrifice, which runs through everything, why, we do not know. Still, be not afraid, for it is you who will win at the last, not she. For the rest, soon you will go away from here, since the year for which you came is almost finished, and you must turn your mind to the bigger life. I pray you when you do, not to forget me, for, my boy, I, who have no son, have learned to love you like a son, better perhaps, than had you been one, since often I have observed that it is not always fathers and sons that love each other most, frequently the other way, indeed.

"Also I pray another thing of you—that if you think I have any wisdom, or any little light in the lamp of this ugly, old body of mine, you will always take me for a counsellor, and write to me concerning your troubles, (as indeed, you must do, for remember I am your trustee of this property,) and perhaps pay attention to the advice I may give. And now let us get to our stars; they are much more amusing than Madame Riennes. It is strange to think that the same God who made the stars also made Madame Riennes. Truly He is a charitable and tolerant God!"

"Perhaps the devil made her," suggested Godfrey.

"It may be so, it may be so, but is it not said in the Book of Proverbs, I believe, that He makes both good and evil for His own infinite ends, though what these may be, I, worm that I am, cannot pretend to understand. And now to our stars that are far away and pure, though who knows but that if one were near to them, they would prove as full of foulness as the earth?"

The Pasteur was right when he said that Madame Riennes would not cease from attempts to do evil to Godfrey, and therefore wrong when he added that the trouble she had caused was finished. Of this, that young man was made painfully aware, when a fortnight or so later another letter from his father reached him. It informed him that Mr. Knight had received an anonymous communication which stated that he, Godfrey, was leading an evil life in Lucerne, also that he was being entrapped into a marriage with Mademoiselle Boiset, whom he had been seen embracing behind some rocks. The letter ended:

"Lacking proof, I do not accept these stories as facts, although, as there is no smoke without fire, I think it probable that there is something in them and that you are drifting into undesirable companionships. At any rate I am sure that the time has come for you to return home and to commence your studies for the Church. I have to request, therefore, that you will do this at once as I am entering your name at my own college for the next term and have so informed the trustees under Miss Ogilvy's will, who will no doubt meet the expense and give you a suitable allowance. I am writing to the Pasteur Boiset to the same effect. Looking forward to seeing you, when we can discuss all these matters in more detail,—I am, your affectionate father, "Richard Knight."

In dismay Godfrey took this letter to the Pasteur. For the last thing Godfrey wished to do was to leave Kleindorf and the house in which he was so welcome and so well treated, in order to return to the stony bosom of Monk's Acre Abbey.

"I have also received a letter," said Monsieur Boiset; "it seems that you and I always receive disagreeable letters together. The last were from the witch-woman Riennes, and these are from your father. He has an unpleasant way of writing, this father of yours, although he is a good man, for here he suggests that I am trying to trap you for a son- in-law, wherein I see the fat finger of that witch Riennes, who has so great a passion for the anonymous epistle. Well, if he had said that I wished to trap you for a son, he would have shot nearer to the bulls'- eye, but for a son-in-law, as you know, it is not so. Still, you must go; indeed, it is time that you went, now that you talk French so well, and have, I hope, learnt other things also, you to whom the big world opens. But see, your father talks of your entering the Church. Tell me, is this so? If so, of course, I shall be happy."

"No," said Godfrey, shaking his head.

"Then," replied the Pasteur, "I may say that I am equally happy. It is not everyone that has a call for this vocation, and there are more ways of doing good in the world than from the floor of a pulpit. Myself, I have wondered sometimes—but let that be; it is the lot of certain of us, who think in our vanity that we could have done great things, to be obliged to do the small things, because God has so decreed. To one He gives the ten talents, to the other only one talent, or even but a franc. Whatever it be, of it we must make the best, and so long as we do not bury it, we have done well. I can only say that I have tried to use my franc, or my fifty centimes, to such advantage as I could, and hope that in some other place and time I may be entrusted with a larger sum. Oh! my boy, we are all of us drawn by the horses of Circumstance, but, as I believe, those horses have a driver who knows whither he is guiding us."

A few days later Godfrey went. His last midday meal at the Maison Blanche, before he departed to catch the night train for Paris, was rather a melancholy function. Madame, who had grown fond of him in her somewhat frivolous way, openly dropped tears into her soup. Juliette looked sad and distraite, though inwardly supported by the knowledge that her distant cousin, the notary Jules, was arriving on the morrow to spend his vacation at the Maison Blanche, so that Godfrey's room would not be without an occupant. Indeed, in her pretty little head she was already planning certain alterations in the arrangement of the furniture, to make it more comfortable to the very different tastes of the new comer.

Still, she was truly sorry to lose her friend the Hibou, although she had not been able to fulfil her mother's wish, and make him fall in love with her, or even to fall in love with him herself. As she explained to Madame Boiset, it was of no use to try, since between their natures there were fixed not only a great gulf, but several whole ranges of the Alps, and whereas the Hibou sat gazing at the stars from their topmost peak, she was picking flowers in the plain and singing as she picked them.

The Pasteur did not make matters better by the extremely forced gaiety of his demeanour. He told stories and cracked bad jokes in the intervals of congratulating Godfrey at his release from so dull a place as Kleindorf. Godfrey said little or nothing, but reflected to himself that the Pasteur did not know Monk's Acre.

At last the moment came, and he departed with a heavy heart, for he had learned to love these simple, kindly folk, especially the Pasteur. How glad he was when it was over and he had lost sight of the handkerchiefs that were being waved at him from the gate as the hired vehicle rolled away. Not that it was quite over, for the Pasteur accompanied him to the station, in order, as he said, to take his last instructions about the Villa Ogilvy, although, in truth, Godfrey had none to give.

"Please do what you think best," was all that he could say. Also, when several miles further on, they came to a turn in the road, there, panting on a rock, stood Juliette, who had reached the place, running at full speed, by a short cut through the woods. They had no time to stop, because the Pasteur thought that they were late for the train, which, as a matter of fact, did not leave for half-an-hour after they reached the station. So they could only make mutual signals of recognition and farewell. Juliette, who looked as though she were crying, kissed her hand to him, calling out:

"Adieu, adieu! cher ami," while he sought refuge in the Englishman's usual expedient of taking off his hat.

"It is nothing, nothing," said the Pasteur, who had also noted Juliette's tear-swollen eyes, "to-morrow she will have Jules to console her, a most worthy young man, though me he bores."

Here, it may be added, that Jules consoled her so well, that within a year they were married, and most happily.

Yet Godfrey was destined never to see that graceful figure and gay little face again, since long before he revisited Lucerne Juliette died on the birth of her third child. And soon, who thought of Juliette except perhaps Godfrey, for her husband married again very shortly, as a worthy and domestic person of the sort would do. Her children were too young to remember her, and her mother, not long afterwards, was carried off by a sudden illness, pneumonia, to join her in the Shades. Except the Pasteur himself none was left.

Well, such is the way of this sad world of change and death. But Godfrey never forgot the picture of her standing breathless on the rock and kissing her slim hand to him. It was one of those incidents which, when they happen to a man in his youth, remain indelibly impressed upon his mind.

At the station there were more farewells, for here was the notary, who had managed Miss Ogilvy's Swiss affairs and now, under the direction of Monsieur Boiset, attended to those of Godfrey. Also such of the servants were present as had been kept on at the Villa, while among those walking about the platform he saw Brother Josiah Smith and Professor Petersen, who had come evidently to see the last of him, and make report to a certain quarter.

The Pasteur talked continually, in his high, thin voice, to cover up his agitation, but what it was all about Godfrey could never remember. All he recollected of the parting was being taken into those long arms, embraced upon the forehead, and most fervently blessed.

Then the train steamed off, and he felt glad that all was over.

CHAPTER XII

HOME

About forty-eight hours later Godfrey arrived duly at the little Essex station three miles from Monk's Acre. There was nobody to meet him, which was not strange, as the hour of his coming was unknown. Still, unreasonable as it might be, the contrast between the warmth and affection that had distinguished his departure, and the cold vacuum that greeted his arrival, chilled him. He said a few words to the grumpy old porter who was the sole occupant of the platform, but that worthy, although he knew him well enough, did not seem to realise that he had ever been away. During the year in which so many things had happened to Godfrey nothing at all had happened to the porter, and therefore he did not appreciate the lapse of time.

Leaving his baggage to be brought by the carrier's cart, Godfrey took the alpenstock that, in a moment of enthusiasm, the guide had given him as a souvenir of his great adventure, and started for home. It was a very famous alpenstock, which this guide and his father before him had used all their lives, one that had been planted in the topmost snows of every peak in Switzerland. Indeed the names of the most unclimbable of these, together with the dates of their conquest by its owners, sometimes followed by crosses to show that on such or such an expedition life had been lost, were burnt into the tough wood with a hot iron. As the first of these dates was as far back as 1831, Godfrey valued this staff highly, and did not like to leave it to the chances of the carrier's cart.

His road through the fields ran past Hawk's Hall, of which he observed with a thrill of dismay, that the blinds were drawn as though in it someone lay dead. There was no reason why he should have been dismayed, since he had heard that Isobel had gone away to somewhere in "Ameriky," as Mrs. Parsons had expressed it in a brief and illspelt letter, and that Sir John was living in town. Yet the sight depressed him still further with its suggestion of death, or of separation, which is almost as bad, for, be it remembered, he was at an age when such impressions come home.

After leaving the Hall with its blinded and shuttered windows, his quickest road to the Abbey House ran through the churchyard. Here the first thing that confronted him was a gigantic monument, of which the new marble glittered in the afternoon sun. It was a confused affair, and all he made out of it, without close examination, was a life-sized angel with an early-Victorian countenance, leaning against the broken stump of an oak tree and scattering from a basket, of the kind that is used to collect nuts or windfall apples, on to a sarcophagus beneath a profusion of marble roses, some of which seemed to have been arrested and frozen in mid-air. He glanced at the inscription in gold letters. It was "To the beloved memory of Lady Jane Blake, wife of Sir John Blake, Bart., J.P., and daughter of the Right Hon. The Earl of Lynfield, whose bereaved husband erected this monument—'Her husband . . . praiseth her.'"

Godfrey looked, and remembering the gentle little woman whose crumbling flesh lay beneath, shivered at the awful and crushing erection above. In life, as he knew, she had been unhappy, but what had she done to deserve such a memorial in death? Still, she was dead, of that there was no doubt, and oh! the sadness of it all.

He went on to the Abbey, resisting a queer temptation to enter the church and look at the tomb of the Plantagenet lady and her unknown knight, who slept there so quietly from year to year, through spring, summer, autumn and winter, for ever and for ever. The front door was locked, so he rang the bell. It was answered by a new servant, rather a forbidding, middle-aged woman with a limp, who informed him that Mr. Knight was out, and notwithstanding his explanations, declined to admit him into the house. Doubtless she thought that a young man, wearing a foreign-looking hat and carrying such a strange long stick, must be a thief, or worse. The end of it was that she slammed the door in his face and shot the old-fashioned bolts.

Then Godfrey bethought him of the other door, that which led into the ancient refectory, which was now used as a schoolroom. This was open, so he went in and, being tired after his long journey, sat himself down in the chair at the end of the old oak table, that same chair in which Isobel had kissed him when he was a little boy. He looked about him vaguely; the place, of course, was much the same as it had been for the last five hundred years, but, as he could see from the names on the copybooks that lay about, the pupils who inhabited it had changed. Of the whole six not one was the same.

Then, perhaps for the first time, he began to understand how variable is the world, a mere passing show in which nothing remains the same, except the houses and the trees. Even these depart, for a cottage with which he had been familiar from his earliest infancy, as he could see through the open door, was pulled down to make room for "improvements," and the great old elm, where the rooks used to build, had been torn up in a gale. Only its ugly stump and projecting roots were left.

So he sat musing there, very depressed at heart, till at length Mrs. Parsons came and discovered him in a half-doze. She, too, was somewhat changed, for of a sudden age had begun to take a hold of her. Her hair was white now, and her plump, round face had withered like a spring apple. Still, she greeted him with the old affection, for which he felt grateful, seeing that it was the first touch of kindness he had known since he set foot on English ground.

"Dear me, Master Godfrey!" she said, "hadn't I heard that you were coming, I could never have been sure that it was you. Why, you've grown into a regular young gentleman in those foreign parts, and handsome, too, though I sez it. Who could have guessed that you are your father's son? Why, you'd make two of him. But there, they say that your mother was a good-looking lady and large built, though, as I never set eyes on her, I can't say for sure. Well, you must be tired after all this travelling in steamships and trains, so come into the dining-room and have some tea, for I have got the key to the sideboard."

He went, and, passing through the hall, left his alpenstock in the umbrella-stand. In due course the tea was produced, though for it he seemed to have little appetite. While he made pretence to eat the thick bread and butter, Mrs. Parsons told him the news, such as it was. Sir John was living in town and "flinging the money about, so it was said, not but what he had got lots to fling and plenty to catch it," she added meaningly. His poor, dear lady was dead, and "happy for her on the whole." Miss Isobel had "gone foreign," having, it was told, quarrelled with her father, and nothing had been heard of her since she went. She, too, had grown into a fine young lady.

That was all he gathered before Mrs. Parsons was obliged to depart to see to her business—except that she was exceedingly glad to see him.

Godfrey went up to his bedroom, which he found unprepared, for somebody else seemed to be sleeping there. While he was surveying it and wondering who this occupant might be, he heard his father in the hall asking the parlour-maid which of the young gentlemen had left that "ridiculous stick" in the stand. She replied that she did not know, whereupon the hard voice of his parent told her to take it away. Afterwards Godfrey found it thrown into the wood-house to be chopped up for firewood, though luckily before this happened.

By this time a kind of anger had seized him. It was true that he had not said by what train he was coming, for the reason that until he reached London he could not tell, but he had written that he was to arrive that afternoon, and surely some note might have been taken of the fact.

He went downstairs and confronted his father, who alone amid so much change seemed to be exactly the same. Mr. Knight shook him by the hand without any particular cordiality, and at once attacked him for not having intimated the hour of his arrival, saying that it was too late to advise the carrier to call at the station for his baggage and that a trap would have to be sent, which cost money.

"Very well, Father, I will pay for it myself," answered Godfrey.

"Oh, yes, I forgot!" exclaimed Mr. Knight, with a sneer, "you have come into money somehow, have you not, and doubtless consider yourself independent?"

"Yes, and I am glad of it, Father, as now I hope I shall not be any more expense to you."

"As you have begun to talk business, Godfrey," replied his father in an acid manner, "we may as well go into things and get it over. You have, I presume, made up your mind to go into the Church in accordance with my wish?"

"No, Father; I do not intend to become a clergyman."

"Indeed. You seem to me to have fallen under very bad influences in Switzerland. However, it does not much matter, as I intend that you shall."

"I am sorry, but I cannot, Father."

Then, within such limits as his piety permitted, which were sufficiently wide, Mr. Knight lost his temper very badly indeed. He attacked his son, suggesting that he had been leading an evil life in Lucerne, as he had learned "from outside sources," and declared that either he should obey him or be cast off. Godfrey, whose temper by this time was also rising, intimated that he preferred the latter alternative.

"What, then, do you intend to do, young man?" asked Mr. Knight.

"I do not know yet, Father." Then an inspiration came to him, and he added, "I shall go to London to-morrow to consult my trustees under Miss Ogilvy's will."

"Really," said Mr. Knight in a rage. "You are after that ill-gotten money, are you? Well, as we seem to agree so badly, why not go to- night instead of to-morrow; there is a late train? Perhaps it would be pleasanter for both of us, and then I need not send for your luggage. Also it would save my shifting the new boy from your room."

"Do you really mean that, Father?"

"I am not in the habit of saying what I do not mean. Only please understand that if you reject my plans for your career, which have been formed after much thought, and, I may add, prayer, I wash my hands of you who are now too old to be argued with in any other way."

Godfrey looked at his father and considered the iron mouth cut straight like a slit across the face, the hard, insignificant countenance and the small, cold, grey eyes. He realised the intensity of the petty anger based, for the most part, on jealousy because he was now independent and could not be ordered about and bullied like the rest of the little boys, and knew that behind it there was not affection, but dislike. Summing up all this in his quick mind, he became aware that father or not, he regarded this man with great aversion. Their natures, their outlook, all about them were antagonistic, and, in fact, had been so from the beginning. The less that they saw of each other the better it would be for both. Although still so young, he had ripened early, and was now almost a man who knew that these things were so without possibility of doubt.

"Very well, Father," he said, "I will go. It is better than stopping here to quarrel."

"I thought you would, now that your friend, Isobel, who did you so much harm with her bad influence, has departed to Mexico, where, I have no doubt, she has forgotten all about you. You won't be able to run after her money as you did after Miss Ogilvy's," replied Mr. Knight with another sneer.

"You insult me," said Godfrey. "It is a lie that I ran after Miss Ogilvy's money, and I will never forgive you for saying such a thing of me in connection with Isobel," and turning he left the room.

So did his father, for Godfrey heard him go to his study and lock the door, doubtless as a sign and a token.

Then Godfrey sought out Mrs. Parsons and told her everything. The old woman was much disturbed, and wept.

"I have been thinking of late, Master Godfrey," she said, "that your father's heart is made of that kind of stone which Hell is paved with, only with the good intentions left out—it's that hard. Here you are come back as fine a young man as a body can wish to see, of whom his begetter might well be proud, though, for the matter of that, there is precious little of him in you—and he shuts the door in your face just because you won't be a parson and have come into fortune—that's what rankles. I say that your mother, if she was a fool when she married him, was a wise woman when she died. Parson or not, he will never go where she is. Well, it's sad, but you'll be well out of this cold house, where there's so much praying but not a spark of love."

"I think so," said Godfrey with a sigh.

"I think so, too, for myself, I mean. But, look here, my boy, I only stopped on looking after this dratted pack of young gentlemen because you were coming home again. But, as you ain't, I'm out of it; yes, when the door shuts on you I give my month's notice, which perhaps will mean that I leave to-morrow, for he won't be able to abide the sight of me after that."

"But how will you live, Nurse, till I can help you?"

"Lord bless you, dear, that's all right. I've been a careful woman all my life, and have hard on £500 put away in the Savings Bank, to say nothing of a bit of Stock. Also, my old brother, who was a builder, died last year and left me with a nice little house down in Hampstead, which he built to live in himself, but never did, poor man, bit by bit when he was short of business, very comfortable and in a good neighbourhood, with first-rate furniture and real silver plate, to say nothing of some more Stock, yes, for £1,000 or more. I let it furnished by the month, but the tenant is going away, so I shall just move into it myself, and perhaps take in a lodger or two to keep me from being idle."

"That's capital!" said Godfrey, delighted.

"Yes, and I tell you what would be capitaller. Mayhap you will have to live in London for a bit, and, if so, you are just the kind of lodger I should like, and I don't think we should quarrel about terms. I'll write you down the address of that house, the Grove as it is called, though why, I don't know, seeing there isn't a tree within half a mile, which I don't mind, as there are too many about here, making so much damp. And you'll write and let me know what you are going to do, won't you?"

"Of course I will."

"And now, look here. Likely you will want a little money till you square up things with your trustee people that the master hates so much."

"Well, I had forgotten it, but, as a matter of fact, I have only ten shillings left, and that isn't much when one is going to London," confessed Godfrey.

"I thought so; you never were one to think much of such things, and so it's probable that you'll get plenty of them, for it's what we care about we are starved in, just to make it hot for us poor humans. Take your father, for instance; he loves power, he does; he'd like to be a bishop of the old Roman sort what could torture people who didn't agree with them. And what is he? The parson of a potty parish of a couple of hundred people, counting the babies and the softies, and half of them Dissenters or Salvation Army. Moreover, they can't be bullied, because if they were they'd just walk into the next chapel door. Of course, there's the young gentlemen, and he takes it out of them, but, Lord bless us! that's like kicking a wool sack, of which any man of spirit soon gets tired. So, you see, he is sick-hearted, and will be more so now that you have stood up to him; and, in this way or that, it's the same with everyone, none of us gets what we want, while of what we don't want there's always plenty."

While the old lady held forth thus in her little room which, although she did not know it, had once been the penitential cell of the Abbey, wherein for hundreds of years many unhappy ones had reflected in a very similar vein, she was engaged in trying key after key upon a stout oak chest. It was part of the ancient furniture of the place, that indeed in former days had served as the receptacle for hair shirts, scourges and other physical inducements to repentance and piety.

Now it had a different purpose and held Mrs. Parsons' best dresses, also, in a bandbox, an ornament preserved from her wedding-cake, for once in the far past she was married to a sailor, a very great black- guard, who came to his end by tumbling from a gangway when he was drunk. Among these articles was a tin tea-canister which, when opened, proved to be full of money; gold, silver and even humble copper, to say nothing of several banknotes.

"Now, there you are, my dear, take what you like," she said, "and pay it back if you wish, but if you don't, it might have been worse spent." And she pushed the receptacle, labelled "Imperial Pekoe," towards him across the table, adding, "Drat those moths! There's another on my best silk."

Godfrey burst out laughing and enjoyed that laugh, for it was his first happy moment since his return to England.

"Give me what you like," he said.

So she extracted from the tea-tin a five-pound note, four sovereigns and a pound's worth of silver and copper.

"There," she said, "that will do to begin with, for too much money in the pocket is a temptation in a wicked place like London, where there's always someone waiting to share it. If it's wanted there's more where that came from, and you've only to write and say so. And now you have got the address and you've got the cash, and if you want to catch that last train it's time you were off. If I took the same to-morrow night, why, it wouldn't surprise me, especially as I want to hear all you've been a-doing in those foreign parts, tumbling over precipices and the rest. So good-bye, my dear, and God bless you. Lord! it seems only the other day that I was giving you your bottle."

Then they kissed each other and, having retrieved his alpenstock from the stick-house, Godfrey trudged back to the station, where he picked up his luggage and departed for London. Arriving at Liverpool Street rather late, he went to the Great Eastern Hotel, and after a good meal, which he needed, slept like a top. His reception in England had been bitter, but the young soon shake off their troubles, from which, indeed, the loving kindness of his dear old nurse already had extracted the sting.

On the following morning, while breakfasting at a little table by one of the pillars of the big dining-room, he began to wonder what he should do next. In his pocket he had a notebook, in which, at the suggestion of the Pasteur, he had set down the address of the lawyers who had written to him about his legacy. It was in a place called the Poultry, which, on inquiry from the hall-porter, he discovered was quite close by the Mansion House.

So a while later, for the porter told him that it was no use to go to see lawyers too early, he sallied forth, and after much search discovered the queer spot called the Poultry, also the offices of Messrs. Ranson, Richards and Son. Here he gave his name to a clerk, who thrust a very oily head out of a kind of mahogany box, and was told that Mr. Ranson was engaged, but that, if he cared to wait, perhaps he would see him later on. He said he would wait, and was shown into a stuffy little room, furnished with ancient deed-boxes and a very large, old leather-covered sofa that took up half the place. Here he sat for a while, staring at a square of dirty glass which gave what light was available, and reflecting upon things in general.

While he was thus engaged he heard a kind of tumult outside, in which he recognised the treble of the oily-headed clerk coming in a bad second to a deep, bass voice. Then the door opened and a big, burly man, with a red face and a jovial, rolling eye, appeared with startling suddenness and ejaculated:

"Damn Ranson, damn Richards, or damn them both, with the Son thrown in! I ask you, young man"— here he addressed Godfrey seated on the corner of the sofa—"what is the use of a firm of lawyers whom you can never see? You pay the brutes, but three times out of four they are not visible, or, as I suspect, pretend not to be, in order to enhance their own importance. And I sent them a telegram, too, having a train to catch. What do you think?"

"I don't know, Sir," Godfrey answered. "I never came to a lawyer's office before, and I hope I shan't again if this is the kind of room they put one into."

"Room!" ejaculated the irate gentleman, "call it a dog kennel, call it a cesspool, for, by heaven, it smells like one, but in the interests of truth, young man, don't call it a room."

"Now that you mention it, there is a queer odour. Perhaps a dead rat under the floor," suggested Godfrey.

"Twenty dead rats, probably, since I imagine that this hole has not been cleaned since the time of George II. We are martyrs in this world, Sir. I come here to attend to the affairs of some whippersnapper whom I never saw and never want to see, just because Helen Ogilvy, who was my first cousin, chooses to make me a trustee of her confounded will, in which she leaves money to the confounded whippersnapper, God knows why. This whippersnapper has a father, a parson, who can write the most offensive letters imaginable. I received one of them this morning, accusing the whippersnapper of all sorts of vague things, and me and my fellow trustee, who is at present enjoying himself travelling, of abetting him. I repeat, damn Ranson, Richards and Son; damn the parson, damn Helen—no, I won't say that, for she is dead—and especially damn the whippersnapper. Don't you agree with me?"

"Not quite, Sir," said Godfrey. "I don't mind about Ranson, Richards and Son, or anybody else, but I don't quite see why you should damn me, who, I am sure, never wished to give you any trouble."

"You! And who the Hades may you be?"

"I am Godfrey Knight, and I suppose that you are my trustee, or one of them."

"Godfrey Knight, the young man whose father gives us so much trouble, all at our own expense, I may remark. Well, after hearing so much of you on paper, I'm deuced glad to meet you in the flesh. Come into the light, if you can call it light, and let me have a look at you."

Godfrey stepped beneath the dirty pane and was contemplated through an eyeglass by this breezy old gentleman, who exclaimed presently:

"You're all right, I think; a fine figure of a young man, not bad looking, either, but you want drilling. Why the devil don't you go into the army?"

"I don't know," answered Godfrey, "never thought of it. Are you in the army, Sir?"

"No, not now, though I was. Commanded my regiment for five years, and then kicked out with the courtesy title of Major-General. Cubitte is my name, spelt with two 't's' and an 'e,' please, and don't you forget that, since that 'e' has been a point of honour with our family for a hundred years, the Lord knows why. Well, there we are. Do you smoke?"

"Only a pipe," said Godfrey.

"That's right; I hate those accursed cigarettes, still they are better than nothing. Now sit down and tell me all about yourself."

Godfrey obeyed, and somehow feeling at ease with this choleric old General, in the course of the next twenty minutes explained many things to him, including the cause of his appearance in that office.

"So you don't want to be a parson," said the General, "and with your father's example before your eyes, I am sure I don't wonder. However, you are independent of him more or less, and had better cut out a line for yourself. We will back you. What do you say to the army?"

"I think I should rather like that," answered Godfrey. "Only, only, I want to get out of England as soon as possible."

"And quite right, too—accursed hole, full of fog and politicians. But that's not difficult with India waiting for you. I'm an Indian cavalry officer myself, and could put you up to the ropes and give you a hand afterwards, perhaps, if you show yourself of the right stuff, as I think you will. But, of course, you will have to go to Sandhurst, pass an entrance examination, and so forth. Can you manage that?"

"Yes, Sir, I think so, with a little preparation. I know a good deal of one sort or another, including French."

"All right, three months' cramming at Scoones' or Wren's, will do the trick. And now I suppose you want some money?"

Godfrey explained that he did, having only £10 which he had borrowed from his old nurse.

Just then the oily-headed clerk announced that Mr. Ranson was at liberty. So they both went in to see him, and the rest may be imagined. The trustees undertook to pay his expenses, even if they had to stretch a point to do so, and gave him £20 to go on with, also a letter of introduction to Scoones, whom he was instructed to see and arrange to join their classes. Then General Cubitte hustled off, telling him to come to dine at an address in Kensington two nights later and "report himself."

So within less than an hour Godfrey's future career was settled. He came out of the office feeling rather dazed but happier than when he went in, and inquired his way to Garrick Street, where he was informed that Mr. Scoones had his establishment. He found the place and, by good luck, found Mr. Scoones also, a kindly, keen, white-haired man, who read the letter, made a few inquiries and put him through a brief examination.

"Your information is varied and peculiar," he said, "and not of the sort that generally appeals to Her Majesty's examiners. Still, I see that you have intelligence and, of course, the French is an asset; also the literature to some extent, and the Latin, though these would have counted more had you been going up for the Indian Civil. I think we can get you through in three months if you will work; it all depends on that. You will find a lot of young men here of whom quite seventy per cent. do nothing, except see life. Very nice fellows in their way, but if you want to get into Sandhurst, keep clear of them. Now, my term opens next Monday. I will write to General Cubitte and tell him what I think of you, also that the fees are payable in advance. Good-bye, glad you happened to catch me, which you would not have done half an hour later, as I am going out of town. At ten o'clock next Monday, please."

After this, not knowing what to do, Godfrey returned to the Great Eastern Hotel and wrote a letter to his father, in which, baldly enough, he explained what had happened.

Having posted it in the box in the hall, he bethought him that he must find some place to live in, as the hotel was too expensive for a permanence, and was making inquiries of the porter as to how he should set about the matter when a telegram was handed to him. It ran: "All up as I expected. Meet me Liverpool Street 4.30.—Nurse."

So Godfrey postponed his search for lodgings, and at the appointed hour kept the assignation on the platform. The train arrived, and out of it, looking much more like her old self than she had on the previous day, emerged Mrs. Parsons with the most extraordinary collection of bundles, he counted nine of them, to say nothing of a jackdaw in a cage. She embraced him with enthusiasm, dropping the heaviest of the parcels, which seemed to contain bricks, upon his toe, and in a flood of language told him of the peculiar awfulness of the row between his father and herself which had ensued upon his departure.

"Yes," she ended, "he flung my money at my head and I flung it back at his, though afterwards I picked it up again, for it is no use wasting good gold and silver. And so here I am, beginning life again, like you, and feeling thirty years younger for it. Now, tell me what you are going to do?"

Then they went and had tea in the refreshment room, leaving the jackdaw and the other impediments in charge of a porter, and he told her.

"That's first-rate," she said. "I always hated the idea of seeing you with a black coat on your back. The Queen's uniform looks much better, and I want you to be a man. Now you help me into a cab and by dinner time to-morrow I'll be ready for you at my house at Hampstead, if I have to work all night to do it. Terms—drat the terms. Well, if you must have them, Master Godfrey, ten shillings a week will be more than you will cost me, and I ought to give you five back for your company. Now I'll make a start, for there will be a lot to do before the place is fit for a young gentleman. I've never seen it but twice, you know."

So she departed, packed into a four-wheeled cab, with the jackdaw on her lap, and Godfrey went to Madame Tussaud's, where he studied the guillotine and the Chamber of Horrors.

On the following morning, having further improved his mind at the Tower, he took a cab also, and in due course arrived at Hampstead with his belongings. The place took some finding, for it was on the top of a hill in an old-fashioned, out of the way part of the suburb, but when found proved to be delightful. It was a little square house, built of stone, on which the old builder had lavished all his skill and care, so that in it everything was perfect, with a garden both in front and behind. The floors were laid in oak, the little hall was oak-panelled, there were hot and cold water in every room, and so forth. Moreover, an odd man was waiting to carry in his things, and in one of the front sitting-rooms, which was excellently furnished, sat Mrs. Parsons knitting as though she had been there for years.

"Here you are," she said, "just as I was beginning to get tired of having nothing to do. Lord! what a fuss we make about things before we face 'em. After all they ain't nothing but bubbles. Blow them and they burst. Look here, Master Godfrey," and she waved her hand about the sitting-room. "Pretty neat, ain't it? Well, I thought it would be all of a hugger-mugger. But what did I find? That those tenants had been jewels and left everything like a new pin, to say nothing of improvements, such as an Eagle range. Moreover, the caretaker is a policeman's wife and a very nice woman always ready to help for a trifle, and that man that brought in your boxes is a relative of hers who does gardening jobs and such-like. Now, come and see your rooms," and she led him with pride into a capital back apartment with a large window, in fact an old Tudor one which the builder had produced somewhere, together with the panelling on the walls.

"That's your study," she said, "bookshelves and all complete. Now, follow me," and she took him upstairs to a really charming bedroom.

"But," said Godfrey, surveying these splendours, "this must be the best room in the house. Where do you sleep?"

"Oh! at the back there, my dear. You see, I am accustomed to a small chamber and shouldn't be happy in this big one. Besides, you are going to pay me rent and must be accommodated. And now come down to your dinner."

A very good dinner it was, cooked by the policeman's wife, which Mrs. Parsons insisted on serving, as she would not sit at the table with him. In short, Godfrey found himself in clover, a circumstance that filled him with some sadness. Why, he wondered, should he always be made so miserable at home and so happy when he was away? Then he remembered that famous line about the man who throughout life ever found his warmest welcome at an inn, and perceived that it hid much philosophy. Frequently enough homes are not what fond fancy paints them, while in the bosom of strangers there is much kindliness.

CHAPTER XIII

THE INTERVENING YEARS

Now we may omit a great deal from Godfrey's youthful career. Within a few days he received a letter from his father forwarded to him from the hotel, that was even more unpleasant than the majority of the paternal epistles to which he was accustomed. Mr. Knight, probably from honest conviction and a misreading of the facts of life, was one of those persons who are called Pacifists. Although he never carried out the doctrine in his own small affairs, he believed that nations were enjoined by divine decree to turn the other cheek and indeed every portion of their corporate frame to the smiter, and that by so doing, in some mysterious way, they would attain to profound peace and felicity. Consequently he hated armies, especially as these involved taxation, and loathed the trade of soldiering, which he considered one of licensed murder.

The decision of his son to adopt this career was therefore a bitter blow to him, concerning which he expressed his feelings in the plainest language, ending his epistle by intimating his strong conviction that Godfrey, having taken the sword, was destined to perish by the sword. Also he pointed out to him that he had turned his back upon God Who would certainly remember the affront, being, he remarked, "a jealous God," and lastly that the less they saw of each other in future—here he was referring to himself, not to the Divinity as the context would seem to imply—the better it would be for both of them.

Further there was a postscript about the disgraceful conduct of the woman, Mrs. Parsons, who, after receiving the shelter of his house for many years, had made a scene and departed, leaving him in the lurch. His injunction was that under no circumstances should he, Godfrey, have anything more to do with this violent and treacherous female who had made him a pretext of quarrel, and, having learned that he had money, doubtless wished to get something out of him.

Godfrey did not answer this letter, nor did his father write to him again for quite a long while.

For the rest, on the appointed Monday he presented himself at Garrick Street, and began his course of tuition under the general direction of the wise Mr. Scoones, "cramming" as it was called. This, indeed, exactly describes the process, for all knowledge was rejected except that which was likely to obtain marks in the course of an examination by hide-bound persons appointed to ascertain who were the individuals best fitted to be appointed to various branches of the Public Service. Anything less calculated to secure the selection of suitable men than such a system cannot well be imagined. However, it was that which certain nebulous authorities had decreed should prevail, and there was an end of it, although in effect it involved, and still involves, the frequent sacrifice of those qualities and characteristics which are essential to a public servant, to others that are quite the reverse. For instance, to a parrot-like memory and the power of acquiring a superficial acquaintance with much miscellaneous information and remembering the same for, say, six months.

Although he hated the business and thought with longing of his studies, stellar and other, in the Kleindorf observatory, Godfrey was quite clever enough to collect what was needed. In fact, some three months later he passed his examination with ease about half-way up the list, and duly entered Sandhurst.

He found the establishment at Garrick Street just such a place as its owner had described. In it were many charming but idle young men, often with a certain amount of means, who were going up for the Diplomatic Service, the Foreign Office, the Indian Civil, or various branches of the army. Of these a large proportion enjoyed life but did little else, and in due course failed in their competitive encounters with the examiners.

Others were too stupid to succeed, or perhaps their natural talents had another bent, while the remainder, by no means the most brilliant, but with a faculty for passing examinations and without any disturbing originality, worked hard and sailed into their desired haven with considerable facility, being of the stuff of which most successful men are made. For the rest, there was the opportunity, and if they did not avail themselves of it Scoones' was not to blame. It was, and perhaps still remains, a most admirable institution of its sort, one, indeed, of which the present chronicler has very grateful recollections.

Among the pupils studying there was a young man named Arthur Thorburn, an orphan, with considerable expectations, who lived with an aunt in a fine old house at Queen Anne's Gate. He was a brilliant young man, witty and original, but rash and without perseverance, whom his guardians wished to enter the Diplomatic Service, a career in which, without doubt, had he ever attained to it, he would have achieved a considerable failure. In appearance he was of medium height, round- faced, light-haired, blue-eyed, with a constant and most charming smile, in every way a complete contrast to Godfrey. Perhaps this was the reason of the curious attachment that the two formed for each other, unless, indeed, such strong and strange affinities have their roots in past individual history, which is veiled from mortal eyes. At any rate, it happened that on Godfrey's first day at Scoones' he sat next to Arthur Thorburn in two classes which he attended. Godfrey listened intently and made notes; Arthur caricatured the lecturer, an art for which he had a native gift, and passed the results round the class. Godfrey saw the caricature and sniggered, then when the lectures were over gravely reproved the author, saying that he should not do such things.

"Why not?" asked Arthur, opening his blue eyes. "Heaven intended that stuffy old parrot" (he had drawn this learned man as a dilapidated fowl of that species) "to be caricatured. Observe that his nose is already half a beak. Or perhaps it is a beak developing into a nose; it depends whether he is on the downward or upward path of evolution."

"Because you made me laugh," replied Godfrey, "whereby I lost at least eighteenpennyworth of information."

"A laugh is worth eighteenpence," suggested Arthur.

"That depends upon how many eighteenpences one possesses. You may have lots, some people are short of them."

"Quite true. I never looked at it in that way before. I am obliged to you for putting it so plainly," said Arthur with his charming smile.

Such was the beginning of the acquaintance of these two, and in some cases might have been its end. But with them it was not so. Arthur conceived a sincere admiration for Godfrey who could speak like this to a stranger, and at Scoones' and as much as possible outside, haunted him like a shadow. Soon it was a regular thing for Godfrey to go to dine at the old Georgian house in Queen Anne's Gate upon Sunday evenings, where he became popular with the rather magnificent early- Victorian aunt who thought that he exercised a good influence upon her nephew. Sometimes, too, Arthur would accompany Godfrey to Hampstead and sit smoking and making furtive caricatures of him and Mrs. Parsons, while he worked and she beamed admiration. The occupation sounds dull, but somehow Arthur did not find it so; he said that it rested his overwrought brain.

"Look here, old fellow," said Godfrey at length, "have you any intention of passing that examination of yours?"

"In the interests of the Diplomatic Service and of the country I think not," replied Arthur reflectively. "I feel that it is a case where true altruism becomes a duty."

"Then what do you mean to do with yourself?"

"Don't know. Live on my money, I suppose, and on that of my respected aunt after her lamented decease which, although I see no signs of it, she tells me she considers imminent."

"I don't wonder, Arthur, with you hanging about the house. You ought to be ashamed of yourself. A man is made to work his way through the world, not to idle."

"Like a beetle boring through wood, not like a butterfly flitting over flowers; that's what you mean, isn't it? Well, butterflies are nicer than beetles, and some of us like flowers better than dead wood. But, I say, old chap, do you mean it?"

"I do, and so does your aunt."

"Let us waive my aunt. Like the poor she is always with us, and I, alas! am well acquainted with her views, which are those of a past epoch. But I am not obstinate; tell me what to do and I'll do it—anything except enter the Diplomatic Service, to lie abroad for the benefit of my country, in the words of the ancient saying."

"There is no fear of that, for you would never pass the examination," said the practical Godfrey. "You see, you are too clever," he added by way of explanation, "and too much occupied with a dozen things of which examiners take no account, the merits of the various religious systems, for instance."

"So are you," interrupted Arthur.

"I know I am; I love them. I'd like to talk to you about reincarnation and astronomy, of which I know something, and even astrology and the survival of the dead and lots of other things. But I have got to make my way in the world, and I've no time. You think me a heavy bore and an old fogey because I won't go to parties to which lots of those nice fellows ask me. Do you suppose I shouldn't like the parties and all the larks afterwards and the jolly actresses and the rest? Of course I should, for I'm a man like others. But I tell you I haven't time. I've flouted my father, and I'm on my honour, so to speak, to justify myself and get on. So I mean to pass that tomfool examination and to cram down a lot of stuff in order to do so, which is of no more use to me than though I had swallowed so much brown paper. Fool-stuff, pulped by fools to be the food of fools—that's what it is. And now I'm going to shove some spoonfuls of it down my throat, so light your pipe, and please be quiet."

"One moment more of your precious time," interrupted Arthur. "What is the exact career that you propose to adorn? Something foreign, I think—Indian Civil Service?"

"No, as I have told you a dozen times, Indian Army."

"The army has points—possibly in the future it might give a man an opportunity of departing from the world in a fashion that is generally, if in error, considered to be decent. India, too, has still more points, for there anyone with intelligence might study the beginnings of civilisation, which, perhaps, are also its end. My friend, I, too, will enter the Indian Army, that is if I can pass the examination. Provide me at once with the necessary books and, Mrs. Parsons, be good-hearted enough to bring some of your excellent coffee, brewed double strong. Do not imagine, young man, who ought, by the way, to have been born fifty years earlier and married my aunt, that you are the only one who can face and conquer facts, even those advanced by that most accursed of empty-headed bores, the man or the maniac called Euclid."

So the pair of them studied together, and by dint of private tuition in the evening, for at Scoones' where his talent for caricature was too much for him, Arthur would do little or nothing, Godfrey dragged his friend through the examination, the last but one in the list. Even then a miracle intervened to save him. Arthur's Euclid was hopeless. He hated the whole business of squares and angles and parallelograms with such intensity that it made him mentally and morally sick. To his, as to some other minds, it was utter nonsense devised by a semi-lunatic for the bewilderment of mankind, and adopted by other lunatics as an appropriate form of torture of the young.

At length, in despair, Godfrey, knowing that Arthur had an excellent memory, only the night before the examination, made him learn a couple of propositions selected out of the books which were to be studied, quite at hazard, with injunctions that no matter what other propositions were set he should write out these two, pretending that he had mistaken the question. This Arthur did with perfect accuracy, and by the greatest of good luck one of the two propositions was actually that which he was asked to set down, while the other was allowed to pass as an error.

So he bumped through somehow, and in the end the Indian Army gained a most excellent officer. It is true that there were difficulties when he explained to his aunt and his trustees that in some inexplicable manner he had passed for Sandhurst instead of into the Diplomatic Service. But when he demonstrated to them that this was his great and final effort and that nothing on earth would induce him to face another examination, even to be made a king, they thought it best to accept the accomplished fact.

"After all, you have passed something," said his aunt, "which is more than anyone ever expected you would do, and the army is respectable, for, as I have told you, my grandfather was killed at Waterloo."

"Yes," replied Arthur, "you have told me, my dear Aunt, very often. He broke his neck by jumping off his horse when riding towards or from the battlefield, did he not? and now I propose to follow his honoured example, on the battlefield, if possible, or if not, in steeplechasing."

So the pair of them went to Sandhurst together, and together in due course were gazetted to a certain regiment of Indian cavalry, the only difference being that Godfrey passed out top and Arthur passed out bottom, although, in fact, he was much the cleverer of the two. Of the interval between these two examinations there is nothing that need be reported, for their lives and the things that happened to them were as those of hundreds of other young men. Only through all they remained the fastest of friends, so much so that by the influence of General Cubitte, as has been said, they managed to be gazetted to the same regiment.

During those two years Godfrey never saw his father, and communicated with him but rarely. His winter vacations were spent at Mrs. Parsons' house in Hampstead, working for the most part, since he was absolutely determined to justify himself and get on in the profession which he had chosen. In the summer he and Arthur went walking tours, and once, with some other young men, visited the Continent to study various battlefields, and improve their minds. At least Godfrey studied the battlefields, while Arthur gave most of his attention to the younger part of the female population of France and Italy. At Easter again they went to Scotland, where Arthur had some property settled on him—for he was a young man well supplied with this world's goods—and fished for salmon and trout. Altogether, for Godfrey, it was a profitable and happy two years. At Sandhurst and elsewhere everyone thought well of him, while old General Cubitte became his devoted friend and could not say enough in his praise.

"Damn it! Sir," he exclaimed once, "do you mean to tell me that you never overdraw your allowance? It is not natural; almost wrong indeed. I wonder what your secret vices are? Well, so long as you keep them secret, you ought to be a big man one day and end up in a very different position to George

Cubitte—called a General—who never saw a shot fired in his life. There'll be lots of them flying about before you're old, my boy, and doubtless you'll get your share of gunpowder—or nitro-glycerine—if you go on as you have begun. If I weren't afraid of making you cocky, I'd tell you what they say about you down at that Sandhurst shop, where I have an old pal or two.

Shortly after this came the final examination, through which, as has been said, Godfrey sailed out top, an easy first indeed—a position to which his thorough knowledge of French and general aptitude for foreign languages, together with his powers of work and application, really entitled him. All his friends were delighted, especially Arthur, who looked on him as a kind of lusus naturæ, and from his humble position at the bottom of the tree, gazed admiringly at Godfrey perched upon its topmost bough. The old Pasteur, too, with whom Godfrey kept up an almost weekly correspondence, continuing his astronomical studies by letter, was enraptured and covered him with compliments, as did his instructors at the College.

All of this would have been enough to turn the heads of many young men, but as it happened Godfrey was by nature modest, with enough intelligence to appreciate the abysmal depths of his own ignorance by the light of the little lamp of knowledge with which he had furnished himself on his journey into their blackness. This intense modesty always remained a leading characteristic of his, which endeared him to many, although it was not one that helped him forward in life. It is the bold, self-confident man, who knows how to make the most of his small gifts, who travels fastest and farthest in this world of ours.

When, however, actually he received quite an affectionate and pleased letter from his father, he did, for a while, feel a little proud. The letter enclosed a cutting from the local paper recording his success, and digging up for the benefit of its readers an account of his adventure on the Alps. Also, it mentioned prominently that he was the son of the Rev. Mr. Knight, the incumbent of Monk's Abbey, and had received his education in that gentleman's establishment; so prominently, indeed, that even the unsuspicious Godfrey could not help wondering if his father had ever seen that paragraph before it appeared in print. The letter ended with this passage:

"We have not met for a long while, owing to causes to which I will not allude, and I suppose that shortly you will be going to India. If you care to come here I should like to see you before you leave England. This is natural, as after all you are my only child and I am growing old. Once you have departed to that far country who knows whether we shall ever meet again in this world?"

Godfrey, a generous-hearted and forgiving person, was much touched when he read these words, and wrote at once to say that if it were convenient, he would come down to Monk's Abbey at the beginning of the following week and spend some of his leave there. So, in due course, he went.

As it happened, at about the same time Destiny had arranged that another character in this history was returning to that quiet Essex village, namely Isobel Blake.

Isobel went to Mexico with her uncle and there had a most interesting time. She studied Aztec history with her usual thoroughness; so well, indeed, that she became a recognised authority on the subject. She climbed Popocatepetl, the mysterious "Sleeping Woman" that overhands the ancient town, and looked into its crater. Greatly daring, she even visited Yucatan and saw some of the pre-Aztec remains. For this adventure she paid with an attack of fever which never quite left her system. Indeed, that fever had a peculiar effect upon her, which may have been physical or something else. Isobel's fault, or rather characteristic, as the reader may have gathered, was that she built too much upon the material side of things. What she saw, what she knew, what her body told her, what the recorded experience of the world taught—these were real; all the rest, to her, was phantasy or imagination. She kept her feet upon the solid ground of fact, and left all else to dreamers; or, as she would have expressed it, to the victims of superstition inherited or acquired.

Well, something happened to her at the crisis of that fever, which was sharp, and took her on her return from Yucatan, at a horrible port called Frontera, where there were palm trees and zopilotes—a kind of vile American vulture—which sat silently on the verandah outside her door in the dreadful little hotel built upon piles in the mud of the great river, and mosquitoes by the ten million, and sleepy-eyed, crushed-looking Indians, and horrible halfbreeds, and everything else which suggests an earthly hell, except the glorious sunshine.

Of a sudden, when she was at her worst, all the materiality—if there be such a word—which circumstances and innate tendency had woven about her as a garment, seemed to melt away, and she became aware of something vast in which she floated like an insect in the atmosphere—some surrounding sea which she could neither measure nor travel.

She knew that she was not merely Isobel Blake, but a part of the universe in its largest sense, and that the universe expressed itself in miniature within her soul. She knew that ever since it had been, she was, and that while it existed she would endure. This imagination or inspiration, whichever it may have been, went no further than that, and afterwards she set it down to delirium, or to the exaltation that often accompanies fever. Still, it left a mark upon her, opening a new door in her heart, so to speak.

For the rest, the life in Mexico City was gay, especially in the position which she filled as the niece of the British Minister, who was often called upon to act as hostess, as her aunt was delicate and her cousin was younger than herself and not apt at the business. There were Diaz and the foreign Diplomatic Ministers; also the leading Mexicans to be entertained, for which purpose she learned Spanish. Then there were English travellers, distinguished, some of them, and German nobles, generally in the Diplomatic Service of their country, whom by some peculiar feminine instinct of her own, she suspected of being spies and generally persons of evil intentions. Also there was the British colony, among whom were some very nice people that she made her friends, the strange, adventurous pioneers of our Empire who are to be bound in every part of the world, and in a sense its cream.

Lastly, there were the American tourists and business men, many of whom she thought amusing. One of these, a millionaire who had to do with a "beef trust," though what that might be she never quite understood, proposed to her. He was a nice young fellow enough, of a real old American family whose ancestors were supposed to have come over in the Mayflower, and possessed of a remarkable vein of original humour; also he was much in love. But Isobel would have none of it, and said so in such plain, unmistakable language that the millionaire straightway left Mexico City in his private railway car, disconsolately to pursue his beef speculations in other lands.

On the day that he departed Isobel received a note from him which ran:

"I have lost you, and since I am too sore-hearted to stay in this antique country and conclude the business that brought me here, I reckon that I have also lost 250,000 dollars. That sum, however, I would gladly have given for the honour and joy of your friendship, and as much more added. So I think it well spent, especially as it never figured in my accounts. Good-bye. God bless you and whoever it may be with whom you are in love, for that there is someone I am quite sure, also that he must be a good fellow."

From which it will be seen that this millionaire was a very nice young man. So, at least, thought Isobel, though he did write about her being in love with someone, which was the rankest nonsense. In love, indeed! Why, she had never met a man for whom she could possibly entertain any feelings of that sort, no, not even if he had been able to make a queen of her, or to endow her with all the cash resources of all the beef trusts in the world. Men in that aspect were repellent and hateful to her; the possibility of such a union with any one of them was poisonous, even unnatural to her, soul and body.

Once, it is true, there had been a certain boy—but he had passed out of her life—oh! years ago, and, what is more, had affronted her by refusing to answer a letter which she had written to him, just, as she imagined—though of course this was only a guess—because of his ridiculous and unwarrantable jealousy and the atrocious pride that was his failing. Also she had read in the papers of a very brave act which he had done on the Alps, one which filled her with a pride that was not atrocious, but quite natural where an old playmate was concerned, and had noticed that it was a young lady whom he had rescued. That, of course, explained everything, and if her first supposition should be incorrect, would quite account for her having received no answer to her letter.

It was true, however, that she had heard no more of this young lady, though scraps of gossip concerning Godfrey did occasionally reach her. For instance, she knew that he had quarrelled with his father because he would not enter the Church and was going into the army, a career which she much preferred, especially as she did not believe in the Church and could not imagine what Godfrey would look like in a black coat and a white tie.

By the way, she wondered what he did look like now. She had an old faded photograph of him as a lanky youth, but after all this time he could not in the least resemble that. Well, probably he had grown as plain and uninteresting—as she was herself. It was wonderful that the American young man could have seen anything in her, but then, no doubt he went on in the same kind of way with half the girls he met.

Thus reflected Isobel, and a little while later paid a last visit to the museum, which interested her more than any place in Mexico, perhaps because its exhibits strengthened her theories as to comparative religion, and shook off her feet the dust of what her American admirer had called that "antique land." It was with a positive pang that from the deck of the steamship outside Vera Cruz she looked her last on the snows of the glorious peak of Orizaba, but soon these faded away into the skyline and with them her life in Mexico.

Returning to England via the West Indies in the company of her uncle who was coming home on leave before taking up an appointment as Minister to one of the South American republics, she was greeted on the platform at Waterloo by her father. Sir John Blake had by this time forgotten their previous disagreements, or, at any rate, determined to ignore them, and Isobel, who was now in her way a finished woman of the world, though she did not forget, had come to a like conclusion. So their meeting was cordial enough, and for a while, not a very long while, they continued to live together in outward amity, with a tacit understanding that they should follow their respective paths, unmolested by each other.

CHAPTER XIV

TOGETHER

On the afternoon of the first day after his arrival at the Abbey, some spirit in his feet moved Godfrey to go into the church. As though by instinct, he went to the chancel, and stood there contemplating the brass of the nameless Plantagenet lady. How long it was since he had looked upon her graven face and form draped in the stately habiliments of a bygone age! Then, he remembered with a pang, Isobel was with him, and they had seemed to be very near together. Now there was no Isobel, and they were very far apart, both in the spirit and in the flesh. For he had not heard of her return to England and imagined that she was still in Mexico, whence no tidings of her came to him.

There he stood among the dead, reflecting that we do not need to pass out of the body to know the meaning of death, since, as once Isobel had said herself, some separations are as bad, or worse. The story of the dead is, at any rate, completed; there is nothing more to be learned about them, and of them we imagine, perhaps quite erroneously, that we have no need to be jealous, since we cannot conceive that they may form new interests in another sphere. But with the living it is otherwise. Somewhere their life is continued; somewhere they are getting themselves friends or lovers and carrying on the daily round of being, and we have no share in them or in aught that they may do. And probably they have forgotten us. And, if we still happen to be attached to them, oh! it hurts.

Thus mused Godfrey, trying to picture to himself what Isobel looked like when she had stood by his side on that long-past autumn eve, and only succeeded in remembering exactly what she looked like when she was kissing a rose with a certain knight in armour in a square garden, since for some perverse reason it was this picture that remained so painfully clear to his mind. Then he drifted off into speculations upon the general mystery of things of a sort that were common with him, and in these became oblivious of all else.

He did not even hear or see a tall young woman enter the church, clad in summer white, no, not when she was within five pace and, becoming suddenly aware of his presence, had stopped to study him with the acutest interest. In a flash Isobel knew who he was. Of course he was much changed, for Godfrey, who had matured early, as those of his generation were apt to do, especially if they had led a varied life, was now a handsome and well-built young man with a fine, thoughtful face and a quite respectable moustache.

"How he has changed, oh! how he has changed," she thought to herself. The raw boy had become a man, and as she knew at once by her woman's instinct, a man with a great deal in him. Isobel was a sensible member of her sex; one, too, who had seen something of the world by now, and she did not expect or wish for a hero or a saint built upon the mid- Victorian pattern, as portrayed in the books of the lady novelists of that period. She wanted a man to be a man, by preference with the faults pertaining to the male nature, since she had observed that those who lacked these, possessed others, which to her robust womanhood seemed far worse, such as meanness and avarice and backbiting, and all the other qualities of the Pharisee.

Well, in Godfrey, whether she were right or wrong, with that swift glance of hers, she seemed to recognise a man as she wished a man to be. If that standard of hers meant that very possibly he had admired other women, the lady whom he had pulled up a precipice, for instance, she did not mind particularly, so long as he admired her, Isobel, most of all. That was her one sine qua non, that he should admire her most of all, or rather be fondest of her in his innermost self.

What was she thinking about? What was there to show that he cared one brass farthing about her? Nothing at all. And yet, why was he here where she had parted from him so long ago? Surely not to stare at the grave of a dead woman with whom he could have had nothing to do, since she left the world some five centuries before. And another question. What had brought her here, she who hated churches and all the mummery that they signified?

Would he never wake up? Would he never realise her presence? Oh! then he could care nothing about her. Probably he was thinking of the girl he had pulled up a cliff in the Alps. But why did he come to this place to think of her?

Isobel stood quite still there and waited in the shadow of a Georgian tomb, till presently Godfrey did seem to grow aware that he was no longer alone. Something or somebody had impinged upon his intelligence. He began to look about him, though always in the wrong direction. Then, convinced that he was the victim of fancy, he spoke aloud as he had a bad habit of doing when by himself.

"It's very curious," he said, "but I could have sworn that Isobel was here, as near me as when we parted. I suppose that is what comes of thinking so much about her. Or do people leave something of themselves behind in places where they have experienced emotion? If so, churches ought to be very full of ghosts. I dare say that they are, only then no one could know it except those who had shared the emotion, and therefore they remain intangible. Still, I could have sworn that Isobel was here. Indeed, I seem to feel her now, and I hope that the dream will go on."

Listening there in the shadow, she heard, and flushed in her flesh and rejoiced in her innermost being. So he had not forgotten her, which is the true and real infidelity that never can be forgiven, at any rate, by a woman. So she was still something in his life, although he had not answered her letter years ago.

Then she grew angry with herself. What did it matter to her what he was, or thought, or did? It was absurd that she could be dependent morally upon anyone, who must rely in life or death upon herself alone and on the strong soul within her. She was wroth with Godfrey for exciting such disturbance in— what was it—her spirit or her body? Nonsense, she had no spirit. That was a phantasy. Therefore it must be in her body which was her own particular property that should remain uninfluenced by any other body.

So it came about that the first words she spoke to him were somewhat rough in their texture. She stepped forward out of the shadow of the Georgian tomb and confronted him with a defiant air, her head thrown back, looking, to tell the truth, rather stately.

"I hoped that by this time you had given up talking to yourself, Godfrey, which, as I always told you, is a bad habit. I did not hear much of what you were mumbling, but I understood you to say that you thought I was here. Well, why shouldn't I be here?"

He stared at her blankly and answered:

"God knows, I don't! But since you ask the question, why are you here, Isobel? It is Isobel, isn't it, or am I still dreaming? Let me touch you and I shall know."

She drew back a little way, quite three inches.

"Of course it is Isobel, don't your senses tell you that without wanting to touch me? Why, I knew it was you from the end of the church. But you ask me why I am here. I wish you would tell me. I was passing, and something drew me into this place. I suppose it was you, and if so, I say at once that I resent it; you have no right—"

"No, no, certainly not, but do let me touch you to make sure that you are Isobel."

"Very well," she said, and stretched out a hand towards him.

He caught it with his left which was nearest, and then with his right hand reached forward and seized her other hand. With a masterful movement he draw her towards him, and though she was a strong woman she seemed to have no power to resist. She thought that he was going to kiss her and did not care greatly if he did.

But he checked himself in time, and instead of pressing his lips upon hers, only kissed her hands, first one and then the other, for quite a long while: nor did she attempt to deny him, perhaps because a wild impulse took possession of her to kiss his in answer. Yes, his hands, or his lips, or even his coat or anything about him. Oh! it made her very angry, but there it was, for something rushed up in her which she had never felt before, something mad and wild and sweet.

She wrenched herself away at last and began to scold him again.

"What have you been doing all these years? Why did you never write to me?"

"Because I was too proud, as you never wrote to me."

"Too proud! Pride will be your ruin; it goes before every sort of fall. Besides, I did write to you. I can show you a copy of the letter, if I haven't torn it up."

"I never got it; did you post it yourself?"

"Yes, that is I took it to the Abbey House and left it to be addressed there."

"Oh! then perhaps it is there still," and he looked at her.

"Nonsense, no one could have been so mean, not even—"

He shrugged his shoulders, a trick he had learned abroad, then said:

"Well, it doesn't matter now, does it, Isobel?"

"Yes, it matters a lot. Years of misunderstanding and doubt and loss, when life is so short. I might have married or all sorts of things."

"What has my not receiving your letter got to do with that?" he asked, astonished.

"Nothing at all. Why do you ask such silly questions? I only meant that if I had married I should not have been here, and we should never have met again."

"Well, you are here and we have met in this church, where we parted."

"Yes, it's odd, isn't it? I wish it had been somewhere else. I don't like this gloomy old place with its atmosphere of death. Come outside."

They went, and when they were through the churchyard gates walked at hazard towards the stream which ran through the grounds of Hawk's Hall. Here they sat down upon a fallen willow, watching the swallows skim over the surface of the placid waters, and for a while were silent. They had so much to say to each other that it seemed as though scarcely they knew where to commence.

"Tell me," she said at length, "were you in the square garden on the night of that dance at which I came out? Oh! I see by your look that you were. Then why did you not speak to me instead of standing behind a bush, watching in that mean fashion?"

"I wasn't properly dressed for parties, and—and—you seemed to be—very much engaged—with a rose and a knight in armour."

"Engaged! It was only part of a game. I wrote and told you all about it in the letter you did not get. Did you never kiss a flower for a joke and give it to someone, not knowing that you were being watched?"

Godfrey coloured and shifted uneasily on his log.

"Well, as a matter of fact," he said, "it is odd that you should have guessed—for something of the sort did once happen quite by accident. Also I was watched."

"I!—you mean we. One doesn't kiss flowers by oneself and give them to the air. It would be more ridiculous even than the other thing."

"I will tell you all about it if you like," he stammered confusedly.

She looked at him with her large, steady grey eyes, and answered in a cold voice:

"No, thank you, I don't like. Nothing bores me so much as other people's silly love affairs."

Baffled in defence, Godfrey resorted to attack.

"What has become of the knight in armour?" he asked.

"He is married and has twins. I saw the announcement of their birth in the paper yesterday. And what has become of the lady with the flower? For since there was a flower, there must have been a lady; I suppose the same whom you pulled up the precipice."

"She is married also, to her cousin, but I don't know that she has any children yet, and I never pulled her up any precipice. It was a man I pulled, a very heavy one. My arm isn't quite right yet."

"Oh!" said Isobel. Then with another sudden change of voice she went on. "Now tell me all about yourself, Godfrey. There must be such lots to say, and I long to hear."

So he told her, and she told him of herself, and they talked and talked till the shadows of advancing night began to close around them. Suddenly Godfrey looked at his watch, of which he could only just see the hands.

"My goodness!" he said, "it is half-past seven."

"Well, what about it? It doesn't matter when I dine, for I have come down alone here for a few days, a week perhaps, to get the house ready for my father and his friends."

"Yes, but my father dines at seven, and if there is one thing he hates it is being kept waiting for dinner."

She looked as though she thought that it did not much matter whether or no Mr. Knight waited for his dinner, then said:

"Well, you can come up to the Hall and dine with me."

"I think I had better not," he answered. "You see, we are getting on so well together—I mean my father and I, and I don't want to begin a row again. He would hate it."

"You mean, Godfrey, that he would hate your dining with me. Well, that is true, for he always loathed me like poison, and I don't think he is a man to change his mind. So perhaps you had better go. Do you think we shall be allowed to see each other again?" she added with sarcasm.

"Of course. Let's meet here to-morrow at eleven. My father is going to a Diocesan meeting and won't be back till the evening. So we might spend the day together if you have nothing better to do."

"Let me see. No, I have no engagement. You see, I only came down half an hour before we met in the church."

Then they rose from their willow log and stood looking at each other, a very proper pair. Something welled up in him and burst from his lips.

"How beautiful you have grown," he said.

She laughed a little, very softly, and said:

"Beautiful! I? Those Alpine snows affect the sight, don't they? I felt like that on Popocatepetl. Or is it the twilight that I have to thank? Oh! you silly old Godfrey, you must have been living among very plain people."

"You are beautiful," he replied stubbornly, "the most beautiful woman I ever saw. You always were, and you always will be."

Again she laughed, for who of her sex is there that does not like to be called beautiful, especially when she knows that it is meant, and that whatever her personal shortcomings, to the speaker she is beautiful? But this time the only answer she attempted was:

"You said you were late, and you are getting later. Run home, there's a good little boy."

"Why do you laugh at me?" he asked.

"Because I am laughing at myself," she answered, "and you should have your share."

Then very nearly he kissed her, only he was in such a hurry, also the willow log, a large one, was between them; possibly she had arranged that this should be so. So he could only press her hand and depart, muttering something indistinguishable. She watched him vanish, after which she sat down again on the log and really did laugh. Still, it was a queer kind of merriment, for by degrees it turned into little sobs and tears.

"You little fool, what has happened to you?" she asked herself. "Are you—are you—and if so, is he—? Oh! nonsense, and yet, something has happened, for I never felt like this before. I thought it was all rubbish, mere natural attraction, part of Nature's scheme and so on, as they write in the clever books. But it's more than that—at least it would be if I were— Besides, I'm ages older than he is, although I was born six months later. I'm a woman full-grown, and he is only a boy. If he hadn't been a boy he would have taken his advantage when he must have known that I was weak as water, just for the joy of seeing him again. Now he has lost his chance, if he wanted one, for by to-morrow I shall be strong again, and there shall be no more—"

Then she looked at the backs of her hands which she could not see because of the gathering darkness, and as they were invisible, kissed them instead, just as though they belonged to someone else. After this she sat a while brooding and listening to the pulsing of her heart, which was beating with unusual strength this night. As she did so in that mysterious hour which sometimes comes to us in English summers, a great change fell upon her. When she sat down upon that fallen tree she was still a girl and virginal; when she rose from it she was a developed, loving woman. It was as though a spirit had visited her and whispered in her ear. She could almost hear the words. They were:

"Fulfil your fate. Love and be loved with body and with spirit, with heart and soul and strength."

At length she rose, and as she did so said aloud:

"I do not know who or what I have to thank for life and all that makes me, me. But I am glad to have been born, now, who have often wished that I had never been born. Even if I knew that I must pass away to-night, I should still be glad, since I have learned that there is something in me which cannot die. It came when that man kissed my hands, and it will endure for ever."

Godfrey was late for dinner, very late, and what was worse, his father had waited for him.

"I suppose you forgot that I dined at seven, not at eight," was his cold greeting, for Mr. Knight, a large eater like many teetotallers, was one of those people who make a fetish of punctuality at meals, and always grow cross when they are hungry.

Godfrey, whose mind had not been steadied by the events of the afternoon, became confused and replied that he was extremely sorry, but the fact was he had met Isobel and, in talking to her, had not noticed the time.

"Isobel!" exclaimed his father, whose voice was now icy. "What Isobel?"

"I never knew but one, Father."

"Oh! I suppose you mean Miss Blake. I had no idea she was here; indeed, I thought she was still in Mexico. But doubtless you were better informed."

"No, Father, I met her accidentally. She has returned to England."

"That is obvious, Godfrey—"

"She has come down," he continued in a hurry, "to get the house ready for Sir John, who arrives shortly."

"Oh! has she? What a strange coincidence! All the years of our separation while you were way she was away, but within two days of your return she returns."

"Yes, it does seem odd," agreed the flustered Godfrey, "but it's lucky, isn't it, for, of course, I am glad to see her again."

Mr. Knight finished carving himself a helping of beef, and let the knife fall with a clatter into the dish. Then he said in carefully chosen words:

"You may think it lucky—or well arranged—but I must differ. I tell you at once that I consider Miss Blake a most pernicious young woman, and as your father I can only express the hope that you do not intend to allow her to re-assert her evil influence over you."

Godfrey was about to answer with wrath, but changed his mind and remained silent. So the topic dropped, but that it stood very straight upon its feet in Mr. Knight's mind was clear from the compression of his thin lips and the ill-humour of his remarks about the coldness and overdone character of the beef and sundry other household matters. As soon as the meal was concluded and he had washed it down with a last glass of water and with a very wry face thanked Providence for all that he had received, he retired into his study and was seen no more till prayer-time.

Nor was he seen then by Godfrey, who had gone out to smoke his pipe since his father could not bear the smell of tobacco in the house, and wandered unconsciously towards the Hall. There he stood, gazing at a light which he knew came from Isobel's window, and lost in this unfruitful contemplation, once more forgot the time. When he arrived home it was to find the house in darkness and a note in his father's handwriting on the hall table requesting him to be careful to lock the door, as everyone had gone to bed.

He went, too, but could not sleep, for, strangely enough, that disturbance of body and spirit which had afflicted Isobel possessed him also. It seemed wonderful to him that he should have found her again, whom he thought to be so utterly lost, and grown so sweet and dear. How could he have lived all this while without her, he wondered, and, another thought, how could he bear to part with her once more? Oh! she was his life, and—why should they part? She had not minded when he kissed her hands, at which, of course, she might have been angry; indeed, she left them to be kissed for quite a long while, though not half long enough. Perhaps she did not wish that they should part either, or perhaps she only desired that they should be just friends as before. It seemed almost impossible that they could become more than friends, even if she cared to do so, which he could scarcely hope.

What was he? A young fellow, twenty, with only a little money and all his way to make in the world. And what was she? A grand young lady, rather younger than himself, it was true, but seeming years older, who was a great heiress, they said, and expected to marry a lord, someone born with a silver spoon in his mouth, whose fortune had been made for him by other people. Moreover, his father hated her because their religious views were different, and her father hated him, or used to, for other reasons.

Yes, it was quite impossible—and yet Nature seemed to take no account of that: Nature seemed to tell him that it was absolutely possible, and indeed right, and what she, Nature, wished. Also this same persistent Nature seemed to suggest to him that Isobel was her most willing and obedient pupil, and that perhaps if he could look into her heart he would find that she did care, and very much more than for the wealth and the hypothetical lord.

Nature seemed to suggest, too, that Isobel's thoughts were with him at that moment; that she was uncommonly near to him in soul if not in body; that she was thinking about him as he was thinking about her, and saying much the same things to herself as he was saying to himself. Indeed, he even began a whispered conversation with her, of a sort he would not have ventured upon had she been there, pausing between the sentences for her answers, which, as he imagined them, were very satisfactory indeed.

By degrees, however, question and answer grew less frequent and further apart as he dozed off and finally sank into a deep sleep. So deep was it, indeed, that he was awakened only by the clamour of the breakfast bell, and when he arrived downstairs, to be confronted by some cold bacon on an uncovered dish, his father had departed to the Diocesan Conference. Well, this fact had its consolations, and bacon, however cold, with contentment is better than bacon hot where contention is.

So he ate it and anything else he could find with appetite, and then went upstairs to shave and do his hair nicely and to put on a new suit of clothes, which he considered became him. Also, as he had still three-quarters of an hour to spare, he began to write a little poem about Isobel, which was a dismal failure, to tell the truth, since he could think of no satisfactory rhyme to her name, except "O well!" which, however he put it, sounded silly.

At last, rather too early, he threw the sheet of paper into the fireplace and started, only to find that although it still lacked a quarter of an hour to eleven, Isobel was already seated on that tree.

"What have you been doing to yourself?" she asked, "putting on those smart London clothes? I like the old grey things you had on last night ever so much better, and I wanted you to climb a tree to get me some young jackdaws. And—good gracious! Godfrey, your head smells like a whole hairdresser's shop. Please come to the other side, to leeward of me."

He murmured something about liking to look tidy, and then remarked that she seemed rather finely dressed herself.

"It's only my Mexican hat," she answered, touching the big sombrero, woven from the finest Panama grass, which she was wearing, "and the necklace is made of little gold Aztec idols that were found in a grave. They are very rare; a gentleman gave them to me, and afterwards I was horrified to find that he had paid an awful lot for them, £200, I believe. Do you understand about the Aztec gods? If not I will explain them all to you. This big one in the middle is Huitzilcoatl, the god of—"

"No, no," interrupted Godfrey, "I don't and I don't want to. I think them very ugly, and I always understood that ladies did not accept such expensive presents from gentlemen. Who was he?"

"An American millionaire who didn't wear armour," she answered blandly. Then she changed the subject with the original remark that the swallows were flying higher than they had done on the previous evening, when they looked as though one could almost catch them with one's hand.

Godfrey reflected to himself that other things which had seemed quite close on the previous night were now like the swallows, far out of reach. Only he took comfort in the remembrance that swallows, however near, are evasive birds, not easy to seize unless you can find them sleeping. Next she began to tell him all about the Mexican gods, whether he wanted to listen or not, and he sat there in the glory of his new clothes and brilliantined hair, and gazed at her till she asked him to desist as she felt as though she were being mesmerised.

This led him to his spiritualistic experiences of which he told her all the story, and by the time it was finished, behold! it was the luncheon hour.

"It is very interesting," she said as they entered the Hall, "and I can't laugh at it all as I should have done once, I don't quite know why. But I hope, Godfrey, that you will have no more to do with spirits."

"No, not while—" and he looked at her.

"While what?"

"While—there are such nice bodies in the world," he stammered, colouring.

She coloured also, tossed her head, and went to wash her hands.

The afternoon they spent in hunting for imaginary young jackdaws in a totally nebulous tree. Isobel grew rather cross over its non- discovery, swearing that she remembered it well years ago, and that there were always young jackdaws there.

"Perhaps it has been cut down," suggested Godfrey. "I am told that your father has been improving the place a great deal in that kind of way, so as to make it up to date and scientific and profitable, and all the rest of it. Also if it hasn't, there would have been no young jackdaws, since they must have flown quite six weeks ago."

"Then why couldn't you say that at once, instead of making us waste all this time?" asked Isobel with indignation.

"I don't know," replied Godfrey in a somewhat vacuous fashion. "It was all the same to me if we were hunting for young jackdaws or the man in the moon, as long as we were together."

"Godfrey, it is evident that you have been overworking and are growing foolish. I make excuses for you, since anybody who passed first out of Sandhurst must have overworked, but it does not alter the fact. Now I must go home and see about that house, for as yet I have arranged nothing at all, and the place is in an awful state. Remember that my father is coming down presently with either six or eight terrible people, I forget which. All I know about them is that they are extremely rich and expect to be what is called 'done well.'"

"Must you?" remarked Godfrey, looking disappointed.

"Yes, I must. And so must you. Your father is coming back by the five o'clock train, and I advise you to be there to meet him. Perhaps I shall see you to-morrow some time."

"I can't," exclaimed Godfrey in a kind of wail. "I am to be taken off to a school in some town or other, I forget which, that my father has been examining. I suppose it is the speech day, and he proposes to introduce me as a kind of object lesson because I have passed first in an examination."

"Yes, as a shining example and—an advertisement. Well, perhaps we shall meet later," and without giving him an opportunity of saying more she vanished away.

CHAPTER XV

FOR EVER

Godfrey managed to be late again, and only reached home five minutes after his father, who had bicycled instead of walking from the station as he supposed that he would do.

"I forgot to give orders about your lunch," said Mr. Knight tentatively. "I hope that you managed to get some."

"Oh, yes, Father; that is, I lunched out, at the Hall."

"Indeed! I did not know that Sir John had arrived."

"No, he hasn't; at least I have not seen him. I lunched with Isobel."

"Indeed!" remarked Mr. Knight again, and the subject dropped.

Next day, Godfrey, once more arrayed in his best clothes, attended the prize-giving and duly was made to look foolish, only getting home just in time for dinner, after which his father requested him to check certain examination papers. Then came Sunday and church at which Isobel did not appear; two churches in fact, and after these a tea party to the churchwardens and their wives, to whom Godfrey was expected to explain the wonders of the Alps. Before it was over, if he could have managed it, these stolid farmers with their families would have lain at the bottom of the deepest moraine that exists amid those famous mountains. But there they were, swallowing tea and munching cake while they gazed on him with ox-like eyes, and he plunged into wild explanations as to the movements of glaciers.

"Something like one of them new-fangled machines what carry hay up on to the top of stacks," said Churchwarden No. 1 at length.

"Did you ever sit on a glacier while it slided from the top to the bottom of a mountain, Master Godfrey, and if so, however did you get up again?" asked Churchwarden No. 2.

"Is a glacier so called after the tradesman what cuts glass, because glass and ice are both clear-like?" inquired Churchwarden No. 1, filled with sudden inspiration.

Then Godfrey, in despair, said that he thought it was and fled away, only to be reproached afterwards by his father for having tried to puzzle those excellent and pious men.

On Monday his luck was better, since Mr. Knight was called away immediately after lunch to take a funeral in a distant parish of which the incumbent was absent at the seaside. Godfrey, by a kind of instinct, sped at once to the willow log by the stream, where, through an outreaching of the long arm of coincidence, he found Isobel seated. After casually remarking that the swallows were flying neither high nor low that day, but as it were in mid-air, she added that she had not seen him for a long while.

"No, you haven't—say for three years," he answered, and detailed his tribulations.

"Ah!" said Isobel, "that's always the way; one is never left at leisure to follow one's own fancies in this world. To-morrow, for instance, my father and all his horrible friends—I don't know any of them, except one, but from past experience I presume them to be horrible—are coming down to lunch, and are going to stop for three days' partridge shooting. Their female belongings are going to stop also, or some of them are, which means that I shall have to look after them."

"It's all bad news to-day," remarked Godfrey, shaking his head. "I've just had a telegram saying that I must report myself on Wednesday, goodness knows why, for I expected to get a month's leave."

"Oh!" said Isobel, looking a little dismayed. "Then let us make the best of to-day, for who knows what to-morrow may bring forth?"

Who indeed? Certainly not either of these young people.

They talked awhile seated by the river; then began to walk through certain ancient grazing grounds where the monks used to run their cattle. Their conversation, fluent enough at first, grew somewhat constrained and artificial, since both of them were thinking of matters different from those that they were trying to dress out in words; intimate, pressing, burning matters that seemed to devour their intelligences of everyday with a kind of eating fire. They grew almost silent, talking only at random and listening to the beating of their own hearts rather than to the words that fell from each other's lips.

The sky clouded over, and some heavy drops of rain began to fall.

"I suppose that we must go in," said Isobel, "we shall be soaked presently," and she glanced at her light summer attire.

"Where?" exclaimed Godfrey. "The Abbey? No, my father will be back by now; it must be the Hall."

"Very well, but I dare say my father is there by now, for I understand that he is coming down this afternoon to arrange about the shooting."

"Great heavens!" groaned Godfrey, "and I wanted to—tell you a story which I thought perhaps might interest you, and I don't know when I shall get another chance—now."

"Then why did you not tell your story before?" she inquired with some irritation.

"Oh! because I have only just thought of it," he replied rather wildly.

At this moment they were passing the church, and the rain began to fall in earnest. By some mutual impulse they entered through the chancel door which was always unlocked, and by some mutual folly, left it open.

Advancing instinctively to the tombs of the unknown Plantagenet lady and her knight which were so intimately connected with the little events of their little lives, they listened for a while to the rush of the rain upon the leaden roof, saying nothing, till the silence grew irksome indeed. Each waited for the other to break it, but with a woman's infinite patience Isobel waited the longer. There she stood, staring at the brass of the Plantagenet lady, still as the bones of that lady which lay beneath.

"My story," said Godfrey at last with a gasp, and stopped.

"Yes," said Isobel. "What is it?"

"Oh!" he exclaimed in an agony, "a very short one. I love you, that's all."

A little quiver ran through her, causing her dress to shake and the gold Mexican gods on her necklace to tinkle against each other. Then she grew still as a stone, and raising those large and steady eyes of hers, looked him up and down, finally fixing them upon his own.

"Is that true?" she asked.

"True! It is as true as life and death, or as Heaven and Hell."

"I don't know anything about Heaven and Hell; they are hypothetical, are they not? Life and death are enough for me," and she stopped.

"Then by life and death, for life and death, and for ever, I love you, Isobel."

"Thank you," she said, and stopped once more.

"You don't help one much. Have you nothing to say?"

"What is there to say? You made a statement for which I thanked you. You asked no question."

"It is a question," he exclaimed indignantly. "If I love you, of course I want to know if you love me."

"Then why did you not say so? But," she added very deliberately, "since you want to know, I do and always have and always shall, in life or death—and for ever—if that means anything."

He stared at her, tried to utter something and failed. Then he fell back upon another very primitive and ancient expedient. Flinging his arms about her, he pressed her to his heart and kissed her again and again and again; nor, in her moment of complete surrender, did she scruple to kiss him back.

It was while they were thus engaged, offering a wonderful spectacle of love triumphant and rejoicing in its triumph, that another person who was passing the church bethought him of its shelter as a refuge from the pouring rain. Seeing the open door, Mr. Knight, for it was he, slipped into the great building in his quiet, rather cat-like fashion, but on its threshold saw, and stopped. Notwithstanding the shadows, he recognised them in a moment. More, the sight of this pair, the son whom he disliked and the woman whom he hated, thus embraced, thus lost in a sea of passion, moved him to white fury, so that he lifted his clenched hands above his head and shook them, muttering:

"And in my church, my church!"

Then unable to bear more of this spectacle, he slipped away again, heedless of the pouring skies.

By nature, although in obedience to a rash promise once he had married, Mr. Knight was a true woman-hater. That sex and everything to do with it were repellent to him. Even the most harmless manifestations of natural affection between male and female he considered disgusting, indeed indecent, and if these were carried any further he held it to be among the greatest of crimes. He was one of those who, if he had the power, would have hounded any poor girl who, in the country phrase, "had got into trouble," to the river brink and over it, as a creature not fit to live; or if she escaped destruction, would have, and indeed often had, pursued her with unceasing malignity, thinking that thereby he did God service. His attitude towards such a person was that of an Inquisitor towards a fallen nun.

Moreover, he could do this with a clear conscience, since he could truly say that he was qualified to throw the first stone, being of those who mistake personal aversion for personal virtue. Because his cold-hearted nature rejected it, he loathed this kind of human failing and felt good in the loathing. Nor did it ever occur to him to reflect that others, such as secret malice, jealousy and all uncharitableness on which his heart fed, might be much worse than the outrush of human passion in obedience to the almighty decree of Nature that is determined not to die.

These being his views, the feelings that the sight awoke in him of this pair declaring their holy love in the accustomed, human fashion, can scarcely be measured and are certainly beyond description. Had he been another sort of man who had found some devil flogging a child to death, the rage and indignation aroused in his breast could not have been greater, even if it were his own child.

The one thing that Mr. Knight had feared for years was that Godfrey, who, as he knew, was fonder of Isobel than of any other living creature, should come to love her in a fuller fashion: Isobel, a girl who had laughed at and flouted him and once told him to his face that a study of his character and treatment of others had done more to turn her from the Christian religion than anything else.

In a sense he was unselfish in this matter, or rather his hate mastered his selfishness. He knew very well that Isobel would be a great match for Godfrey, and he was by no means a man who underrated money and position and their power. He guessed, too, that she really loved him and would have made him the best of wives; that with her at his side he might do almost anything in the world. But these considerations did not in the least soften his loathing of the very thought of such a marriage. Incredible as it may seem, he would rather have seen Godfrey dead than the happy husband of Isobel.

Mr. Knight, drunk with rage, reeled rather than walked away from the church door, wondering what he might do to baulk and shame that living, loving pair who could kiss and cling even among the tombs. A thought came to him, a very evil thought which he welcomed as an inspiration sent straight from an offended Heaven. Sir John Blake had come home; he knew it, for he had passed him on the road seated alone in a fine motor-car, and they had waved their hands to each other not ten minutes before. He would go and tell him all; in the character of an upright man who does not like to see his rich neighbour harmed by the entanglement of that neighbour's daughter in an undesirable relationship. That Sir John would consider himself to be harmed, he was sure enough, being by no means ignorant of his plans and aspirations for the future of that daughter, who was expected to make a great alliance in return for the fortune which she would bring to her husband.

No sooner said than done. In three minutes he was at the Hall and, as it chanced, met Sir John by the front door.

"Hullo, Reverend! How are you? You look very wet and miserable; taking refuge from the rain, I suppose, though it is clearing off now. Have a brandy and soda, or a glass of port?"

"Thank you, Sir John, I am an abstainer, but a cup of hot tea would be welcome."

"Tea—ah! yes, but that takes time to make, so I should have to leave you to drink it by yourself. Fact is I want to find my daughter. Some of those blessed guests of mine, including Mounteroy, the young Earl, you know, whom I wish her to meet particularly, are coming down to-night by the last train and not to-morrow, so I must get everything arranged in a hurry. Can't make out where the girl has gone."

"I think I can tell you, Sir John," said Mr. Knight with a sickly smile; "at least I saw her a little while ago rather peculiarly engaged."

"Where, and how was she engaged?"

Without asking permission Mr. Knight entered the house and stepped into a cloak-room that opened out of the hall. Being curious, Sir John followed him. Mr. Knight shut the door and, supporting himself against the frame of a marble wash-basin with gilded taps, said:

"I saw her in the chancel of the Abbey Church and she was kissing my son, Godfrey; at least he was kissing her, and she seemed to be responding to his infamous advances, for her arms were round his neck and I heard sounds which suggested that this was so."

"Holy Moses!" ejaculated Sir John, "what in the name of hell are they after?"

"Your question, stripped of its unnecessary and profane expletives, seems easy to answer. I imagine that my immoral son has just proposed to your daughter, and been accepted with—well, unusual emphasis."

"Perhaps you are right. But if he had I don't see anything particularly immoral about it. If I had never done anything worse than that I shouldn't feel myself called to go upon my knees and cry peccavi. However, that ain't the point. The point is that a game of this sort don't at all suit my book, but," here he looked at the clergyman shrewdly, "why do you come to tell about it? I should have thought that under all the circumstances you should have been glad. Isobel isn't likely to be exactly a beggar, you know, so it seems devilish queer that you should object, as I gather you do; unless it is to the kissing, which has been heard of before."

"I do object most strongly, Sir John," replied Mr. Knight in his iciest tones. "I disapprove entirely of your daughter, whose lack of any Christian feeling is notorious, and whose corrupting influence will, I fear, make my son as bad as herself."

"Damn her lack of Christian feeling, and damn yours and your impudence too, you half-drowned church rat! Why don't you call her Jezebel at once, and have done with it? One of the things I like about her is that she has the pluck to snap her fingers at such as you and all your ignorant superstitions. What are you getting at? That is what I want to know."

"I put aside your insults to which as a clergyman it is my duty to turn the other cheek," replied Mr. Knight, with a furious gasp. "As to the rest I am trying to get at the pure and sacred truth."

"You look as though you would do better to get at the pure and sacred brandy," remarked Sir John, surveying him critically, "but that's your affair. Now, what is the truth?"

"Alas! that I must say it. I believe my son to be that basest of creatures, a fortune-hunter. How did he get that money left to him by another woman?"

"Don't know, I'm sure. Perhaps the old girl found the young chap attractive, and wished to acknowledge favours received. Such things have been known. You don't suppose he forged her will, do you?"

"You are ribald, Sir, ribald."

"Am I? Well, and you are jolly offensive. Thank God you weren't my father. Now, from what I remember of that boy of yours, I shouldn't have thought that he was a fortune-hunter. I should have thought that he was a young beggar who wished to get hold of the girl he fancies, and that's all. Still, you know him best, and I dare say you are right. Anyway, for your own peculiar and crack-brained reasons, you don't want this business, and I say at once you can't want it less than I do. Do you suppose that I wish to see my only child, who will have half a million of money and might be a countess, or half a dozen countesses, to-morrow, married to the son of a beggarly sniveller like you, for as you are so fond of the pure and sacred truth, I'll give it you—a fellow who can come and peach upon your own boy and his girl."

"My conscience and my duty—" began Mr. Knight.

"Oh! drat your conscience and blow your duty. You're a spy and a backbiting tell-tale, that's what you are. Did you never kiss a girl yourself?"

"Never until after I was married, when we are specially enjoined by the great Apostle—"

"Then I'm sorry for your wife, for she must have had a lot to teach you. But let's stop slanging, we have our own opinions of each other and there's an end. Now we have both the same object, you because you are a pious crank and no more human than a dried eel, and I because I am a man of the world who want to see my daughter where she ought to be, wearing a coronet in the House of Lords. The question is: How is the job to be done? You don't understand Isobel, but I do. If her back is put up, wild horses won't move her. She'd snap her fingers in my face, and tell me to go to a place that you are better acquainted with than I am, or will be, and take my money with me. Of course, I could hold her for a few months, till she is of age perhaps, but after that, No. So it seems that the only chance is your son. Now, what's his weak point? Can he be bought off?"

"Certainly not," said Mr. Knight.

"Oh! that's odd in one who, you say, is a fortune-hunter. Well, what is it? Everyone has a weak point, and another girl won't do just now."

"His weakest point is his fondness for that treacherous and abominable sex of which I have just had so painful an example; and in the church too, yes, in my church."

"And a jolly good place to get to in such a rain, for of course they didn't know that you were hiding under the pews. But I've told you that cock won't fight at present. What's the next?"

At these accumulated insults Mr. Knight turned perfectly livid with suppressed rage. But he did suppress it, for he had an object to gain which, to his perverted mind, was the most important in the whole world—namely, the final separation of his son and Isobel.

"His next bad point," he went on, "is his pride, which is abnormal, although from childhood I have done my best to inculcate humility of spirit into his heart. He cannot bear any affront, or even neglect. For instance, he left me for some years just because he did not consider that he was received properly on his return from Switzerland; also because he went into a rage, for he has a very evil temper if roused, when I suggested that he wanted to run after your daughter's money."

"Well, it wasn't a very nice thing to say, was it? But I think I see light. He's proud, is he, and don't like allusions to fortune-hunting. All right; I'll rub his nose in the dirt and make him good. I'm just the boy for a job of that sort, as perhaps you will agree, my reverend friend; and if he shows his airs to me, I'll kick him off the premises. Come on! I dare say we shall find them still in the church, where they think themselves so snug, although the rain has stopped."

So this precious pair started, each of them bent, though for different reasons, upon as evil a mission as the mind of man can conceive. For what is there more wicked than to wish to bring about the separation and subsequent misery of two young people who, as they guessed well enough, loved each other body and soul, and thereby to spoil their lives? Yet, so strange is human nature, that neither of them thought that they were committing any sin. Mr. Knight, now and afterwards, justified himself with the reflection that he was parting his son from a "pernicious" young woman of strong character, who would probably lead him away from religion as it was understood by him. One also whom he looked upon as the worst of outcasts, who deserved and doubtless was destined to inhabit hell, because hastily she had rejected his form of faith, as the young are apt to do, for reasons, however hollow, that seemed to her sufficient.

He took no account of his bitter, secret jealousy of this girl, who, as he thought, had estranged his son from him, and prevented him from carrying out his cherished plans of making of him a clergyman like himself, or of his innate physical hatred of women which caused him to desire that Godfrey should remain celibate. These motives, although he was well aware of them, he set down as naught, being quite sure, in view of the goodness of his aims, that they would be overlooked or even commended by the Power above Whom he pictured in his mind's eye as a furious old man, animated chiefly by jealousy and a desire to wreak vengeance on and torture the helpless. For it is the lessons of the Old Testament that sink most deeply into the souls of Mr. Knight and his kind.

Sir John's ends were quite different. He was the very vulgarest of self-made men, coarse and brutal by nature, a sensualist of the type that is untouched by imagination; a man who would crush anyone who stood in his path without compunction, just because that person did stand in his path. But he was extremely shrewd—witness the way he saw through Mr. Knight—and in his own fashion very able— witness his success in life.

Moreover, since a man of his type has generally some object beyond the mere acquiring of money, particularly after it has been acquired, he had his, to rise high, for he was very ambitious. His natural discernment set all his own failings before him in the clearest light; also their consequences. He knew that he was vulgar and brutal, and that as a result all persons of real gentility looked down upon him, however much they might seem to cringe before his money and power, yes, though they chanced to be but labouring men.

For instance, his wife had done so, which was one of the reasons why he hated her, as indeed had all her distinguished relatives, after they came to know him, although he lent them money. He knew that even if he became a peer, as he fully expected to do, it would be the same story; outward deference and lip service, but inward dislike and contempt. In short, there were limits which he could never hope to pass, and therefore so far as he was concerned, his ambitious thirst must remain unslaked.

But he had a daughter whom Nature, perhaps because of her mother's blood, had set in quite a different class. She had his ability, but she was gentle-born, which he was not, one who could mix with and be welcomed by the highest in the world, and this without the slightest question. If not beautiful, she was very distinguished; she had presence and what the French call "the air." Further, she would be one of the richest women in England. Considered from his point of view, therefore, it was but natural that he should desire her to make a brilliant marriage and found a great family, which he would thus have originated—at any rate, to some extent. Night and day he longed that this should come about, and it was the reason why the young Lord Mounteroy was visiting Hawk's Hall.

Mounteroy had met Isobel at a dinner-party in London the other day and admired her. He had told an old lady—a kind of society tout—who had repeated it to Sir John, that he wished to get married, and that Isobel Blake was the sort of girl he would like to marry. He was a clever man, also ambitious, one who had hopes of some day ruling the country, but to do this he needed behind him great and assured fortune in addition to his ancient but somewhat impoverished rank. In short, she suited his book, and he suited that of Sir John. Now, the thing to do was to bring it about that he should also suit Isobel's book. And just at the critical moment this accursed accident had happened. Oh! it was too much.

No wonder that Sir John was filled with righteous wrath and a stern determination to "make things hot" for the cause of the "accident" as, led to the attack by the active but dripping Mr. Knight whom he designated in his heart as that "little cur of a parson," much as an overfed and bloated bloodhound might be by some black and vicious mongrel, he tramped heavily towards the church. Indeed they made a queer contrast, this small, active but fierce-faced man in his sombre, shiny garments and dingy white tie, and the huge, ample-paunched baronet with his red, flat face, heavy lips and projecting but intelligent eyes, clothed in a new suit, wearing an enormous black pearl in his necktie and a diamond ring on his finger; the very ideal of Mammon in every detail of his person and of his carefully advertised opulence.

Isobel, whose humour had its sardonic side, and who was the first to catch sight of them when they reached the church, Mr. Knight tripping ahead, and Sir John hot with the exercise in the close, moist air, lumbering after him with his mouth open, compared them in her mind to a fierce little pilot fish conducting an overfed shark to some helpless prey which it had discovered battling with the waters of circumstance; that after all, was only another version of the mongrel and the bloodhound. Also she compared them to other things, even less complimentary.

Yet none of these, perhaps, was really adequate, either to the evil intentions or the repellent appearance of this pair as they advanced upon their wicked mission of jealousy and hate.

CHAPTER XVI

LOVE AND LOSS

All unaware that they had been seen and by no friendly eyes, Godfrey and Isobel remained embracing each other for quite a long while. At length she wrenched herself away and, sinking on to a chancel bench, motioned to him to seat himself beside her.

"Let us talk," she said in a new voice, a strange voice that was low and rich, such as he had never heard her use, "let us talk, my dear."

"What of?" he asked almost in a whisper as he took his place, and her hand, which he held against his beating heart. "My soul has been talking to yours for the last five minutes, or is it five seconds or five years? It does not seem to have anything more to say."

"Yet I think there is plenty to be said, Godfrey. Do you know that while we were kissing each other there some very queer ideas got hold of me, not only of the sort which might be expected in our case? You remember that Plantagenet lady who lies buried beneath where we were standing, she whose dress I once copied to wear at the ball when I came out."

"Don't speak of that," he interrupted, "for then you were kissing someone else."

"It is not true. I never kissed anyone else in that way, and I do not think I ever shall. I kissed a rose, that's all, and I gather that you have done as much and very likely a great deal more. But it is of the lady I am speaking, not of the ball. She seemed to come up from her grave and enter into me, and say something."

"Well, what did she say, Isobel?" he asked dreamily.

"That's it, I don't know, although she talked to me as one might to oneself. All I know is that it was of trouble and patience and great joy, and war and tragedy in which I must be intimately concerned, and—after the tragedy—of a most infinite rest and bliss."

"I expect she was telling you her own story, which seems to have ended well," he replied in the same dreamy fashion.

"Yes, I think so, but also that she meant that her story would be my story, copied you know, as I copied her dress. Of course it is all nonsense, just the influence of the place taking hold of me when overcome by other things, but at the time it seemed very real."

"So does a bad dream," said Godfrey, "but for all that it isn't real. Still it is odd that everything important seems to happen to us within a few feet of that lady's dust, and I can't quite disbelieve in spirits and their power of impressing themselves upon us; I wish I could. The strange thing is that you should put any faith in them."

"I don't, though I admit that my views about such matters are changing. You know I used to be sure that when we die everything is over with us. Now I think differently, why I cannot say."

Then the subject dropped, because really they were both wrapped in the great joy of a glorious hour and disinclined to dwell upon fancies about a woman who had died five hundred years ago, or on metaphysical speculations. Also the fear of what might follow upon that hour haunted them more vividly than any hovering ghost, if such there were.

"My dear," said Isobel, "I am sorry, but I must say it; I am sure that there will be trouble about this business."

"No doubt, Isobel; there always is trouble, at least where I am concerned; also one can't be happy without paying. But what does it matter so long as we stick to each other? Soon we shall both be of age and can do what we like."

"One always thinks that, Godfrey, and yet, somehow, one never can. Free will is a fraud in that sense as in every other."

"I have something, as you know, enough with my pay to enable us to get on, even if you were disinherited, dear, though, of course, you could not live as you have been accustomed to do."

"Oh! don't talk to me of money," she said impatiently, "though for the matter of that, I have something, too, a little that comes to me from my mother. Money won't divide us, Godfrey."

"Then what will, Isobel?"

"Nothing in the long run," she answered with conviction, "not even death itself, since in a way we are one and part of each other and therefore cannot be separated for always, whatever happens for a while, as I am sure that something will happen which will make you leave me."

"I swear that I will never leave you, I will die with you first," he exclaimed, springing up.

"Such oaths have been made often and broken—before the dawn," she answered, smiling and shaking her head.

"I swear that I will always love you," he went on.

"Ah! now I believe you, dear!" she broke in again. "However badly you may behave, you will always love me because you must."

"Well, and will you always love me however badly I behave?"

"Of course," she answered simply, "because I must. Oh! whatever we may hear about each other, we may be quite certain that we still love each other—because we must—and all your heaven and hell cannot make any difference, no, not if they were both to join forces and try their best. But that does not mean that necessarily we shall marry each other, for I think that people who love like that rarely do marry, because, you see, they would be too happy, which something is always trying to prevent. It may mean, however," she added reflectively, "that we shall not marry anybody else, though even that might happen in your case—not in mine. Always remember, Godfrey, that I shall never marry anybody else, not even if you took three wives one after the other."

"Three wives!" gasped Godfrey.

"Yes, why not? It would be quite natural, wouldn't it, if you wouldn't marry me, and even proper. Only I should never take one—husband, I mean—not from any particular virtue, but just because I couldn't. You see, it would make me ill. And if I tried I should only run away."

"Oh! stop talking nonsense," said Godfrey, "when so soon you will have to go to see about those people," and he held out his arms.

She sank into them, and for a little while they forgot their doubts and fears.

The rain had ceased, and the triumphant sun shining gloriously through the west window of stained glass, poured its rays upon them, dyeing them all the colours of an angel's wings. Also incidentally it made them extremely conspicuous in that dusky church, of which they had all this while forgotten to shut the door.

"My word!" said Sir John to Mr. Knight in tones of savage sarcasm as they surveyed the two through this door. "We've got here just at the right time. Don't they look pretty, and don't you wish that you were his age and that was someone else's daughter? I tell you, I do."

Mr. Knight gurgled something in his inarticulate wrath, for at that moment he hated Isobel's father as much as he did Isobel, which was saying a great deal.

"Well, my pretty pair of cooing turtle-doves," went on Sir John in a sort of shout, addressing himself to them, "be so good as to stop that, or I think I shall wring both your necks, damn you."

"Not in this Holy House, which these infamous and shameless persons have desecrated with their profane embraces," interrupted Mr. Knight.

"Yes, according to your ideas it will be almost a case of re- consecration. You'll have to write to the bishop about it, Mr. Parson. Oh! confound you. Don't stand there like a couple of stuck pigs, but come out of that and let us have a little chat in the churchyard."

Now, at the first words that reached their ears Godfrey and Isobel had drawn back from each other and stood side by side quite still before the altar, as a pair about to be married might do.

They were dumbfounded, and no wonder. As might be expected Isobel was the first to recover herself.

"Come, my dear," she said in a clear voice to Godfrey, "my father and yours wish to speak to us. I am glad we have a chance of explaining matters so soon."

"Yes," said Godfrey, but in a wrathful voice, for he felt anger stirring in him. Perhaps it was excited by that ancient instinct which causes the male animal to resent the spying upon him when he is courting his female as the deadliest of all possible insults, or perhaps by some prescience of affronts which were about to be offered to him and Isobel by these two whom he knew to be bitterly hostile. At least his temper was rising, and like most rather gentle-natured men when really provoked and cornered, he could be dangerous.

"Yes," he repeated, "let us go out and see this matter through."

So they went, Sir John and Mr. Knight drawing back a little before them, till they were brought to a halt by the horrible memorial which the former had erected over his wife's grave. Here they stood, prepared for the encounter. Sir John was the first to take the lists, saying:

"Perhaps you will explain, Isobel, why I found you, as I thought, kissing this young fellow—like any village slut beneath a hedge."

Isobel's big eyes grew steely as she answered:

"For the same reason, Father. Like your village slut, I kissed this man because he is my lover whom I mean to marry. If, as I gather, you are not certain as to what you saw, I will kiss him again, here in front of you."

"I have no doubt you will; just like your cheek!" ejaculated Sir John, taken a little aback.

Then Mr. Knight took up the ball, addressing himself to his son:

"Could you find no other place for your immoral performances except the church, Godfrey, and my chancel too?"

"No," answered Godfrey, "because it was raining and we sheltered there. And what do you mean by your talk about immorality? Is it not lawful for a man to love a woman? I should have thought that the Bible, which you are always quoting, would have taught you otherwise. Also, once you were married yourself else I should not be here, for which I am not sure that I thank you; at least, I shouldn't were it not for Isobel."

For a moment Mr. Knight could think of no answer to these arguments, but Sir John having recovered his breath, attacked again:

"Look here, young fellow, I have no time to listen to jaw about the Bible and moral and immoral and all that bosh, which you can have out with your reverend parent afterwards. I am a plain man, I am, and want a plain answer to a plain question. Do you think that you are going to marry my daughter, Isobel?"

"Such is my desire and intention," replied Godfrey, with vague recollections of the baptismal service, though of these at the moment he was not aware.

"Oh, is it? Then you are jolly well mistaken in your desire and intention. Let's make things clear. You are a beggarly youngster who propose to enter the army at some future date, which you may or may not do. And you have the impudence to wish to marry one of the biggest heiresses in England against my will."

"And against mine," burst in Mr. Knight, "who consider her a most pernicious young woman, one who rejects the Christian faith and will lead you to perdition. That is why, when I chanced to espy you in such a compromising position, I hastened to inform the lady's father."

"Oh! you did that, did you?" interposed Isobel, contemplating him steadily. "Well, I am glad to know who could have been so cowardly," she added with withering contempt. "Now I begin to wonder whether a letter which some years ago, I brought to the Abbey House to be forwarded to Godfrey, was ever posted to him who did not receive it, or whether, perhaps, it fell into the hands of—someone like you."

"It did," said Mr. Knight. "I read it and have it to this day. In my discretion as a father I did not consider it desirable that my young son should receive that letter. What I have witnessed this afternoon shows me how right was my judgment."

"Thank you so much," said Isobel. "That takes a great weight off my mind. Godfrey, my dear, I apologise to you for my doubts. The truth did occur to me, but I thought it impossible that a clergyman," here she looked again at Mr. Knight, "could be a thief also who did not dare to own to his theft."

"Never mind all that," went on Sir John in his heavy, masterful voice. "It stands like this. You," and he pointed a fat finger at Godfrey, "are—well, I'll tell you what you are—you're just a cunning young fortune-hunter. You found out that this property and a good bit besides are coming to Isobel, and you want to collar the sag, like you did that of the old woman out in Lucerne. Well, you don't do it, my boy. I've other views for Isobel. Do you think I want to see her married to—to—the son of a fellow like that— a canting snuffler who prigs letters and splits on his own son?" and swinging the fat finger round he thrust it almost into the face of Mr. Knight.

"What did you say?" gasped Godfrey. "That I am a fortune-hunter?"

"Yes, that's what I said, and I'll repeat it if you like."

"Then," went on Godfrey, speaking in a thick, low voice, for now his temper had mastered him thoroughly, "I say that you are a liar. I say that you are a base and vulgar man who has made money somehow and thinks that this justifies him in insulting those who are not base or vulgar, because they have less money."

"You infernal young scamp," shouted Sir John in a roar like to that of an angry bull. "Do you dare to call me a liar? Apologise at once, or—" and he stopped.

"I do not apologise. I repeat that you are a liar, the greatest liar I ever met. Now—or what?"

Thus spoke Godfrey, drawing up his tall, slim young form to its full height, his dark eyes flashing, his fine face alight with righteous rage. Isobel, who was standing quite still and smiling a little, rather contemptuously, looked at him out of the corners of her eyes and thought that anger became him well. Never before had he seemed so handsome to her approving judgment.

"Or this," bellowed Sir John, and, lifting the tightly rolled umbrella he carried, he struck Godfrey with all his strength upon the side of the head.

Godfrey staggered, but fortunately the soft hat he was wearing, upon the brim of which the stroke fell, broke its weight to some extent, so that he was not really hurt. Only now he went quite mad in a kind of icy way, and, springing at Sir John with the lightness of a leopard, dealt him two blows, one with his left hand and the next with his right.

They were good, straight blows, for boxing had been his favourite amusement at Sandhurst where he was a middleweight champion. The first caught Sir John upon his thick lips which were badly cut against the teeth, causing him to stagger; while the second, that with the right, landed on the bridge of his nose and blacked both his eyes. This, so strong and heavy was it, notwithstanding Sir John's great weight, knocked him clean off his feet. Back he went, and in his efforts to save himself gripped Mr. Knight with one hand and with the other the legs of the early Victorian angel that surmounted Lady Jane's grave against which they were standing. Neither of these could withstand the strain. The angel, which was only pinned by lead-coated rivets to its base and the column behind, flew from its supports, as did Mr. Knight from his, so that in another second, the men having tripped against the surround of the grave, all three rolled upon the path, the marble luckily falling clear of both of them.

"Now I've done it," said Godfrey in a reflective voice as he contemplated the tangled ruin.

"Yes," exclaimed Isobel, "I think you have."

Then they remained grim and silent while the pair, who were not really much injured, picked themselves up with groans.

"I am sorry that I knocked you down, since I am young and you are not," said Godfrey, "but I repeat that you are a liar," he added by an afterthought.

Sir John spat out a tooth, and began to mop the blood from his nose with a silk pocket-handkerchief.

"Oh! you do, do you?" he said in a somewhat subdued voice. "Well, you'll find out that I'm other things too before I'm done with you. And I repeat that you are fortune-hunting young rascal and that I would rather see my daughter dead than married to you."

"And I say, Godfrey, I would rather see you dead than married to her!" broke in Mr. Knight, spitting out his words like an angry cat.

"I don't think that you need be afraid, Father," answered Godfrey quietly, although his rage burned as fiercely as ever. "You have worked this business well, and it seems a little impossible now, doesn't it? Listen, Sir John Blake. Not even for the sake of Isobel will I submit to such insults. I will not give her up, but I swear by God that while you are alive I will not marry Isobel, nor will I write to her or speak to her again. After you are dead, which I dare say will be before so very long," and he surveyed the huge, puffy-fleshed baronet with a critical eye, "then—if she cares to wait for me—I will marry her, hoping that in the meanwhile you may lose your money or dispose of it as you like."

Sir John stared, still mopping his face, but finding no words. He feared death very much and this prophecy of it, spoken with such a ring of truth, as though the speaker knew, frightened him. At that moment in his heart he cursed the Reverend Mr. Knight and his tale- bearing, and wished most earnestly that he had never been led into interference with this matter. After all Godfrey was a fine young man whom his daughter cared for, and might do well in life, and he had struck him first after offering him intentional and pre-arranged insult. Such were the thoughts that flashed through his somewhat muddled brain. Also another, that they were too late. The evil was done and never could be undone.

Then Isobel spoke in cold, clear tones, saying:

"Godfrey is quite right and has been right all through. Had you, Father, and that man," and she pointed contemptuously at Mr. Knight, "left us alone we should have come and told you what had happened between us, and if you disapproved we would have waited until we were of full age and have married as we should have been free to do. But now that is impossible, for blows have passed between you. After slandering him vilely, you struck Godfrey first, Father, and he would not have been a man if he had not struck you back; indeed I should have thought little of him afterwards. Well, he has made an oath, and I know that he will keep it. Now I, too, make an oath which certainly I shall keep. I swear in the presence of both of you, by myself and by Godfrey, that neither in this world or in any other, should I live again and have remembrance, will I marry any man or exchange tendernesses with any man, except himself. So all your plans come to nothing; yes, you have brought all this misery upon us for nothing, and if you want to found a great family, as I know you do, you had better marry again yourself and let me go my way. In any case, if I should survive you and should Godfrey live, I will marry him after your death, even if we have to wait until we are old to do so. As to your fortune, I care nothing for it, being quite ready to work in the world with the help of the little I have."

She paused as though for an answer, but none came, for if Sir John had been frightened before, now he was terrified of this outraged young woman who, tall, commanding and stern-eyed, looked to him like an avenging angel.

"There doesn't seem much more to say, does there?" she went on, "except that I think, Father, you had better telegraph to your guests that you are not well and cannot receive them, for I won't. So good- bye, dearest Godfrey. I shall remember all that you have said, and you will remember all that I have said, and as I believe, we shall live to meet again one day. Meanwhile, don't think too bitterly of my father, or of your own, because they have acted according to their natures and lights, though where these will lead them I am sure I do not know. Good-bye, dearest, dearest Godfrey. Do your best in the world and keep out of troubles if you can. Oh! what a lot we shall have to tell each other when we meet again."

Then before them both she kissed him, and he kissed her back, saying:

"I will remember. I am glad you think there was nothing else to be done. God bless you, Isobel. Make the best of your life, as I will try to do with mine. Good-bye."

"Good-bye, dear," she answered, "think of me always when you wake and before you go to sleep, as I will think of you."

Then she turned and went, never looking behind her.

Godfrey watched her tall form vanish through the churchyard gate and over the slope of a little hill that lay between it and Hawk's Hall, and that was the last sight he had of her for many a year. When she was quite lost to view, he spoke to the two men who still stood irresolute before him.

"Isobel I shall meet again," he said, "but not either of you, for I have done with you both. It is not for me to judge you. Judge yourself and be judged."

Then he turned, too, and went.

"It's all right," said Sir John to Mr. Knight, "that is, he won't marry her, at any rate at present, so I suppose that we should both be pleased, if anyone can be pleased with cut lips and two black eyes. And yet somehow we seem to have made a mess of it," and he glanced at the shattered marble statue of the Victorian angel of which both the wings were broken off.

"We have done our duty," replied Mr. Knight, pursing up his thin lips, "and at least Godfrey is freed from your daughter."

"I'm not so sure of that, my reverend friend. But of one thing I am sure, that I am freed from her also, or rather that she is freed from me. Also you are freed from him. Don't you understand, you vicious little viper, that you will never see that young man again, and that thanks to your cursed advice I shall never see my daughter again, at least not really? What devil was it that sent you to play upon my weaknesses and ambition? If you had left things alone and they had come to me in a natural way there would have been a row, of course, but I dare say it would have ended all right. But you told me how to work on him and I overdid the part. Now nothing can ever be all right for either of us, or for them either, until we are both dead. Do you understand also that we have made two young people who should have been the supports of our old age desire above everything our deaths because we have given them cause to hate us, and since they are of the sort that keep their word, only by our deaths can they become free, or, at any rate, by mine? Well, it doesn't matter what you understand, you little bigot, but I know what I do."

"I have done my duty," repeated Mr. Knight sullenly, "and I don't care what happens afterwards. 'Fiat justita ruat cœlum,'" he added in the Latin tag.

"Oh, yes. Justice may say fie and the sky may be rude, and anything else may happen, but we've dished our lives and theirs, my friend, and—damn you! get out of my sight. Rows I am accustomed to with Isobel and others, but this isn't a row, it's an earthquake; it's a catastrophe, for which I have to thank you. Lord! how my mouth hurts, and I can't see out of my right eye. Talk of a mailed fist, that young beggar has one like a pole-axe. Now I must go to telegraph to all those people. Temporary indisposition, yes—temporary indisposition, that's it. Good-bye, my holy friend. You won't do as much mischief in one day again in a hurry, spy as hard as you like."

Then Sir John departed, nursing his cut lips with one hand and his broken umbrella with the other.

Mr. Knight watched him go, and said to himself:

"I thought that I disliked the daughter, but the father is worse. Offensive, purse-proud, vulgar beast! How dare he speak to me like that! I'm glad, yes, I'm glad Godfrey knocked him down, though I suppose there will be a scandal. Well, my hands are clean; I have done my duty, and I must not complain if it is unpleasant, since I have dragged Godfrey back from the mouth of the pit. I think I'll take a walk to steady my nerves; it may be as well not to meet Godfrey again just now."

CHAPTER XVII

INDIA

On his road to the house to pack his portmanteau Godfrey went a little way round to arrange with a blacksmith, generally known as Tom, who jobbed out a pony-trap, to drive him to the station to catch the 7.15 train. The blacksmith remarked that they would have to hurry, and set to work to put the pony in, while Godfrey ran on to the Abbey House and hurriedly collected his clothes. He got them packed and down into the hall just as the trap arrived.

As he was entering it the servant put a letter into his hand which she said had come for him by the afternoon post. He thrust it into his pocket unlooked at, and off they went at the pony's best pace.

"You are going away oncommon quick, Master Godfrey. Coming back to these parts soon?" queried the blacksmith.

"No, not for a long while, Tom."

"I think there must have been lightning with that rain," went on Tom, after a pause, "although I heard no thunder. Else how ever did that marble angel over poor Lady Jane's grave come down with such a smash?"

Godfrey glanced at him, but Tom remained imperturbable and went on:

"They du say it wor a wunnerful smash, what broke off both the wings and nearly flattered out some as stood by. Rum thing, Master Godfrey, that the lightning should have picked out the grave of so good a lady to hit; ondiscriminating thing, lightning is."

"Stop talking humbug, Tom. Were you there?" asked Godfrey.

"Well, not exactly there, Master Godfrey, but I and one or two others was nigh, having heard voices louder than the common, just looking over the churchyard wall, to tell truth."

"Oh!" ejaculated Godfrey, and Tom continued in a reflective voice.

"My! they were two beuties, what you gave that old fat devil of a squire. If he'd been a bull instead of only roaring like one, they'd have brought him down, to say nothing of parson and the angel."

"I couldn't help it, Tom. I was mad."

"And no wonder, after being crumped on the nut with a tight umbrella. Why, I'd have done the same myself, baronite or no baronite. Oh! there's no need to explain; I knows everything about it, and so does every babe in the village by now, not to mention the old women. Master Godfrey, you take my advice, the next time you go a-courtin' shut the door behind you, which I always made a point o' doing when I was young. Being passing that way, I seed parson peeping in, and knowing you was there, guessed why. Truth is I came to warn you after he'd gone up to the Hall, but seein' how you was engaged, thought it a pity to interrupt, though now I wish I had."

Godfrey groaned; there was nothing to say.

"Well, all the soot's in the cooking-pot now, so to speak," proceeded Tom blandly, "and we're downright sad about it, we are, for as my missus was saying, you'd make a pretty pair. But, Lord, Master Godfrey, don't you take it too much to heart, for she's an upright young lady, she is, and steadfast. Or if she ain't, there's plenty of others; also one day follows another, as the saying goes, and the worst of old varmints don't live for ever. But parson, he beats me, and you his son, so they tell, though I never could think it myself. If he ain't the meanest ferret I ever clapped eyes on, may the old mare fall down and break my neck. Well, he'll hear about it, I can promise him, especially if he meets my missus what's got a tongue in her head, and is a chapel woman into the bargain. Lord! there comes the train. Don't you fear, we'll catch her. Hold tight, Master Godfrey, and be ready to jump out. No, no, there ain't nothing to pay. I'll stick it on to parson's fare next time I've druve him. Good-bye, Master Godfrey, and God bless you, if only for that there right and left which warmed my heart to see, and mind ye," he shouted after him, "there's more young women in the world than ye meets in an afternoon's walk, and one nail drives another out, as being a smith by trade I knows well."

Godfrey bundled into an empty carriage with his portmanteau and his coat, and covered his face with his hands that he might see no more of that accursed station whence he seemed always to be departing in trouble. So everything had been overheard and seen, and doubtless the story would travel far and wide. Poor Isobel!

As a matter of fact it did, but it was not Isobel who suffered, since public sympathy was strong on the side of her and of her lover. The indignation of the neighbourhood concentrated itself upon the square and the parson, especially the latter. Indeed the village showed its sympathy with the victims and its wrath with the oppressors, by going on strike. Few beaters turned up at Sir John's next shooting party, and on the following Sunday Mr. Knight preached to empty benches, a vacuum that continued from week to week. The end of it was he became so unpopular and his strained relations with Sir John grew so notorious that the bishop, who like everyone else knew the whole story, gently suggested to him that a change of livings would be to his advantage; also to that of the church in Monk's Acre and its neighbourhood.

So Mr. Knight departed to another parish in a remote part of the diocese which, having been inundated by the sea, was almost devoid of inhabitants, and saw the Abbey and Hawk's Hall no more.

In searching his pockets for matches, Godfrey found the letter which had been given to him as he left the Abbey. He knew the writing on the envelope at once, and was minded not to open it, for this and the foreign stamp told him that it came from Madame Riennes. Still curiosity, or a desire to take his mind off the miseries by which it was beset, prevailed, and he did open the envelope and read. It ran thus:

"Ah! my little friend, my godson in the speerit, Godfrey

"I daresay you thought that poor old Madame was dead, gone to join the Celestials, because you have not heard from her for so long a while. Not a bit, my little Godfrey, though perhaps I should not call you little, since my crystal shows me that you have grown taller even than you were in the old days at Lucerne, and much broader, quite a good-made man and nice to look at. Well, my Godfrey, I hear things about you sometimes, for the most part from the speerit called Eleanor who, I warn you, has a great bone to pick with you. Because, you see, people do not change so much as you think when they get to the other side. So a woman remains a woman, and being a woman she stays jealous, and does not like it when her affinity turns the back on her, as you have done on Eleanor. Therefore she will give you a bad trick if she can, just as a woman would upon the earth. Also I hear of you sometimes from Miss Ogilvy or, rather, her speerit, for she is as fond of you as ever, so fond that I think you must have mixed up together in a previous life, because otherwise there is nothing to account for it. She tries to protect you from Eleanor the indignant, with whom she has, I gather, much row.

"Now for my message, which come to me from all these speerits. I hear you have done very well in what they call examinations, and have before you a shining future. But do not think that you will be happy, my Godfrey, for you will not get that girl you want for a long, long while, and then only for the shortest of time, just enough to kiss and say, 'Oh! my pretty, how nice you are!' And then au revoir to the world of speerits. Meanwhile, being a little fool, you will go empty and hungry, since you are not one of those who hate the woman, which, after all, is the best thing in life for the man while he is young, like, so the spirits tell me, does your dear papa. And oh! how plenty this woman fruit hang on every tree, so why not pluck and eat before the time come, when you cannot, because if you still have appetite those nice plums turn your stomach? So you have a bad time before you, my Godfrey, waiting for the big fat plum far away which you cannot see or touch and much less taste, while the other nice plums fall into different hands, or wither—wither, waiting to be eaten.

"At end, when you get your big, fat plum, just as you set your teeth in it, oh! something blow it out of your mouth, I know not what, the speerits will not say, perhaps because they do not know, for they have not prescience of all things. But of this be sure, my Godfrey, when that happen, that it is your own fault, for had you trusted to your godmamma Riennes it never would have chanced, since she would have shown you how to get your plum and eat it to the stone and then throw away the stone and get other plums and be happy—happy and full instead of empty. Well, so it is, and as I must I tell you. There is but one hope for you, unless you would go sorrowful. To come back to your godmamma, who will teach you how to walk and be happy—happy and get all you want. Also, since she is now poor, you would do well to send her a little money to this address in Italy, since that old humbug of a Pasteur, whom she cannot harm because of the influences round him, still prevents her from returning to Switzerland, where she has friends. Now that big plum, it is very nice and you desire it much. Come to your godmamma and she will show you how to get it off the tree quickly. Yes, within one year. Or do not come and it will hang there for many winters and shrivel as plums do, and at last one bite and it will be gone. And then, my godson, then, my dear Godfrey—well, perhaps I will tell you the rest another time. You poor silly boy, who will not understand that the more you get the more you will always have. "Your Godmamma, "Who love you still although you treat her so badly, "The Countess of Riennes.

"(Ah! you did not know I had that title, did you, but in the speerit world I have others which are much higher.)"

Godfrey thrust this precious epistle back into his pocket with a feeling of physical and mental sickness. How did this horrible woman know so much about him and his affairs, and why did she prophesy such dreadful things? Further, if her knowledge was so accurate, although veiled in her foreign metaphor, why should not her prophecies be accurate also? And if they were, why should he be called upon to suffer so many things?

He could find no answer to these questions, but afterwards he sent her letter to the Pasteur, who in due course returned it with some upright and manly comments both upon the epistle itself and the story of his troubles, which Godfrey had detailed to him. Amongst much else he wrote in French:

"You suffer and cannot understand why, my dear boy. Nor do I, but it is truth that all who are worth anything are called upon to suffer, to what end we do not know. Nothing of value is gained except by suffering. Why, again we do not know. This wretched woman is right in a way when she refers all solutions to another world, only her other world is one that is bad, and her solutions are very base. Be sure that there are other and better ones that we shall learn in due time, when this little sun has set for us. For it will rise elsewhere, Godfrey, in a brighter sky. Meanwhile, do not be frightened by her threats, for even if they should all be true, to those evils which she prophesies there is, be sure, another interpretation. As I think one of your poets has said, we add our figures until they come even. So go your way and keep as upright as you can, and have no fear since God is over all, not the devil."

Thus preached the Pasteur, and what he said gave Godfrey the greatest comfort. Still, being young, he made one mistake. He did send Madame Riennes some money, partly out of pity—ten pounds in a postal order without any covering letter, a folly that did not tend to a cessation of her epistolatory efforts.

On reaching town Godfrey went straight to Hampstead. There to his surprise he found all prepared for his reception.

"I was expecting you, my dear," said Mrs. Parsons, "and even have a little bit extra in the house in case you should come."

"Why, when I told you I had gone home for a month?" asked Godfrey.

"Why? For the same reason as I knows that oil and vinegar won't abide mixed in the same bottle. I was sure enough that being a man grown, you and your father could never get on together in one house. But perhaps there is something else in it too," she added doubtfully.

Then Godfrey told her that there was something else, and indeed all about the business.

"Well, there you are, and there's nothing to be said, or at least so much that it comes to the same thing," remarked Mrs. Parsons, in a reflective tone, when he had finished his story. "But what I want to know," she went on, "is why these kind of things happen. You two—I mean you and Miss Isobel—are just fitted to each other, appointed together by Nature, so to speak, and fond as a couple of doves upon a perch. So why shouldn't you take each other and have done? What is there to come between a young man and a young woman such as you are?"

"I don't know," groaned Godfrey.

"No, nor don't I; and yet something does come between. What's the meaning of it all? Why do things always go cussed in this 'ere world? Is there a devil about what manages it, or is it just chance? Why shouldn't people have what they want and when it's wanted, instead of being forced to wait until perhaps it isn't, or can't be enjoyed, or often enough to lose it altogether? You can't answer, and nor can't I; only at times I do think, notwithstanding all my Christian teachings and hundreds and hundreds of your father's sermons, that the devil, he's top-dog here. And as for that there foreign woman whose letter you've read to me, she's his housemaid. Not but what I'm sure it will all come right at last," she added, with an attempt at cheerfulness.

"I hope so," replied Godfrey, without conviction, and went to bed.

Presently he descended from his room again, bearing a pill-box in which was enclosed a certain ring that years before he had bought at Lucerne, a ring set with two hearts of turquoise.

"I promised not to write," he said, "but you might address this to her. She'll know what it is, for I told her about it."

"Yes," said Mrs. Parsons, "the young lady shall have that box of pills. Being upset, it may do her good."

In due course Isobel did have it; also the box came back addressed to Mrs. Parsons. In it was another ring, a simple band of ancient gold—as a matter of fact, it was Roman, a betrothal ring of two thousand years ago. Round it was a scrap of paper on which was written:

"This was dug up in a grave. My great-grandmother gave it to my great-grandfather when they became engaged about a hundred years ago, and he wore it all his life, as in a bygone age someone else had done. Now the great-granddaughter gives it to another. Let him wear it all his life, whatever happens to her, or to him. Then let it go to the grave again, perhaps to be worn by others far centuries hence."

Godfrey understood and set it on the third finger of his left hand, where it remained night and day, and year by year.

So that matter ended, and afterwards came silence and darkness which endured for ten years or more. From his father he heard nothing, nor on his part did he ever write to him again. Indeed the first news concerning him which reached Godfrey was that of his death which happened some seven years later, apparently after a brief illness. Even of this he would not have learned, since no one took the trouble to put it in any paper that he saw, had it not chanced that the Rev. Mr. Knight died intestate, and that therefore his small belongings descended to Godfrey as his natural heir. With them were a number of papers, among which in the after days Godfrey found the very letter that Isobel wrote to him which his father "posted" in his desk.

For his son there was no word, a circumstance that showed the implacability of this man's character. Notwithstanding his continual profession of the highest Christian principles he could never forget or forgive, and this although it was he who was in fault. For what wrong had Godfrey done to him in loving a woman whom he did not chance to like? So he died silent, bearing his resentment to the grave. And yet some odd sense of justice prevented him from robbing Godfrey of his little inheritance, something under two thousand pounds, that came on a policy of insurance and certain savings, a sum which in after years when money was plentiful with him Godfrey appointed to the repair and beautifying of the Abbey Church at Monk's Acre.

Strangely enough, although from his childhood they had been always estranged, Godfrey felt this conduct of his father very much indeed. It seemed dreadful to him that he should vanish thus into the darkness, taking his wrath with him; and often he wondered if it still animated him there. Also he wondered what could be the possible purpose of it all, and indeed why his father was so fashioned that he could grow venomous over such a matter. To all of which questions no answer came, although one suggested itself to him—namely, that he was the victim of some hereditary taint, and therefore not in fact to blame.

In the case of Isobel the darkness was equally dense, for both of them kept their word, and with the single exception of the episode of the exchange of rings, neither attempted to communicate with the other directly or indirectly. From Mrs. Parsons he heard that Hawk's Hall was shut up, and that Sir John and his daughter lived mostly in London or at a place that the former had bought in Scotland. Once indeed Mrs. Parsons did write, or got someone else to write, to him that she had seen Isobel drive past her in the street, and that she looked well, though rather "stern and quiet-like."

That was all the news Godfrey had of Isobel during those ten years, since she was not a person who advertised her movements in the papers, although for her sake he became a great student of society gossip. Also he read with care all announcements of engagements and marriages in The Times, and the deaths, too, for the matter of that, but happily quite without result. Indeed in view of her declaration he ought to have been, and, in fact, was, ashamed of his research; but then, who could be quite sure of anything in this world?

Sir John, he knew, was living, because from time to time he saw his name in lists of subscriptions of a sort that appear under royal patronage and are largely advertised.

So between these two swung a veil of darkness, although, had he but known it, this was not nearly so impenetrable to Isobel as to himself. Somehow—possibly Arthur Thorburn had friends with whom he corresponded in England who knew Isobel—she acquired information as to every detail of his career. Indeed when he came to learn everything he was absolutely amazed at the particulars with which she was acquainted, whereof there were certain that he would have preferred to have kept to himself. But she had them all, with dates and surrounding circumstances and the rest; thousands of miles of ocean had been no bar to her searching gaze.

For his part he was not without consolations, since, strangely enough, he never felt as if she were lost to him, or indeed far away; it was always as though she were in the next room, or at any rate in the next street. There are individuals of sensitive mind, and he was one of them, who know well enough when such a total loss has occurred. It has been well said that the dead are never really dead to us until they are forgotten, and the same applies to the living. While they remember us, they are never so very far away, and what is more we, or some of us, are quite aware if they have ceased to remember, for then the door is shut and the doorway built up and our hearts tell us that this has been done.

In Godfrey's case with Isobel, not only did the doorway remained unfilled—the door itself was always ajar. Although seas divided them and over these no whisper came, yet he felt her thought leaping to him across the world. Especially did this happen at night when he laid himself down to sleep, perhaps because then his mind was most receptive, and since their hours of going to rest must have been different, he being in India and she in England, she could scarcely have been reflecting on him as he fondly believed, at the moment when she, too, entered into the world called sleep.

Therefore, either it was all imagination or he caught her waking thoughts, or perhaps those that haunted her upon this border land were delayed until his subtler being could interpret them. Who knows? At least, unless something had happened to disturb him, those nights were rare when as he was shutting his eyes, Godfrey did not seem to be sensible of Isobel's presence. At any rate, he knew that she had not forgotten; he knew that somewhere in the vast world she was ever thinking of him with more intensity than she thought of any other man or thing. And during all those lonely years this knowledge or belief was his greatest comfort.

Not that Godfrey's life in India was in any way unhappy. On the contrary it was a full and active life. He worked hard at his profession and succeeded in it to a limited extent, and he had his friends, especially his great friend Arthur Thorburn, who always clung to him. He had his flirtations also; being a man of susceptibility who was popular with women, how could they be avoided? For above all things Godfrey was a man, not a hermit or a saint or an æsthete, but just a man with more gifts of a sort than have some others. He lived the life of the rest, he hunted, he shot tigers, doing those things that the Anglo-Indian officer does, but all the same he studied. Whether it were of his trade of soldiering, or of the natives, or of Eastern thought and law, he was always learning something, till at last he knew a great deal, often he wondered to what end.

And yet, with all his friends and acquaintances, in a way he remained a very lonely man, as those who are a little out of the ordinary often do. In the common groove we rub against the other marbles running down it, but once we leap over its edge, then where are we? We cannot wander off into space because of the attraction of the earth that is so near to us, and yet we are alone in the air until with a bump we meet our native ground. Therefore for the most of us the groove is much better. And yet some who leave it have been carried elsewhere, if only for a little while, like St. Paul into the third heaven.

CHAPTER XVIII

FRANCE—AND AFTER

Nothing so very remarkable happened to Godfrey during those ten years of his life in India, or at least only one or two things. Thus once he got into a scrape for which he was not really responsible, and got out of it again, as he imagined, without remark, until Isobel showed her common and rather painful intimacy with its details, of which she appeared to take a somewhat uncharitable view, at any rate so far as the lady was concerned.

The other matter was more serious, since it involved the loss of his greatest friend, Arthur Thorburn. Briefly, what happened was this. There was a frontier disturbance. Godfrey, who by now was a staff officer, had been sent to a far outpost held by Thorburn with a certain number of men, and there took command. A reconnaissance was necessary, and Thorburn went out for that purpose with over half of the available garrison of the post, having received written orders that he was not to engage the enemy unless he found himself absolutely surrounded. In the end Thorburn did engage the enemy with the result that practically he and his force were exterminated, but not before they had inflicted such a lesson on the said enemy that it sued for peace and has been great friends with the British power ever since.

First however a feeble attack was made on Godfrey's camp that he beat off without the loss of a single man, exaggerated accounts of which were telegraphed home representing it as a "Rorke's Drift defence."

Godfrey was heartbroken; he had loved this man as a brother, more indeed than brothers often love. And now Thorburn, his only friend, was dead. The Darkness had taken him, that impenetrable, devouring darkness out of which we come and into which we go. Religion told him he should not grieve, that Thorburn doubtless was much better off whither he had gone than he could ever have been on earth, although it was true the same religion said that he might be much worse off, since thither his failings would have followed him. Dismissing the latter possibility, how could he be happy in a new world, Godfrey wondered, having left all he cared for behind him and without possibility of communication with them?

In short, all the old problems of which he had not thought much since Miss Ogilvy died, came back to Godfrey with added force and left him wretched. Nor was he consoled by the sequel of the affair of which he was bound to report the facts. The gallant man who was dead was blamed unjustly for what had happened, as perhaps he deserved who had not succeeded, since those who set their blind eye to the telescope as Nelson did must justify their action by success.

Godfrey, on the other hand, who had done little but defeat an attack made by exhausted and dispirited men, was praised to the skies and found himself figuring as a kind of hero in the English Press, which after a long period of peace having lost all sense of proportion in such matters, was glad of anything that could be made to serve the purposes of sensation. Ultimately he was thanked by the Government of India, made a brevet-Major and decorated with the D.S.O., of all of which it may be said with truth that never were such honours received with less pleasure.

So much did he grieve over this unhappy business that his health was affected and being run down, in the end he took some sort of fever and was very ill indeed. When at length he recovered more or less he went before a Medical Board who ordered him promptly to England on six months' leave.

Most men would have rejoiced, but Godfrey did not. He had little wish to return to England, where, except Mrs. Parsons, there were none he desired to see, save one whom he was sworn not to see. This he could bear while they were thousands of miles apart, but to be in the same country with Isobel, in the same town perhaps, and forbidden to hear her voice or to touch her hand, how could he bear that? Still he had no choice in this matter, arranged by the hand of Fate, and went, reflecting that he would go to Lucerne and spent the time with the Pasteur. Perhaps even he would live in the beautiful house that Miss Ogilvy had left to him, or a corner of it, seeing that it was empty, for the tenants to whom it had been let had gone away.

So he started at the end of the first week in July, 1914.

When his ship reached Marseilles it was to find that the world was buzzing with strange rumours. There was talk of war in Europe. Russia was said to be mobilising; Germany was said to be mobilising; France was said to be mobilising; it was even rumoured that England might be drawn into some Titanic struggle of the nations. And yet no accurate information was obtainable. The English papers they saw were somewhat old and their reports vague in the extreme.

Much excited, like everyone else, Godfrey telegraphed to the India Office, asking leave to come home direct overland, which he could not do without permission since he was in command of a number of soldiers who were returning to England on furlough.

No answer came to his wire before his ship sailed, and therefore he was obliged to proceed by long sea. Still it had important consequences which at the moment he could not foresee. In the Bay the tidings that reached them by Marconigram were evidently so carefully censored that out of them they could make nothing, except that the Empire was filled with great doubt and anxiety, and that the world stood on the verge of such a war as had never been known in history.

At length they came to Southampton where the pilot-boat brought him a telegram ordering him to report himself without delay. Three hours later he was in London. At the India Office, where he was kept waiting a while, he was shown into the room of a prominent and harassed official who had some papers in front of him.

"You are Major Knight?" said the official. "Well, here is your record before me and it is good, very good indeed. But I see that you are on sick leave. Are you too ill for service?"

"No," answered Godfrey, "the voyage has set me up. I feel as well as ever I did."

"That's fortunate," answered the official, "but there is a doctor on the premises, and to make sure he shall have a look at you. Go down and see him, if you will, and then come back here with his report," and he rang a bell and gave some orders.

Within half an hour Godfrey was back in the room with a clean bill of health. The official read the certificate and remarked that he was going to send him over to the War Office, where he would make an appointment for him by telephone.

"What for, Sir?" asked Godfrey. "You see I am only just off my ship and very ignorant of the news."

"The news is, Major Knight, that we shall be at war with Germany before we are twelve hours older," was the solemn answer. "Officers are wanted, and we are giving every good man from India on whom we can lay our hands. They won't put you on the Staff, because you have everything to learn about European work, but I expect they will find you a billet in one of the expeditionary regiments. And now good-bye and good luck to you, for I have lots of men to see. By the way, I take it for granted that you volunteered for the job?"

"Of course," replied Godfrey simply, and went away to wander about the endless passages of the War Office till at length he discovered the man whom he must see.

A few tumultuous days went by, and he found himself upon a steamer crossing to France, attached to a famous English regiment.

The next month always remained in Godfrey's mind as a kind of nightmare in which he moved on plains stained the colour of blood, beneath a sky black with bellowing thunder and illumined occasionally by a blaze of splendour. It would be useless to attempt to set out the experience and adventures of the particular cavalry regiment to which he was attached as a major, since, notwithstanding their infinite variety, they were such as all shared whose glory it was to take part with what the Kaiser called the "contemptible little army" of England in the ineffable retreat from Mons, that retreat which saved France and Civilisation.

Godfrey played his part well, once or twice with heroism indeed, but what of that amid eighty thousand heroes? Back he staggered with the rest, exhausted, sleepless, fighting, fighting, fighting, his mind filled alternately with horror and with wonder, horror at the deeds to which men can sink and the general scheme of things that makes them possible, wonder at the heights to which they can rise when lifted by the inspiration of a great ideal and a holy cause. Death, he reflected, could not after all mean so very much to man, seeing how bravely it was met every minute of the day and night, and that the aspect of it, often so terrible, did but encourage others in like fashion to smile and die. But oh! what did it all mean, and who ruled this universe with such a flaming, blood-stained sword?

Then at last came the turn of the tide when the hungry German wolf was obliged to abandon that Paris which already he thought between his jaws and, a few days after it, the charge, the one splendid, perfect charge that consoled Godfrey and those with him for all which they had suffered, lost and feared. He was in command of the regiment now, for those superior to him had been killed, and he directed and accompanied that charge. They thundered on to the mass of the Germans who were retreating with no time to entrench or set entanglements, a gentle slope in front, and hard, clear ground beneath their horses' feet. They cut through them, they trod them down, they drove them by scores and hundreds into the stream beyond, till those two battalions, or what remained of them, were but a tangled, drowning mob. It was finished; the English squadron turned to retreat as had been ordered.

Then of a sudden Godfrey felt a dull blow. For a few moments consciousness remained to him. He called out some command about the retirement; it came to his mind that thus it was well to die in the moment of his little victory. After that—blackness!

When his sense returned to him he found himself lying in the curtained corner of a big room. At least he thought it was big because of the vast expanse of ceiling which he could see above the curtain rods and the sounds without, some of which seemed to come from a distance. There was a window, too, through which he caught sight of lawns and statues and formal trees. Just then the curtain was drawn, and there appeared a middle-aged woman dressed in white, looking very calm, very kind and very spotless, who started a little when she saw that his eyes were open and that his face was intelligent.

"Where am I?" he asked, and was puzzled to observe that the sound of his voice seemed feeble and far away.

"In the hospital at Versailles," she answered in a pleasant voice.

"Indeed!" he murmured. "It occurred to me that it might be Heaven or some place of the sort."

"If you looked through the curtain you wouldn't call it Heaven," she said with a sigh, adding, "No, Major, you were near to 'going west,' very near, but you never got to the gates of Heaven."

"I can't remember," he murmured again.

"Of course you can't, so don't try, for you see you got it in the head, a bit of shell; and a nice operation, or rather operations, they had over you. If it wasn't for that clever surgeon—but there, never mind."

"Shall I recover?"

"Of course you will. We have had no doubt about that for the last week; you have been here nearly three, you know; only, you see, we thought you might be blind, something to do with the nerves of the eyes. But it appears that isn't so. Now be quiet, for I can't stop talking to you with two dying just outside, and another whom I hope to save."

"One thing, Nurse—about the war. Have the Germans got Paris?"

"That's a silly question, Major, which makes me think you ain't so right as I believed. If those brutes had Paris do you think you would be at Versailles? Or, at any rate, that I should? Don't you bother about the war. It's all right, or as right as it is likely to be for many a long day."

Then she went.

A week later Godfrey was allowed to get out of bed and was even carried to sit in the autumn sunshine among other shattered men. Now he learned all there was to know; that the German rush had been stayed, that they had been headed off from Calais, and that the armies were entrenching opposite to each other and preparing for the winter, the Allied cause having been saved, as it were, by a miracle, at any rate for the while. He was still very weak, with great pain in his head, and could not read at all, which grieved him.

So the time went by, till at last he was told that he was to be sent to England, as his bed was wanted and he could recover there as well as in France. Two days later he started in a hospital train and suffered much upon the journey, although it was broken for a night at Boulogne. Still he came safely to London, and was taken to a central hospital where next day several doctors held a consultation over him. When it was over they asked him if he had friends in London and wished to stay there. He replied that he had no friends except an old nurse at Hampstead, if she were still there, and that he did not like London. Then there was talk among them, and the word Torquay was mentioned. The head doctor seemed to agree, but as he was leaving, changed his mind.

"Too long a journey," he said, "it would knock him up. Give me that list. Here, this place will do; quite close and got up regardless, I am told, for she's very rich. That's what he wants—comfort and first- class food," and with a nod to Godfrey, who was listening in an idle fashion, quite indifferent as to his destination, he was gone.

Next day they carried him off in an ambulance through the crowded Strand, and presently he found himself at Liverpool Street, where he was put into an invalid carriage. He asked the orderly where he was going, but the man did not seem to know, or had forgotten the name. So troubling no more about it he took a dose of medicine as he had been ordered, and presently went to sleep, as no doubt it was intended that he should do. When he woke up again it was to find himself being lifted from another ambulance into a house which was very dark, perhaps because of the lighting orders, for now night had fallen. He was carried in a chair up some stairs into a very nice bedroom, and there put to bed by two men. They went away, leaving him alone.

Something puzzled him about the place; at first he could not think what it was. Then he knew. The smell of it was familiar to him. He did not recognise the room, but the smell he did seem to recognise, though being weak and shaken he could not connect it with any particular house or locality. Now there were voices in the passage, and he knew that he must be dreaming, for the only one that he could really hear sounded exactly like to that of old Mrs. Parsons. He smiled at the thought and shut his eyes. The voice that was like to that of Mrs. Parsons died away, saying as it went:

"No, I haven't got the names, but I dare say they are downstairs. I'll go and look."

The door opened and he heard someone enter, a woman this time by her tread. He did not see, both because his eyes were still almost closed and for the reason that the electric light was heavily shaded. So he just lay there, wondering quite vaguely where he was and who the woman might be. She came near to the bed and looked down at him, for he heard her dress rustle as she bent. Then he became aware of a very strange sensation. He felt as though something were flowing from that woman to him, some strange and concentrated power of thought which was changing into a kind of agony of joy. The woman above him began to breathe quickly, in sighs as it were, and he knew that she was stirred; he knew that she was wondering.

"I cannot see his face, I cannot see his face!" she whispered in a strained, unnatural tone. Then with some swift movement she lifted the shade that was over the lamp. He, too, turned his head and opened his eyes.

Oh, God! there over him leant Isobel, clad in a nurse's robes—yes, Isobel—unless he were mad.

Next moment he knew that he was not mad, for she said one word, only one, but it was enough.

"Godfrey!"

"Isobel!" he gasped. "Is it you?"

She made no answer, at least in words. Only she bent down and kissed him on the lips.

"You mustn't do that," he whispered. "Remember—our promise?"

"I remember," she answered. "Am I likely to forget? It was that you would never see me nor come into this house while my father lived. Well, he died a month ago." Then a doubt struck her, and she added swiftly: "Didn't you want to come here?"

"Want, Isobel! What else have I wanted for ten years? But I didn't know; my coming here was just an accident."

"Are there such things as accidents?" she queried. "Was it an accident when twenty years ago I found you sleeping in the schoolroom at the Abbey and kissed you on the forehead, or when I found you sleeping a few minutes ago twenty whole years later—?" and she paused.

"And kissed me—not upon the forehead," said Godfrey reflective, adding, "I never knew about that first kiss. Thank you for it."

"Not upon the forehead," she repeated after him, colouring a little. "You see I have faith and take a great deal for granted. If I should be mistaken—"

"Oh! don't trouble about that," he broke in, "because you know it couldn't be. Ten years, or ten thousand, and it would make no difference."

"I wonder," she mused, "oh! how I wonder. Do you think it possible that we shall be living ten thousand years hence?"

"Quite," he answered with cheerful assurance, "much more possible than that I should be living to-day. What's ten thousand years? It's quite a hundred thousand since I saw you."

"Don't laugh at me," she exclaimed.

"Why not, dear, when there's nothing in the whole world at which I wouldn't laugh at just now? although I would rather look at you. Also I wasn't laughing, I was loving, and when one is loving very much, the truth comes out."

"Then you really think it true—about the ten thousand years, I mean?"

"Of course, dear," he answered, and this time his voice was serious enough. "Did we not tell each other yonder in the Abbey that ours was the love eternal?"

"Yes, but words cannot make eternity."

"No, but thoughts and the will behind them can, for we reap what we sow."

"Why do you say that?" she asked quickly.

"I can't tell you, except because I know that it is so. We come to strange conclusions out yonder, where only death seems to be true and all the rest a dream. What we call the real and the unreal get mixed."

A kind of wave of happiness passed through her, so obvious that it was visible to the watching Godfrey.

"If you believe it I dare say that it is so, for you always had what they call vision, had you not?" Then without waiting for an answer, she went on, "What nonsense we are talking. Don't you understand, Godfrey, that I am quite old?"

"Yes," he answered, "getting on; six months younger than I am, I think."

"Oh! it's different with a man. Another dozen years and I'm finished."

"Possibly, except for that eternity before you."

"Also," she continued, "I am even—"

"Even more beautiful than you were ten years ago, at any rate to me," he broke in.

"You foolish Godfrey," she murmured, and moved a little away from him.

Just then the door opened, and Mrs. Parsons, looking very odd in a nurse's dress with the cap awry upon her grey hair, entered, carrying a bit of paper.

"The hunt I had!" she began; "that silly, new-fangled kind of a girl- clerk having stuck the paper away under the letter O—for officers, you know, Miss—in some fancy box of hers, and then gone off to tea. Here are the names, but I can't see without my specs."

At this point something in the attitude of the two struck her, something that her instincts told her was uncommon, and she stood irresolute. Isobel stepped to her as though to take the list, and, bending down, whispered into her ear.

"What?" said Mrs. Parsons. "Surely I didn't understand; you know I'm getting deaf as well as blind. Say the name again."

Isobel obeyed, still in a whisper.

"Him!" exclaimed the old woman, "him! Our Godfrey, and you've been and let on who you were—you who call yourself a nursing Commandant? Why, I dare say you'll be the death of him. Out you go, Miss, anyway; I'll take charge of this case for the present," and as it seemed to Godfrey, watching from the far corner, literally she bundled Isobel from the room.

Then she shut and locked the door. Coming to the bedside she knelt down rather stiffly, looked at him for a while to make sure, and kissed him, not once, but many times.

"So you have come back, my dear," she said, "and only half dead. Well, we won't have no young woman pushing between you and me just at present, Commandant or not. Time enough for love-making when you are stronger. Oh! and I never thought to see you again. There must be a good God somewhere after all, although He did make them Germans."

Then again she fell to kissing and blessing him, her hot tears dropping on his face and upsetting him ten times as much as Isobel had done.

Since in this topsy-turvy world often things work by contraries, oddly enough no harm came to Godfrey from these fierce excitements. Indeed he slept better than he had done since he found his mind again, and awoke, still weak of course, but without any temperature or pains in his head. Now it was that there began the most blissful period of all his life. Isobel, when she had recovered her balance, made him understand that he was a patient, and that exciting talk or acts must be avoided. He on his part fell in with her wishes, and indeed was well content to do so. For a while he wanted nothing more than just to lie there and watch her moving in and out of his room, with his food or flowers, or whatever it might be, for a burst of bad weather prevented him from going out of doors. Then, as he strengthened she began to talk to him (which Mrs. Parsons did long before that event), telling him all that for years he had longed to know; no, not all, but some things. Among other matters she described to him the details of her father's end, which occurred in a very characteristic fashion.

"You see, dear," she said, "as he grew older his passion for money- making increased more and more; why, I am sure I cannot say, seeing that Heaven knows he had enough."

"Yes," said Godfrey, "I suppose you are a very rich woman."

She nodded, saying: "So rich that I don't know how rich, for really I haven't troubled even to read all the figures, and as yet they are not complete. Moreover, I believe that soon I shall be much richer. I'll tell you why presently. The odd thing is, too, that my father died intestate, so I get every farthing. I believe he meant to make a will with some rather peculiar provisions that perhaps you can guess. But this will was never made."

"Why not?" asked Godfrey.

"Because he died first, that's all. It was this way. He, or rather his firm, which is only another name for him, for he owned three-fourths of the capital, got some tremendous shipping contract with the Government arising out of the war, that secures an enormous profit to them; how much I can't tell you, but hundreds and hundreds of thousands of pounds. He had been very anxious about this contract, for his terms were so stiff that the officials who manage such affairs hesitated about signing them. At last one day after a long and I gather, stormy interview with I don't know whom, in the course of which some rather strong language seems to have been used, the contract was signed and delivered to the firm. My father came home to this house with a copy of it in his pocket. He was very triumphant, for he looked at the matter solely from a business point of view, not at all from that of the country. Also he was very tired, for he had aged much during the last few years, and suffered occasionally from heart attacks. To keep himself up he drank a great deal of wine at dinner, first champagne and then the best part of a bottle of port. This made him talkative, and he kept me sitting there to listen to him while he boasted, poor man, of how he had 'walked round' the officials who thought themselves so clever, but never saw some trap which he had set for them."

"And what did you do?" asked Godfrey.

"You know very well what I did. I grew angry, I could not help it, and told him I thought it was shameful to make money wrongfully out of the country at such a time, especially when he did not want it at all. Then he was furious and answered that he did want it, to support the peerage which he was going to get. He said also," she added slowly, "that I was 'an ignorant, interfering vixen,' yes, that is what he called me, a vixen, who had always been a disappointment to him and thwarted his plans. 'However,' he went on, 'as you think so little of my hard-earned money, I'll take care that you don't have more of it than I can help. I am not going to leave it to be wasted on silly charities by a sour old maid, for that's what you are, since you can't get hold of your precious parson's son, who I hope will be sent to the war and killed. I'll see the lawyers to-morrow, and make a will, which I hope you'll find pleasant reading one day.'

"I answered that he might make what will he liked, and left the room, though he tried to stop me.

"About half an hour later I saw the butler running about the garden where I was, looking for me in the gloom, and heard him calling: 'Come to Sir John, miss. Come to Sir John!'

"I went in and there was my father fallen forward on the dining-room table, with blood coming from his lips, though I believe this was caused by a crushed wineglass. His pocket-book was open beneath him, in which he had been writing figures of his estate, and, I think, headings for the will he meant to make, but these I could not read since the faint pencilling was blotted out with blood. He was quite dead from some kind of a stroke followed by heart failure, as the doctors said."

"Is that all the pleasant story?" asked Godfrey.

"Yes, except that there being no will I inherited everything, or shall do so. I tried to get that contract cancelled, but could not; first, because having once made it the Government would not consent, since to do so would have been a reflection on those concerned, and secondly, for the reason that the other partners in the shipping business objected. So we shall have to give it back in some other way."

Godfrey looked at her, and said:

"You meant to say that you will have to give it back."

"I don't know what I meant," she answered, colouring; "but having said we, I think I will be like the Government and stick to it. That is, unless you object very much, my dear."

"Object! I object!" and taking the hand that was nearest to him, he covered it with kisses. As he did so he noted that for the first time she wore the little ring with turquoise hearts upon her third finger, the ring that so many years before he had bought at Lucerne, the ring that through Mrs. Parsons he had sent her in the pill-box on the evening of their separation.

This was the only form of engagement that ever passed between them, the truth being that from the moment he entered the place it was all taken for granted, not only by themselves, but by everyone in the house, including the wounded. With this development of an intelligent instinct, it is possible that Mrs. Parsons had something to do.

CHAPTER XIX

MARRIAGE

In that atmosphere of perfect bliss Godfrey's cure was quick. For bliss it was, save only that there was another bliss beyond to be attained. Remember that this man, now approaching middle life, had never drunk of the cup of what is known as love upon the earth.

Some might answer that such is the universal experience; that true, complete love has no existence, except it be that love of God to which a few at last attain, since in what we know as God completeness and absolute unity can be found alone. Other loves all have their flaws, with one exception perhaps, that of the love of the dead which fondly we imagine to be unchangeable. For the rest passion, however exalted, passes or at least becomes dull with years; the most cherished children grow up, and in so doing, by the law of Nature, grow away; friends are estranged and lost in their own lives.

Upon the earth there is no perfect love; it must be sought elsewhere, since having the changeful shadows, we know there is a sky wherein shines the sun that casts them.

Godfrey, as it chanced, omitting Isobel, had walked little even in these sweet shadows. There were but three others for whom he had felt devotion in all his days, Mrs. Parsons, his tutor, Monsieur Boiset, and his friend, Arthur Thorburn, who was gone. Therefore to him Isobel was everything. As a child he had adored her; as a woman she was his desire, his faith and his worship.

If this were so with him, still more was it the case with Isobel, who in truth cared for no other human being. Something in her nature prevented her from contracting violent female friendships, and to all men, except a few of ability, each of them old enough to be her father, she was totally indifferent; indeed most of them repelled her. On Godfrey, and Godfrey alone, from the first moment she saw him as a child she had poured all the deep treasure of her heart. He was at once her divinity and her other self, the segment that completed her life's circle, without which it was nothing but a useless, broken ring.

So much did this seem to her to be so, that notwithstanding her lack of faith in matters beyond proof and knowledge, she never conceived of this passion of hers as having had a beginning, or of being capable of an end. This contradictory woman would argue against the possibility of any future existence, yet she was quite certain that her love for Godfrey had a future existence, and indeed one that was endless. When at length he put it to her that her attitude was most illogical, since that which was dead and dissolved could not exist in any place or shape, she thought for a while and replied quietly:

"Then I must be wrong."

"Wrong in what?" asked Godfrey.

"In supposing that we do not live after death. The continuance of our love I know to be beyond any doubt, and if it involves our continuance as individual entities—well, then we continue, that is all."

"We might continue as a single entity," he suggested.

"Perhaps," she answered, "and if so this would be better still, for it must be impossible to lose one another while that remained alive, comprising both."

Thus, and in these few words, although she never became altogether orthodox, or took quite the same view of such mysteries as did Godfrey, Isobel made her great recantation, for which probably there would never have been any need had she been born in different surroundings and found some other spiritual guide in youth than Mr. Knight. As the cruelties and the narrow bitterness of the world had bred unfaith in her, so did supreme love breed faith, if of an unusual sort, since she learned that without the faith her love must die, and the love she knew to be immortal. Therefore the existence of that living love presupposed all the rest, and convinced her, which in one of her obstinate nature nothing else could possibly have done, no, not if she had seen a miracle. Also this love of hers was so profound and beautiful that she felt its true origin and ultimate home must be elsewhere than on the earth.

That was why she consented to be married in church, somewhat to Godfrey's surprise.

In due course, having practically recovered his health, Godfrey appeared before a Board in London which passed him as fit for service, but gave him a month's leave. With this document he returned to Hawk's Hall, and there showed it to Isobel.

"And when the month is up?" she asked, looking at him.

"Then I suppose I shall have to join my regiment, unless they send me somewhere else."

"A month is a very short time," she went on, still looking at him and turning a little pale.

"Yes, dear, but lots can happen in it, as we found out in France. For instance," he added, with a little hesitation, "we can get married, that is, if you wish."

"You know very well, Godfrey, that I have wished it for quite ten years."

"And you know very well, Isobel, that I have wished it—well, ever since I understood what marriage was. How about to-morrow?" he exclaimed, after a pause.

She laughed, and shook her head.

"I believe, Godfrey, that some sort of license is necessary, and it is past post time. Also it would look scarcely decent; all these people would laugh at us. Also, as there is a good deal of property concerned, I must make some arrangements."

"What arrangements?" he asked.

She laughed again. "That is my affair; you know I am a great supporter of Woman's Rights."

"Oh! I see," he replied vaguely, "to keep it all free from the husband's control, &c."

"Yes, Godfrey, that's it. What a business head you have. You should join the shipping firm after the war."

Then they settled to be married on that day week, after which Isobel suggested that he should take up his abode at the Abbey House, where the clergyman, a bachelor, would be very glad to have him as a guest. When Godfrey inquired why, she replied blandly because his room was wanted for another patient, he being now cured, and that therefore he had no right to stop there.

"Oh! I see. How selfish of me," said Godfrey, and went off to arrange matters with the clergyman, a friendly and accommodating young man, with the result that on this night once more he slept in the room he had occupied as a boy. For her part Isobel telephoned, first to her dressmaker, and secondly to the lawyer who was winding up her father's estate, requesting these important persons to come to see her on the morrow.

They came quickly, since Isobel was too valuable a client to be neglected, arriving by the same train, with the result that the lawyer was kept waiting an hour and a half by the dressmaker, a fact which he remembered in his bill. When at last his turn came, Isobel did not detain him long.

"I am going to be married," she said, "on the twenty-fourth to Major Godfrey Knight of the Indian Cavalry. Will you kindly prepare two documents, the first to be signed before my marriage, and the second, a will, immediately after it, since otherwise it would be invalidated by that change in my condition."

The lawyer stared at her, since so much legal knowledge was not common among his lady clients, and asked for instructions as to what the documents were to set out.

"They will be very simple," said Isobel. "The first, a marriage settlement, will settle half my income free of my control upon my future husband during our joint lives. The second, that is the will, will leave to him all my property, real and personal."

"I must point out to you, Miss Blake," said the astonished lawyer, "that these provisions are very unusual. Does Major Knight bring large sums into settlement?"

"I don't think so," she answered. "His means are quite moderate, and if they were not, it would never occur to him to do anything of the sort, as he understands nothing about money. Also circumstanced as I am, it does not matter in the least."

"Your late father would have taken a different view," sniffed the lawyer.

"Possibly," replied Isobel, "for our views varied upon most points. While he was alive I gave way to his, to my great loss and sorrow. Now that he is dead I follow my own."

"Well, that is definite, Miss Blake, and of course your wishes must be obeyed. But as regards this will, do not think me indelicate for mentioning it, but there might be children."

"I don't think you at all indelicate. Why should I at over thirty years of age? I have considered the point. If we are blessed with any children, and I should predecease him, my future husband will make such arrangements for their welfare as he considers wise and just. I have every confidence in his judgment, and if he should happen to die intestate, which I think very probable, they would inherit equally. There is enough for any number of them."

"Unless he loses or spends it," groaned the lawyer.

"He is much more likely to save it from some mistaken sense of duty, and to live entirely on what he has of his own," remarked Isobel. "If so, it cannot be helped, and no doubt the poor will benefit. Now if you thoroughly understand what I wish done, I think that is all. I have to see the dressmaker again, so good-bye."

"Executors?" gasped the lawyer.

"Public Trustee," said Isobel, over her shoulder.

"They say that she is one of these Suffragette women, although she keeps it dark. Well, I can believe it. Anyway, this officer is tumbling into honey, and there's no fool like a woman in love," said the lawyer to himself as he packed his bag of papers.

Isobel was quite right. The question of settlements never even occurred to Godfrey. He was aware, however, that it is usual for a bridegroom to make the bride a present, and going to London, walked miserably up and down Bond Street looking into windows until he was tired. At one moment he fixed his affections upon an old Queen Anne porringer, which his natural taste told him to be quite beautiful; but having learned from the dealer that it was meant for the mixing of infant's pap, he retired abashed. Almost next door he saw in a jeweller's window a necklace of small pearls priced at three hundred pounds, and probably worth about half that amount. Having quite a handsome balance at his back, he came to the conclusion that he could afford this and, going in, bought it at once, oblivious of the fact that Isobel already had ropes of pearls the size of marrowfat peas. However, she was delighted with it, especially when she saw what it had cost him, for he had never thought to cut the sale ticket from the necklace. It was those pearls, and not the marrowfat peas, that Isobel wore upon her wedding day. Save for the little ring with the two turquoise hearts, these were her only ornament.

A question arose as to where the honeymoon, or so much as would remain of one, was to be spent. Godfrey would have liked to go to Lucerne and visit the Pasteur, but as this could not be managed in war time, suggested London.

"Why London?" exclaimed Isobel.

"Only because most ladies like theatres, though I confess I hate them myself."

"You silly man," she answered. "Do you suppose, when we can have only a few days together, that I want to waste time in theatres?"

In the end it was settled that they would go to London for a night, and then on to Cornwall, which they hoped fondly might be warm at that time of year.

So at last, on the twenty-fourth day of December of that fateful year 1914, they were married in the Abbey Church. Isobel's uncle, the one with whom she had stayed in Mexico, and who had retired now from the Diplomatic Service, gave her away, and a young cousin of hers was the sole bridesmaid, for the ceremony was of the sort called a "war wedding." Her dress, however, was splendid of its kind, some rich thing of flowing broidered silk with a veil of wondrous lace.

Either from accident or by design, in general effect it much resembled that of the Plantagenet lady which once she had copied from the brass. Perhaps, being dissatisfied with her former effort, she determined to recap it on a more splendid scale, or perhaps it was a chance. At any rate, the veil raised in two points from her head, fell down like that of the nameless lady, while from her elbows long narrow sleeves hung almost to the ground. Beautiful Isobel never was, but in this garb, with happiness shining in her eyes, her tall, well-made form looked imposing and even stately, an effect that was heightened by her deliberate and dignified movements. The great church was crowded, for the news of this wedding had spread far and wide, and its romantic character attracted people both from the neighbouring villages and the little town.

Set in the splendid surroundings of the old Abbey, through the painted windows of which gleamed the winter sun, Godfrey in his glittering Indian uniform and orders, and his bride in her quaint, rich dress, made a striking pair at the altar rail. Indeed it is doubtful whether since hundreds of years ago the old Crusader and his fair lady, whose ashes were beneath their feet, stood where they stood for this same purpose of marriage, clad in coat of mail and gleaming silk, a nobler- looking couple had been wed in that ancient fane.

Oddly enough, with the strange inconsequence of the human mind, especially in moments of suppressed excitement, it was of this nameless lady and her lord that Godfrey kept thinking throughout the service, once more wondering who they were and what was their story. He remembered too how the graves of that unknown pair had been connected with his fortunes and those of Isobel. Here It was that they plighted the troth which now they were about to fulfil. Here it was that he had bidden her farewell before he went to Switzerland. He could see her now as she was then, tall and slender in her white robe, and the red ray of sunshine gleaming like a splash of blood upon her breast. He glanced at her by his side as she turned towards him, and behold! there it shone again, splendid yet ominous.

He shivered a little at the sight of it—he knew not why—and was glad when a dense black snow-cloud hid the face of the sun and killed it.

It was over at last, and they were man and wife.

"Do these words and vows and ceremonies make any difference to you?" she whispered as they walked side by side down the church, the observed of all observers. "They do not to me. I feel as though all the rites in the world would be quite powerless and without meaning in face of the fact of our eternal unity."

It was a queer little speech for her to make, with its thought and balance; Godfrey often reflected afterwards, expressing as it did a great truth so far as they were concerned, since no ceremonial, however hallowed, could increase their existing oneness or take away therefrom. At the moment, however, he scarcely understood it, and only smiled in reply.

Then they went into the vestry and signed their names, and everything was over. Here Godfrey's former trustee, General Cubitte, grown very old now, but as bustling and emphatic as of yore, who signed the book as one of the witnesses, buttonholed him. At some length he explained how he had been to see an eminent swell at the War Office, a "dug-out" who was an old friend of his, and impressed upon him his, Godfrey's, extraordinary abilities as a soldier, pointing out that he ought at once to be given command of a regiment, and how the eminent swell had promised that he would see to it forthwith. Oh! if he had only known, he would not have thanked him.

At last they started for the motor-car, which was to drive them in pomp three hundred yards to the Hall. Some delay occurred. Another motor-car at the church gate would not start, and had to be drawn out of the way. Three or four of the nurses from the hospital and certain local ladies surrounded Isobel, and burst into talk and congratulations, thus separating her from Godfrey.

Overhearing complimentary remarks about himself, he drew back a little from the porch into the church which had now emptied. As he stood there someone tapped him on the shoulder. The touch disturbed him; it was unpleasant to him and he turned impatiently to see from whom it came. There in front of him, bundled up in a rusty black cloak of which the hood covered the head, was a short fat woman. Her face was hidden, but from the cavernous recesses of the hood two piercing black eyes shone like to those of a tiger in its den. After all those years Godfrey recognised them at once; indeed subconsciously he had known who had touched him even before he turned. It was Madame Riennes.

"Ah!" she said, in her hateful, remembered voice, "so my little Godfrey who has grown such a big Godfrey now—yes, big in every way, had recognition of his dear Godmamma, did he? Oh! do not deny it; I saw you jump with joy. Well, I knew what was happening—never mind how I knew—and though I am so poor now, I travelled here to assist and give my felicitations. Eleanor, too, she sends hers, though you guess of what kind they are, for remember, as I told you long ago, speerits are just as jealous as we women, because, you see, they were women before they were speerits."

"Thank you," broke in Godfrey; "I am afraid I must be going."

"Oh! yes. You are in a great hurry, for now you have got the plum, my Godfrey, have you not, and want to eat it? Well, I have a message for you, suck it hard, for very, very soon you come to the stone, which you know is sharp and cold with no taste, and must be thrown away. Oh! something make me say this too; I know not what. Perhaps that stone must be planted, not thrown away; yes, I think it must be planted, and that it will grow into the most beautiful of plum trees in another land."

She threw back her hood, showing her enormous forehead and flabby, sunken face, which looked as though she had lived for years in a cellar, and yet had about it an air of inspiration. "Yes," she went on, "I see that tree white with blossom. I see it bending with the golden fruit—thousands upon thousands of fruits. Oh! Godfrey, it is the Tree of Life, and underneath it sit you and that lady who looks like a queen, and whom you love so dear, and look into each other's eyes for ever and for ever, because you see that tree immortal do not grow upon the earth, my Godfrey."

The horrible old woman made him afraid, especially did her last words make him afraid, because he who was experienced in such matters knew that she had come with no intention of uttering them, that they had burst from her lips in a sudden semi-trance such as overtakes her sisterhood from time to time. He knew what that meant, that Death had marked them, and that they were called elsewhere, he or Isobel, or both.

"I must be going," he repeated.

"Yes, yes, you must be going—you who are going so far. The hungry fish must go after the bait, must it not, and oh! the hook it does not see. But, my leetle big Godfrey, one moment. Your loving old Godmamma, she tumble on the evil day ever since that cursed old Pasteur"—here her pale face twisted and her eyes grew wicked—"let loose the law- dogs on me. I want money, my godson. Here is an address," and she thrust a piece of paper upon him.

He threw it down and stamped on it. In his pocket was a leather case full of bank-notes. He drew out a handful of them and held them to her. She snatched them as a hungry hawk snatches meat, with a fierce and curious swiftness.

Then at last he escaped, and in another minute, amidst the cheers of the crowd, was driving away at the side of the stately Isobel.

At the Hall, where one of the wards had been cleared for the purpose, there was a little informal reception, at which for a while Godfrey found himself officiating alone, since Isobel had disappeared with General Cubitte and the brother officer who had acted as his best man. When at length they returned he asked her where she had been, rather sharply perhaps, for his nerves were on edge.

"To see to some business with the lawyer," she answered.

"What business, dear?" he inquired. "I thought you settled all that this morning?"

"It could not be settled this morning, Godfrey, because a will can only be signed after marriage."

"Good gracious!" he exclaimed. "Give me a glass of champagne."

An hour later they were motoring to London alone, at last alone, and to this pair Heaven opened its seventh door.

They dined in the private sitting-room of the suit which under the inspiration of Isobel he had taken at a London hotel, and then after the curious-eyed waiters had cleared the table, sat together in front of the fire, hand in hand, but not talking very much. At length Isobel rose and they embraced each other.

"I am going to bed now," she said; "but before you come, and perhaps we forget about such matters, I want you to kneel down with me and say a prayer."

He obeyed as a child might, though wondering, for somehow he had never connected Isobel and Prayer in his mind. There they knelt in front of the fire, as reverently as though it burned upon an altar, and Isobel said her prayer aloud. It ran thus:

"O Unknown God Whom always I have sought and Whom now I think that I have found, or am near to finding; O Power that sent me forth to taste of Life and gather Knowledge, and Who at Thine own hour wilt call me back again, hear the prayer of Isobel and of Godfrey her lover. This is what they ask of Thee: that be their time together on the earth long or short, it may endure for ever in the lives and lands beyond the earth. They ask also that all their sins, known and unknown, great or small, may be forgiven them, and that with Thy gifts they may do good, and that if children come to them, they may be blessed in such fashion as Thou seest well, and afterwards endure with them through all the existences to be. O Giver of Life and Love Eternal, hear this, the solemn marriage prayer of Godfrey and of Isobel."

Then she rose and with one long look, left him, seeming to his eyes no more a woman, as ten thousand women are, but a very Fire of spiritual love incarnate in a veil of flesh.

CHAPTER XX

ORDERS

Godfrey and his wife never went to Cornwall after all, for on Christmas Day the weather turned so bad and travelling was so difficult that they determined to stop where they were for a few days.

As for them the roof of this London hotel had become synonymous with that of the crystal dome of heaven, this did not matter in the least. There they sat in their hideous, over-gilded, private sitting-room, or, when the weather was clear enough, went for walks in the Park, and once to the South Kensington Museum, where they enjoyed themselves very thoroughly.

It was on the fourth morning after their marriage that the blow fell. Godfrey had waked early, and lay watching his wife at his side. The grey light from the uncurtained window, which they had opened to air the over-heated room, revealed her in outline but not in detail and made her fine face mysterious, framed as it was in her yellow hair. He watched it with a kind of rapture, till at length she sighed and stirred, then began to murmur in her sleep.

"My darling," she whispered, "oh! my darling, how have I lived without you? Well, that is over, since alive or dead we can never be parted more, not really—not really!"

Then she opened her grey eyes and stretched out her arms to receive him, and he was glad, for he seemed to be listening to that which he was not meant to hear.

A little later there came a knocking at the door, and a page boy's squeaky voice without said:

"Telegram for you, Sir."

Godfrey called to him to put it down, but Isobel turned pale and shivered.

"What can it be?" she said, clasping him. "No one knows our address."

"Oh, yes, they do," he answered. "You forget you telephoned to the Hall yesterday afternoon about the hospital business you had forgotten and gave our number, which would be quite enough."

"So I did, like a fool," she exclaimed, looking as though she were going to cry.

"Don't be frightened, dear," he said. "I dare say it is nothing. You see we have no one to lose."

"No, no, I feel sure it is a great deal and—we have each other. Read it quickly and get the thing over."

So he rose and fetched the yellow envelope which reposed upon Isobel's boots outside the door. A glance showed him that it was marked "official," and then his heart, too, began to sink. Returning to the bed, he switched on the electric light and opened the envelope.

"There's enough of it," he said, drawing out three closely written sheets.

"Read, read it!" answered Isobel.

So he read. It was indeed a very long telegram, one of such as are commonly sent at the expense of the country, and it came from the War Office. The gist of it was that attempts had been made to communicate with him at an address he had given in Cornwall, but the messages had been returned, and finally inquiry at Hawk's Hall had given a clue. He was directed to report himself "early to-morrow" (the telegram had been sent off on the previous night) to take up an appointment which would be explained to him. There was, it added, no time to lose, as the ship was due to sail within twenty-four hours.

"There!" said Isobel, "I knew it was something of the sort. This," she added with a flash of inspiration, "is the result of the meddling of that old General Cubitte. You see it must be a distant appointment, or they would not talk about the ship being due to sail."

"I dare say," he answered as cheerfully as he could. "Such things are to be expected in these times, are they not?"

"Too bad!" she went on, "at any rate they might have let you have your leave."

Then they rose because they must and made pretence to eat some breakfast, after which they departed in one of Isobel's motors, which had been summoned by telephone from her London house, to the Department indicated in the telegram.

They need not have hurried, since the important person whom Godfrey must see did not arrive for a full hour, during all which time Isobel sat waiting in the motor. However, when he appeared he was very gracious.

"Oh! yes," he said, "you are Major Knight, and we have a mutual friend in old General Cubitte. In fact it was he who put an idea into our heads, for which, as I understand you are just married—a pretty hunt you gave us, by the way—perhaps you won't altogether bless him, since otherwise, as you are only just recovered from your wounds, I have no doubt we could have given you a month or two extra leave. However, I know you are very keen, for I've looked up your record, and private affairs must give way, mustn't they? Also, as it happens, Mrs. Knight need not be anxious, as we are not going to send you into any particular danger; I dare say you won't see a shot fired.

"Look here, Major, you have been a Staff officer, haven't you, and it is reported of you that you always got on extremely well with natives, and especially in some semi-political billets which you have held when you had to negotiate with their chiefs. Well, to cut it short, a man of the kind is wanted in East Africa, coming out direct from home with military authority. He will have to keep in touch with the big chiefs in our own territory and arrange for them to supply men for working or fighting, etc., and if possible, open negotiations with those in German territory and win them over to us. Further, as you know, there are an enormous number of Indians settled in East Africa, with whom you would be particularly qualified to deal. We should look to you to make the most of these in any way required. You see, the appointment is a special one, and if the work be well done, as I have no doubt it will be, I am almost sure," he added significantly, "that the results to the officer concerned will be special also.

"Now, I don't ask you if you decline the appointment, because we are certain in time of war you will not do so, and I think that's all, except that you will be accredited ostensibly to the staff of the General in command in East Africa, and also receive private instructions, of which the General and the local Governments will have copies. Now, do you understand everything, especially that your powers will be very wide and that you will have to act largely on your own discretion?"

"I think so, Sir," said Godfrey, concealing the complete confusion of his mind as well as he was able. "At any rate, I shall pick things up as I go along."

"Yes, that's the right spirit—pick things up as you go on, as we are all doing in this war. I have to pick 'em up, I can tell you. And now I won't keep you any longer, for, you see, you'll have to hustle. I believe a special boat for East Africa with stores, etc., sails to-morrow morning, so you'll have to take the last train to Southampton. An officer will meet you at Waterloo with your instructions, and if he misses you, will go on down to the boat. Also, you will have details of your pay and allowances, which will be liberal, though I am told you are not likely to want money in future. So good-bye and good luck to you. You must report officially through the General or the local Governors, but you will also be able to write privately to us. Indeed, please remember that we shall expect you to do so."

So Godfrey went, but as he neared the door the big man called after him:

"By the way, I forgot to congratulate you. No, no, I don't mean on your marriage, but on your promotion. You've been informed, haven't you? Well, it will be gazetted to-morrow or in a day or two, and letters will be sent to you with the other papers."

"What promotion?" asked Godfrey.

"Oh! to be a colonel, of course. You did very well out there in France, you know, and it is thought advisable that the officer undertaking this special work should have a colonel's rank, just to begin with. Good-bye."

So Godfrey went, and said vaguely to the waiting Isobel:

"I'm afraid, dear, that I shall have to ask you to help me to do some shopping. I think there are some stores near here. We had better drive to them."

"Tell me everything," said Isobel.

So he told her, and when he had finished she said slowly:

"It is bad enough, but I suppose it might be worse. Will they let me go with you to Southampton?"

"I expect so," he answered. "At any rate, we will try it on. I think it is an ordinary train, and you have a right to take a ticket."

Then they shopped, all day they shopped, with the result, since money can do much, that when they reached Waterloo his baggage containing everything needful, or at least nearly everything, was already waiting for him. So was the messenger with the promised papers, including a formal communication notifying to him that he was now a lieutenant- colonel.

"And to think that they have painted 'Major' on those tin cases!" said Isobel regretfully, for no objection had been raised to her accompanying Godfrey, with whom she was seated in a reserved carriage.

They reached Southampton about midnight, and on Godfrey presenting himself and asking when the boat sailed he was informed that this was uncertain, but probably within the next week. Then remembering all he had gone through that day, he swore as a man will, but Isobel rejoiced inwardly, oh! how she rejoiced, though all she said was that it would give him time to complete his shopping.

Save for the advancing shadow of separation and a constant stream of telegrams and telephone messages to and from his chiefs in London, which occupied many of the hours, these were very happy days, especially as in the end they spread themselves out to the original limit of his leave.

"At least we have not been cheated," said Isobel when at last they stood together on the deck of the ship, waiting for the second bell to ring, "and others are worse off. I believe those two poor people," and she pointed to a young officer and his child-like bride, "were only married yesterday."

The scene on the ship was dreary, for many were going in her to the various theatres of war, Egypt, Africa, and other places, and sad, oh! sad were the good-byes upon that bitter winter afternoon. Some of the women cried, especially those of the humbler class. But Isobel would not cry. She remained quite calm to the last, arranging a few flowers and unpacking a travelling bag in Godfrey's cabin, for as a colonel he had one to himself.

Then the second bell rang, and to the ears upon which its strident clamour fell the trump of doom could not have been more awful.

"Good-bye, my darling," she said, "good-bye, and remember what I have told you, that near or far, living or dead, we can never really be apart again, for ours is the Love Eternal given to us in the Beginning."

"Yes," he answered briefly, "I know that it is so and—enduring for ever! God bless us both as He sees best."

The ship cast off, and Isobel stood in the evening light watching from the quay till Godfrey vanished and the vessel which bore him was swallowed up in the shadows. Then she went back to the hotel and, throwing herself upon that widowed bed, kissed the place where his head had lain, and wept, ah! how she wept, for her joy-days were done and her heart was breaking in her.

After this Isobel took a night train back to town and, returning to Hawk's Hall, threw herself with the energy that was remarkable in her, into the management of her hospital and many another work and charity connected with the war. For it was only in work that she could forget herself and her aching loneliness.

Godfrey had a comfortable and a prosperous voyage, since it was almost before the days of submarines, at any rate so far as passenger steamers were concerned, and they saw no enemy ships. Therefore, within little more than a month he landed on the hot shores of Mombasa, and could cable to Isobel that he was safe and well and receive her loving answer.

His next business was to report himself in the proper quarter, which he did. Those over him seemed quite bewildered as to what he had come for or what he was to do, and could only suggest that he should travel to Nairobi and Uganda and put himself in touch with the civil authorities. This he did also and, as a result, formulated a certain scheme of action, to which his military superiors assented, intimating that he might do as he liked, so long as he did not interfere with them.

What happened to him may be very briefly described. In the end he started to visit a great chief on the borders of German East Africa, but in British territory, a man whose loyalty was rumoured to be doubtful. This chief, Jaga by name, was a professed Christian, and at his town there lived a missionary of the name of Tafelett, who had built a church there and was said to have much influence over him. So with the Reverend Mr. Tafelett Godfrey communicated by runners, saying that he was coming to visit him. Accordingly he started with a guard of native troops, a coloured interpreter and some servants, but without any white companion, since the attack on German territory was beginning and no one could be spared to go with him upon a diplomatic mission.

The journey was long and arduous, involving many days of marching across the East African veld and through its forests, where game of all sorts was extraordinarily plentiful, and at night they were surrounded by lions. At length, however, with the exception of one man who remained with the lions, they arrived safely at the town of Jaga and were met by Mr. Tafelett, who took Godfrey into his house, a neat thatched building with a wide verandah that stood by the church, which was a kind of whitewashed shed, also thatched.

Mr. Tafelett proved to be a clergyman of good birth and standing, one of those earnest, saint-like souls who follow literally the scriptural injunction and abandon all to advance the cause of their Master in the dark places of the earth. A tall, thin, nervous-looking man of not much over thirty years of age; one, too, possessed of considerable private means, he had some five years before given up a good living in England in order to obey what he considered to be his "call." Being sent to this outlying post, he found it in a condition of the most complete savagery, and worked as few have done. He built the church with native labour, furnishing it beautifully inside, mostly at his own expense. He learned the local languages, he started a school, he combated the witch-doctors and medicine-men.

Finally he met with his reward in the conversion of the young chief Jaga, which was followed by that of a considerable portion of his people.

But here came the trouble. The bulk of the tribe, which was large and powerful, did not share their chief's views. For instance, his uncle, Alulu, the head rain-maker and witch-doctor, differed from them very emphatically. He was shrewd enough to see that the triumph of Christianity meant his destruction, also the abandonment of all their ancient customs. He harangued the tribe in secret, asking them if they wished to bring upon themselves the vengeance of their ancestral and other spirits and to go through their days as the possessors of only one miserable wife, questions to which they answered that emphatically they did not. So the tribe was rent in two, and by far the smaller half clung to Jaga, to whom the dim, turbulent heathen thousands beneath his rule rendered but a lip service.

Then came the war, and Alulu and his great following saw their opportunity. Why should they not be rid of Jaga and the Christian teacher with his new-fangled notions? If it could be done in no other way, why should they not move across the border which was close by, into German territory? The Germans, at any rate, would not bother them about such matters; under their rule they might live as their forefathers had done from the beginning, and have as many wives as they chose without being called all sorts of ugly names.

This was the position when Godfrey arrived. His coming made a great sensation. He was reported to be a very big lord indeed, as big, or bigger than the King's governor himself. Alulu put it about that he had come to make a soldier of every fit man and to enslave the women and the elders to work on the roads or in dragging guns. The place seethed with secret ferment.

Mr. Tafelett knew something of all this through Jaga, who was genuinely frightened, and communicated it to Godfrey. In the result a meeting of all the headmen was held, which was attended by thousands of the people. Godfrey spoke through his interpreter, saying that in this great war the King of England required their help, and generally set out the objects of his mission, remarks that were received in respectful silence. Then Alulu spoke, devoting himself chiefly to an attack upon the Christian faith and on the interference of the white teacher with their customs, that, he observed, had resulted in their ancestral spirits cursing them with the worst drought they had experienced for years, which in the circumstances he, Alulu, could and would do nothing to alleviate. How could they fight and work for the Great King when their stomachs were pinched with hunger owing to the witchcraft and magical rites which the white teacher celebrated in the church?

"How, indeed?" shouted the heathen section, although in fact their season had been very good; while the Christians, feeling themselves in a minority, were silent.

Then the Chief, Jaga, spoke. He traversed all the arguments of Alulu, whom he denounced in no measured terms, saying that he was plotting against him. Finally he came down heavily on the side of the British, remarking that he knew who were the would-be traitors and that they should suffer in due course.

"It has been whispered in my ears," he concluded, "that there is a plot afoot against my friend, the white Teacher, who has done us all so much good. It has even been whispered that there are those," here he looked hard at Alulu, "who have declared that it would be well to kill this great white Lord who is our guest," and he pointed to Godfrey with his little chief's staff, "so that he may not return to tell who are the true traitors among the people of Jaga. I say to you who have thought such things, that this Lord is the greatest of all lords, and as well might you lay hands on our father, the mighty King of England himself, as upon this his friend and counsellor. If a drop of his blood is shed, then surely the King's armies will come, and we shall die, every one of us, the innocent and the guilty together. For terrible will be the vengeance of the King."

This outburst made a great impression, for all the multitude cried:

"It is so! We know that it is so," and Alulu interposed that he would as soon think of murdering his own mother (who, Mr. Tafelett whispered to Godfrey, had been dead these many years) as of touching a hair of the great white chief's head. On the contrary, it was their desire to do everything that he ordered them. But concerning the matter of the new custom of having one wife only, etc.

This brought Mr. Tafelett to his feet, for on monogamy he was especially strong, and the meeting ended on a theological discussion which nearly resulted in blows between the factions. Finally it was adjourned for a week, when it was arranged that an answer should be given to Godfrey's demands.

Three nights later an answer was given and one of a terrible sort.

Shortly after sundown Godfrey was sitting in the missionary's house writing a report. Mr. Tafelett, it being Sunday, was holding an evening service in the church, at which Jaga and most of the Christians were present. Suddenly a tumult arose, and the air was rent with savage shouts and shrieks. Godfrey sprang up and snatched his revolver just as some of his servants arrived and announced that the people in the church were being killed. Acting on his first impulse, he ran to the place, calling to his guard to follow him, which they did so tardily that he entered it alone. Here a sight of horror met his eyes.

The building was full of dead and dying people. By the altar, dressed in his savage witch-doctor's gear, stood Alulu, a lamp in his hand, with which evidently he had been firing the church, for tongues of flame ran up the walls. On the altar itself was something that had a white cloth thrown over it, as do the sacred vessels. Catching sight of Godfrey, with a yell the brute tore away the napkin, revealing the severed head of Mr. Tafelett, whose surplice-draped body Godfrey now distinguished lying in the shadows on one side of the altar!

"Here is the white medicine-man's magic wine," he screamed, pointing to the blood that ran down the broidered frontal. "Come, drink! come, drink!"

Godfrey ran forward up the church, his pistol in his hand. When he reached the chancel he stopped and fired at the mouthing, bedizened devil who was dancing hideously in front of the altar. The heavy service-revolver bullet struck him in some mortal place, for he leapt into the air, grabbed at the altar cloth and fell to the ground. There he lay still, covered by the cloth, with the massive brass crucifix resting face downwards on his breast and the murdered man's head lying at his side—as though it were looking at him.

This was the last sight that Godfrey saw for many a day, for just then a spear pierced his breast, also something struck him on the temple. A curious recollection rose in his mind of the head of a mummy after the Pasteur had broken it off, rolling along the floor in the flat at Lucerne. Then he thought he heard Madame Riennes laughing, after which he remembered no more; it might have been a thousand years, or it might have been a minute, for he had passed into a state that takes no reck of time.

Godfrey began to dream. He dreamed that he was travelling; that he was in a house, and then, a long while afterwards, that he was making a journey by sea.

Another vacuum of nothingness and he dreamed again, this time very vividly. Now his dream was that he had come to Egypt and was stretched on a bed in a room, through the windows of which he could see the Pyramids quite close at hand. More, he seemed to become acquainted with all their history. He saw them in the building; multitudes of brown men dragging huge blocks of stone up a slope of sand. He saw them finished one by one, and all the ceremonies of the worship with which they were connected. Dead Pharaohs were laid to rest there beneath his eyes, living Pharaohs prayed within their chapels and made oblation to the spirits of those who had gone before them, while ever the white-robed, shaven priests chanted in his ears.

Then all passed, and he saw them mighty as ever, but deserted, standing there in the desert, the monuments of a forgotten greatness, till at length a new people came and stripped off their marble coverings.

These things he remembered afterwards, but there were many more that he forgot.

Again Godfrey dreamed, a strange and beautiful dream which went on from day to day. It was that he was very ill and that Isobel had come to nurse him. She came quite suddenly and at first seemed a little frightened and disturbed, but afterwards very happy indeed. This went on for a while, till suddenly there struck him a sense of something terrible that had happened, of an upheaval of conditions, of a wrenching asunder of ties, of change utter and profound.

Then while he mourned because she was not there, Isobel came again, but different. The difference was indefinable, but it was undoubted. Her appearance seemed to have changed somewhat, and in the intervals between her comings he could never remember how she had been clothed, except for two things which she always seemed to wear, the little ring with the turquoise hearts, though oddly enough, not her wedding ring, and the string of small pearls which he had given her when they were married, and knew again by the clasp, that was fashioned in a lover's knot of gold. Her voice, too, seemed changed, or rather he did not hear her voice, since it appeared to speak within him, in his consciousness, not without to his ears. She told him all sorts of strange things, about a wonderful land in which they would live together, and the home that she was making ready for him, and the trees and flowers growing around it, that were unlike any of which Godfrey had ever heard. Also she said that there were many other matters whereof she would wish to speak to him, only she might not.

Finally there came a vivid dream in which she told him that soon he would wake up to the world again for a lIttle whIle (she seemed to lay emphasIs on thIs "lIttle whIle") and, If he could not fInd her In It, that he must not grieve at all, since although their case seemed sad, it was much better than he could conceive. In his dream she made him promise that he would not grieve, and he did so, wondering. At this she smiled, looking more beautiful than ever he could have conceived her to be. Then she spoke these words, always, as it appeared, within him, printing them, as it were, upon his mind:

"Now you are about to wake up and I must leave you for a while. But this I promise you, my most dear, my beloved, my own, that before you fall asleep again for the last time, you shall see me once more, for that is allowed to me. Indeed it shall be I who will soothe you to sleep and I who will receive you when you awake again. Also in the space between, although you do not see me, you will always feel me near, and I shall be with you. So swear to me once more that you will not grieve."

Then in his vision Godfrey swore, and she appeared to lean over him and whisper words into his ear that, although they impressed themselves upon his brain as the others had done, had no meaning for him, since they were in some language which he did not understand.

Only he knew that they conveyed a blessing to him, and not that of Isobel alone!

CHAPTER XXI

LOVE ETERNAL

Godfrey awoke and looked about him. He was lying in a small room opposite to an open window that had thin gauze shutters which, as an old Indian, he knew at once were to keep out mosquitoes. Through this window he could see the mighty, towering shapes of the Pyramids, and reflected that after all there must have been some truth in those wonderful dreams. He lifted his hand; it was so thin that the strong sunlight shone through it. He touched his head and felt that it was wrapped in bandages, also that it seemed benumbed upon one side.

A little dark woman wearing a nurse's uniform, entered the room and he asked her where he was, as once before he had done in France and under very similar conditions. She stared and answered with an Irish accent:

"Where else but at Mena House Hospital. Don't the Pyramids tell you that?"

"I thought so," he replied. "How long have I been here?"

"Oh! two months, or more. I can't tell you, Colonel, unless I look at the books, with so many sick men coming and going. Shure! it's a pleasure to see you yourself again. We thought that perhaps you'd never wake up reasonably."

"Did you? I always knew that I should."

"And how did you know that?"

"Because someone whom I am very fond of, came and told me so."

She glanced at him sharply.

"Then it's myself that should be flattered," she answered, "or the night nurse, seeing that it is we who have cared for you with no visitors admitted except the doctors, and they didn't talk that way. Now, Colonel, just you drink this and have a nap, for you mustn't speak too much all at once. If you keep wagging your jaw you'll upset the bandages."

When he woke again it was night and now the full moon, such a moon as one sees in Egypt, shone upon the side of the Great Pyramid and made it silver. He could hear voices talking outside his door, one that of the Irish nurse which he recognised, and the other of a man, for although they spoke low, this sense of hearing seemed to be peculiarly acute to him.

"It is so, Major," said the nurse. "I tell you that except for a little matter about someone whom he thought had been visiting him, he is as reasonable as I am, and much more than you are, saving your presence."

"Well," answered the doctor, "as you speak the truth sometimes, Sister, I'm inclined to believe you, but all I have to say is that I could have staked my professional reputation that the poor chap would never get his wits again. He has had an awful blow and on the top of an old wound, too. After all these months, it's strange, very strange, and I hope it will continue."

"Well, of course, Major, there is the delusion about the lady."

"Lady! How do you know it was a lady? Just like a woman making up a romance out of nothing. Yes, there's the delusion, which is bad. Keep his mind off it as much as possible, and tell him some of your own in your best brogue. I'll come and examine him to-morrow morning."

Then the voices died away and Godfrey almost laughed because they had talked of his "delusion," when he knew so well that it was none. Isobel had been with him. Yes, although he could neither hear nor see her, Isobel was with him now for he felt her presence. And yet how could this be if he was in Egypt and she was in England? So wondering, he fell asleep again.

By degrees as he gathered strength, Godfrey learned all the story of what had happened to him, or rather so much of it as those in charge of the hospital knew. It appeared, according to Sister Elizabeth, as his nurse was named, that when he was struck down in the church, "somewhere in Africa" as she said vaguely, the guards whom he had with him, rushed in, firing on the native murderers who fled away except those who were killed.

Believing that, with the missionary, they had murdered the King's Officer, a great man, they fled fast and far into German East Africa and were no more seen. The Chief, Jaga, who had escaped, caused him to be carried out of the burning church to the missionary's house, and sent runners to the nearest magistracy many miles away, where there was a doctor. So there he lay in the house. A native servant who once acted as a hospital orderly, had washed his wounds and bound them up. One of these, that on the head, was caused by a kerry or some blunt instrument, and the other was a spear-stab in the lung. Also from time to time this servant poured milk down his throat.

At length the doctor came with an armed escort and, greatly daring, performed some operation which relieved the pressure on the brain and saved his life. In that house he lay for a month or more and then, in a semi-comatose condition, was carried by slow stages in a litter back to Mombasa. Here he lay another month or so and as his mind showed no signs of returning, was at length put on board a ship and brought to Egypt.

Meanwhile, as Godfrey learned afterwards, he was believed to have been murdered with the missionary, and a report to that effect was sent to England, which, in the general muddle that prevailed at the beginning of the war, had never been corrected. For be it remembered it was not until he was carried to Mombasa, nearly two months after he was hurt, that he reached any place where there was a telegraph. By this time also, those at Mombasa had plenty of fresh casualties to report, and indeed were not aware, or had forgotten what exact story had been sent home concerning Godfrey who could not speak for himself. So it came about through a series of mischances, that at home he was believed to be dead as happened to many other men in the course of the great war.

After he came to himself at the Mena House Hospital, Godfrey inquired whether there were not some letters for him, but none could be found. He had arranged with the only person likely to write to him, namely Isobel, to do so through the War Office, and evidently that plan had not succeeded, for her letters had gone astray. The truth was, of course, that some had been lost and after definite news of his death was received, the rest had not been forwarded. Now he bethought him that he would cable home to Isobel to tell her that he was recovering, though somehow he imagined that she would know this already through the authorities. With great difficulty, for the hurt to his side made it hard for him to use his arm, he wrote the telegram and gave it to Sister Elizabeth to send, remarking that he would pay the cost as soon as he could draw some money.

"That won't matter," she replied as she took the cable. Then with an odd look at him she went away as though to arrange for its despatch.

After she had gone, two orderlies helped Godfrey downstairs to sit on the broad verandah of the hospital. Here still stood many of the little tables which used to serve for pleasant tea-parties when the building was an hotel in the days before the war. On these lay some old English newspapers. Godfrey picked up one of them with his left hand, and began to read idly enough. Almost the first paragraph that his eye fell on was headed:

"Heroic Death of a V.A.D. Commandant."

Something made him read on quickly, and this was what he saw:

"At the inquest on the late Mrs. Knight, the wife of Colonel Knight who was reported murdered by natives in East Africa some little time ago, some interesting evidence was given. It appeared from the testimony of Mrs. Parsons, a nurse in the Hawk's Hall Hospital, that when warning was given of the approach of Zeppelins during last week's raid on the Eastern Counties and London, the patients in the upper rooms of the hospital were removed to its lower floors. Finding that one young man, a private in the Suffolk Regiment who has lost both his feet, had been overlooked, Mrs. Knight, followed by Mrs. Parsons, went upstairs to help him down. When Mrs. Parsons, whom she outran, reached the door of the ward there was a great explosion, apparently on the roof. She waited till the dust had cleared off and groped her way down the ward with the help of an electric torch. Reaching Private Thompson's bed, she saw lying on it Mrs. Knight who had been killed by the fallen masonry. Private Thompson, who was unhurt beneath the body, said that when the bricks began to come down Mrs. Knight called to him to lie still and threw herself on him to protect him. Then something heavy, he believed the stone coping of a chimney, fell on her back and she uttered one word, he thought it was a name, and was silent. Mrs. Knight, who was the only child of the late Sir John Blake, Bart., the well-known shipowner, is said to have been one of the richest women in England. She married the late Colonel Knight some months ago, immediately before he was sent to East Africa. Under the provisions of her will the cremated remains of Mrs. Knight will be interred in the chancel of the Abbey Church at Monk's Acre."

Godfrey read this awful paragraph twice and looked at the date of the paper. It was nearly two months old.

"So she was dead when she came to me. Oh! now I understand," he muttered to himself, and then, had not a passing native servant caught him, he would have fallen to the ground. It was one of the ten thousand minor tragedies of the world war, that is all.

Three months later, still very crippled and coughing badly, because of the injury to his lung, he reported himself in London, and once more saw the Under-Secretary who had sent him out to East Africa. There he sat in the same room, at the same desk, looking precisely the same.

"I am sorry, Sir, that my mission has failed through circumstances beyond my control. I can only add that I did my best," he said briefly.

"I know," answered the official; "it was no fault of yours if those black brutes tried to murder you. Everything goes wrong in that cursed East Africa. Now go home and get yourself fit again, my dear fellow," he went on very kindly, adding, "Your services will not be overlooked."

"I have no home, and I shall never be fit again," replied Godfrey, and left the room.

"I forgot," thought the Under-Secretary. "His wife was killed in a Zeppelin raid. Odd that she should have been taken and he left."

Then, with a sigh and a shrug of the shoulders he turned to his business.

Godfrey went to the little house at Hampstead where he used to live while he was studying as a lad, for here Mrs. Parsons was waiting for him. Then for the first time he gave way and they wept in each other's arms.

"We were too happy, Nurse," he said.

"Yes," she answered, "love like hers wasn't for this world, and more than once she said to me that she never expected to see you again in the flesh, though I thought she meant it was you who would go, as might have been expected. Stop, I have something for you."

Going to a desk she produced from it a ring, that with the turquoise hearts; also a canvas-covered book.

"That's her diary," she said, "she used to write in it every day."

That night Godfrey read many beautiful and sacred things in this diary. From it he learned that the shock of his supposed death had caused Isobel to miscarry and made her ill for some time, though underneath the entries about her illness and the false news of his death she had written:

"He is not dead. I know that he is not dead."

Afterwards there were some curious sentences in which she spoke joyfully of having seen him in her sleep, ill, but living and going to recover, "at any rate for a while," she had added.

On the very day of her death she had made this curious note:

"I feel as though Godfrey and I were about to be separated for a while, and yet that this separation will really bring us closer together. I am strangely happy. Great vistas seem to open to my soul and down them I walk with Godfrey for ever and a day, and over them broods the Love of God in which are embodied and expressed all other loves. Oh! how wrong and foolish was I, who for so many years rejected that Love, which yet will not be turned away and in mercy gave me sight and wisdom and with these Godfrey, from whose soul my soul can never more be parted. For as I told you, my darling, ours is the Love Eternal. Remember it always, Godfrey, if ever your eyes should see these words upon the earth. Afterwards there will be no need for memory."

So the diary ended.

They invalided Godfrey out of the service and because of his lung trouble, he went to the house that Miss Ogilvy had left him in Lucerne, taking Mrs. Parsons with him. There too he found the Pasteur, grown an old man but otherwise much the same as ever, and him also he brought to live in the Villa Ogilvy.

The winter went on and Godfrey grew, not better, but worse, till at last he knew that he was dying, and rejoiced to die. One evening a letter was brought to him. It was from Madame Riennes, written in a shaky hand, and ran thus:

"I am going to pass to the World of Speerits, and so are you, my Godfrey, for I know all about you and everything that has happened. The plum is eaten, but the stone—ah! it is growing already, and soon you will be sitting with another under that beautiful Tree of Life of which I told you in the English church. And I, where shall I be sitting? Ah! I do not know, but there is this difference between us that whereas I am afraid, you have no cause for fear. You, you rejoice, yes, and shall rejoice—for though sometimes I hate you I must tell it. Yet I am sorry if I have harmed you, and should you be able, I pray you, say a good word in the World of Speerits for your sinful old godmamma Riennes. So fare you well, who thinking that you have lost, have gained all. It is I, I who have lost. Again farewell, and bid that old Pasteur to pray for me, which he, who is good, will do, although I was his enemy and cursed him."

"See that she lacks for nothing till the end, and comfort her if you can," said Godfrey to the Pasteur.

That night a shape of glory seemed to stand by Godfrey's bed and to whisper wonderful things into his ears. He saw it, ah, clearly, and knew that informing its changeful loveliness was all which had been Isobel upon the earth.

"Fear nothing," he thought it said, "for I am with you and others greater than I. Know, Godfrey, that everything has a meaning and that all joy must be won through pain. Our lives seem to have been short and sad, but these are not the real life, they are but its black and ugly door, whereof the threshold must be watered with our tears and the locks turned by the winds of Faith and Prayer. Do not be afraid then of the blackness of the passage, for beyond it shines the immortal light in that land where there is understanding and all forgiveness. Therefore be glad, Godfrey, for the night of sorrows is at an end and the dawn breaks of peace that passes understanding."

Godfrey woke and spoke to the old Pasteur who was watching by his bed while Mrs. Parsons wept at its foot.

"Did you see anything?" he asked.

"No, my son," he answered, "but I felt something. It was as though an angel stood at my side."

Then Godfrey told him all his vision, and much else besides, of which before he had never spoken to living man.

"It well may be, my son," answered the Pasteur, "since to those who have suffered greatly, the good God gives the great reward. He Who endured pain can understand our pains, and He Who redeemed sin can understand and be gentle to our sins, for His is the true Love Eternal. So go forward with faith and gladness, and in the joy of that new world and of the lost which is found again, think sometimes of the old Pasteur who hopes soon to join you there."

Then he shrove and blessed him.

After this Godfrey slept awhile to wake elsewhere in the Land of that Love Eternal which the soul of Isobel foreknew.

H. Rider Haggard – A Short Biography

Sir Henry Rider Haggard, KBE was born on June 22nd, 1856 at Bradenham in Norfolk, England.

More familiarly known as H. Rider Haggard, he was the eighth of ten children born to Sir William Meybohm Rider Haggard, a barrister (born, incidentally, in St Petersburg, Russia), and Ella Doveton, an author, poet and daughter of a merchant in the East India Trading Company.

Haggard was initially schooled at Garsington Rectory in Oxfordshire where he studied under the tutelage of Reverend H. J. Graham. His elder brothers, who seemed to find more favour with their father, graduated from various private schools whilst Haggard was sent to Ipswich Grammar School, saving his father a considerable sum in fees.

He failed his army entrance exam, and was therefore sent to a private crammer in London in preparation for the entrance exam to the British Foreign Office, which he appears never to have sat. However, it was during his two years in London that Haggard came into contact with a circle of people interested in the study of psychical phenomena and for which he too now developed a life-long interest together with a series of enduring friendships.

In 1875, Haggard's father used his family's connections to send him to Southern Africa to take up an unpaid position as assistant to the secretary to Sir Henry Bulwer, Lieutenant-Governor of the Colony of Natal. In 1876 he was transferred to the staff of Sir Theophilus Shepstone, Special Commissioner for the Transvaal. It was in this role that Haggard was present in Pretoria in April 1877 for the official announcement of the British annexation of the Boer Republic of the Transvaal. The official who had been nominated to read out the Proclamation lost his voice and Haggard was his replacement. It was a moment in history.

Haggard was to remain in the country for six years, during which time he served as Master of the High Court of the Transvaal and an adjutant of the Pretoria Horse.

It was here that he fell in love with Mary Elizabeth "Lilly" Jackson. He hoped to marry her once he obtained more certainty in his career path.

In 1878 he became Registrar of the High Court in the Transvaal and now the time seemed opportune to write to his father to tell him of his hope to marry. The reply from his father was uncompromising. He forbade it until his son had made a proper career for himself.

The following year, 1879, Lily married Frank Archer, a well-to-do banker.

Haggard returned briefly to England to marry a friend of his sister's, Marianna Louisa Margitson, a 21 year old, in 1880, and the couple travelled to Africa together. Haggard's years in Africa had proved, at least on a writing level, rich and inspirational for him, and while still in Natal he wrote two articles for The Gentleman's Magazine describing his experiences.

Moving back to England in (and accounts here differ as to whether it was 1881 or 1882) the couple settled in Ditchingham, Norfolk, Louisa's ancestral home. Later they moved to Kessingland and established connections with the church in Bungay, Suffolk. The marriage produced four children. A son named Jack (who tragically died at age 10 of measles) and three daughters, Angela, Dorothy and Lilias. (Lilias grew to become an author and her father's biographer.)

In England Law was to be the fulcrum of his career. However, although he studied, writing was growing in its appeal to him. His first book, Cetywayo and His White Neighbours, was an account and study of Britain's policies in South Africa.

From this point his career as a writer began to take substantial hold and with it a dramatic shift to fiction. Two years later he published his first fiction, Dawn followed in 1885 by arguably his most popular novel, King Solomon's Mines—detailing the life of the adventurer Allan Quatermain. This was followed the following year, 1886, by She: A History of Adventure, which introduced the female character Ayesha. Both characters, Quatermain and Ayesha, developed a series of books about their adventures.

The study of Law now fell away entirely. He appeared also to have a keen sense of his commercial appreciation. Rather than sell the copyright of his first best-seller, King Solomon's Mines, for a £100 fee he, instead, accepted a 10% royalty. This book is also generally accepted as the first of the Lost World writing genre.

Haggard obviously thought there were many further adventures to tell and it would be hard to find a publisher who would disagree given the start he had made. Sequels soon followed. Allan Quatermain continued his epic and swash-buckling adventures in Africa whilst the sequel to She entitled Ayesha played out her adventures in Tibet. Interestingly Haggard would later extend his characters adventures around the world with Eric Brighteyes, being the basis for an epic Viking romance.

The Haggard family lived at 69 Gunterstone Road in Hammersmith, London, from mid-1885 to mid-1888. It was here that he wrote his most famous works. His time in Africa had given him the experience and atmosphere as well as several observations and friendships of the people who would so influence his fictional characters. Chief among them were the larger-than-life adventurers Frederick Selous and Frederick Russell Burnham. Both were men of Empire and huge ambition as they helped uncover the great mineral wealth of Africa, as well as the ruins of ancient lost civilisations of the continent, such as Great Zimbabwe.

Three of Haggard's books, The Wizard (1896), Black Heart and White Heart; a Zulu Idyll (1896), and Elissa; the Doom of Zimbabwe (1898), are dedicated to Burnham's daughter Nada, the first white child born in Bulawayo; she had been named after Haggard's 1892 book Nada the Lily.

As is typical of the writing of the time his novels contain many of the stereotypes associated with colonialism, yet they also sympathise, to a degree, with the native populations. Africans often play heroic roles in the novels, although the protagonists are more often than not European. The time around the turn of the century was, after all, the great sprint to Empire by many European countries intent on gaining possessions of land, people and resources.

Three of Haggard's novels were written in collaboration with his friend Andrew Lang who shared his interest in the spiritual realm and paranormal phenomena and who was also a greatly admired editor.

Haggard's stories are still widely read today. Ayesha, the female protagonist of She, has been cited as a prototype by psychoanalysts such as Sigmund Freud (in The Interpretation of Dreams) and Carl Jung. Her epithet is, of course, "She Who Must Be Obeyed" and has for decades been used tongue-in-cheek to describe the presumed balance of influence between the sexes.

As a legacy it is easy to establish Haggard, and his pioneering work, as the author of the Lost World branch of writing and its influence of such other writers as Edgar Rice Burroughs, Robert E. Howard and Talbot Mundy. The Allan Quatermain character influenced many 'serials' in Hollywood during the 30s & 40s and can readily be seen as a template for Indiana Jones, the American archaeologist and explorer and huge box office film character.

Years later, when Haggard was a successful novelist, he was contacted by his former love, Lilly Archer, née Jackson. Lily had been deserted by her husband, who had embezzled funds and fled bankrupt to Africa. Haggard installed her and her sons in a house and saw to the children's education. Lilly eventually followed her husband to Africa, where he infected her with syphilis before dying of it himself. Lilly returned to England in late 1907, where Haggard again supported her until her death on April 22nd, 1909.

Haggard also wrote about agricultural and social reform, in part inspired by his experiences in Africa, but also based on what he saw in Europe. By the end of his life, he was adamantly opposed to Bolshevism, a position that he shared with his life-long friend Rudyard Kipling. The two had found friendship upon Kipling's arrival at London in 1889 largely on the strength of their shared opinions.

Haggard was extremely interested in the social affairs of the Country and eager to play a more active part in attempting reform. In 1895 he stood unsuccessfully for Parliament as a Conservative candidate for the Eastern division of Norfolk losing by 198 votes.

Also in 1895 he served on a government commission to examine Salvation Army labour colonies. This, and his heavy involvement in agriculture reform, led to him being a member of several further commissions on land use and related affairs, work that involved several trips to the Colonies and Dominions. This work, in part, helped lead to the passage of the 1909 Development Bill.

In 1911 he served on the Royal Commission examining coastal erosion.

He was an absorbed and dedicated writer of letters to The Times, nearly one hundred were published by them and the bibliography attached below reveals much in the range of subjects he wished to bring attention to.

He was made a Knight Bachelor in 1912 and a Knight Commander of the Order of the British Empire in 1919. Haggard was a member of several clubs including the Athenaeum, Savile, and Authors' clubs.

The district of Rider in British Columbia, Canada, was named in his honour.

Henry Rider Haggard died on May 14th, 1925 at the age of 68. His ashes were buried at Ditchingham Church. His papers are held at the Norfolk Record Office.

The first chapter of his book People of the Mist (1894) is credited with inspiring the 1912 motto of the Royal Air Force (formerly the Royal Flying Corps), Per ardua ad astra. "Through adversity to the stars" (or alternately "Through struggle to the stars") it is also used by other Commonwealth air forces such as the RAAF, RCAF, RNZAF, and the SAAF.

H. Rider Haggard – A Concise Bibliography

Novels
Dawn (1884) Published in three volumes
The Witch's Head (1884) Published in three volumes
King Solomon's Mines (1885) Allan Quatermain series
She: A History of Adventure (1886) Ayesha series
Allan Quatermain (1887) Allan Quatermain series
Jess (1887)
A Tale of Three Lions (1887) Allan Quatermain series

Maiwa's Revenge, or the War of the Little Hand (1888) Allan Quatermain series
Colonel Quaritch, VC (1889) Published in three volumes
Cleopatra (1889)
Beatrice (1890)
The World's Desire (1890) Co-written with Andrew Lang
Eric Brighteyes (1891)
Nada the Lily (1892)
An Heroic Effort (1893)
Montezuma's Daughter (1893)
The People of the Mist (1894)
Heart of the World (1895)
Joan Haste (1895)
The Wizard (1896)
Doctor Therne (1898)
Swallow: A Tale of the Great Trek (1899)
Lysbeth (1901)
Pearl Maiden (1903)
Stella Fregelius: A Tale of Three Destinies (1903)
The Brethren (1904)
Ayesha: The Return of She (1905) Ayesha series
The Way of the Spirit (1906)
Benita (1906)
Fair Margaret (1907)
The Ghost Kings(1908)
The Yellow God (1908)
The Lady of Blossholme (1909)
Morning Star (1910)
Queen Sheba's Ring (1910)
Red Eve (1911)
The Mahatma and the Hare (1911)
Marie (1912) Allan Quatermain series
Child of Storm (1913) Allan Quatermain series
The Wanderer's Necklace (1914)
The Holy Flower (1915) Allan Quatermain series
The Ivory Child (1916) Allan Quatermain series
Finished (1917) Allan Quatermain series]
Love Eternal (1918)
Moon of Israel (1918)
When the World Shook (1919)
The Ancient Allan (1920) Allan Quatermain series
She and Allan (1921) Allan Quatermain series / Ayesha series
The Virgin of the Sun (1922)
Wisdom's Daughter (1923) Ayesha series
Heu-Heu (1924) Allan Quatermain series]
Queen of the Dawn (1925)
The Treasure of the Lake (1926) Allan Quatermain series
Allan and the Ice-Gods (1927) Allan Quatermain series
Mary of Marion Isle (1929)

Belshazzar (1930)

The Government and the Land (letter) (8 May 1907) The Times
Miss Jebb on Small Holdings (15 June 1907) Country Life
Rural Housing and Sanitation Association (27 June 1907) The Times
St Thomas Hospital Medical School (28 June 1907) The Times
The Land Question (4 July 1907) The Times
A Plea for the Sitting Tenant (letter) (12 August 1907) The Times
A Literary Coincidence (letter) (19 October 1907) The Spectator
Town Planning Conference (26 October 1907) The Times
Dr Barnardo's Homes (16 November 1907) The Times
The Proposed Agricultural Party (5 December 1907) The Times
Mr Rider Haggard and Small Holdings (10 January 1908) The Times
Mr Haggard and Children's Legislation (13 March 1908) The Times
The Drink Trade and Common Sense (letter) (2 April 1908) The Times
The Zulus: The Finest Savage Race in the World (June 1908) The Pall Mall Magazine
Sparrows (letter) (18 August 1908) The Times
Sparrows, Rats and Humanity (letter) (5 September 1908) The Times
The Letters of Queen Victoria (letter) (26 November 1908) The Times
The Romance of the World's Greatest Rivers (December 1908) Travel Magazine
Afforestation. Mr Rider Haggard's View (1 March 1909) The Times
The Late Sir Marshal Clarke (letter) (13 April 1909) The Times
Mr Rider Haggard on Agriculture (27 November 1909) The Times
Mr Rider Haggard on South Africa (11 March 1910) The Times
Why? (letter) (25 April 1910) The Times
Mr Rider Haggard on Irish Agriculture (23 May 1910) The Times
Why Not? (letter) (12 July 1910) The Times
Mr Rider Haggard on Agriculture (16 September 1910) The Times
Mr Rider Haggard on Vermin (8 November 1910) The Times
Danish High Schools (21 December 1910) The Times
Sugar Beet Growing in Norfolk (6 March 1911) The Times
Rural Denmark (letter) (22 March 1911) The Times
Rural Denmark (letter) (3 April 1911) The Times
The Copyright Bill (letter) (6 June 1911) The Times
Mr Rider Haggard on Poverty. The Burden of Civilization (15 July 1911) The Times
Mr Rider Haggard and the Public Records (28 July 1911) The Times
The Farmers' Burden (1 December 1911) The Times
Egyptian Date Farm. The Financial Aspect (11 October 1912) The Times
Umslopogaas and Makokel. Sir H. Rider Haggard on Zulu Types (letter) (16 August 1913) The Times
The Death of Mark Haggard (letter) (10 October 1914) The Times
On the Land. Old Problems and New Ways. The War—and After. (15 March 1915) The Times
Soldiers as Settlers. After-War Problem for the Empire (20 August 1915) The Times
Raids by Air. Zeppelins and Zeppelins (letter) (22 October 1915) The Times
Women's Work on the Land. A Palliative in Hard Times (letter) (29 November 1915) The Times
Women on the Land. Town Girls' Unfitness for Farm Work (letter) (9 December 1915) The Times
Soldiers as Settlers. Sir Rider Haggard's Oversea Mission (2 February 1916) The Times
Soldiers as Settlers (letter) (7 February 1916) The Times
Soldier Settlers. The Future of Rural England (letter) (10 February 1916) The Times
Farewell Luncheon to Sir Rider Haggard (March 1916) United Empire
Soldier Settlers for the Empire. Offer from Victoria (18 April 1916) The Times

Sir R Haggard's Tour. Land for Ex-Service Men (22 July 1916) The Times
Sir H. Rider Haggard's Mission. Land for Ex-Soldiers (1 August 1916) The Times
Land for Ex-Soldiers. Outline of Sir R. Haggard's Report   (12 August 1916) The Times
Empire Land Settlement Deputation to the Secretary of State for the Colonies and the President of the Board of Agriculture (September 1916) United Empire
Empire Land Settlement by Sir Rider Haggard (December 1916) United Empire
A Journey through Zululand by Sir H Rider Haggard (December 1916) The Windsor Magazine
Mr Wilson's Note. British Publicity (28 December 1916) The Times
Home Produce (letter) (22 February 1917) The Times
The Milk Supply (letter) (11 April 1917) The Times
Corn Production Bill. A National Measure (letter) (13 June 1917) The Times
A Protest and a Plea. Farmers and Meat (letter) (9 October 1917) The Times
Pig-Breeding. A Subject for Municipal Enterprise (letter) (22 February 1918) The Times
The German Colonies. Interests of the Dominions (letter) (5 November 1918) The Times
Light—More Light! (letter) (19 November 1918) The Times
A Great American. Tributes to the Late Mr Roosevelt (letter) (8 January 1919) The Times
Shut the Door (letter) (10 March 1919) The Times
Population and Housing. Emigration v Birth Control (25 March 1919) The Times
The Ex-Kaiser (letter) (11 April 1919) The Times
Empire Birth-Rate. Sir Rider Haggard on Emigration (17 April 1919) The Times
Ex-Service Men Abroad. Warnings from California (letter) (10 May 1919) The Times
Edith Cavell (letter) (16 May 1919) The Times
The Ex-Kaiser. Uncertainties of Trial (letter) (8 July 1919) The Times
Race Suicide Peril. Western Civilization Threatened (11 October 1919) The Times
The British Cinema. Production of Reputable Films (letter) (5 November 1919) The Times
Horrors on the Film. Limits of Publicity (letter) (19 November 1919) The Times
The British Museum (letter) (24 January 1920) The Times
Air Exploration and Empire (letter) (7 February 1920) The Times
The Liberty League. A Campaign Against Bolshevism (letter) (3 March 1920) The Times
Bolshevist Peril. Counter-Propaganda (4 March 1920) The Times
The Empire's Vacant Lands. Settlers and the Food Supply (14 April 1920) The Times
Films and Happy Endings. The Tyranny of a Convention (letter)   (21 April 1921) The Times
Land and its Burdens. Evil of Grinding Taxation (letter) (8 August 1921) The Times
Boy Emigrants (letter) (31 March 1922) The Times
Migration and Morals. Declining Birther Rate (7 April 1922) The Times
Labour Party's Programme. Confiscation and Class Hatred (letter) (28 October 1922) The Times
Efficient Denmark. Keeping the People on the Land (7 December 1922) The Times
The Egyptian Find. Tombs of Eighteenth Dynasty Queens (letter) (19 December 1922) The Times
King Tutankhamen. Reburial in Great Pyramid (letter) (13 February 1923) The Times
The Norfolk Dispute. A Truce while There is Time (letter) (3 April 1923) The Times
Rural Post and Telephone. Minister's Reply to Deputation (19 April 1923) The Times
Liberalism and Land Reform (letter) (1 May 1923) The Times
Small Holdings. Influence of Heredity (letter) (4 July 1923) The Times
Agricultural Parcel Post (26 July 1923) The Times
Country Houses for Sale. Empty East Anglian Mansions (letter) (14 June 1924) The Times
Plight of Agriculture (24 July 1924) The Times
Loans From the British Museum (letter) (30 July 1924) The Times
Zinovieff Letter. Mr MacDonald and a Political Plot (letter) (29 October 1924) The Times

Two Centuries of Publishing. Tributes to Messrs. Longmans (6 November 1924) The Times
Imagination and War (26 November 1924) The Times

Film Adaptations

King Solomon's Mines
This novel has been adapted at least six times. The first version, King Solomon's Mines, directed by Robert Stevenson, premiered in 1937. The best known version premiered in 1950: King Solomon's Mines, directed by Compton Bennett and Andrew Marton, was followed in 1959 by a sequel, Watusi. In 1979 a low-budget version directed by Alvin Rakoff, King Solomon's Treasure, combined both King Solomon's Mines and Allan Quatermain in one story. The 1985 film King Solomon's Mines was a tongue-in-cheek parody of the story, with a 1987 sequel in the same vein, Allan Quatermain and the Lost City of Gold. Around the same time an Australian animated TV film came out, King Solomon's Mines. In 2008 a direct-to-video adaptation, Allan Quatermain and the Temple of Skulls, was released.

She
She has been adapted for the cinema at least ten times, and was one of the earliest films to be made, in 1899 as La Colonne de feu (The Pillar of Fire), by Georges Méliès. A 1911 version starred Marguerite Snow, a British-produced version appeared in 1916, and in 1917 Valeska Suratt appeared in a production for Fox which is lost. In 1925 a silent film of She, starring Betty Blythe, was produced with the active participation of Rider Haggard, who wrote the intertitles. This film combines elements from all the books in the series.

A decade later another cinematic version of the novels was released, featuring Helen Gahagan, Randolph Scott and Nigel Bruce. Unlike the book and the other films, this 1935 version was set in the Arctic, rather than Africa, and depicts the ancient civilisation of the story in an Art Deco style, with music by Max Steiner.

The 1965 film She was produced by Hammer Film Productions; it starred Ursula Andress as Ayesha and John Richardson as her reincarnated love, with Peter Cushing and Bernard Cribbins as other members of the expedition.

In 2001 another adaption was released direct-to-video with Ian Duncan as Leo Vincey, Ophélie Winter as Ayesha and Marie Bäumer as Roxane.

Dawn
The film Dawn was released in 1917, starring Hubert Carter and Annie Esmond.

Jess
This book was filmed in 1912, featuring Marguerite Snow, Florence La Badie and James Cruze, in 1914 with Constance Crawley and Arthur Maude, and in 1917 as Heart and Soul, starring Theda Bara in the title role.

Beatrice
The book was adapted into a 1921 Italian silent drama film called The Stronger Passion, directed by Herbert Brenon and starring Marie Doro and Sandro Salvini.

Swallow
The novel was adapted into a 1922 South African film.

Stella Fregelius
The book was adapted into a 1921 British film, Stella.

Moon of Israel
This novel was the basis of a script by Ladislaus Vajda, for film-director Michael Curtiz in his 1924 Austrian epic known as Die Sklavenkönigin (Queen of the Slaves).